I, PLAGUE

Maurice Johns

MAURICE JOHNS

Please review Links at MauriceJohns-Author

Maurice Johns

All rights reserved, no part of this publication may be reproduced by any means, electronic, mechanical photocopying, documentary, film or in any other format without prior written permission of the publisher.

>Published by
>Chipmunkapublishing
>PO Box 6872
>Brentwood
>Essex CM13 1ZT
>United Kingdom

http://www.chipmunkapublishing.com

Copyright © M Johns 2025

Edited by Aleks Lech

Chipmunkapublishing gratefully acknowledge the support of Arts Council England.

I, Plague

For Abi and Tristan

Maurice Johns

I, Plague

"And there went out another horse that was red:
and power was given to him that sat thereon to take peace
from the earth, and that they should kill one another:
and there was given unto him a great sword."

Book of Revelations

Maurice Johns

CHAPTER ONE

The walls of the office shimmered and wavered as the light from the street below passed through windows streaked with droplets of rain. The light gave the oak desk and leather chairs the appearance of life as it reflected off the polished surfaces, constantly moving, the sheets of water running down the panes, forcing the scene to continually shimmer and change shape.

The window comprised the complete front of the office. Its view from the fifth floor overlooked a magnificent panorama over Edinburgh's Princes Street, the gardens, and up to the Mound, where the buildings, all the way to the dominating castle, were floodlit, the light being absorbed into, and lighting, the low, gray clouds that hung over the city.

There was a constant stream of late shoppers and buses on the street below, however, no sound penetrated the glass. Occasional headlight beams swept across the ceiling as a taxi or bus turned from the Mound onto Princes Street.

Against a shadowed wall, a black leather settee lurked, and the long sofas, black yawning chasms, invited the unwary to sink into their depths. Two pale forms had done just that. They were moving, slowly, writhing in each other's grasp, tossing and turning, fighting the enveloping comfort of the leather and the outstretched arms. Their groans and moans of pleasure broke the silence of the office.

A door on the wall across the office slowly opened, and a barely discernible figure slipped through the narrow gap, softly closing the door behind him. No light from the outside office had filtered through the brief gap in the door, leaving the occupants of the sofa blissfully unaware of the intruder, who watched their, now frantic, coupling with amusement.

The figure, dressed completely in black, only the slits of his eyes showing through a balaclava, moved quietly on sneakered feet around the wall to a position at the feet of the gasping couple. He stood, unmoving, quietly observing their antics.

He had time, he knew their routine, had been observing this ritual for two weeks. Besides, it amused him that, when the moment came for their ultimate pleasure and release, he would provide another form of release. He found the thought poetic, and regretted that others would never know of it.

The female turned her lover on his back and, leaning on his chest, impaled herself upon him, throwing back her head, arching her back as she ground and jerked her way to satisfaction.

The man underneath began thrusting his hips upwards, trying to keep in time with her ever more frantic movements. One final thrust, a moan from him, some muffled words from her, and she collapsed forward to lie on top of him. Their heavy breathing mingled, their eyes closed as they savoured the moment.

The figure moved forward, stepping around the front of the sofa, stopping and positioning himself at the shoulders of the woman. He listened to their breathing even off. When he lifted his right hand it held a revolver, a Colt Python, the barrel extended, made ungainly by a silencer.

He placed his thumb on the hammer and drew it back. The double click was loud in the office, echoing around the walls. The man opened his eyes, not believing what he was seeing.

A slight pressure on the trigger and the hammer fell. A hollow point .357 Magnum round fled from its resting place, down the barrel, through the silencer and into the back of the woman's head. A soft *plop* accompanied the flight of the bullet. The man's eyes were still staring at the gaping hole as the bullet exited the woman's head and buried itself in the armrest of the sofa. Eyes turned to horror as blood, bone and brain were blown from the cavity that once was a forehead, covering the head and shoulders of the man trapped underneath her now still body.

He still did not move, he did not make a sound, he watched silently as the gun moved a few inches to a point where he was staring down the bottomless pit. At the last minute, recognition of what was about to happen worked its way through his paralyzed thought process. It was too late. The hammer clicked back and fell instantly, a second round left the chamber and buried itself in the sofa, leaving a bloody mess where the back of his head had rested.

The figure in black unscrewed the silencer and placed it, and the gun, in a back pack. He moved out of the office as quietly as he had appeared, closing the door gently behind him.

I, Plague

In the outer office he removed all the black outer clothing he had been wearing, replacing the sneakers with a pair of black leather shoes, and put them in the back pack.

The man, who left the office building, turning up the collar of his coat and pulling the hat forward over his eyes, against the rain, was dressed in a business suit and overcoat. He was no different from thousands of others who walked the streets of Edinburgh on their way to or from bars and restaurants, or going home to their families after an honest day's labour.

CHAPTER TWO

Detective Inspector Andy McNeish sat quietly fuming in the traffic congestion in Shandwick Place. The day had started off poorly with the call, at six thirty, from his second in command informing him of the double murder. His wife had then complained incessantly while he prepared to leave her. He had promised that the time away at St Andrews would not be interrupted by work – that he would devote himself to their fifteenth wedding anniversary. Not even an assurance that he would return that afternoon served to appease her. Then, because of the time, he had encountered the morning rush hour long before he had hit the Forth Bridge.

In frustration, he reached down into the passenger well and placed the blue light on the roof of his Rover. Ignoring the other motorists, he pulled out into the central reservation and threaded his way through the traffic until he could see Princes Street stretching in front of him, a never ending stream of buses blocking his view of the parked scene of crime vehicle and the ambulances. The flow of pedestrians was broken as they skirted the area blocked off by uniformed constables. He pulled over, driving onto the kerb to ease the traffic congestion, and sat for a minute to gather his thoughts.

Detective Sergeant Will Taylor had told him who the victims were, which was why he had deemed it necessary to call him out. It was Steven Hawkins and his secretary, Mhairi McDonald. The significance of the victim was that he was allegedly - modern terminology which Andy hated (in his book there was nothing alleged about it) - involved in the major crimes in Scotland. He was strongly suspected of heading up the whole operation which included prostitution, drugs, money laundering and any other nefarious activity which sprang to mind. All of these suspected activities were, to Andy's mind, carried out under the cover of a large property portfolio, which had netted him millions. No concrete evidence had ever been found against him, despite the best efforts of the Serious Crime Squad. To all intents and purposes, he was a successful businessman. With a shrug Andy told himself that was now a thing of the past and opened the door.

He took his ready bag out of the boot of the car and made his way into the building, flashing his warrant card at the constable watching the door. He took the lift to the fifth floor and slipped on the white suit and shoe covers before moving to the entrance of the offices.

"Morning Will, what have we got here then?" He grimaced to himself as he said that. He always vowed to try and find something else to say when he arrived on a crime scene, but it always came out the same.

"Morning, boss," came the cheery reply. Will Taylor was always cheerful, no matter the time or how many hours he had worked. "Both shot in the head, point blank and personal. They were having sex in his office. Pathologist and crime scene people are in there now. So far though, there doesn't appear to be anything for them to go on. Only thing we'll have are the rounds. Powerful handgun they say. Want to go in?"

McNeish grumbled his assent and they moved through the outer office to the door, where they saw a demarcated area on which they could make their way to the bodies.

"Morning Doc, what happened?" It was almost a rhetorical question. The mess on the sofa was pretty self-explanatory.

"Hi, Andy. One shot to the woman's head, in the back, exited through the forehead. One round in through the forehead for the man. Only thing I can say for sure now is that they were having a good time." He paused. "Also, the killer has a sense of the poetic. He waited until they had climaxed before shooting them."

McNeish turned to the Scene of Crime officer, silently waiting for the information he was waiting to give.

"Andy, there's nothing so far. I can tell you he stood at the end of the sofa for a good few minutes before moving around to take his shots. If you look, you can see the heavier imprints in the carpet. If the pile hadn't been so lush and untouched in this area we wouldn't have picked it up. As far as any other forensics, there's absolutely nothing so far."

"Professional hit, boss?" Will asked, as he straightened up from looking at the carpet.

"Looks that way, doesn't it? Considering what we know about our friend here, it could be business related – drugs, something like that. Looks like the girl was collateral damage. Classic case of the wrong place at the wrong time, but I have a feeling that is one question we are not going to have the answer to for some time."

He gestured to Will to follow him to the secretary's office, where he started to pull off the protective clothing. "Any witnesses, anyone hear the shots? Damn it, anything to go on?"

"Nothing, nada. Shirley's interviewing the cleaning lady who found the bodies and called it in. She's pretty shaken up. Doc estimates the time of death as last night between six and ten. Mike's going through the CCTV footage from the building and street to see if we can pick up the shooter. One thing it does show though, is that the building was empty apart from the victims and the shooter."

"OK, keep Mike on that, and give him any help you can if he turns up something. We're bound to have the killer on CCTV, but if he's a professional, he'll have taken the CCTV into consideration. It seems pretty cold; standing watching like that and then waiting for them to finish before shooting them. Will, I have a real bad feeling about this." McNeish could see his concerns mirrored in the face of his second in command.

"Me too. I never even saw this kind of killing in the Met." Will had joined the Lothian and Borders Police from the Met, where he had been a rising young star. McNeish had been glad to add him to his team.

As McNeish repacked his ready bag, Will observed "Who says crime doesn't pay? Look at this place – its luxury, no expense spared."

McNeish took a closer look at the office and furnishings. It was as opulent as any director's office he had ever seen. In fact, better equipped than most. "Alleged crime – remember the political correctness brigade. No, you're right, crime does pay. Always bugged me that we never had anything on him." As he turned to the door, Mike, the most junior of his team, arrived.

"I think we've got him on the CCTV, both from the building and the street. Not much to go on, an overcoat with the collar turned up and a hat pulled low over his face obscures any features. We're tapping into all the tapes trying to trace his movements. Last I heard, he was crossing North Bridge heading to the Royal Mile."

"Well, nothing in life is that easy. Get whatever you've got across to those computer wizards. Maybe they can live up to their boast that they can do anything with the smallest thing. Get them to try the facial recognition thing, build up the face from what we've got. Know what I mean?"

"Yes boss." Both Will and Mike tried to conceal their smiles. McNeish's lack of computer skills was legendary among the force. He argued that he preferred the old fashioned way and anyway, he had a team of experts to deal with things computer related.

"All right Will, lets get back to the office and set up an incident room. We can look at what little we've got, see what we need and try and get a bit organized before the brass start breathing down my neck. Grab Shirley on the way out. She should be finished with the cleaner by now."

As the Senior Investigating Officer, he would have to coordinate the various lines of investigation, and he was busy thinking about all the things he needed to do in the next few hours.

"Will, the families, have any family liaison officers been assigned?"

Will answered promptly. " Yes, they're standing by. Waiting for the go ahead from you."

McNeish knew all the FLOs, and trusted their judgment, preferring to allow them to handle the initial notification.

"OK, send them in. Tell them to watch for reactions, particularly the wife. See what they can dig up. If she knew about the affair, state of the marriage, the usual. But tell them to tread gently. We'll have a chat with them later; take in a bit more detail. Ask them to report to me by," he looked at his watch, "twelve. Right, let's see if the press guru is at his desk. Might as well prepare some kind of statement; ask for the public's help. Don't think it will do much good, but you never know."

Standing next to his car, McNeish looked at the sunny, clear blue sky, and thought about the things he should have been doing – a leisurely breakfast with Eileen, his long suffering wife, a walk on the beach, maybe a round of golf. An audible sigh escaped his lips and he climbed into the car. He made a mental note to give her a call from the office.

CHAPTER THREE

The rider sat motionless on the horse, his unseeing gaze taking in the wide green field in front of him. The hustle and bustle of the stables on his right could barely be heard, sounds of wheelbarrows and chatter only occasionally carrying on the light breeze. They sat in the long morning shadow of an ancient oak tree, rider and horse, solitary on the small rise. Behind them the sun was still low in the sky, a hazy shimmering ball of light struggling to warm the air.

Ending his morning ride here had been a habit for as long as he had been living in this part of Leicestershire, which was now pushing three and a half years. It had often been asked of him what he thought about while sitting there. In the past he had always answered that it was where his best ideas came to him. Now, however, he would only reply that he was not thinking – just remembering. He closed his eyes for a moment and imagined he could hear the sound of his or Marie's laughter coming from the stables. A sad smile formed on his lips, to be quickly replaced by a frown as the image of her lifeless body lying on the ground intruded, as it always did, on the memories of her living, her smile, the way she moved her head, her incessant chatter about the horses and the pupils. He pushed the thought away and tried to recapture her face with the smile, failed, and opened his eyes. God, how he missed her. She had been for the briefest, but happiest, of times Mrs. James Hawk.

He gathered the reins, adjusting his seat in the saddle and quietly spoke. "Well, Darling, better be going and get ready for the madding crowd. I think it'll be good to see them all again, at least I'll be sober this time."

He applied gentle pressure with his legs and the horse moved slowly forward down the slope and in the direction of the stables. He knew it was a funny sort of name for a horse, but when he had first seen her, she had nuzzled his chest and he had said that she was an absolute darling, and the name had stuck.

As they walked slowly back to the stables, James thought about the upcoming weekend. It had been three months since he had entertained his friends. Not since the funeral. It still wrenched his gut when he used that word. With the exception of Mike, who could only be described as the nearest thing he had to a best friend, he had withdrawn from all contact and sought solace and answers in bottle after bottle of whiskey. When Mike had visited, he had joined him and they both got drunk. When James thought of that time he felt ashamed at the loss of control, the way he must have behaved. The housekeeping staff had been bloody marvels, taking care of him. He knew that without them he might have drunk himself to death, they had made sure he ate something every day, had kept things turning over. It had been the same with the stable business; the girls there had run things very capably and, as he later learned, always stopped by the house to see how he was.

When he had sobered up, he found it all touching, had in fact been surprised at their loyalty. It was not something he had been accustomed to during his previous life. They had even been some of the many to offer advice. It had actually been young Jean who had told him that it was because he had not known grief on this scale before that he did not know how to handle it, and that was why he'd resorted to the bottle to reduce the pain and shut down the memories. Very astute for someone so young, James thought.

At the stables he was met by Vicky, one of the managers, and she took Darling from him, asking if he had a good ride. He chatted briefly with her, not wanting to appear rude, but his mind was already working on the final preparations that needed to be taken care of before the arrival of his guests, and he quickly excused himself.

As James walked up the curved drive and the house came fully into sight, he stopped and gazed at it, he had never become accustomed to the size and quiet grandeur of the building. It had been the home to much laughter and joy since he had moved in. All of it had been down to Marie, both before and after their marriage. He felt the same emptiness as he looked, and fought to conquer it, although he knew it was useless. Perhaps not conquer it, rather control it. He knew that if he did not control it, he would be reduced to a blubbering wreck again. James supposed that feeling would remain with him for the rest of his life. Squaring his shoulders, he strode through the back gate and into the cavernous kitchen.

"Morning, Madge. How are we this morning? Looking forward to wild hordes descending on us, upsetting your schedule and getting under your feet?" He liked to joke with her. He knew very well that she had been looking forward to this weekend since he had first mentioned it. The house had a feeling about it that had been lacking, almost as if it, like him, was shaking the cobwebs of sorrow away, ready for some jovial, happy conversation, even laughter, resounding around the old halls and rooms.
"Oh, yes sir." No matter how hard he had tried he could not get her to

call him anything but *Sir*. One time he had overheard her telling Pippa that *"the master would not be happy"*. It sounded a bit Victorian to his ears, but he'd learned to accept her old-school manners. "The girls and James are all looking forward to seeing everyone again, particularly young Pippa. It'll be just like old times..." She immediately looked contrite. "I'm so sorry sir, I didn't mean..."

James stopped her. "It's alright, Madge. I know what you mean, yes it will be a bit like old times. So everything under control? I can get changed and have a drink?"

She almost shooed him out of the kitchen. He found himself smiling, not a frequent occurrence of late, catching her good mood. He showered and changed. As he dressed he looked at his reflection in the mirror. At least the drinking binge had not done too much harm, and the workouts in the gym since he had sobered up had also helped to maintain his body in good shape. Better than he deserved.

James expected the first of the guests to arrive in the early afternoon. They were driving up from London. He was looking forward to seeing them again, especially Mike, who now worked for Lou Carter, an anglicised version of his old name, who would be coming with his family. They had met again after a break of two years and re-established their friendship during a time when James' sister had been in trouble. Only one of their daughters would be with them, Mona, the youngest.

The eldest, Monique, worked in Paris as a Corporate Lawyer and had excused herself because of business commitments. It was a shame; James had always liked her, her independence and strong character. Mike, he knew, had had a crush on her since their first meeting.

Also coming would be young Pippa, and her parents. She would hate being called that, she was quite the young lady. Marie and he had become very attached to this plucky girl who had battled cancer for most of her young life, but was now in remission. She had always brought happiness with her.

James poured himself a small whiskey, Glenfiddich, his favourite tipple, to calm the nerves he felt jangling. He supposed his nervousness was based more on having to face them all after his binge. Still, he told himself, it had to be done. They had been good and true friends. God, he was thinking like an old man.

I, Plague

It was about three o' clock when he was dragged from his reverie by Madge announcing that the first of them were coming up the drive. James roused himself and wandered to the front door. Madge was busy organising the staff, needlessly making sure they knew which rooms were which.

The two cars were pulling up at the front door as he went down the steps. First out was Mona, as usual. He was surprised by the amount she had grown. No longer a pubescent girl, she was blossoming into an attractive young woman. She had not, however, lost her child like exuberance, and covered the short distance at a gallop, throwing her arms around his neck and hugging him. James looked over the top of her head and threw his hands up in despair as her parents and Mike approached. He would never tell anyone, but he did like being the uncle figure. He managed to disentangle himself and shake hands with the men, kissing Carmen on the cheek and leading them inside.

In the lounge he started on his rehearsed opening. He had agonised over it for hours, and, with a deep breath he started.

"Good to see you all again. I just wanted to say that I appreciate the support you've given me over the last few months. I know I must have been a regal pain in the a...sorry, bum. Anyway, thank you." James ended lamely, having completely forgotten what he had been going to say. There was a silence, not an awkward one, before Mona jumped up. She hugged him again, eliciting smiles all around.

"It's because we love you, James." Without pausing for a breath, she leapt to the subject, which James knew she had been bottling up. "Do you think I can go down to the stables now? Right, I'll go and get changed." She was off before James had finished nodding his head.
"Anyone for a drink?" A relief to be doing something with his hands.

He had barely handed out the drinks when Mona bounced into the room, now clad in her riding gear. James knew Lou had bought her the best clothing and equipment that money could buy, but she still managed to look like any other girl who came to the stables.

"I saw another car coming down the drive. Do you think it's Pippa?" She didn't wait for a reply before dashing out, bumping into Madge and Jean on her way. "Look Madge, Pippa's here."
James had nicknamed Pippa the *"Pocket Hurricane"* shortly after he and Marie first met her. She had energy in abundance. As he walked to

the door James realised that he probably loved these girls as much as he would his own daughters. That said, however, he did not know if he could keep up with them, and unlike daughters they tended to leave after a while.

James again endured the hugs and led Pippa and her folks into the house. Everyone already knew each other, so there were no uncomfortable introductions. He could stand back and watch, instead of forcing conversation. Pippa had disappeared with Mona as soon as she arrived, and it wasn't long before the two of them came back down stairs, dressed for the stables.

They were a complete contrast. Pippa, fair with blonde hair and blue eyes, which were always smiling, and Mona, with her dark hair and eyes; relatively speaking she was the more sombre of the two. "You two bunking off school to get here so early?" he teased.

"James, you really are out of touch, it's still the holidays, silly." They grabbed a hand each. "Come on James, let's go to the stables."

"Good idea." It was Mike who spoke. "It will be good to stretch the old legs after the drive."

The women said they would stay behind and the men were dragged through the kitchen and onto the road. Pippa and Mona could not contain their impatience and were soon well ahead of them.

"How are you, James? Good to see you back on track." The rest was unspoken.

"Doing good thanks, Lou. How's this old reprobate shaping up? I hope you keep him busy."

They spent the next hour watching the girls and catching up on all the news. As they returned to the house, James knew that it was going to be a good weekend. The part he had been dreading had passed, it was just like it had been prior to the accident.

I, Plague

CHAPTER FOUR

The rain was falling straight down in sheet after sheet, blurring the scene through the windscreen. Low, dark, and motionless clouds reinforced the impression that Manchester was indeed a gray and drab part of the country, where it always rained. *Раин, раин, алваыс раин ин тхис цоунтры*. Stop, he thought. Always think in English, otherwise you'll make a mistake. It was easy to remember someone who spoke in Russian, and that was the last thing he wanted. He had always prided himself on his ability to blend into the background, wherever he happened to be. His clothing, his attitude, his accent, all were calculatedly neutral. There was nothing that made him standout from the crowd. That was one of the reasons for his fifteen years of success at his chosen career of assassin. But he did manage to smile to himself, it was true, it seemed like it never stopped raining. He had spent the night at the Old Trafford Hotel, overlooking the football ground. He would have liked to have seen a Manchester United game, but it was a weekend when they were playing away. One of the perks of working for Gregori was that he could always attend games where Gregori's club was playing. Still, he thought, there would be plenty of time for that once he was retired. Not too long to go now.

He checked his watch, a run of the mill Seiko, and looked through the windscreen of the rented Audi at the fourth house down the cul de sac. If the normal Sunday morning routine was to be followed, the garage door should open and the car washing ritual would begin in the next two or three minutes. He supposed that the rain was a good cover; it would allow him to cover most of his features with hat and umbrella as he walked to and from the house. During the time spent observing his subject, he had noticed the tendency of the British towards Sunday morning sloth. Any churchgoers only came out of their houses around eleven thirty, and even then they drove off straight away, not paying any attention to their surroundings. All these things worked in his favour.

As he sat, he contemplated his next few moves. He knew that, after this killing, the police would surely link the two. He was using the same gun, that was a habit, but it did lessen the chance of it being found while he was filling the contract. After the next hit all the alarm bells would start ringing, and he would have to exercise extreme care. He was not, however, concerned by this, they would have no physical description to go on, no DNA and no fingerprints, just the rounds found in the victims.

The automatic garage door swung up and open. He touched the revolver in his coat pocket and decided to wait a few minutes before making his move. He knew, from the time spent watching his subject, that he started washing the car's roof first before moving to the front. It was there he preferred to find him, at the back of the garage where no one would see him fall. A small thing, but one which could buy him extra minutes to clear the scene. He opened the car door and swung the umbrella out, flicking the switch that opened it, before stepping out and closing the door behind him.

He turned into the cul de sac, walking slowly, wanting to appear to examine the house numbers as he went. The houses were large with a wide expanse of garden at the front, each of them having double garages and generally at least one car parked in front. It was obviously an affluent area, befitting someone who had made a fortune from the illegal enterprises he ran in this part of England. The suburb was in stark contrast to some of the ones he had driven through on his way from the hotel he had stayed in. There was no difference to his home city of Moscow; in recent years wealth had been accumulated by a few, and they had segregated themselves in comfortable surroundings, much as these people were doing here. The only difference being that in England it had been this way for hundreds of years, and Russia had only started back on the capitalist road since the collapse of the USSR.

He sauntered to the front of the house with the open garage and stood for a minute, wanting to give the impression to anyone who happened to be watching that he was confused, then, pretending to notice for the first time that there was someone inside, he walked slowly up the drive. He kept his hands in his pockets as he approached the rear of the BMW 7 series, closing his fist around the butt of the Colt Python and shaking it slightly to loosen it from the folds of his pocket.

As he neared the driver's side of the car, he saw a tall black man bent over the bonnet, vigorously applying a soapy sponge to the surface. He went unnoticed as he passed the rear of the car and stood at the rear door. He had pulled the gun halfway out of the pocket, only the six inch barrel and silencer extension still concealed. He relaxed his grip on the umbrella permitting it to rest on his shoulder, the hood deliberately dropping to conceal the top half of his body from any passers by on the street.

"Excuse me, I wonder if you can help me?" he said softly. As the bent figure straightened, not showing any sign of surprise, he saw a tall, handsome man with good strong cheekbones, clear eyes and closely cropped hair. He was still holding the sponge, water dripping onto the floor at his feet.

The gun barrel cleared the pocket, lifting its extended length to point directly at the forehead of the car washer. His face registered shock at the sight, and the sound of the hammer being pulled back, but he did not have time to move before a .357 hollow point jerked his head back, spraying the white wall and wooden workbench behind with blood. The gunman stepped forward over the prostate body and fired one more round into the head before pocketing the gun and turning. To an onlooker he wanted to appear to be thanking someone, and with brief wave he walked back the way he came, this time with the more purposeful stride of a man who knows where he is going. The whole episode had taken less than three minutes, and the whole time his face had been concealed by the hat and the umbrella. There was no sound of alarm as he reached the car and started the engine. He had not expected any, and maintained a steady pace as he left the area, ensuring he did not attract the unwanted attention of a bored policeman by keeping to the speed limits.

He followed a circuitous route around the suburbs, which would take him well away from the house and the area before he was picked up by the CCTV cameras. It was also a different exit point from the road he had used to access the estate. It was time consuming, but it was another detail which he used to buy himself time. It was entirely possible that the car would not be identified anyway, but taking care was what had kept him alive and out of jail.

He drove to Manchester Airport, where he took his bag from the car and returned the keys to the Avis desk. After the formalities, and being wished a pleasant flight by the receptionist, he walked into the terminal building and retraced his steps to catch a shuttle bus into the city centre. To all appearances, he was just another bored and tired businessman finishing his trip.

Leaving the airport shuttle, he made his way into Manchester's main line train station. He knew he had time before his Virgin train left for Bristol. He had pre-booked his first class ticket over the Internet. Hefting his bag over one shoulder, and putting the umbrella under one arm, he pushed open the door to the cafeteria, inadvertently bumping into two Transport Policemen who were leaving, their hands full with cups of coffee.

"Sorry", he murmured, and held the door open for them. It amused him that they would never know how close they had come to someone who would soon be the most sought after man in Britain. One of them had actually brushed against his bag, and had probably, unknowingly, been within an inch of the Colt Python. Sitting at a corner table, nursing his cappuccino, he reviewed the operation. It had all gone easily and according to the schedule he had worked out. The first two killings were the easiest, but that had not been the reason for placing them at the top of the list. It was merely geography; he wanted to work his way down and then across the country.

Gregori Yegenovich would be pleased if he was following the events. He would already be moving in on the Scottish operation, and would start on the Manchester operation the next day. By the end of the week he would have control over most of Britain, with the exception of London. Even then, it would only be a matter of days before he controlled the extremely lucrative drug market, illegal immigrants and sex market. Gregori had laid out his plans and timetable for him when he offered him the job. It was ambitious and brutal. Necessarily brutal, to ensure that the lower echelons fell into line without a fight after they lost the figureheads. Anyone who complained too much would be dealt with swiftly and extremely harshly. That side of the business did not involve him; he was being paid to kill a list of nine people. He knew that five of them were heads of various parts of the country, but the last four were a family. An old man, his wife and two children. Gregori had been specific about it; the children were to be killed first, then the wife, and finally the old man. He would make sure that they knew what was going to happen, and who was behind it.

When his operation moved to London he would call in the rest of team. To complete the contract in London and Paris would be the most difficult part of the operation. They would be alert and waiting for him. He would need the specialists who comprised the rest of his murder team.

Still, enough time to think about all that after he had finished the next job. He finished his coffee and made his way to Platform 11, walking to the front of the Bristol train. He actually detested travelling by train, but it was anonymous and free of the security checks found at airports, which allowed him to carry a small arsenal on board with him. This time, however, he only had the Colt Python and a Browning 9mm, which was back up for unexpected eventualities.

I, Plague

CHAPTER FIVE

Andy McNeish looked round the small incident room at his team. They were quiet, almost sombre, and he knew that it had nothing to do with the fact that it was three o' clock on a Sunday afternoon. Andy cleared his throat to silence the subdued talk and started.

"First, thank you all for the time you've put in on this case." He glanced down at his notes, an unnecessary act, considering the brevity of them. "I know it's been frustrating, everything we've done has drawn a blank, but let's review it a final time before we close this off. Right, Forensics, anything new?"

"Nothing, boss. We've rerun everything we have, gone through the place with a fine tooth comb. We have nothing."

"Thanks, anything else on ballistics?"

"Nothing new. .357 hollow point magnum load, probably a revolver with a six inch barrel. We think it would be with a sound suppressor considering the noise a gun like that makes. No match on the rounds recovered."

"Anything from Interpol or any of our friends on the continent or America?"

This time it was Will who answered. "No, Andy. But it's still early days, especially for Interpol. I would guess that this is business related, a takeover maybe. The killing is too clean. It's the work of a professional, and we know they don't come cheap, ergo - business. I believe the wife doesn't have a clue as to what's going on. You agree Meg?" turning to the FLO on his left.

"I do," she did not hesitate. "Can't act the stuff she's been through."

"All right, forget the facts. Anyone have a feeling, heard rumours, anything?" Andy trusted their instincts, and if they believed something they heard then he was always prepared to run with it. It was Shirley who spoke up.

"Word is - there's a change of supplier for the drugs hitting the streets. New faces moving in, taking over the key points of the distribution network. Nothing concrete, but a lot of the guys out there are scared, a couple have disappeared, and the rest aren't too inclined to talk. You know what these guys are like; must be something pretty hairy going on to get them this riled up. But, just rumour, boss, nothing to go on. Although I have asked Narcotics to keep a finger on things and let us know if anything pops up."

Andy sighed, he hated this part. "Well, it looks like we have to put this on the back burner for now, get on with something more pressing where we might be able to do something constructive." He held up his hand to silence the protests, just as the phone rang. He gestured for Will to answer it and continued.

"I know, and I don't like it any more than you, but there's no point in chasing dead ends day after day. We have to call it quits. Right, let's get on with the cases lying on our desks. Thanks again."

The movement towards the door was halted by Will holding up his hand waving them back into the room. They listened to his answers of yes and his goodbye, waiting patiently for him to tell them about the call. Will looked at Andy, who told him the floor was his.

"I don't know if this is a break or not, probably not. But that was Manchester Police, a DCI Farrington. They've just had a similar shooting down there. Marcus Bering, shot twice in the head in his garage this morning, while he was washing his car. No witnesses, no forensics so far, their lab boy says that one of the rounds recovered from the wall might be a .357 hollow point, but he needs more time to confirm that. That was the reason for the call; they saw our bulletin. Main point of interest is that Bering was the kingpin in organised crime for the north of England, just like our Mr Hawkins used to be up here." There were nods of assent at this theory. "Right, they're going to e mail all they have to us and we'll do the same from this end. Maybe between the two sides, we'll catch a break. That OK with you, Andy?"

"Let's get on with it. Put everything we have on the two vics, profiles of the organisation, all that stuff. Make sure we cross the t's and dot the i's. I think this is going to be taken from us by the Organised Crime boys. Try get finished today, then we'll be ready to hand it over and get on with the usual stuff that's on our desks."

Andy left them to it and went back to his office to do his bit. He was just finishing his report when the Assistant Chief Constable came in and sat down. Waving Andy to stay seated, he came straight to the point.

"Andy, just finished a call from OCU in London. They're concerned that the two killings here and in Manchester are a part of a nationwide takeover. I'd guess that you have already figured that out, but they added that they have some intelligence to back that up. It would appear that it might be the Russians who are moving in, and that is a worry for us."

"Too true." Andy was thoughtful. "Word has it that they are brutal and ruthless. That would explain why some of the guys on the street are running so scared. I'd hazard a guess that we're going to find some more bodies scattered around before things settle down. I don't suppose they mentioned if they have any idea who'll be taking over up here?"

"Unfortunately not. They say they are in the dark at this stage, but will obviously keep us informed. I'll sit on them to make sure they do that. I'll hold a briefing for everyone as soon as I know something." The AC managed a rueful smile. Co-operation on a national level sometimes left a lot to be desired; it had improved recently, but each force and department were traditionally very territorial about the investigations.

"We will, of course, do everything we can to cooperate from this end, sir." There was nothing he could think of to say.

"Thanks, Andy." The ACC stood and stopped at the door. "I know this is unnecessary, but you will keep me up to speed if anything turns up about this situation?" He didn't wait for a reply and closed the door softly behind him.

CHAPTER SIX

The weekend had gone smoothly. The house had been full of laughter again, and the delightful gibberish of teenage girls. Pippa and Mona had been joined by Beth and Cindy, two girls from the local village, and the four of them had alternated between the house and the stables all weekend. James felt relaxed and in more control than he had been in months.

Mike and Lou were preparing to head back to London, and another week's work. They had told him of plans to further expand his restaurant network. Mike was taking on more of an executive role - a big leap from the security consultant he had started out as, a result of their first meeting. The two mothers were trying in vain to get their daughters to sit still and eat breakfast. Madge and the girls were running around fussing, serving the eggs, toast and coffee, as well as making efforts to pack cases.

James sipped his coffee and watched it all with a small smile playing on his lips. During a late Saturday night, while consuming copious amounts of whiskey, he had finally been able to discuss Marie's accidental death, and his own lack of ability to cope with it. He had discussed his future plans for the estate. And James and Mike had reminisced about their first meeting, how much they had come on since that day. More particularly, they talked about the evening when James had killed two men who had burst into a family dinner with the intention of killing Lou. It had been after that when James had suggested that Mona and her mother visit, an effort to take her mind off the events she had witnessed. That had solidified their friendship. James had grown to like and trust this man, who had once controlled the majority of organised crime in Britain. He liked to think he would still have liked him in the old days, but knew that it was easier now that Lou was retired and a respectable businessman.

When only Mike and James were left at the table the conversation turned, as it mostly did, to their old days.

"We've both come quite a long way in the last few years since we last worked together in some smelly country." Mike's gaze was far away; James guessed he was picturing the plains and jungles of some African republic. "Still pop down to the Lamb and Flag and catch up with some of the lads. Another couple didn't make it back from their last job."

"We're way too old for that kind of soldiering now. Too used to the comfortable life. Don't know about you, but I can't imagine sleeping on anything but a bed. As for guns, well mine are locked away, and they're going to stay that way. Yes, old friend, it's a better life we have now than either of us deserves."

Mike stood and went into the lounge, returning with two glasses. "Bit early for whiskey?"

"Not at all, I'm not driving, and one isn't going to hurt." He handed James a glass and lifted his in a toast.

"Here's to a comfortable life and to those guys who never made it."

"Starting a bit early, aren't you boys?" Lou had entered the room unheard. Mona and Pippa stood quietly beside him.

"Just remembering." It was all James could say. It was true, in that brief moment all the faces from the old days had marched across his vision.

"I understand. How about one for me, if you don't mind me joining you?" Mike left and returned again with three glasses, each with a generous shot. When James looked askance at the level of the amber fluid, Mike grinned. "Always did enjoy handing out your booze."

They toasted each other silently. Mona and Pippa stood on either side of James and held onto his elbows, heads resting lightly on his shoulder. It was a good feeling.

As with the rest of the weekend the moment passed too soon and James was standing in the drive, watching the three cars disappearing onto the country road which would take them home.

He decided that the Monday morning would be dedicated to catching up on his finances. He knew that he was more than comfortable. He would never have to worry about money again in his life. The stables were doing well, despite the economy, the classes were full, the rented space was full, and the training centre was occupied with British Horse Society courses. On top of all this, he had a half share in a country house hotel owned by his sister and her husband. They were doing a really good job of running at a profit. He made a note to go and visit in the not too distant future.

He went through to the kitchen and sat at his normal morning place at the long table. Jean came through with an armful of sheets and towels. He stood and helped her, despite her protestations that she could manage. "Put that load in, then come and have a coffee, Jean. Don't worry, we've got all day to do the rooms, it's not as if someone else is coming tonight. Did you enjoy the weekend, not too much work for all of you?"

"No, of course not, it was great to have people here again, especially the girls." Jean paused for a moment, then reached across the table and took his hand. "It was also good to see you back to your normal self. James, we were all so worried about you. We never told you, but we took turns checking on you through the night, making sure you were all right. You don't mind, do you?"

"No, I don't mind. Do you realize, that's the first time you called me by my name since that night?" He might have had too much to drink that night about two weeks ago but it stayed with him.

James had been lying on the sofa listening to some soppy CD, feeling low and worse than that, lonely. Jean had come in to clear up some of the mess, dirty glasses and plates. He had started talking and she had listened. He could not remember what they talked about. It was not about Marie, any other subject but that. Eventually James had asked her to sit and had sat up to give her room on the sofa. He had taken another drink since Jean had entered the room, and thought how pleasant it was to have someone to listen to him. He didn't know how long they talked. She told him about the breakup with her boyfriend and started crying. James had taken her in his arms and cradled her, trying to soothe her. Then he felt the old familiar ache. This was not Marie and he so wanted it to be her. He in turn had started sobbing.

He had managed to whisper in her ear. "A right pair we are, crying away like babies. The split up hit you that hard?" He could barely make out her reply, her face was so buried in his shoulder.

"No, it's not the actual break-up. It's more that I fell in love with someone else."

"Why the tears then? Whoever it is, I hope he knows how lucky he is."

"That's just it, he doesn't know. Probably doesn't even know I exist, never mind finding me attractive."
James had held her up to look at her face. Jean's eyes were red and still

brimming with tears. Her cheeks were streaked and he reached out and gently wiped the tears away with his thumbs. With her short hair framing her face, and the way the light shone on her skin it attained a porcelain quality. This close her eyes looked like blue suns against the paleness. She raised her hand and held his against her cheek, leaning her head into it, cradling her face. He had a thought that in all the years she had worked for him, he had never been this close to her, or anyone else, apart from Marie.

He found it strangely easy. Imperceptibly, she had moved closer to him. James looked at her parted lips and moved his head down to kiss her. Eyes closed, he permitted himself to drown in the kiss, enjoying the softness, lips still moist and tasting of salt from the tears. Jean had responded, slipping her tongue between his lips, teasing the tip of his tongue and the insides of his lips. He knew he wasn't kissing Marie, but did not want the moment to pass. The kiss was not the familiar one of lovers, rather one of exploration, tender, ever so sweet. The embrace was a comfort beyond comprehension. They parted and she had buried her head on his shoulder again. James had been bewildered; what had he let happen?

He was going to push her upright and away from him when he felt that she was sobbing again.

James stroked her hair and mumbled. "I'm sorry. I'm so sorry. Please don't cry."

That was the first time Jean called him by name. "Oh James, don't be sorry, please just hold me for a bit longer. I'm fine, really I am."

They had held each other for some time before she pushed him away and stood to pick up the tray she had left on the table. James had asked her if she would come back when she finished, and she said she would. He must have dozed, and was in that half awake state, eyes still closed, when he felt that his head was being stroked, fingers lightly tracing the outline of his jaw and cheekbones. Over his eyelids and nose. All the time he heard her soothing voice.

"My James, my poor James. How you must hurt. I wish I could take that from you, but you wouldn't let me, would you? Oh, if only things were different, if only I could tell you all the things I feel, how I could help you."

All he could do was put his arm around her shoulders and hold her close. As far as James could remember, not another word was spoken until he woke with daylight streaming through the windows and Jean asleep in his arms. James had gently disengaged himself and gone to the bathroom. When he returned she was gone.

That had been the start of recovery. They had never spoken of the incident, although he had resolved to broach the subject at some appropriate time. He supposed that now was as good a time as any.

"It's good to hear you call me James." God, he thought what an asinine opening. He saw she was framing something to say and held up his hand to stop her. "Don't you dare apologise. I promise that I won't tell Madge if you don't." James couldn't help feeling a certain tenderness towards her, and knew that he was smiling. "I would like, no, I was wandering - no. Look, what I'm trying to say is that I would like for us to have a chat, alone without fear of someone walking in on us. Would you be willing to do that?"

"Of course, yes. When? I do have the afternoon and evening off, after we finish the cleaning."

"That's good. Look, why don't we go to the pub. You tell me when you're leaving, and I'll leave at the same time. That way you won't have to do any embarrassing explaining."

"It'll be around two. I better get on or we'll have Madge storming through here looking for me."

When James caught up with Madge he told her not to prepare anything for his lunch, rather to give everyone the rest of the day off; they had done well. When asked, he said he would go to the pub for lunch. "Glad to hear it, do you good to get back out again. All the locals will be pleased to see you."

It was raining heavily in a steady stream when he went out to the Range Rover. James was just starting the engine when he realised that he forgotten his wallet. He had become so used to not going out that it was no longer part of the ritual of dressing. In the hall, he met Madge and Jean. "Glad I caught you, sir, Jean here is going into the village and I was going to ask if you would give her a lift."

James shared a brief conspirator's smile with Jean as he picked up his wallet.

Maurice Johns

The pub was busy when they walked through the doors. James saw a vacant table near the window and suggested Jean take a seat and he would fetch them some drinks. All his friends were there. These were the same people who had been guests at his wedding. Eight months later, the same people had attended the funeral. James had not seen them for the months he had been on a bender. It took forever to get to the bar and order the drinks, and almost as long to get back to the table.

Apologising for the delay in getting back to her, he decided to broach the subject right away, only to be thwarted by a waitress asking if they were going to order any food. They made their choices, both opting for a simple Ploughman's lunch.

As James watched Jean read the menu and order he was concerned about what he was going to say. He didn't have the foggiest idea as to how to handle the situation. He didn't want to hurt her, he didn't want to give her the wrong impression. Maybe he didn't want to do anything. That would be the easy solution.

Jean took the initiative. "Do you really not mind me calling you James? It sort of slipped out this morning. I'm sorry if I did wrong." She looked at him with those eyes he remembered so well from the close up view. The memory of the kiss flashed across his mind with a pang of longing that so surprised him he almost physically started. What could he say, except to reassure her that she hadn't done anything wrong, that he didn't mind. Truth be known, he actually liked it, but he didn't tell her that.

"I suppose this is about that night when...well, you know." Jean held his eyes, drawing him into the blue depths. Now he had no choice in the matter.

"Yes." Is honesty the best policy? That was the question on his mind. James jumped in. "Look, I feel terrible about that, I wanted to apologise for taking advantage of you when you were upset. I don't know what came over me. I really am sorry."

"Oh, bugger. Oops, sorry." Jean was looking down digging into her handbag, eventually coming out with a tissue. When she wiped her eyes James knew that he had said the wrong thing. He tried to apologise again. "James, please stop saying you're sorry. I think Pippa would say you were being silly." That brought a smile. "Truly, it's *me* who should be apologising for taking advantage of *you*." Now she had completely lost him. Was he just plain simple minded? Or was it he did not understand women? Both would apply, James thought.

"May I be honest with you?" Jean asked and he nodded, wondering what was coming. "You have to promise that you won't be annoyed with me?" James promised, now even more intrigued. Jean almost finished her vodka and coke before turning back to him. Unfortunately, the food arrived at the same time. He ordered another round of drinks and they ate in silence while they waited for them.

Again she took a healthy swig before putting down her knife and leaning towards him. As she did so, he picked up the scent of a perfume whose name he could not think of, but it was very pleasant. James immediately felt guilty. It was as if such a thought was an infringement of his memory of Marie. Pull yourself together, he admonished himself.

"Right, do you remember that night, what we talked about?" James assured her he remembered vividly. Jean blushed slightly. "Well, it was all true. I cried more because I was worried about you, we all were, you know. Each and every one of us shared your pain and your grief. Hell, I'm not doing a good job of this. Anyway, you didn't take advantage of me, like I said, it was the other way around. I wanted you to kiss me. I didn't know it was going to happen. I didn't plan it or anything like that. But when we were sitting there, I wanted you to kiss me. There, I've said it. Do you forgive me? God, that sounded awful."

"First, of course I forgive you, but there's nothing to forgive. I honestly don't know what to say." He thought for a minute. "You've been honest, so you deserve the same from me. I don't know if what we did was right or wrong. I can tell you that I enjoyed the time spent with you. You made me feel good, no that's the wrong word. I don't know. For the first time since the accident I felt at ease, comfortable, if you will." It was his turn to blush, but Jean didn't smile. "I should probably thank you, I enjoyed it so much, but that doesn't seem right. Honestly, I wanted to kiss you too. There, I've said it." James busied himself cutting some cheese, feeling her eyes on him. He was going to continue but she stopped him.

"You feel guilty, about the feelings, I mean. You feel you're betraying the memory. Even now I can see you're feeling some guilt, just by being here."
"That's very astute for one so young, but true. When did you gain such wisdom?"

Jean laughed. "I watch too much TV."

James swallowed half his pint. "I suppose it comes down to two things. Tell me if I'm making any wrong assumptions here. Yes, I feel guilty. It does feel like I'm cheating on Marie, when we kissed, and now. I know it's stupid, but I think its part of the process. I have no idea when I'll be ready to move on. Maybe it's already started, I don't know. I do know that it would be unfair of me to start something I could not finish. Also, you're still very young, much younger than Marie. I'm sorry, I'm not doing very well at this." James took a sip of his beer. "The last thing in the world I would want is to hurt you. You know the saying that it's better to have loved and lost than never to have loved at all?" Jean nodded. "Well, I think it implies that the love is lost with the person, but I know that you never lose the love, only the object of that love. My word, that's quite profound for an old soldier. But do you know what I mean?"

"I understand. I hope one day someone will love me like that. You remember everything, don't you? Even the things I said when I thought you were asleep?"

James nodded.

"God, I'm sorry. You weren't meant to hear that."

"Really, it's all right. I didn't even have a clue before then. Even when you told me about your ex. I wish I could tell you I felt the same, but the truth is, I don't, not right now. I would like us to be friends. God, that's something out of a really corny movie. Can we still be friends, do you think? See what happens? I also have to protect your reputation. Just think what everyone would say. Sad, old man has to find his girlfriends by hiring them." James smiled to show it was a poor attempt at humour.

"I'd like that," Jean offered her hand for a shake. "Friends." He shook her hand.

CHAPTER SEVEN

At last it had stopped raining. The sky was clear and blue, and a gentle breeze barely moved the branches and leaves on the trees. It was pleasantly warm, even this early in the morning. It would not be long before the day was hot enough to make his vigil uncomfortable. He did not mind having to lie and wait in the rain, but that did not mean he had to like it. This was far better. That was the trouble with this modus operandi, it could take hours before a reasonable target presented itself.

He had arrived, after a long train journey, at the Coomb Grove Manor Hotel three miles outside Bath, late on Sunday night, and spent Monday relaxing, acting like a tourist. His case had been kept by the concierge after his first visit and had, judging by the layer of dust, been untouched. After a tour of Bath, he had picked up the car he bought in London for cash, from the lock up he hired. On the Tuesday morning he had driven to a wooded lane two kilometers from the house and parked in the undergrowth. He had not made any special effort to hide the car. Sometimes, hiding in the open was the best disguise. Anyway, he reasoned, there would be very few walkers out on a weekday.

An estate agent would have described the property as a luxury farmhouse with outbuildings, set in spacious grounds, convenient to both Bristol and Bath. From the observations he had made, it was certainly luxurious. There was a tennis court and, at the rear, a swimming pool in an extension of the house. He knew that that the glass roof and door all slid back on good days to convert it into an open air pool. It was a Tuesday, and he didn't think that would happen today; his target would be busy with the running of his part of the country.

He had approached the house from the west, using a stand of trees and thick undergrowth as cover. He carried a case, slightly longer than a briefcase, but inconspicuous. Once in the undergrowth he located the tree he had marked as a good shooting platform. Before climbing up he slid on a tight fitting pair of gloves, a brown overall and head covering. Opening the case he assembled the Galil 7,62 with care. It slotted smoothly together and, attaching the strap, he climbed the tree slowly, not disturbing the branches or leaving any obvious scratches to mark his progress. He found the fork he wanted. It was wide enough to offer some comfort, and deep enough in the foliage to offer protection from searching eyes. He knew that only the closest scrutiny from directly underneath him would reveal his presence. He settled himself, looped the strap around his left forearm and rested the long barrel on a fork between two smaller branches. The house sprang into focus and, adjusting the sights, he swung the rifle over the windows and grounds around the house.

He grunted in satisfaction as his assumption that things would tighten up were proved correct. There were three men in the grounds, and an entrance gate had been swung closed.

Counting the windows from the left, he found the third one which permitted a view into an office and a broad desk with a high backed chair, currently empty. No cause for alarm, it was still early, and his target was probably still having breakfast. He rested the rifle across his lap and took a sip from the bottle of water he had in his overalls. When he saw a woman and three children exit the house and climb into a Range Rover, he picked up the rifle again. He was aware of the sound of the vehicle leaving and the gate being closed behind them as he picked out the office window.

From the night he had spent checking the outside of the house, he knew that the window glass was standard double glazing. There had been no dogs in evidence and the men that now patrolled the grounds were not resident on the property. He moved the rifle to check the other rooms he could see, and found them empty. Good; in all likelihood they were the only ones present, apart from the target. A brief smile etched its way onto his face. They had certainly drawn the short straw for their guard duty. He watched the patterns of their patrols and saw that they rarely went to the rear of the building. They were making the mistake of assuming that any threat would be from the front. He selected the order in which he would take them down, based on their proximity to each other. He knew the shock factor would allow the necessary seconds to swing from one to the other.

When he swung back to the office window he did a mental calculation about the distance and the strength of the breeze. It was just over 500 metres and the breeze now was barely noticeable. He adjusted the sight by a fraction and focused on the chair. He was now in the "*zone*" and would remain there until the job was finished. Every part of his mind and body was concentrated through the eyepiece of the scope. The rifle was an extension of his arms and hands. He was aware of the birds landing and taking off around him, the soft rustle of the leaves as the breeze gusted with sufficient force to stir them.

Routine; in his job it was essential. And the morning routine was adhered to. Clear up the paperwork, make a few phone calls. The target settled into the comfort of his chair and leaned forward to pick up some papers. With them in his hands he leaned back, resting his head on the back of the chair to read them. A brief stirring of the leaves and it was still again. Anticipation of the next move, only a movement of the hands as a page was turned and the gentle pressure on the trigger increased, the finger taking up the slack and then squeezing further until the sub sonic round left the barrel, whispering its way through the window and hitting the target in the centre of the forehead. Appropriately nicknamed *"Whispering Death"*, the birds in the trees did not interrupt their own version of a routine. Through the scope, he could see the head jerking backwards against the restraint of the chair. The blossoming of fine, red spray lingering like motes of dust. A perfect shot. There were no self congratulations; such a shot was expected. He moved the barrel sighting on the furthest guard and squeezed the trigger again, moving and firing another two times, each time lingering only long enough to be sure that the head shot had been achieved. Each of them dead before they hit the ground. Now there would be no pursuit, no alarm.

Climbing down from his shooting platform as carefully as he had climbed into it, he scanned the ground for the empty brass casings, picking up each one until all four were accounted for and placing them in his overall pocket. He then carefully disassembled the rifle and packed it away.

A look around before leaving the cover of the trees and he was walking back to the car, stripping off the overall and replacing the sneakers with leather shoes, and driving away.

CHAPTER EIGHT

Mike was quietly fuming as he sat in front of Lou's desk. It was Wednesday morning, and only thirty minutes ago information had reached him about the deaths in Scotland, Manchester, and Bristol. Mike blamed himself for the incompetence of his information network. To him, it was irrelevant that Lou had retired years ago and did not keep in touch with any of old associates. It was simply the fact that no-one had deemed it necessary to tell him right away. Some of the blame, if not all of it, was his own.

He had thrown himself into the role he had been offered, that of heading up the restaurant chain. It was part of the expansion of the solely legitimate business that Lou now controlled. Mike had been flattered by the offer. His experience in this field was severely limited, but, as Lou had pointed out, if he could run one business he could run another. The principles stayed the same, even if the product was vastly different.

Across the desk Lou remained unperturbed by the news. He had only said that it was a shame and had ordered that some flowers and a condolence card be sent to the families.

"It's all I can do, Mike. I'm keeping myself well away from that sort of thing. It does look like there's some sort of takeover going on though. It will be interesting to see what develops out of this." Lou had dismissed Mike's apologies for the tardiness of the news, pointing out what Mike had already known. The matter was now closed, and the business of the day resumed.

In the afternoon, Mike left the house. Lou always liked to spend time with Mona; as he was fond of reminding everyone, she had come late in his life. This in itself was a blessing, as he now had time for her, time he had not been able to make for his eldest. Mike drove to Oxford Street, where the latest restaurant was undergoing changes and decoration. He checked with the foreman, suggested some small changes and signed off on work completed. He was still finding it difficult to adjust to his new role. He always felt he should be doing more. Quite what, he didn't know, but it nagged at him nonetheless.

Feeling out of place, he decided he would go the Lamb and Flag and see if anyone he knew was there. It was a small, local pub, standing on a corner. It was the type of place where you could stand and imagine the bombs of the blitz falling around. There were always the same faces scattered around, regulars who jealously guarded their spot at the bar, or at tables where they played dominoes. How it evolved into a meeting and recruiting place for ex soldiers looking for mercenary work, Mike did not know. It had always been that way apparently.

Way back, in the days of the Congo, the back room had been used to interview for contracts, and it had remained that way. Even though he was no longer in that line of business, he still liked to visit and catch up. It was his only contact with the outside world. Sometimes, he felt he should make some sort of effort to try and find that *"special"* person. Maybe one day.

Mike had never managed to find a steady girlfriend. This he blamed on the lifestyle he had followed prior to settling down in Lou's employ. Reluctant to admit it, even to James, he had maintained a soft spot for Monique. He had never even hinted to her about a date. He felt she was way outside his league, successful corporate lawyer that she was, living in Paris. She moved there to escape the stigma she felt because of her father's business dealings, which she had disapproved of strongly since she had been old enough to understand. Time, and the fact that he had retired, had mellowed her to a large extent, but there were times when Mike felt he was regarded in much the same way as her father had been.

As soon as he walked through the pub's door, Mike saw a face he recognised. "Ethan? Is that you? God, it's good to see you again, kid."

He was full of questions for this youngster. Mike supposed Ethan could not be described as a youngster anymore. He was a full grown man, although he still retained his youthful looks, which was probably down to the blond hair, unwrinkled, tanned face, and a certain sparkle in his blue eyes.

Ethan told him what he had been doing in the four years since they had worked together. It had been his first job as a mercenary, and Mike and James had taken the youngster under their wing in the hope they could teach him enough to keep him alive. It had been close, and almost cost James his own life. Now he was telling Mike about his last job, having only returned two days previously. He mentioned the names of two men who had been killed. Mike recognised the names, but could not put a face on them.

"Been thinking about jacking the whole thing in, trying to settle a bit, you know? Get a respectable job." Mike was wondering if it was the loss of two comrades that brought this on. "Truth be known, I'm tired of walking into villages and seeing men, women and children with bits missing. Hearing the stories of the gangs who raid their villages. Getting a bit sick of it all. Miss the money, though."

Mike told him that he might be able to help in the work department, and gave him his card, making him promise to call him as soon as he settled back down. He knew that after a hard job it took a couple of weeks, at least, to get back into a civilised routine. He took the number of Ethan's boarding house and promised that he would call if he heard of anything. He was already putting together an idea in his mind about what he could do for him. Something in the restaurant line, but he would figure that out later.

Mike lingered over his beer and explained to Ethan how he had managed to get his present job. As he recounted the story, he thought just how lucky he had been. He had actually ridden on the back of James' luck. If James had not contacted him to get the information he needed, he would not have been with him when he met Lou and Marcus. Then he would not have been invited to the dinner, so rudely interrupted by the two youths with shotguns. Not that, he explained to Ethan, he had done much there.

He had been sitting with his back to the door and by the time he realised what James had been up to, it was all over. Mike told Ethan about James' place, the stables and the way he had settled down. He assured him that James would be pleased to see him again and promised to take him with him on his next visit.

"That's some story. You guys really landed on your feet. I hope I'm as lucky. I can't imagine James as the country gentleman, I never really had much to do with you two outside the job. Why do you think he prefers James instead of Jim, or Jimmy?"

"I don't know, is the answer. I mean, I prefer Mike to Michael. Not much you can do with your name, probably why we call you kid, or youngster."

"Tell me, does he still come out with those quotes of his? He always had one."
"He does indeed. Let's see if I can remember the one he used at that meeting I told you about. It was from the Bible - "*A pale horse whose rider is called Plague appears, and Hell follows at his heels*" - it worked, as well. James explained that we would be the plague and that

hell would surely descend on him and his people. Yes, really did the trick."

Mike could see the curiosity on the young man's face, and was expecting the next question. "What happened? Is that how you got into this work now?"

"Yes. It was a direct result of that meeting." Mike looked at his watch. "I've got time, if you want to hear the story, I'll tell you." Ethan nodded, and Mike bought another round of drinks before starting. "James has a sister and she and her husband made a bad deal with a guy called Marcus. It ended up they got into trouble with him, and he was going to take the hotel they had bought as payment for the loan. They asked James for help, and he got in touch with me." Mike smiled at the memory. He remembered it as clearly as if it had happened only that morning.

They walked back to St Martin's Place and the coffee shop. True to his word, the waiter had kept the table for them and they sat, ordering medium lattes for the wait. To the casual observer, they were two work colleagues taking a break. They were relaxed; any nerves were gone. It was an old and familiar routine for the two of them as they waited. James was the first to see the car drop off Lou and a tall, well dressed black man. He nudged Mike, and indicated them with his head. Further up the road another car had stopped and two more black men got out. They were both dressed in business suits and Mike idly wondered if they were the same two who had made the threats. As Lou approached James stood and offered his hand. He was introduced to Marcus and shook the well manicured hand. Mike knew he would have noticed the expensive cut of the suit, the highly polished shoes and the watch on the wrist. James gestured for them to sit. Lou started the small talk.

"Brought your valet along with you, I see." James smiled and introduced Mike as an old friend. They both ordered cappuccinos and when they had been brought to the table, Marcus spoke for the first time.

"I'm told by Lou here that you're a serious man. That you have a proposition for me, regarding Morag and Tony. He tells me they're family. Anyway, I'm listening."

James leaned forward, elbows on the table, and put forward his proposition, explaining that he had the banker's draft in his inside pocket and how the profit share scheme would work. He went into as much detail as he could about the arrangements he proposed. They had finished their coffee by the time James had finished, and were silent as the waiter brought refills. James had been aware that the old man had been watching throughout his story, although he had maintained steady eye contact with Marcus.

"That sounds very reasonable, however, it closes a business opportunity for me. One that I was rather looking forward to." Marcus sounded too polite and well spoken to be a crook. This made James smile as he replied.

"Well, I would agree with you there. If you agree to this, then the only laundry that will be done at the hotel is the sheets and towels."

He was pleased to see this brought a smile first to the face of the old man and then, slowly, to Marcus.

"Very droll, I must say. But what if I turn down your offer, and proceed with my original plan? Did you bring the paperwork that my men dropped off, by the way?"

"No, that's now ashes. I'm sorry, but that isn't an option. What will I do?" He paused. James waited, prolonging the pause. He looked directly at Marcus. There was not a trace of humour in his demeanour or voice when he spoke. Mike could see he felt cold, emotionless. He had reverted to what he had been three years previously. "If I may," he said eventually, "I'd like to draw your attention to a passage from Revelations." He was met with a blank stare. "The Bible." Recognition from Marcus. On the periphery of his vision he saw the old man smile. "A pale horse whose rider is called Plague appears, and Hell follows at his heels." He paused again, "If any harm comes to my family, you won't see the pale horse, you may not even see me, but I promise you, Hell, of the kind you cannot even imagine, will follow at my heels."

Marcus held his stare. "Do you think you can take me and all my men?"

Without breaking his gaze, feeling this was some kind of test, he asked Mike "How long to put a fully equipped strike force in the field?"

"Two, three days. Four at the very outside. That's on the ground."

"Our projected casualties?"

Again Mike answered immediately, "Less than five per cent. Up against amateurs, have to count on bad luck."

"Mortality for the opposition?"

"One hundred per cent. There'll be collateral damage, can't help that going up against civilians. Hard to tell what that'll be."

"Estimated time from start to finish?"

"If we started after finishing here, all over by next Friday."

James had still not broken his stare. "There you have it. If you make a move against my family, I will kill you and everyone associated with you."

Mike chipped in, speaking in an equally soft voice. "If anything happened to James, from a lightning strike to a bird crapping on his head. I will kill you."

Marcus leaned back. He was not smiling, and did not break eye contact. The old man looked tense. James decided to try and take the menace from the air, where it hung like a black cloud.

"I'm going to put my hand into my pocket to show the banker's draft, nothing else." He pulled back his jacket, knowing that the weapon in the shoulder rig would be in full view, and pulled the draft from his pocket, allowing the jacket to fall closed. He had seen Marcus' eyes follow his hand and the tightening of his mouth when he saw the weapon. However, when his hand came out with only the draft he visibly relaxed. He held it up in front of him.

"It's made out to you. It's as good as cash, but you know that. It's here, and it's yours. All you have to do is say the word."

Marcus reached out and took the banker's draft, looking at it and placing it back on the table, mid way between them. "You're very confident, but then again, I suppose in your line of work you have to be. Run through, again, the arrangement whereby I would get some profit from the hotel."

James did, this time explaining that, based on projections, he would receive £100,000. He waited.

"Very well, I accept. Such an action against me as you described would be very bad for business, and very expensive. It would take a long time to recover. One last thing – how do I know you will not carry out such an action anyway?"

"You forgot, it would be somewhat injurious to your health. You have my word on it. In the same way as I will have your word that any action against my family will cease."

"I give you my word." He picked up the banker's draft, folded it neatly in half and put it in his jacket pocket. James stood with them, Marcus offered his hand, and James shook it. Lou waited, telling Marcus that he would meet him at the car.

"Well, young man. I thought I had heard it all in my time, but that was priceless. I wish I had you working for me thirty years ago."

Mike had to smile.

"I must be off," Lou said, *"but I wanted to invite you to dinner tonight. As I told you yesterday, you interest me. It's my eldest daughter's birthday, hence the dinner, no business. I'll send a car to pick you up, seven thirty?"*

James looked at Mike, and Lou added, "Your valet is invited, of course. Mike is it?"

Mike drew his attention back to the present, and saw Ethan was smiling. "Valet?"

"Yeah, little joke. Anyway, that was the beginning of it really, that invitation to dinner. Don't suppose much else would have come of it if something hadn't happened during the dinner, which sort of put us in the spotlight, so to speak. In the old man's debt; his words, not mine." Mike took a drink and continued. "It should have been a quiet dinner, but you know how sometimes things happen, over which you have no control?" He again allowed his mind to picture the events as he narrated the story.

Ethan was still full of curiosity. "You mentioned the dinner earlier. What really happened, if you don't mind telling me?"

I, Plague

"Not at all, it was pretty much as I said, it was all over in a flash, but I'll tell it from the beginning, I'll tell it from James' perspective since he was the hero of the day."

The driver held the door and showed them inside. The only patrons were seated at a long table at the back of the restaurant. James saw Lou coming forward to meet them, shaking them both by the hand and welcoming them.

As he led them to the rear, he explained his eldest daughter was now thirty and had just been offered a junior partnership with the law firm she worked for. Cause for a double celebration. He signalled a waiter, who took their drinks order. They were introduced to the group of twenty five, mainly men and women, but with younger, teenage, children. They were told they would find the names of everyone for themselves. They were, however, introduced more formally to Lou's wife Carmen and his daughters, Monique being the eldest, and Mona. Lou told them he had met James only the previous day, and had been able to assist in a negotiation.

They were both made to feel welcome, and James found himself talking to Monique. She told him, in reply to his questions, that she worked in Paris for a law firm. When he queried that, he was told that she had studied at the Sorbonne and decided to remain. She loved Paris, and had built a good life for herself there. She asked if he was aware of her father's occupation prior to his retirement. He told her he was, to which she said that had been the primary reason for her choice of university. She had a way of looking at a person, he thought, almost as if she was reading his mind.

He tried to steer the conversation away from her father's past, asking her about the part of Paris she had her apartment in. He saw, during a lull in the conversation, that Mike was fully occupied with Carmen and Mona. He had them laughing as he recounted some story or the other. Monique had meanwhile thrown a question about his occupation. He was glad to be on neutral and safe ground, telling her about his home and the stables.

They were seated at a long table for dinner. James found himself next to Monique, who was on her father's left and opposite Mona who had Mike next to her. He supposed that being so close to the host was an honour. He was also glad that his place had his back against the wall; he could never have sat for a whole meal with his back to the door, as Mike now was. Not after the events of the last few days. Again, old habits dying hard, it had been astounding how they had all come flooding back, movements and action, such as sitting with his back to the wall coming naturally.

During the meal, he kept the conversation on the stables, much to Mona's interest. She declared she was passionate about horses, but being in London, she never really had the chance to ride. James entertained them with stories about the riding classes and some of the funnier incidents. At one point, as Mona was busy telling Mike about a ride on Wimbledon Common, he was asked by Monique, "Were you ever in the same business as my father?" He was surprised at the directness of the question. Her eyes were boring into his. At least he could answer honestly, he thought.

"No, I never even met your father until this week. I asked him for a favour, facilitating a meeting. But the answer is no, I've never been involved in any criminal activity." He smiled at her as he bent his head towards her ear. "To be honest, when I read about it, I thought it was a bit like a movie script, you know, The Godfather."

This, at least, brought a small smile to her lips, crinkling her eyes at the corners. "I didn't think you were the type. You obviously love your home. I'm glad."

James had debated with himself about telling her about his past, and his association with Mike, but decided against it. They would, in all likelihood, never meet again; there was no point.

The table had been cleared, leaving only the glasses and the bottles of wine. Lou had given a short speech about Monique and had given her a present, to much applause. Being next to her, James could see that it was a beautiful gold Rolex watch.

James looked up from the watch as the front door opened. He knew that the restaurant had been closed to all other patrons, and saw the manager walking to the two young black men who had entered. The hair on the back of James' neck bristled. They were wearing long raincoats and black knitted head coverings. There was something wrong with the picture. He moved his right hand under his jacket and unclipped the leather strap retaining his pistol in the holster. He moved his hand around the grip, thumb on the hammer. The manager had reached the intruders, who had stopped inside the door. He was saying something to them, when he was pushed to one side, falling against the till point. The two youths started walking towards the table, coats

I, Plague

falling open. James had a glimpse of a shotgun barrel. He withdrew his hand from under his jacket, pulling back the hammer in the same movement and standing. He pushed Monique back in her chair and moved to stand in front of her. Mike had seen his initial movement and had looked around in time to see the manager fall. He reacted as quickly as James, pulling Mona to him and pushing her behind her father, remaining in front of Lou as he tried to clear his weapon.

James, however, had the edge. His weapon was lining up on the youths as the coats fell away and they started to raise short, obviously sawn off, shotguns. James fired two rounds into the chest of the one who was proving quicker at lifting his shotgun, moving slightly to place two more rounds in the chest of the second youth. When hit they both dropped their shotguns, raising hands to their wounds before falling against the wall and to the floor. James knew that they were both dead before their heads bounced off the tiles.

There was a shocked, stunned silence, which James took advantage off. "Mike, check the front door and street." He took off.

James turned to the driver. "You, through the kitchen and check the back." He hesitated, looking to his boss. "Move!" James shouted. He moved to the two gunmen. They were dead. He picked up the shotguns, broke them and took out the shells. He helped the manager to his feet. "Can you close curtains, blinds anything, to cover the windows?" He nodded blankly, staring at the two dead bodies, blood beginning to pool under their backs, bright against the paleness of the floor. James looked at them; it wasn't too bad, as there were two holes in the coats, and hardly any blood on their fronts. He grabbed the manager's arm. "Do it now, the windows."

Mike came through the front door, ignoring the pistol which had swung in his direction as the door opened. "Clear in the street."

James told him to stay there and keep an eye open. He went back to Lou and his family, asking if everyone was all right. The gunmen hadn't managed to get a shot off, but there was always shock.

He told a waiter to take a table cloth and cover the bodies as best he could. The driver came back from the kitchen, telling him that it was clear. James had not finished with him. "For Christ's sake, tell me your name." He did. "Right Mario, any other drivers here?" There was only one other. "Both of you, bring the cars round to the back door, can we get cars down there?" He was told they could and they left to do that task, Mike going with them.

James checked that Lou and the daughters were unharmed by the pushing they had received. They were shaken, but all right. He stood in front of Mona, blocking her view of the bodies now being covered. James put his hand under her chin and lifted her face to look in his eyes.

"Mona, I need you to listen to me. What you saw just now was terrible, horrible. But I need you to be brave, just like you are now, for a short time longer. Can you do that for me?" She nodded. He added, "When Mike comes back he's going to take you, your sister and mother and father home. OK, you can trust Mike, he'll take good care of you." She nodded again and he pushed her gently into the arms of her sister. As he did this he saw that Monique was looking at him strangely. He barely heard the whisper, "Who are you?" he ignored the question and made his way to Lou, telling him that the cars were coming to the back door and that he should get himself and all his family into them.

He went to the back door and waited, gun still drawn, ready. The two cars came down the alley and Mike got out to cover the front, seeing that James was already there. James shepherded and cajoled as many people as he could into each of the cars. Lou was talking to the drivers, leaving them as the cars filled to stand next to James. Mike too came to his side. "No, Mike, I need you to go with Carmen and the girls, please." He nodded and climbed in the front of the Mercedes.

Lou waved the cars away before turning back to James. "Don't say it, they've gone to my house. Mario will be calling in some more help. I'm not leaving you with this mess. These people don't know you." He gestured to the stunned staff standing in the kitchen. "We'll get sorted here and by that time Mario will be back for us."

James could do nothing but follow his lead. Lou had all the staff gathered together and spoke to them, telling them that he didn't know why the shooting had happened. He asked them to stay quiet, telling the manager to send them all home, after giving them a cash bonus. After the back door had been locked behind them, there was only the manager and one more staff member standing in the kitchen. Lou sent the manager to the front to fetch them all a strong drink. James looked down and saw he was still holding a cocked weapon. He thumbed the hammer back into place and holstered it. They moved back into the restaurant, Lou going to the bodies and lifting the cloth to look at the

I, Plague

faces.

"Don't know them, never seen them before. Now we have to find out who sent them." He started making calls.

He took James back to the table. "Some guys will be along shortly. They'll clean up the mess and get rid of the bodies. The place will be as good as new by the morning." James voiced his concern about all the witnesses, but was assured that nothing would ever be said. A knocking on the front door interrupted them. It was a group of men in overalls. Lou greeted each by name and showed them what he needed done. They went to work straight away, only looking up when Mario came through the kitchen door to tell them the car was in the alley. Lou had a last word with the manager and his 'cleaning crew' before guiding James out to the car. "Just as well I own the company."

They sat in silence, Lou only speaking when his phone rang, issuing short, sharp instructions. There was a wrought iron gate at the entrance to the house. It was closed and there were two men on the inside. It was opened for them and closed immediately behind them. As they drove to the front of the house, James could see two men patrolling the front of the building. No guns were evident, but he was sure they would be armed.

Inside James was taken to a spacious and well appointed, comfortable room where the group from dinner were sitting and standing, talking in small groups. They fell silent as they entered and James could feel their eyes on him as he walked to stand next to Mike.

Mike handed James a glass of Scotch. "You think they were after us?"

It was a good question and James took a sip before answering. "Don't think so. They could have taken us down on the street, going in or out. Anywhere, really. Why chose such a public place? No I don't think they were after us."
"I think you're right there." Lou had walked to stand behind James. "It was something else." He moved around to stand in between them, accepting a glass from Mario. "I want to thank you. Even in the heat of the moment, I saw what you did. Moving like that to stand in front of me and my daughters. Thank you, I'm glad you were there."

Mike and James lifted their glasses. There was nothing that could be said. Lou turned to the group and held up his hands for quiet. The *hubbub died down and he started speaking.*

"I'm very sorry for tonight. I cannot tell you how sorry I am that you were put in danger. Nothing like this has ever happened before, especially not at a family gathering, as you all know. I don't know what happened. One thing I can tell you, it has nothing to do with these men." Putting his arms around James' and Mike's shoulders. "Another thing I can tell you, is that if they hadn't been there, well, what might have happened doesn't even bear thinking about."

"These two men acted selflessly, putting themselves between Mona and Monique and the gunmen. They did this without thinking about their own safety. If a shot had been fired at us then they would have died, not Mona and Monique. For this I owe these men more than I can ever repay." To applause, he hugged both of them.

After that, Lou organized for various drivers to take his guests home and arrangements were made for James' family at the hotel to be picked up and brought to Lou's house. They weren't told about the shooting, for which James was grateful. For much of the night Lou met with a string of men whom James did not know while James and Mike wondered if they'd got themselves into a shooting war.

"Now," he continued, "we must get you all home. I am sure that you are all safe. If I find out something different I will take the appropriate measures. Mario has organised for cars and drivers to take you home. Again, my apologies."

As the talk resumed Mike took James' arm. "Do you think we should get someone to look in on the hotel? I can probably get someone there in an hour."

Again, Lou had overheard. "No, what we'll do is have your family picked up and brought here. Just to be on the safe side, eh?"

James agreed and phoned Tony, telling them to be ready in the lobby within half an hour. They didn't need to pack, they would be going back. He put off the questions, reminding him that he agreed to do whatever James told them. James did, however, try to assure him that there was nothing to worry about.

"I've sent a good man to fetch them," Lou came back and told them.

James voiced a concern that had been nagging at him. "I hope we

I, Plague

haven't brought this to you. You helping us out and all?"

"I'm sure you haven't, but we can't discount anything. We'll know soon enough, this kind of thing is hard to keep quiet for long. Trust me. On this, I have more experience than you."

There was nothing to do but wait. Gradually all the dinner guests had left and the room was quiet, only the tinkling of ice against glass breaking the silence.

Mike and James were still standing in the corner drinking their whiskey. "Not bad for an old man!" James looked at him. "I mean, the reactions are still sharp. And the shots, haven't lost the old touch."

James was about to make a retort when he felt a hand on his arm. He turned and was face to face with Monique. He hadn't spoken to her since the restaurant. "Who are you guys? You tell me about stables and your life there, but then you shoot two men in front of us."

James in turn took her arms and led her to a sofa, sitting next to her. "I'll try and explain before my sister arrives."

He spent the next ten minutes giving her a very short version of how they had come to find themselves at dinner, also telling her how Mike and he had come to be friends. She sat, quietly taking it all in. He could see her working through her thoughts, placing them in categories and coming to a decision, before finally speaking. "That's quite a story. I'm looking forward to meeting this family of yours, that you're willing to risk so much for."

That reminded James that they should be arriving any minute, and he excused himself to rejoin Mike and go to the front door. They stood outside. Mike offered him a cigarette which he gratefully accepted. As it was lit he told Mike "Never worked out why I stopped. This is the second this week and I've enjoyed them both."

They saw the gate open and a car pulled up in front of them. Morag and Isobel almost ran to them, asking if they were all right, wanting to know why they had been brought here. James quieted them, taking them inside to meet their host. He introduced them around. It was Tony who spoke first. "You're the chap who helped us out with Marcus. Thank you."

Maurice Johns

Once they were seated James let it fall to Mike to explain what had happened. He was glad when Mike made no mention of the shooting, only saying that there was reason for caution and that Lou and his family had kindly offered to put them up for the night. It appeared to work, and soon the women were talking amongst themselves, plates of sandwiches being produced. Lou had disappeared, seeming to be meeting with a string of men who came to the door, taking them into another room and closing the door firmly behind them.

"Think we've got ourselves into a shooting war?" Mike asked James.

"None of our business, Mike. Not as long as we're not the targets. The old man looks as if he has everything under control. A turn up for the books, though."

Carmen announced that the women folk were going to bed and offered to show everyone where they would be sleeping. James and Mike said that they would stay downstairs for a while. They replenished their glasses and relaxed on the sofa vacated by the women. As they were alone they felt they were able to take off their jackets, leaving the holsters in place. It felt incongruous, sitting in an expensive house, in one of the expensive suburbs of London, wearing a gun. But again, the whole week had been incongruous, unreal.

It was two in the morning when the old man showed the last of his visitors to the door and joined them. "I'll know, hopefully by lunch tomorrow, what's going on. Marcus swears it was nothing to do with him."

"And that was that. It turned out that it had nothing to do with us and our meeting earlier. The old man was so grateful he offered me a job, which I was glad to accept, to get out of the soldiering work. James went back to his place and we've stayed in touch ever since."

He glanced at his watch. "Anyway, I have to get back. Stay well, and I'll find something for you, that's a promise." He stood up to leave and stopped, turning back.

"Ethan, there's something you should know about James, for when you see him again. He was married, a really nice girl. He loved her, worshipped the ground she walked on. He was as happy as any man can be. Well, she was killed in a riding accident a few months ago. Really broke him up. He hit the bottle for a while, trying to chase the pain away, I guess. Well, he's still hurting. Just thought you should know.

I, Plague

Not that he's changed, he thinks he hides it well, but he doesn't. Right now I'm for the off."

CHAPTER NINE

He was leaning on the railings, watching the sea break on Brighton beach. The squabbling of seagulls over scraps of food almost masked the quiet ring of the mobile phone. Only one person had the number. "Da, Gregori."

"Anatoly, my old friend, you've been busy. Nice to see you still manage to keep to your schedule, despite your advancing years. Is everything going well?"

Anatoly laughed. Gregori was the only man who would dare speak to him like that. "All the business will be completed by Friday, then I'll take some time for personal matters. That might take a bit longer, but I'm bringing in my colleagues to help. Especially the Paris job."

"That's good. I will now send word and Carter will know in the next day or two what is going to happen to him. Enough business. Are you looking forward to your retirement? I have kept you a place in my box for the game against Moscow Dynamo."

"Thank you. I will look forward to that. As for retirement, I think I will enjoy living in one place for more than a few days. I'll be glad to get home, the traffic in this bloody country is murder."

"Good Anatoly. I will meet you when this business is over."

Anatoly put the phone back in his pocket. It had been good to have some form of contact. His line of work was a lonely one. His mind slipped back to the first time he had met Gregori. It had been in Afghanistan. They were both in the Army and had been selected, based on their aptitude with weapons, for a special squad. They would move into the mountains and take out targets within the Taliban. It had been a gruelling assignment, the terrain was punishing, the heat and the cold brutal. Anatoly had spent long stints with Gregori as his partner and they had come to know and then like each other, a mutual respect for the other's abilities building. There was always one big difference between the two men. Anatoly was good at killing, he neither liked nor disliked it. It was a job. On the other hand Gregori had enjoyed the killing, far preferring to be up close and personal, inflicting pain and watching the life force drain out of the body. Not for him the sniper's rifle.
Despite this, or maybe because of it, they were a good team. After

I, Plague

Afghanistan, Anatoly had been recruited by the KGB, as it was then, and trained further in the art of assassination. Gregori had gone on to acquire and sell arms that were being discarded after the pull out, making his first million in a very short time. He had diverted arms for his own purposes, building a small army, which he used to gain control of most of the rackets inside the USSR. By the time the USSR broke up, the Berlin Wall had fallen and the West started their economic invasion of Russia, he was in complete control of most of the illegal activities.

Then Gregori had started to move in on the lucrative market in Western Europe. He had no problems removing the competition, not by negotiation, he had tried that and found it not to his taste, but by brutal and bloody force. Gregori had learned well the lessons from the USA when it came to setting up his empire.

It was while Anatoly had been attached to the Stasi in East Germany that they had met again and a job offer was made. He had been growing increasingly weary of the politics and the machinations within the organisation anyway, and was glad to move on to more lucrative pastures. Anatoly had been well paid for his work and had, in the last year, bought a villa on the Black Sea, near Odessa, where he intended to retire. He had stayed in the job longer that was normal, and was tired. He had begun to feel his forty two years.

He envied the vigour of youth, as seen in his team of three. They were all in their late twenties, ex military or KGB, each with their own skills. He knew they would carry on working for Gregori after he had put himself out to pasture. He also knew they were good enough to work alone. He had spent three years training each and every one of them.

Anatoly straightened and turned to continue his walk along the Brighton Esplanade. There would be plenty of time to reminisce when the job was done.

He had arrived the previous afternoon, checking into the Old Ship Hotel. He enjoyed the older style of hotel. They had an elegance that was missing in the newer, glass, concrete and plastic versions. Character in any establishment was important to him. His preferences were clearly visible in choice of *dacha* in Odessa. It was not new, but it was not rustic. It had a lived in feeling.

There were three hours until he had to take position for the next target. This man was yet another creature of habit. Although only a receiver and distributor of the drugs and people, he had achieved a comfortable standard of living. He behaved more like a senior corporate executive, and this would be the death of him.

This time he planned the action with great care. It was the most risky of all the killings. There were many factors which could come into play. He had spent a whole two weeks following this target and noting his movements. He had decided that the best place would be as he pulled into his drive in the evening. It was the only time he was ever truly alone – those few seconds as he waited for the garage door to swing open.

Anatoly had two choices. One, he could park nearby and walk along the beach which the house overlooked and take a position in the gorse bushes which separated the sand from the sidewalk and road. That was the riskier of the two. Passers by, both on the beach and the sidewalk, were likely to notice someone with a case, taking a stroll. It also increased the time it would take to get away from the scene. The location was too close to the Brighton Marina and adjoining village.

The second option, and the one he preferred, he had already prepared for. He had rigged the back seats of his car to fold down, allowing him to lie flat in the boot of the car. He had fixed the lid to ensure it didn't swing open all the way when released. It opened a matter of three inches. He had spent time on an isolated part of Salisbury Plain ensuring he had enough room to shoot accurately and with a clear line of sight to the target.

Anatoly knew that, to a casual passer by, there would be nothing suspicious. It would take a very close look to notice that the boot lid was ajar. To all intents and purposes the car would appear to be parked, while the driver took a stroll on the beach. The secret to success with this plan lay wholly in assuming the shooting position and straightening up after the shot. It would not do to be seen doing something as conspicuous as lying down in the back of a car. It was something which someone might remember. He was not concerned about the car, it was like millions of others on the roads of Britain. Nothing distinguished it from other cars in that area. Even modern technology had played a part in this, as most cars had the same aerodynamic design, making it often hard to distinguish between a BMW and a Vauxhall.

Anatoly drove off the road and parked facing the sea. He had picked this spot with care. The front and sides of the car were close to the gorse bushes that grew along the coast line. There was a sand dune in front which prevented a walker on the beach from seeing into the car. His own walks had shown that only the top part of the windscreen and roof were visible. The bushes on the side ensured that no-one would pass too close to the car and be able to observe him lying in the back. There was also the golf course stretching its fairways and greens to one side. Good cover.

Making sure that there was no-one around, he reclined the front seat fully, stretched and lay down. He pulled on a strap, which collapsed the right rear seat, and slid onto his stomach into the gap provided. Inside, he released the boot lid and it opened the three inches. Sliding forward, he looked out and saw the driveway, garage and front of the house. Good, he thought, all we do now is wait. He adjusted his case in front of him and picked up the rifle, lining it up on the garage. Squinting through the sight, he adjusted himself, the rifle, and the supporting case to the optimum position. Barring any unforeseen events, he would not have long to wait.

Glancing at his watch, as he eased into his position, stretching his arms, he saw that he had been waiting thirty minutes. Another ten and he would have to consider aborting for the day. He could not afford for the car to be noticed as being there for too long. Something had obviously held the target up. It might be something as simple as traffic, or a meeting. He did not view this as a problem. There would be other opportunities, and he still had a job to finish in the Norwich region.

Anatoly had waited the ten minutes, and was starting to slide backwards out of the boot when he heard a car slowing. He quickly slid back into the firing position and looked through the opening. It was his target's car. He rushed to adjust himself and the rifle, calming his breathing as he squinted through the scope, focusing on the driver's head rest, making the tiny adjustments until he felt it was perfect. There was a gentle wind blowing from his rear. At this distance he did not think it would make any difference. The car slowed and then stopped in front of the garage.

Anatoly knew that he would park the car in the garage straight away. Through the scope, he could see the head turn to the left as he reached for his briefcase. A slight movement of the right shoulder as he reached for the door handle, and he took his shot. He held his position, watching the head rest judder and then the familiar sight of blood spraying onto the windscreen. As the blood settled, he could see the exit hole in the glass, blood quickly obscuring his view as it slid in a viscous gel.

Anatoly pulled back, leaving the rifle on the boot floor, quietly closing the boot lid and then moving into the driver's seat. For the benefit of any onlooker he stretched and adjusted his seat back to the driving position. He pulled out three minutes after he had taken his shot, unhurried, reversing onto the road and driving past the driveway where the car lay silent. Again he obeyed all the rules of the road as he made his way back to the hotel. Only when safe in the underground car park did he replace the seats and disassemble the rifle, carefully replacing it in its case.

"Good." He only realised that he had spoken aloud when the sound of his own voice startled him. This time, his thoughts remained unvoiced as his mind turned to thinking about the shower and the pleasant meal he was going to enjoy.

CHAPTER TEN

Andy McNeish sat in the waiting area outside the chief Constable's office, feeling very much like an errant schoolboy waiting for the attention of the Headmaster. He knew it was a feeling that even the most innocent of people felt when they were summoned to a police station. He had been racking his brains to find a reason for the meeting. Such a summons was unusual, except for commendations or a major bollocking for a cock up of monumental proportions. As far as he was aware, he deserved neither of those. He shifted his position in the extremely uncomfortable chair and watched the Administrative Assistant tapping away on her keyboard.

How things change; a few short years ago she would have been called a secretary or personal assistant. He could hardly keep up with all the nonsensical paperwork that crossed his desk, changing this and that in an effort at political correctness, or health and safety. If the money and effort that went into those decisions went into police work the world would be a better place. Possibly that was the reason for his being here. He must have spoken out once too often, upset the wrong person. The week leading up to this Thursday morning had produced nothing new regarding the double murders. None of the other cases open on his desk showed much progress either. It felt like the one case was screwing up the others. A run of bad luck, no information, no leads, absolutely nothing. Maybe this lack of progress was the reason for the summons.

Andy was surprised when he was eventually called in. The meeting was brief. Opening with a few pleasantries about his workload, and how his team was shaping up, he had answered all the questions while wondering what it was all about. He was finishing his cup of coffee when the Chief Constable came to the point.

Andy had been told to pack a bag for a week, he would be staying in London. That was all he knew, the Chief Constable added. Andy could not brief his team on what was happening, could not even tell his wife how long he would be gone, for the simple reason that the Chief Constable himself did not know. He had only been instructed to send him. He was sorry that he could not tell him more. He added that he had been called to London for a meeting on the Monday, at which time all would be made clear to him.

McNeish had more questions rushing around in his head, but could see that it would be pointless to ask them. With a mental shrug, he accepted the situation and left. All he could do, he decided, was tell Will that he would be in charge for a while. No doubt the rumour mill would kick into full swing at the suddenness of his posting, but there was nothing he could do about that.

The first reaction to the news was that of concern. Had something happened which had resulted in his suspension? Had there been a complaint about the team, for which he was to carry the can? He tried to assuage the fears and concerns. This was precisely the kind of thing he dreaded. It would only require one misinformed innuendo and then it would be all over the Force by the end of the day. As he stressed to Will, there was nothing amiss, he could not tell him anything because he did not know. Having done his best to clear the air, he went home to pack and face the same type of inquisition from his wife.

CHAPTER ELEVEN

Greogori Yegenovich replaced the phone and swung his chair to look from his office window at the expanse of the football stadium he owned. Football was his passion, and he tremendously enjoyed owning a successful team. He did not flaunt his wealth in the face of the world, unlike those oligarchs who moved west with their millions.

He was pleased at the way his plans for the takeover of the lucrative drug market were going. The business of illegals into the UK had been growing steadily for years, and he now had enough people on the ground to replace those who opposed his move. It amused him to compare his organisation to that of the KGB during the Cold War. With one notable exception, his infiltration of Western European society was infinitely more successful. He was now making millions every month from his enterprises. He was proud of the fact that he cared little for the suffering of the great unwashed masses. They had no-one to blame but themselves for their dependency on the drugs he supplied. The girls from all over Russia and Eastern Europe were far better off in his brothels than they would have been if they plied their trade in their home countries. His only regret was that he was now unable to be more hands on; his profile was too high. He would have very much liked to go to England and deal with the Carter family himself, but knew that would be imprudent. The British police might be ineffectual in dealing with his activities, but he knew that even they would take too much interest in his arrival.

Gregori knew that the ease his operations operated under was down to one major factor. The police force was handicapped by too many rules and regulations. They simply could not compete with him. His most senior lieutenants had bought several medium ranked officers in the areas they worked. This gave them the information well in advance of any police action. Money was a great motivator. It always had been, even in the days of the Soviet Union. He was always careful to control his contempt for the West; too much disdain could result in a mistake, which could be costly.

His conversation with Anatoly had brought on this train of thought. The months spent in Afghanistan, the hardships they had endured, where every face had been the enemy and they only had each other to trust; Gregori smiled as he compared the current situation to the one the USSR had been in. It was much the same. The only difference was the rhetoric. The English and the Americans framed their invasion in terms of democracy and freedom for the people. In truth, he believed that the goals were the same as those of the USSR. Resources. Always resources. The lies about the motives of the politicians were contemptible. In his opinion, most of the western politicians would have worked well within the Politburo.

He buzzed his secretary and asked her to phone London, passing on the message, "Get Carter". That was his attempt at humour, using the title of an old Michael Caine movie as the code word for ensuring that Carter knew he and his family were going to die at the behest of he, Gregori Yegenovich.

When the old man had snubbed his offer of a partnership, Gregori had vowed to have his revenge. He had taken it as a personal matter. The old man had not deemed him worthy of consideration, had written him off as a thug. These things could not be taken lightly, and he had waited a long time for the right moment. Now, with his organisation falling apart, it was time for him to know that Gregori Yegenovich was a man to be taken seriously.

With everything going so smoothly in the UK, he decided it was time to take care of the day-to-day business. He had a meeting with a captain from one of his freighters, which was due to sail on Monday. It carried a lucrative cargo of arms bound for the Middle East and Somalia. As always, he had checked the false end user certificates and the shipping orders himself. Five containers full of weapons, from handguns to surface to air missiles. He did not foresee any problems. The ship would only have three ports of call. Southampton in England, and then onto the Mediterranean, through the Suez Canal and the East coast of Africa. The bulk of the cargo was legitimate, and previous weapons shipments had been well-covered. The freighters he owned were all registered in Panama and plowed through all the world's oceans. A perfect cover to ship anything he wished, giving him complete and utter control over what was probably the most hazardous aspect of his business.

Gregori knew that after this small matter was taken care of he could concentrate on more mundane leisure activities. There was nothing further to be done until the shipment arrived from Afghanistan and the factories in Ukraine, and that was only due on Tuesday. He would personally oversee the loading of that shipment, all of which was destined for the UK. He would spend Friday and Saturday in Moscow, in the arms of his mistress. He smiled at the thought of her young, nubile body. The athletic way she teased him, always prolonging his experience. He had taught her well and it would soon be time to move her on to one of his higher class establishments. He took a perverse pride in having trained most of his better call-girls personally.

CHAPTER TWELVE

Having had a leisurely breakfast and checked out the hotel, Anatoly set off on the drive to the north of London. He had a day of leisure in Brighton. The information he had been given was that the target would only arrive during the course of Friday, no specific time, just sometime during the day. But arrive it would, it had a shipment to drop off. On the way he made one brief call to his team leader, Piotr, who was waiting with the others in a small hotel, anonymous among the proliferation of such small establishments to be found around King's Cross station in London. He told him he would join them later on that Friday and then they would start with the secondary operation, kicking it off on the Sunday with the sending of Alexi to Paris. They needed nothing further, a thorough briefing had taken place a month before and he trusted them implicitly to carry out their tasks.

The detestable highway system in the south of England was as frustrating as it was slow, but he curbed his impatience with it, knowing that there would be plenty of time to arrive and finish this last job. He allowed himself to day dream about his forthcoming retirement. It was now only a matter of days, a week if the last phase did not go according to plan. He was tired of being in this country, with its unpredictable weather, and a population who seemed to complain about everything, if the news broadcasts were to be believed. It seemed to him there was always someone or some group who would find even things which should be beneficial to the whole a problem. They should be shipped off to some camp in the remote highlands of Scotland for re-education. He did not see the necessity for all the consultation and enquiries they held; such a thing would never happen in Russia. People needed to be led, firmly and with discipline, for them to be happy. Clearly happiness was not part of the culture in this country. He permitted himself to muse on this during the three hour drive.

Anatoly eventually passed to the north of London and followed the map firmly ensconced in his mind, from Ipswich taking a road which paralleled the coast to a point between Leiston and Kessingland. It was on this stretch of coast where he expected to find the fifth target. He knew that Gregori's information was always reliable, and expected to find the yacht anchored where it should be. He also knew that it would not move until the cache of drugs aboard had been taken ashore. Something which was better accomplished under cover of darkness.

He drove very slowly along the minor road which took him as close to the coastline as possible, scanning the sea for sight of a yacht. It was almost an hour before he saw one and pulled over to look through his Zeiss binoculars. He scanned the length of the yacht and managed to make out the legend on the stern. The *"Mary Elizabeth – Southampton"*. This was the one he was looking for. It was a good size, ocean going, he guessed. He did not like small boats; the thought of sitting on a plank of wood which was all that separated him from hundreds of metres of nothing honestly terrified him. It was strange, he thought, that he did not feel the same about flying, but put it down to the fact that the ground could be seen, whereas the bottom of the ocean could not.

Back to the task, Anatoly scanned the vessel again. There was no-one in sight as the yacht swung in the current. There was a stiff breeze coming from the sea, and he could feel the chill it brought with it through the open window. He smiled to himself. Something from Mother Russia – a good omen for this day's work.

Discounting the wind, it was a pleasant day. A scattering of clouds moved briskly across the sky and the sea was slightly choppy, an occasional white horse topping a wave. He had a good vantage point and it appeared to be an unfrequented stretch of land. He knew that, sooner or later, his target would come on deck. This was one time he knew he was part of a bigger operation. The drugs on board would be hijacked by Gregori's men when they came ashore. He was aware that, as part of the bigger picture, Gregori intended to decrease the supply, push up the street price before he started placing his own drugs on the streets. Still, he would be back in London before that phase took place.

Anatoly took the case from the boot of his car and walked towards the sand dunes overlooking the beach. He had dressed, copying the styles of bird watchers he had seen, in rough trousers, sturdy boots and a heavy woollen sweater. Selecting a spot in a valley between two dunes and surrounded again by the usual brush found growing on sand, he assembled the Galil. He set up the range finder and noted the distance to the cockpit of the yacht as one thousand and seventy metres. He adjusted the scope and focused on the target area. He measured the wind and calculated the algorithm necessary for a clean shot. Once done he settled himself for the inevitable wait, replacing the cover on the front of his scope to prevent glare, a long standing habit rather than a necessity under the present circumstances.

The sun moved overhead and was now fully behind him. He had been lying there for three and a half hours. He stirred and removed the scope cover. The wind had died to a breeze and the sun was warming his back and the sand around him. He made the adjustments to compensate for the drop in the wind, grateful for something to do after the boredom of waiting. At last there was movement on the yacht. A woman's head and then her body appeared in the cockpit. She was holding a mug and he could see that she was talking to someone in the cabin. She moved and sat leaning against the main sail boom on top of the cabin, and raised her face to the sun. It was a full ten minutes later that the man appeared on deck, moving to stand at the railing and look to land. A clear frontal look at the face confirmed this was the target. Anatoly patiently waited to see what he would do next; rushing a shot would be a waste of time. The man turned to face the woman and, judging by her lips and hand movements, spoke to her. It was a good location for a shot, but he held. The target moved, he swung onto the cabin roof next to the woman but did not sit. Instead he crossed to the seaward side and walked to the bow, checking the anchor, before moving back to stand behind the woman. He stood sipping from his mug, facing the land and, through the scope, it looked as if he was staring directly at the rifle.

Anatoly took a deep breath and let it go, repeating it and holding his breath as the cross hairs settled on the target's forehead. He applied gentle pressure on the trigger, feeling the small amount of pressure and squeezed further. A slight push against his shoulder and he remained glued to the scope. He saw the red hole open at the bridge of the nose, a centimetre low, he chided himself, but still fatal. He fell backwards, tripping over the low railing and into the sea. Anatoly moved the rifle a fraction to the left and picked up the surprised expression on the woman's face, her mouth open as if shouting to find out what had happened. Wasting no time, he repeated the procedure and this time the round landed squarely in the centre of her forehead. He scanned the sea around the yacht and managed to locate the body floating face down, clearing the stern. It had been a bonus that he had fallen into the sea; depending on the tides and currents, it could be days, or longer, before his body would be discovered. He watched the body until it was raised on a small swell and the back of the head became visible. There was no doubt that he was dead; the gaping hole where skull and hair should have been was confirmation if any had been needed. He swung the rifle back and checked on the woman. She was still sitting upright against the boom. From the front, there was not a lot of damage. It would take someone to stand over her to see what had happened. He was pleased with the way it had gone. Now back to London. The next phase should be easy and he would soon be home.

CHAPTER THIRTEEN

A weak sun was hazy behind the high, light clouds of mid-morning. Its warmth was filtered, and only slightly warming to those taking advantage of the park for a quick break in the work routine. It was not busy; a few young families were playing on the grass, old men were sitting on benches, talking or reading newspapers. An island haven in the middle of the hustle and bustle of the city.

Strolling along the side of a man-made lake was a man indistinguishable from others who were not working. He was no longer a young man, his shock of white hair attested to that. He was aware that his age made it more than likely that this would be his last overseas posting. His heyday was well and truly gone. A dinosaur was how he was referred to in the section, not that he minded. His best days had been during the Cold War, before the fall of the Berlin Wall. He had enjoyed and thrived in the old days. He had been placed here only because of his expertise as handler of undercover agents. He carried a folded newspaper under his right arm and stopped frequently to look over the lake at the fountain in the centre. If anyone had bothered to look closely they would have seen that the jeans and sneakers were foreign and very expensive in the Ukraine. His short sleeved shirt had the Polo logo on the breast pocket, another expensive import from the West. His watch would have been the main indicator that he was not a native of Kiev. It was an expensive Seiko, with many dials and a stop watch. None of this mattered. Anyone who had an interest in him knew he worked at the British consulate in the cultural office. Anyone with a deeper interest in him was also aware that he was an officer in the Secret Intelligence Service.

Steve Hudson had spent his whole adult life in the Secret Service, mainly MI6 and most of that on foreign assignments. He had joined in the seventies at the second height of the Cold War, and had enjoyed the life style, although not the pay, of living abroad and being involved in some matters which made the headlines and most that did not. He had always felt that he achieved something of worth for his country. However, lately that feeling was muted. He was now a dinosaur in the new Service. The heady days of Burgess and MacLean were long gone, as he would soon be, as soon as this assignment was over.

Now he remembered those times with a fondness he would not have thought possible at the time. The crossings into East Berlin, the turmoil in the Middle East and Africa. The biggest regret was the fact that the number of friends had declined exponentially as the years had gone by. Unlike agents in novels, they had not all met their end at the hands of the opposition; most had died peacefully, but that was the price paid for getting older.

Even though times had changed, each country was always aware of another country's agents. He knew he was no longer routinely followed, that would be a waste of manpower. His normal duties were very mundane and nondescript. It was only in times of trouble that surveillance stepped up a notch.

Steve had been taken from a desk job in London to work this last assignment in Kiev. It was a straightforward task. He was the handler for a deep cover operative. Steve had never met his agent, had not even spoken to him on the phone. Their only contact had been notes left in a dead letter drop. Frequently, he wondered what this person was like, what he thought about the job and if he ever thought about it ending and going home. He knew such thoughts were a waste of time because, if everything went well, the extraction would be as mundane as catching a plane out of the country and he would be recalled to London to finish out the remaining time till his retirement. Although he bemoaned the fact that he had been chosen to his colleagues, he was secretly pleased to have spent the time in Kiev. A suitable swan song for the long service, and recognition of his proven abilities to cope with the details of handling an undercover agent. Not that this one had caused him any problems, the reports came in regularly and were always useful.

He meandered his way to a small, ornate fountain in the middle of a grassy knoll. Approaching, he moved slightly to his right, lining up his approach as he had done so many time in the past. He sat on the low ledge and opened his newspaper, starting to read the headlines. Removing a packet of cigarettes from his pocket, he lit one. As his left hand dropped the lighter back in his pocket he left it at his side and it dropped behind the low parapet. He counted the bricks with his fingers until he located the one he was searching for. A push against the corner and it swung outwards. Slipping his fingers inside, he felt around and was rewarded as he touched paper. He palmed the small piece of paper and pushed the brick back into place.

He sat reading his newspaper, and smoked another cigarette before standing, stretching, and sauntering off.

It was a drop he and his predecessor had built one dark night at three in the morning when he had first been transferred to the Kiev office. It had only one purpose – to receive information from his one agent in the country. It was more often than not empty. He had had no personal contact with his agent since arriving in the country, but the information had become increasingly more useful. He had passed on to London intelligence about politicians, elections and movements within the crime organisation, which had grown exponentially with the expansion of the EU. He knew that some of the intelligence was shared with Interpol, but had not been informed of any results.

It was only when he was back in his office that he opened and read the piece of paper. Unlike previous reports, which had been brief, this was a detailed account of illegal weapons to be shipped. Sailing times and the numbers of those containers were to be given in the next two days. In addition, there was information about a large drugs shipment destined for the UK. Weights and sailing details of a motor yacht with distribution plans would also follow. A major breakthrough, he thought, as he rushed to the communications centre. All the hard work invested in the years of undercover work was about to pay off big time.

CHAPTER FOURTEEN

Andy McNeish alternated between gazing out of the window, which offered a panoramic view of London, and watching the room fill with faces largely unknown to him. Up river he could make out the imposing shape of Tower Bridge, and on the opposite bank there were some familiar London sights. The office was not what any member of the public would associate with a police operation. They were situated in a modern building, most of which was occupied by corporate head offices, if the board in the foyer was to be believed. The walls on three sides were fitted out with banks of computer terminals and wide screen televisions. Judging by the accents, this appeared to be a gathering of police officers from around the country. The only face he recognised was that of a member of Scotland's Drug Enforcement Agency.

After his meeting in the Chief Constable's office, Andy had gone home to pack and tell his wife about the unexpected posting. She had been, to his surprise, quite excited at the prospect. She had seen the opportunity and had told him she was pleased that he had been given what seemed to be a chance to prove his worth. She had always maintained that he was undervalued in his work, and reassured him that she was quite happy with the brief separation this would involve. It had set his mind at ease on that score; he had to admit to her that he had been worried about her reaction.

Andy had only arrived that morning, catching an early flight from Edinburgh Airport, and had been driven straight here. All the information he could glean was that they would be briefed by a Commander from the Metropolitan Police. From the overheard muted conversations being held around him, he knew that the others were as much in the dark as he was. As everyone was introducing each other they were asked to take their allocated seats by an Assistant Commissioner, who held the door open for a woman in civilian clothes. She was tall, strikingly so, and her auburn hair was loose around her face. She had an air of authority. This was one woman, thought Andy, who was used to getting her own way, and was not shy about taking control of a situation. She was also not afraid to show her femininity; her suit, although a business cut, was designed to compliment her figure. An ACC and a Commander; this was a high-powered briefing and Andy could see others joining him in sitting up and paying attention, curiosity more than a little piqued.

"Good morning, ladies and gentlemen. My name is Bond, Jane Bond."

I, Plague

She waited for the smiles and laughter to subside. "That will be the only joke about my name from here on in. I am going to explain all to you. Any questions you have, I will deal with at the end. Firstly, thank you all for coming, I know you didn't have much say in the matter. We are going to break with long standing rules and etiquette here. You will see that your name cards only bear your first name. That is the first rule; we are all equal, there will be no ranks used, seniority does not count. Why? Because we feel it hinders our interaction. Why you? Each of you has plenty experience in heading up major investigations. Also, and in some ways more importantly, you have the trust and respect of your colleagues, from Chief Constables down, and you are all capable of working in a team. Why are we here? I think all of you are aware of the killings taking place around the country and the belief that it is a professional carrying out these murders. We are not here to deal with that, investigations will continue, and although it is part of the whole, it is secondary to our main objective. To digress a bit here, we do know that this person has been operating successfully for some fifteen years. Not one force has any idea who he is, he never leaves anything but the rounds in his victims. One thing we are sure of is that he is working for this man." A photograph flashed onto the screen. It was grainy and obviously taken covertly from a distance. "He is the reason we are all here - Gregori Yegenovich Zhuravleva. At this point, I have to emphasize that everything, but everything, from the spoken word to blank sheets of paper or computer discs has to remain within these four walls. As you will see, this is of paramount importance. Your Chief Constables and relevant Senior Officers will be given a briefing at the Home Office on Monday. They will not be made aware of the big picture, only we here will know that." She went round the room and waited for each person to acknowledge her.

"We know this man controls the Russian mob, for lack of a better word. He is firmly ensconced across Europe, and has ties to the American operation. We believe that he is making a move to establish himself here. Thus the assassinations. We are working with Interpol, and every force we have a relationship with, to gather facts. Unfortunately, the things I am about to tell you have not been verified as much as we would like. Having said that, the sources are proven Confidential Informants. As new information is received it will be passed on. Gregori, I'll call him that, if for no other reason than I cannot pronounce his surname, has been shipping illegal immigrants into the country for years. He is now virtually the only operator in this game. This has given him a base on which to build his operations. All the background we have on him is contained in the dossiers you will be given. He is a major player. He is an arms dealer, beginning in Afghanistan, he has his supply of the raw product, factories and distribution to the street supply of drugs. He controls a vast percentage of the sex trade. He is known to have contempt for us and other law enforcement agencies. He believes us to be weak, lacking in determination and muscle, and corrupt. He may very well be correct in this. He can probably put more manpower in the field than we can. He can certainly out gun us. He may be correct in that we know that there, as much as it pains me to admit this, are bent coppers out there. Money can buy a lot of information as we know. However, that said, in this instance we are not going to be found lacking in determination. We are going to put together an operation the like of which has never been seen before in this country. We, ladies and gentlemen, are the tip of an iceberg, which will be a national task force to prevent Gregori setting himself up in the UK. You can begin to see the need for absolute secrecy. Icebergs have a habit of sinking things, and I have no intention of becoming a Titanic." She paused to let the murmur settle. "Briefly, what we intend, and I will add here, that this has the highest approval, leaders of all political parties have agreed, is to ascertain when the shipment of drugs is to arrive, let it land, follow it and then seize it. This is not going to be easy. We need inter-agency cooperation, a liaison network, and planning on the scale of the D Day landings. I envisage a rolling type of operation, for example, once the drugs have been off loaded and on their way, the crew will be arrested. And so on down the line."

She smiled at the incredulity etched on the faces of everyone around the table. "Now you begin to understand. The manpower involved is going to stretch us to the limit. The technology we require has brought other agencies into play. MI5, for example is here." She indicated a well dressed younger man with the name plate of Charles. "This gives us access to GCHQ and their monitoring capabilities. Another example is that we are learning lessons from our cousins across the pond, the FBI in particular. We will be using satellite surveillance when the operation gets under way. In short, and I reiterate, this is the biggest thing since sliced bread. We have only two endings, no middle ground, we succeed or we fail. We know that this will not stop the trafficking of drugs, we have to live with that. What it will stop is the influx of an organised crime regime that is unscrupulous and brutal, with the added influx of a large number of firearms onto streets already bursting with illegal weapons." She paused briefly to take a sip of water.

"As I said, we are breaking with tradition here. You will all have a large amount of leeway and autonomy. Anything you want, either in this room or from your respective forces will be given. I cannot guarantee an aircraft carrier, but almost anything else. When we put together the operation, you will be in a position to co-ordinate our movements if they fall into your area. Right, what we do now is have coffee. Through the door at the back of the room a coffee and sandwich station has been set up. Toilet facilities are available down the corridor. You have all been booked into a hotel just around the corner. Please get to know each other, and read the dossiers we will give you. They are as comprehensive as they can be. Liaise with others, for example the Customs guys, and our friend from Scotland's Drug Enforcement Agency. Toss some ideas around, and we'll sit down again at eight this evening and have another chat. I would really like you to throw any ideas into the pot. Finally, we all know that all we need is one break to set the whole shooting match in motion, so we must be prepared for every contingency. Trying to cover all the bases is our first priority. OK, ladies and gentlemen, coffee time."

Andy stood with Stewart, the DEA operative. He had only ever had a nodding relationship with him, and now they sounded each other out, as strangers do.

"Looks like it's going to be another weekend at work," he suggested to Stewart. "Why do these things always happen on Fridays?"

"I know. Bloody criminals have no respect for us hard working innocents. Spend too much time sleeping off their efforts during the day. This is going to piss off the wife, yet again. You married?"

Andy laughed and confirmed that his wife would not be too happy either. A hazard of the job, they joked.

It didn't take too long before they were joined by others, and the conversation turned to what they had just heard. There were some sceptics, some quiet enthusiasm, and some disbelief at the scale of the operation.

The most sensible suggestion was made by Stewart, he put forward that they look at the regional issues, then work up to the big picture. For example, he told them about operations to take various ships and boats off the Scottish coast, which had been quite successful in the past. If they were to concentrate on the smaller parts then the whole would fall into place.
It made the most sense, and they gradually moved into smaller groups, finding opposite numbers from other agencies in the regions and

settling down to study the dossier. Starting to read, Andy knew that it would take a couple of hours just to assimilate the information.

They were left alone, each engrossed in the dossier, an occasional murmured comment made. Like Andy, they found the scale of the criminal empire spread before them almost incomprehensible. He, for one, had no idea this was going on. Sure, he had heard the usual rumours, but had written them off as a bad case of too much TV and movies. The list of violence was staggering, both against persons and property, the sums of money larger than the economy of many countries. All controlled by one man. It was a lot to take in. Doubts about their ability to contain this in the UK assailed him, unbidden. He thought about the rules and regulations they had to adhere to in comparison to Gregori, who had no such hindrances. How could they possibly pull this off with all sorts of Human Rights activists and Health and Safety observers climbing on the bandwagon to condemn their actions?

On the plus side, however, he saw that they had unprecedented access to satellite tracking, as well as the monitoring capabilities of GCHQ. He would have to wait to see just how much clout she had until things really got underway. A personal thought forced its way into his mind. His long suffering wife was not going to be overly happy with a long separation; he would give her a ring from his hotel room later, he decided.

After sandwiches and coffee, taken at their work stations, Commander Bond re-entered the room. It was a brief question and answer session, more to clarify any points that had been raised reading the dossier. There were hardly any questions, but the most interesting one was raised by Customs. He asked if the satellite surveillance of any suspect vessel was really possible. She informed that it was not only possible, it had been arranged. All they needed was to identify the target and the link would be fed directly into the room.

It was Andy who raised the next question. "On a couple of occasions we've been thwarted by the use of mobile phones, when we've knocked down the door but have been unable to stop a call being made. If we raid a ship, do we have the means to stop calls being made to warn people further down the line?"

Bond passed that to the MI5 rep.

"Yes, we can do that. Mobile phones, landline and radio. It will disrupt local services at the same time, but it should not, hopefully, be too noticeable. Phone companies will shut down their masts in the area, and jamming will take place on the radio frequencies. There are some legal aspects to this, but we have always had the cooperation of all the companies in the past. No reason to think that will change."

"On the point of legalities." Bond interrupted. "We will have our own lawyer from the Crown Prosecution Service attached to us when things get moving along a definite line." She consulted her notes. "Bill Fuller. He will make sure the necessary procedures are followed to ensure a successful prosecution, and expedite the necessary warrants for search, arrest, and so on."

There was a short silence while she waited on any further questions. "OK. What I think we should do now that you have all had a chance to absorb the information, is to put together some contingency plans. As you have now gathered, you are seated in regional groups, and you have got to know each other. Each group should now look at their regions and, based on your experiences in the past, put together some ideas on how we would manage the operation if it were found that a shipment was coming into your area. I would suggest, for example, and I would like to emphasise here that I'm not trying to teach you your jobs, take Scotland. In the past there have been several very successful drug seizures. Most of these involved the drugs coming in by some form of boat. This time, however, look at the rolling operation I spoke about before.

Once the initial local plans are in place then we can discuss the liaison between forces that will be required to follow the drugs down the line. We here believe that we may very well be lucky in that the higher echelons, who we are after, may very well get involved in the first shipment. We also hope that we won't have too long to wait. This is based on the fact that the last shipment was hijacked a week ago and the word we are getting is that another shipment is due in the next couple of days. Supply is drying up to a certain extent. If that shipment is taken by Gregori's people then there will be a shortage with resulting price increase. Then, we believe, he will make his move. Therefore, we believe that it is only a matter of days before we start receiving good intelligence about a large shipment. So, ladies and gentlemen, time is of the essence. If you could get together and come up with some ideas for late tomorrow it will give us time to discuss them and, at the very least, have some concept of what we require, should we have to move quickly."

Maurice Johns

CHAPTER FIFTEEN

The sun was a bright orange ball in the west, although it was almost eight in the evening, when Mike took the phone call in his apartment. He saw immediately that it was an internal call from the old man's study. His thought was that he was normally never usually bothered in the evening and almost never over the course of a weekend. For him, since he started here, the weekend started around six on the Friday and he had always been free to do whatever he wanted to fill his leisure hours. He picked up the phone.

"Mike? I'm sorry to trouble you, but would you come down straight away?" Mike told him he would be there in a couple of minutes and paused only to put on a jacket before heading down the stairs. He ignored the exit, which would have taken him out through a private side door and the back of the garages and turned, instead, right to a short corridor which led him to the main house kitchen. He saw no-one as he walked through the house, hearing the sound of a television coming from the family room.

He was waved to a seat across the desk from Lou Carter as soon as he entered the room. His first thought was that someone was ill and he needed to organise a visit or something along those lines. He waited patiently for Lou to speak.

"Straight to the point, Mike. I'm going to need your help with this." The old man looked tired and worried, badly worried, Mike thought, still waiting. "You remember my cousin Albert?" Mike nodded. "I've just come from the hospital. Well, he received a visit from one of Gregori's henchmen this afternoon. Not a pleasant visit by all accounts. Albert was taken from the street and badly beaten. Not badly enough that he could not pass on a message. The beating was to demonstrate that they were serious, he was told that; it would have been too easy just to have given him the message. Anyway, the message has apparently come from Gregori himself. He intends to kill me. Worse, they said that he intends to kill my family before he kills me. Very brief. They told Albert I would understand. That was all. A bad beating for two sentences. God, I thought I had left all that behind." He pushed his hands through his thick white hair.

"How credible is this threat?" To Mike, it seemed far fetched that such a threat could be made at all. "I mean, it seems, from what you've told me, that it wasn't such an insult. It was only business?"

"That's the point, Mike. I believe him. He went to a lot of trouble to deliver this message, and as for the timing, well, look at the last week. His takeover is well under way. I can only think that now business is out of the way, this is his way of settling old scores." He held up his hand, stopping Mike's interruption. "I know it sounds far fetched, even just saying it out loud it sounds unreal. But – I have to take it seriously. What if it is fact? I have to think of the girls, and Carmen. The long and the short of it is that I'm going to need your help to protect them. Will you do it?"

Mike did not even hesitate. "Of course I will. Right, down to business." He was thinking fast. "First, you all have to stay at home. We don't know who is out there or how they will come at you. Second, I need to get some men. We have to protect the house. Shit." He remembered Monique. "You have to phone Monique and see if you can get her to come home, any excuse. I'll have to think about what else to do, but right now everyone is confined to the house." He paused and looked out of the window to gather his thoughts. "One other thing. The curtains on the windows have to be drawn at all times."

Lou was dialling a number as Mike had been speaking. "Hello sweetheart, how are you? I didn't interrupt anything, did I?" There was a pause as he listened to the reply, smiling. "Your mother and I were thinking of having a bit of a celebration for the opening of the new restaurant. Nothing fancy, just something at home, and we were hoping that you could find the time to come across for it. You know we would all love to see you again, it's been too long." Again the pause as he listened. Mike could see a frown develop on his brow. "I understand, but we would really love it if you could come. Will you promise to think about it?" He finished the call before turning to Mike. "She won't come. Says she has too much on her plate at work to get away. Maybe I should have told her the truth."

"No, you did the right thing." Mike was well aware of the antipathy Monique felt towards her father's past. "She would have just dug her heels in further and got all upset for what might still be nothing. We'll have to make a plan to ensure that's looked after."

He tried to gather his thoughts into some logical pattern, while Mario, the driver, was called from his quarters and given instructions about the curtains. "OK, first things first. Do the others know anything about this?" A shake of the head. "Good, we need to keep it that way for the time being. You'll have to think of something to keep them here. Now, I need to make some calls and get some men here. Mind if we use this office as a base?" It was more a rhetorical question than a request for permission. He picked up the phone and dialled the Lamb and Flag. As luck would have it, and as he had hoped on Friday night, some of his old friends were there. It was Ethan who answered the phone. Mike was about to explain what he needed and stopped in mid-sentence. Asking Ethan to hang on, he turned to Lou. "Look, it seems to me that this is well planned; picking up Albert and all. I'm thinking that it wouldn't be hard to bug the phones. It would give them information on your movements." Another thought struck him. "Jeez, I'm getting slow. E-mails for information as well. We have to stop using the phones and e-mails until we can get something done." He picked the phone back up. "Listen young feller, don't say anything. I need to meet you. I'll send someone to pick you up. You know that video shop, the one with more under the counter stuff than usual? Go there and a car will pick you up in," he glanced at his watch, "twenty five to thirty minutes. And do me a favour, ask around and see if any of the others there, only ones who you know, are looking for some short-term work." There was a brief agreement and Mike hung up. He asked for Mario to come back in and explained what he needed him to do. No questions and he was on his way.

"We have to hope that they haven't set anything up yet. But let's not take any chances." He took his mobile and dialled a long unused number. "Tris, long time no speak. I need a favour. I want phone and computer encryption gear set up tonight if possible. The best and most secure you can get your hands on." He listened to the expected moaning about the time and the fact that it was the weekend. He knew that behind the complaints Tristan was working out what he could do. As the complaints ended he was told that he would be there in a few hours. Tristan had worked for the same firm as Mike in the days when he was a security consultant, and most of the equipment was pretty standard stock for the kind of work they undertook. Mike was satisfied that it would be installed by the morning.

Turning to Lou, he had an important question. "All this is not going to come cheap. Am I clear to go ahead and do things as I see fit? Sorry, I should have asked before."

"Of course, my boy. Whatever you think you need, you go ahead and get. But what about Monica?"

Strange, thought Mike, he had reverted to her given name. She had changed her name after moving to France. It had been expedient to accept Monique, as everyone she knew there had called her that.

"That's a good question. I think we should send someone we trust to look after her. Not easy because it will have to be someone she trusts and likes. Someone she knows. I would go but I think I'll be better here where there are three of you to look after. Someone like Ethan springs to mind, but she doesn't know him. I don't think it'll be any good just having someone follow her. Leaves too much to chance if an attempt is made, they have to be close to her all the time." He was almost speaking to himself, trying to engage his brain in tasks which he had not thought of for some time.

There was one name which sprung unbidden, automatically, into his head. He pushed it aside, failed and tried harder. Lou had a suggestion. "Mario could go. She knows him and it won't be too suspicious for him to take a break."

Mike dismissed the idea. "You're right, but Mario's a driver, not a gun hand, he has no experience in this line of work. No we need someone with experience. As much as I hate it, I only know of one man who fits the bill – James." Lou picked up on the reluctance, but said nothing. Mike continued. "Shit, double shit, I know he wanted to be out of this sort of thing. He's well settled and, what with Marie's death and all, I really hate the thought of having to involve him. But he's the most logical choice. If this whole thing is serious and they do come after you, he's the one man I know who would take good care of her."

"I agree." Lou put his head in his hands and his next words were muffled as he spoke into his desk.

"It's a big ask. He would have to know what he was getting into. He wouldn't have anyone with him. Jesus, Mike, anyone we ask to go could get killed along with Monica. Should we phone and put it to him?"

"No phone." It was a difficult decision. "No. I'll go and see him in the morning."

"Why don't you go and join Carmen? I have to start thinking and put together what we're going to do."

Mike stayed at the desk and started putting his thoughts down on paper. The list grew steadily as he tried to think of equipment and manpower he would need. How to apportion the resources to ensure adequate cover. It was the same as planning an operation, the biggest difference being the time frame. The message had been delivered and that could mean that any attempt could be made from that time on. The other difference with this was that there was no discernible enemy. He, or they, were faceless. It could be the refuse collectors, the mailman, anyone. "Stop" he thought. "Don't get too carried away. Think logically, damn you."

He had covered two A4 pages when the door opened and Lou brought Ethan into the room.

Mike made the introductions and gestured Ethan to sit, pouring them all a drink. As he poured he thought how easy the burden of command felt and how quickly he had slipped into it. Sitting, he sipped his drink and started.

"I can't tell you much. I won't tell you much until I know you're in. The thing is Lou, his wife and two daughters have been threatened by a real bad guy. If you agree I would like you to be my second in command. You will have to hire five or six guys, who we must know and can trust, for a close protection assignment. You know the implications of that? No, don't answer yet. We'll fix up someplace here for you all to stay, I don't know how long for. I don't know what shape the threat is. And I don't know how they'll come at us. The only thing is to keep the family safe. On that, I'm afraid, kid, you have to make a decision."

Ethan favoured them both with his boyish grin. "We're going to the mattresses?"

Mike had to laugh and saw Lou grin widely at this. "I've told you before, kid, you watch too many movies."

"I'm in. I reckon I still owe you, I've said it before, but I'll keep saying it until I think I don't any more. Where do we start? Is James coming in on this?" He continued without waiting for an answer. "I spoke with a couple of the lads, you'll remember them and they're up for some work. They say they're getting bored, there's nothing much doing at the moment. It shouldn't be too much of a problem getting them on board."

"Whoa, slow down. First, put together a list of who might be available - you've been around them more - and then we'll go through it. Then I want you to talk to them, pick up some gear for yourself and bring it here. Discretion, kid. You have to be discreet, I don't want half the hard men in London turning up looking for work. I also don't want the opposition to get wind of this until it's up and running. One-on-one conversations only, understand?" He turned to Lou. "Can we set something up where they can sleep, eat, etcetera? Maybe the garage, we can use my place as well, although that should maybe be for Ethan and me. Ethan may be right, after all, we will need some mattresses, blankets, food. Lou, could Mario take care of that?"

"One thing, kid." He looked hard at Ethan. "We won't have the advantage of any weapons, where the opposition will. These guys have to understand that. We can't have a shootout in the middle of an upper class suburb in the middle of London. That makes the whole thing a bit more risky. You have to tell them that."

Ethan left them, assuring them that he understood everything and that he would return in a couple of hours. Mike stopped him as he opened the door. "Ethan, James might be with us on this. I still have to ask him. He won't be here with us, if he joins up he will be in Paris. Point is, I'm going to drive up and see him. When I'm gone you'll be responsible for getting things up and running here."

A wave of the hand and he was gone.

"Isn't he a bit young for this?" Lou, as had everyone whoever met Ethan, had taken his boyish looks at face value.

"He's older than he looks, twenty seven or eight, if I remember correctly. He's been around for a while. Worked with James and me before. A good, honest and reliable lad. I trust him implicitly."

"Good enough for me. Anything I can do to help?" Mike laughed, "Stand by and rest your signing hand. You'll need all your strength to pay for this lot." He added, "You're going to have to tell Carmen something, have you had thoughts on that?"

"I'll tell her the truth. Always have done, well, almost always. Can't see any other way around it, there's going to be too much going on around here for anything else but the truth."

Lou left to join his family and then go to bed. Mike continued with his planning, waiting for Tristan to arrive. Mario joined him, sitting quietly in the corner, keeping mugs of strong coffee in front of him. It was almost three in the morning before Mike's mobile rang and Tristan told him he was outside. Mario went to open the gates and helped him carry the boxes inside.

Tristan positively bounced into the room. "Hi, Mike. Got all the stuff here. Boy, the new boss is going to have kittens when he finds out what I've taken. This is the latest equipment on the market. State of the art, it's…"

"Stop right there, if you're going to tell me all the technical mumbo-jumbo. Just set it up and show me how it works. You know damn well I don't understand half of what you say anyway." He had to smile as he said it; Tristan was always like this. He spent every waking hour engrossed in his work, Mike was sure he dreamed about it when he slept and that he would have serious digestive problems because he ate while he worked. His enthusiasm for technology and his computers was limitless.

He sent Mario off to get some sleep, informing him that he would be driving him to see James first thing in the morning, and settled back to watch the boxes being unpacked and a mountain of gear being assembled. He was only half listening to the nonstop chatter as Tristan assembled it. Occasionally, he had to show him where various junction boxes were, but he was generally left to continue with his planning.

Ethan's idea of a couple of hours was way off base, returning after four, carrying a hold-all. Mike showed him to his apartment and advised him to get some rest, insisting that they would catch up in the morning before he left. He did find out, however, that he had managed to recruit five men, known to both of them, and that they were waiting for the word to move in.

He tried to take a nap in the office as daylight broke, sunlight shafting over the carpet and furniture. It was no use. He could not switch off the thoughts and, he reasoned, it was almost time to leave for Leicestershire. He stirred and picked up his mobile phone, working his way down the list of names and phone numbers which Ethan had left him, arranging for them to be at the house by seven, only two hours distant he was surprised to find.

Tristan announced that he was finished and would now demonstrate how to switch everything on and get it working. Once assembled, it was easy to operate, a fact Tristan took delight in telling him. "It's idiot proof. Could have been designed specifically for you. More like the security services, though. Even they couldn't balls this lot up."

He showed him the bank of twelve mobile phones which were on charge, adding that he hadn't known how many were required, but that more could be arranged if they were needed. He tried, in vain, to explain how the encryption of the phones and computers worked, eventually having to abbreviate it to a demonstration. Once Mike was sure he knew how it all ran he thanked Tristan for his help and, assuring him that the rewards would be great, showed him out of the house.

Mike had closed his eyes and could feel sleep enveloping him when he heard the door open.

"Morning, Mike. Christ, you look terrible. Have you been up all night?" With a groan Mike pulled himself from the comforting warmth of the sofa. He took Lou over the encryption device which had been installed. "How in hell did you manage get hold of this at such short notice?"

Mike explained how his old company used the stuff all the time and how they had been extremely lucky to have it on hand. Half way through, Mario and Ethan came into the room. Mario told them he was ready to leave whenever Mike wanted to. Ethan added he was ready to *"rock and roll".*

"Let me guess – *Full Metal Jacket*? Just please, Ethan, don't tell me to lock and load, all right?"

Mike explained his plans, the positioning of the men around the property, how he wanted each delivery and visitor checked, and how where possible the vehicles were to be left at the front gate. He told Ethan he would meet with the men, and then leave it to him to organise it all.

Promptly at seven the intercom from the front gate buzzed, the first two had arrived. Ethan went to meet them and took them to the kitchen to wait for the rest. Within the next five minutes they had all arrived. Punctual as ever, Mike was glad to note that the discipline remained.

He knew all of them; he had served on three occasions with two, and once with the other three. During their times together they had formed their own small group of Brits and had gotten to know each other pretty well. They were proven under fire and he knew he could rely on them to keep cool heads and obey orders. But more importantly, they could act independently, using their own initiative. He introduced Ethan as his second in command and let him get on with the briefing and placement.

I, Plague

By seven forty five he and Mario were ready to take the north road. He spent a few minutes with Ethan and Lou before he left, more to reassure himself that everything was in place. An unnecessary task, but he knew he was tired and it worried him that he might have forgotten something. It had all happened so fast. He allowed them to herd him into the car and waved Mario away before he had a chance to remember something else.

CHAPTER SIXTEEN

Ten o' clock on a Saturday and James sat in the stable office with Vicky and Helen, the two stable managers. They had been discussing how they could grow the business even further. Both had been with him since the beginning, hired by Marie as grooms and now each running their own enterprise. They were trying to select who they would choose to attend the next BHS courses and then be appointed to a position either within the stable/instructor set-up, or withing the training centre set-up. The choices they had were wide and varied, but they were agreed that it should be someone who had displayed a commitment and eagerness to work with both the horses and the children. He supposed the choice had been obvious from the start. Beth and Cindy worked tirelessly and could not be more enthusiastic.

They had both been so keen on horses when James had first met them he had taken a liking to them. They had lost their mother and their father, Steve, was struggling to do the best for his daughters, but things had definitely been tight financially. James had employed subterfuge in getting the girls started, kitting them out and telling them they could work for their tuition, something which he had to throw in for Steve's benefit. He would never have accepted anything seen as a handout. He had eventually found a way to pay them something for their efforts. They were all now being rewarded by the girls' achievements. They had both made it clear that they wanted to have a career in stable management when they finished school and James, as well as the others, agreed that they should remain with them. It would be a shame to see their investment go to another stable. But it was more than financial, each and every person was dedicated and loyal to his stables and money could not buy that.

He was looking through the window at the bustle in the yard as one class was finishing, removing saddles and moving horses back to their stalls, while another class was fiddling with tack and mounting, ready for whatever instruction they were to receive. Through the group of parents proudly watching their offspring, chatting among themselves, he was surprised to see Mike. He was searching the crowded yard, obviously looking for James. He saw one of the grooms point in the direction of the office, and as he started towards him, James stood at the window and waved.

They shook hands. "I will confess to being surprised. Is this an escape from the big city, a chance to drink some of my whiskey?" He moved to the small fridge and took out two beers. "I know how you city boys like to stay in bed for the weekend, it must have been quite a thing to behold, you getting up so early!"

"Much as it pains me to admit it, I'm not here to take advantage of your hospitality, or to see these lovely ladies again. Just for the record, though, I didn't have to get up early, I haven't been to bed." Grinning at both Vicky and Helen, he raised the bottle of beer to each of them, taking a deep swallow. "Now that's better. James, can we talk?"

The girls stood to leave, James stopping them. "We're finished here?" They both nodded their assent. "Right, why don't we take a walk back to the house?"

James greeted parents he knew as they left the stables, and it was only when they were clear that he saw Mike had that serious look on his face. "Definitely not a social visit if my guess is right. Bad?"

"As it gets. James I need to ask a favour. Well, me and Lou both. Wait," He stopped and leaned against the railings separating the drive from the paddocks. "Don't be so keen to commit yourself until you've heard what I have to say." He watched the class file into the paddock. "God, they're so lucky. So young and innocent. The only thing they have to think about is enjoying their weekend."

This comment worried James more than anything that had been said. He knew Mike well enough to know that when he started talking like this there was something very heavy weighing on his mind. "Why don't we wait until we sit down, have a glass and then you tell me what this is all about?"

They walked the rest of the way in silence, and it was not until they were seated with the doors closed and good measures of whiskey in their glasses that Mike finally spoke.

"You know Lou's history, his associations, sorry, of course you do. Marcus and four others have been shot, at least we assume four others, one has not been found yet, but his mistress was found shot, nine in total. They were all old associates, part of the business, in the past. Anyway, a professional has been going round doing the dirty. That's from my mate at Scotland Yard. Nothing to do with Lou. Well, that would be correct, he's been out of that for years now, again you know all this." He took a deep swallow from his glass. "Anyway, it seems that fifteen years or so ago, a young Russian wanted to come into the UK market. He had a bad reputation, violence, all that, and Lou told him no. The UK didn't need that kind of thing. Lou thought it would be bad for business. A real nasty piece of work, it seems. He took it badly at the time, and little has been heard of him since, except that he has built up quite an empire. Arms dealing, massive drug operation, sex trade, you name it, he's got a finger in it." He paused for another drink, finishing it and standing for a refill.

"Understood, so far. But what's this got to do with Lou, you, or me? As you said, Lou's out of that, or has he quietly retained some interest?" He took the glass and Mike sat down.

"He's out of it all right. Was never really too keen on the drugs thing anyway. That's why it was all fragmented at the start. No, it's not business. It's personal. This Gregori, that's his name by the way, has sat on this grudge from way back. He knew he was thought of as only another thug and he took it really personally. Now he's let word leak to Lou, deliberately so, that the time has come to pay for that insult. Hard to believe, it's so Machiavellian, like something out of the *Godfather* movies. I never thought I'd see this type of thing. So, now the threat, promise, call it what you will, has been made. We know this hit man is around somewhere, and we think it will be him who does the deed. The reason I'm here is simple; I need help. The thing is – it's not just the old man, it's Carmen and the kids as well. We've all heard the stories about these guys, the movies always have this part about the gangster who takes out a man's family before the man himself."

"Holy Shit, Mike. You cannot be serious. Here in England? You're right, it sounds too much like a piece of fiction. I need another drink." As he poured he looked at his friend and read the serious, worried look. "You're taking this as on the up and up? Why are you here if that's the case? Surely you're needed in London?"

"True. We spent all last night talking about this; what we could do. The only thing we came up with so far is for the Wimbledon house to go under a lock down. I've got a few of our old buddies to come in and help. The thing is, we don't know when anything will happen. We are treating this as a credible threat. I've got all my contacts, and Lou is calling in markers, to try and build as much information as we can. Right now, all we have is a big fat zero. The reason I'm here is -" He stopped, looking James straight in the eye. "Hell, neither of us wants to involve you, but we're in a bit of a bind. We racked our brains and all we came up with is you. See, the old man and I trust you implicitly. We can think of no other person alive who we could trust. We want you to go to Paris and look after Monique."

James' mind was racing, trying to assimilate all the information and the implications. "I can see why you're worried." He spoke more to buy himself time to think than for something to say. "Jesus, Mike. Not much to go on, is there? You think they'll try for Monique in Paris? I mean, I go there, what do I tell her? Do Carmen and Mona know anything? Do I get her to go home? Shit, so many questions, I don't know where to begin."

"I'm sorry, James. You don't know how sorry I am to have to ask you this. No, Carmen and Mona know nothing. I wouldn't think that telling Monique would do any good, not until we know more. The main reason for asking you to go to Paris is because, when we spoke to her on the phone last night, we suggested she come for a visit. She said she couldn't, she had too much work and she had things planned. Lou didn't want to push it, so we left it at that. One thing, though," he paused again and waited for James to signal for him to continue. "Before you make any decision Lou wants to talk to you. I will be honest and tell you I have no idea why, he just said he wants to talk to you after I had explained the situation."

James said he would phone, and Mike held out his mobile phone, suggesting he use it instead of the land line. "This is encrypted, same as all the phones down there. He looked at him as he took the phone. "You don't think they would bug the phones, do you?" Mike only shrugged. He was given the speed dial number and heard Lou pick up almost immediately.

"James?" He continued straight on, cutting through the usual pleasantries. "I take it Mike has told you everything?" He waited for James to confirm that. "I also hope he told you that we have not come to you lightly. We talked long and hard about asking for your help. The thing is, I can think of no-one else with whom I would trust the life of my daughter. I would rather have her with you if this thing turns out to be true. I know I'm asking a lot, especially now, well, you know what I mean, Marie and all. But please will you help look after Monique and bring her home to us?"

It was strange to hear the quiet desperation in his voice. James realised that he must be really worried about the threat against his children, to permit that amount of concern to be shown. He made a decision. "I'll do it, Lou. I'll have a word with Mike and make some arrangements. I'll be in Paris either tonight or first thing in the morning. Just think, it's a beautiful city at this time of year. It would be a pleasure to get away and relax a bit. Oh, and Lou, don't worry about Monique, I'll bring her home. Probably kicking and screaming and she won't speak to me again for a while, but I'll think of something."

He handed the phone back to Mike. "Well, we'd better have one more drink and I'll get ready. No, you can't, you're driving." Mike laughed and it sounded good, it lifted the tension.

"No, I'm not. Mario brought me up. He's in the kitchen, probably gorging himself on one of Madge's pies." He watched James pour the drinks. "What are you going to tell Monique?"

"I'll do that now. Improvise, what else. Oh, and lie through my back teeth." He looked up and dialled her mobile phone. He though it was going through to voice mail when she answered in French. "Bonjour, how's the weather in Paris?"

"James, is that you?" At least she sounded pleased to hear from him, he thought, in for a penny, in for a pound.

"I'm going to pop over to Paris for a few days, you know, get away from here for a while. Anyway, I was going to ask you if you'd like to have lunch with me tomorrow. Catch up and all that stuff?"

"That would be lovely, it's been so long since I've seen you. When will you arrive?"

"I haven't made a booking yet, probably tomorrow morning. Take the Eurostar. I might try and get a room at the Champs Elysee Hilton. Nice and central, it's a good place to eat."

As he had hoped she told him emphatically "You'll do no such thing. You will stay here with me. I have two empty bedrooms that are never used. Tell me what time you arrive and I'll meet you at the Gare du Nord."

They made the necessary arrangement for him to tell her what train he would be on and hung up.
"Right now I have to pack. Help yourself to the booze and I'll see if Madge will rustle up some sandwiches. Do me a favour, will you, see if you can get a first class ticket?" Ignoring the jibes about the idle rich

only travelling first class, he briefly told Madge what he was going to do and asked for some sandwiches. After a brief chat with Mario, he went to his room.

As he was moving shoes trying to gain access to the safe installed in his wardrobe, he heard someone come into the room. "Madge sent me up to help pack, well, she didn't exactly send me, I came up to see if I could help." Jean moved to the hanging suits and started selecting some. "How long will you be gone?"

"I have no idea, Jean. Let's say a week. Just popping over to Paris, taking care of some business for Mike." He straightened and she saw the two handguns with shoulder holster in his hands. She didn't say anything but her face told the story of her thoughts, a moving picture of emotions. Jean had seen the guns before when he had put them away, hoping that they would stay hidden for the rest of his life. Sitting on the edge of the bed he unwrapped the cloths and checked them, putting the magazines in and checking others before fitting them into holders.

"Don't worry, kiddo, it's nothing really. Just a precaution, truly." It did nothing to lessen the concern etched on her young face. "Look, neither of us is any kind of trouble, nor will we be. I can't tell you any more because I don't know myself. But obviously this has to stay between the two of us." She nodded and continued packing. As they finished he was about to lift the case but stopped and looked at her, remembering their conversation. He held out his arms and she moved quickly into them, as if afraid the offer would be withdrawn if she hesitated. "Please don't worry." Even as he spoke the words he knew they were useless. "When I get back I promise we'll go out for something to eat and another chat." He lifted her chin. "Just think, a few days in Paris could be just what I need." He smiled down at her. "Come on, how about a smile to send me on my way?" She made an effort and smiled at him. He kissed her lightly on the forehead and picked up his case.

When he got back downstairs Mike handed him a mobile phone. "This is encrypted, same as mine. It should be secure enough but if you have to use any other line to get hold of me, play cautious. We know they're good, but not how good."

CHAPTER SEVENTEEN

The four Russians sat at a table in a quiet restaurant near their hotel. Anatoly watched as the others laughed and joked about some programme they had been watching on the television the night before. It felt good to be able to speak in his mother tongue, to be himself and to relax in the company of the nearest thing he had to friends.

The Saturday had been spent going over the final arrangements for the hit on old man Carter and his family. He had checked in with the communications and computer section of Gregori's business, a business that was largely forgotten about whenever anyone spoke of the crime organisation. It was, in fact, a highly lucrative part of the whole. Computer hacking and the syphoning of money from personal and business accounts totalled millions every year. It also gave him the ability to tap into phone conversations and e-mail messages as required. They had been monitoring Carter's house and had reported that it appeared that he received the message from Gregori, confirmed by a telephone conversation with the eldest daughter in Paris, asking her to come home for a visit. He had been informed that she did not want to, preferring to stay in Paris for business and personal reasons. They had, apparently, not informed her of the reason for the request to visit. Anatoly felt this was a mistake as they would find out soon enough. After that one call, however, they had been informed that the phones and the computers were now protected by an encryption device. They would work on breaking into it but did not hold out much hope for a breakthrough in the short term. He had accepted this as part of the whole. They had been warned, but it was of little consequence now his operation was in place. He had confidence in his own, and his men's, ability to carry it out.

He had decided to send Alexei to Paris to deal with the woman, and two of the others would set themselves up in hideouts already prepared to deal with the rest of the family. Alexei had told him he would deal with the woman on the street, amid the crowds, where he had a good chance of not being seen and for getting away in the confusion afterwards. The others had reconnoitered sniper sites opposite the house in Wimbledon and had made the necessary preparations over the preceding week. It all appeared to be coming together neatly, he thought. Just a pity that Gregori had wanted to warn them of what was coming. It, they had decided, would not make the task any harder, rather, it would make it more time consuming. Alexei was to leave for Paris in the morning and had said that he would watch for a day or two, deciding on the best time as it happened. Anatoly had complete faith in the younger man; he was well suited to working in public places and close up.

On the other hand, the method to be used by the others posed more of a chance of premature discovery. The days were long, and there was always someone wandering around, walking their dog or playing with children. Still, the planning was sound and it would be very bad luck indeed if they were discovered while actually in position. The danger lay in getting into and out of their positions.

Anatoly himself would be the driver of a well-used transit van, taking them to and from the Common. When Alexei returned they would share the workload. No, he decided, it was as good a plan as they could come up with. It was only a matter of time until the contract was filled.

He pulled himself away from the thoughts of the work ahead and joined in the conversation. It had turned to a portrayal of the Russian *Mob* in some crime series.

"The thing is" Anatoly added "is that Westerners have no concept about the Russian people. They do not understand us, how we think. Their arrogance is their downfall. They believe that the rest of the world should be like them. Thank God we're not. They're soft, tied up in their own needs. Greed rules their political classes and business leaders. That is why we are so successful infiltrating their society. They think we're brutal, but that is based only on their own standards. The brutality of their government agencies is concealed from them, but people need discipline. Think of the history of our own country. It has been described as brutal for centuries. Yet it is how we have been governed. It made us strong. Yes, the West is going downhill, what a pity we are no longer in a position to take over."

It was Piotr who added the obvious. "Gregori is well into that, although not in the way that Stalin or the others had in mind. He controls so much of the wealth, his wealth gives him access to much more than the KGB ever had, could only dream of. It sometimes surprises me that he has been able to do so much."

"That's easy. Even the criminals here think small. To do what Gregori has done needs balls and imagination." Alexei was normally the quiet one, speaking only when he had something vital to say. "I must go back to the hotel, it's late, and I have to catch the 8.30 train in the morning."

The others agreed and they made a jovial group as they walked the short distance to the hotel, blending in well with the hundreds of Poles and Czechs who thronged the streets.

CHAPTER EIGHTEEN

James arrived at the Gare du Nord on time, at nine forty five on the Saturday night. True to her word, Monique was waiting at the station to meet him. She surprised him by running to him and hugging him, asking him how his trip had been and the reason behind this sudden visit to Paris. He barely had time to reply to any of her questions before the next one was fired at him. She took him to her Renault and as he dropped his bags in the back seat, she stopped talking.

"I'm sorry, James, I've been rabbiting away since I met you." She leaned across the centre console of the car and gave him another hug. "It's just so good to see you again. I promise, no more questions until we get to my apartment. I hope it's all right, but I've made something to eat. I thought you might not want to go out so late."

He was secretly pleased at this. Not only did he not want to go out, but the more time spent indoors the better, as far as he was concerned. He told her about the journey, honestly impressed by the standards on the Eurostar, as she drove. It was a shorter drive than he had imagined it would be, before she pulled up in front of an elegant building, passing her car keys to the doorman.

"I'm impressed." He smiled at her as they waited for the elevator. "A doorman who also parks your car, very swish. Nice building too." It was more than nice, he thought. The entrance hall was marbled and spotlessly clean. The inside of the elevator was wood veneer, highly polished as was the brass backing for the buttons. "You must be doing all right for yourself, living in a place like this. The sins of the corporate lawyer, or the sins of the clients, paying for this."

She punched him playfully on the arm as the elevator stopped, and she led the way to a door at the end of the hall. The thick door swung silently open onto an open plan entrance way and lounge/dining room. He saw a kitchen full of stainless steel gadgets to the left and a hallway leading to another four doors. The view from the high windows was breathtaking. There was Paris laid out before him, the lit Eiffel Tower towering over the River Seine a centre piece. "Wow." It was the only utterance he could think of saying. "You've really landed a prize place here. Tourists would pay a fortune for this view, and here you have it every time you come home."

"Thank you, kind sir." Monique hugged him again. "Come, let me show your room, it's got the same view, only the windows are smaller." She told him to unpack and come back into the living room, by which time, she added, the food would be ready.

It didn't take long to unpack his few belongings, carefully hiding his guns under the mattress and having a quick wash before joining her in the kitchen.

After eating the plain but good meal she had "thrown together" they sat on the long, white leather sofa gazing out over the panoramic view. Over the meal he had told her about the stables and all the staff she knew from her visits. How Mona and Pippa were the best of friends, inseparable during their time together. "I wonder if they write to each other while they're at school," he mused.

"Of course not, silly." He laughed and told her that was what Mona and Pippa said when he was being particularly dim about something. "They IM each other all the time. Instant Messaging on their computers. Mona says they talk almost every day." They laughed at his lack of understanding of the modern teenager.

After a short, pleasant silence, she put her head on his shoulder and asked him. "How are you getting on? Are things getting any easier? Mike says you've never talked about the accident."

"I'm just fine" he lied, hoping she would let it drop. That wasn't to be the case.

"You know it's been said that things get more bearable as time goes on. Does it still hurt?"

He didn't look down at her. He felt the old wound opening up again and he didn't want her to see the wetness in his eyes. He had never allowed anyone to see the depth of his pain. "Does it?"

"Oh, James I'm sorry if I said something I shouldn't have."

"It's all right. I'll answer." Why he felt the need to answer was beyond him, maybe it was the atmosphere, maybe it was because he liked and trusted her. Maybe it was just because she was a woman. "Yes. It hurts like hell. I miss her every day. I'm angry that I lost her just when we were so happy. I feel guilt because there was nothing I could do to stop it happening. Why have I never talked about it? Well, I think that a man has two things which should remain private, that only he can deal with. Grief and death. Both are very private. No-one can take them away, no-one can feel the pain or take your death on themselves."

"James, that's not altogether wrong, but it's also not altogether correct. Grief can be shared with others. It might not make the pain go away, but others might want to help ease the burden just a bit. You are so lucky that so many people care for you, you have to let them in. They can help."

Bugger, he thought as he felt a tear well out of his eye and run down his cheek. He lifted a hand to brush it away before she saw it, but was too late. "Sorry, I must have got something in my eye."

"Nonsense, here, let me." She took a handkerchief and wiped the tears away. "Don't look like that, there's nothing to be ashamed of. I promise, I won't tell anyone."

She moved and put her arm through his, drawing closer, putting her head back on his shoulder. He was inwardly mortified, but found it strangely comforting. He permitted himself to relax. She was, after all, a good friend, and it wouldn't do any harm to let her think she was helping him.

"Do you know that you're only the second man to have ever sat here?" He knew she was trying to lighten the atmosphere.

"That does surprise me. Is he still around?"

"No, it didn't last long. I'm not very good at relationships. I get scared when they start getting close, you know, when they start talking about the future. Besides, I have my work, and it doesn't allow me much time to get involved. Also I have everything I need right here. Oh, I don't mean the possessions, I mean the feeling this place gives me. Independence, I suppose. Do you understand?"

"I do. I feel the same about my place. Everything a man could want." He straightened. "How about a night cap?" She agreed and he went to pour them both a drink. "I was wondering if you would like to show me some of the sites tomorrow, if you're not doing anything else, of course?" She said she would like that. "Well, I've organised a car and driver. That would mean that we could really relax and not have to worry about how much we drink, or parking, any of that."

"It would be fun. What say we start at the Eiffel Tower and take it from there? I haven't done much of the tourist thing lately. You know, when you live in a place you never really bother too much about the local attractions. Yes, that would be fun. What are you planning for when I'm working?"

"Haven't thought about that yet." Another lie. "I'll just walk around, do some shopping, some sightseeing, maybe take you for lunch if you're free. You can't work all the time, can you? You'll be able to take some time off for an old friend, just for a couple of days."

"Of course I can. I can't take the whole day off till later in the week. Too much to finish off for a client. But, yes, later in the week I'll take some days off."

He had debated how he had been going to handle spending so much time with her, but it was turning out easier than he thought. She should be safe enough while she was in her office, and he could now make sure that he would be with her whenever she wasn't. When he had said goodnight and went to his room he was quite happy to phone Mike and tell him that everything was under control.

First thing on the Sunday morning, he phoned the number given to him for Etienne Le Blanc, a driver recommended by Mike. He arranged for them to be picked up at ten. The driver, he had been told, was well trained in advanced and defensive driving techniques and had been used by Mike before. That was a good enough recommendation for James.

He had coffee ready by the time Monique appeared, still in her pyjamas, her hair sleep tousled, stretching as she crossed the room. "Morning, did you sleep well? God, I went out like a light. Too much wine." She poured herself a coffee and they sat discussing what they could see that day. He told her the car was coming at ten, which caused her to jump up, proclaiming that she had to get ready, and disappear into her bedroom.

James enjoyed the day spent at the Eiffel Tower and then the Louvre. They had wanted to go on to Notre Dame but time had passed so quickly they did not realise how late it had become. As Monique said when they noticed the time "If you hadn't wanted to walk down the stairs at the Tower we would have had plenty of time."
Etienne had proved to be a good driver, quietly confident in his handling of the black Mercedes AMG. As soon as James heard the low

rumble of the idling engine he knew there was plenty of power to deal with any situation. His driving skills were proven in the smooth ride he gave his passengers; he anticipated the movement of others on the road well in advance. James noticed that his eyes were constantly taking in all the mirrors and side views as he drove. The mark of a true professional, who knew exactly what was happening all around him.

He had found it impossible to gain a minute alone with Etienne to discuss what was happening, to find out how much Mike had told him. He had to content himself with waiting until the Monday, after they had dropped Monique off at her office.

That evening, to his relief, they went out to a local restaurant. It was less than a block from her apartment, but he found himself on edge as they walked down the street. He had put one of his guns in his jacket pocket hoping the weight and bulge would not appear too obvious. It was not a position which would enable him to pull it out in a hurry, but it was a hot night and it would be unusual for him not to have taken his jacket off.

CHAPTER NINETEEN

God, there are some things about this job I hate, and hanging around waiting is one of them, Alexei thought. He had arrived at lunchtime from London and had made his way straight to the target's apartment building. He had checked the photographs he had of her and was sure he would recognise her without any problem. She was, after all, quite a looker. He had now spent three hours in the vicinity of the apartment block entrance. He had to keep moving, worried that the doorman would notice him sitting in his rented car festooned with Avis stickers.

He was not concerned by the fact that he had not spotted her. When he had been establishing her routine, he knew that she sometimes spent whole days with girlfriends. Never a man, always girlfriends. He found it curious that a woman as attractive as she was didn't have a steady boyfriend. But it was none of his business, she was a target and that was all. She was no different to a piece of paper stuck on a tree trunk.

He had decided that he would check her routine on the Monday, and then seize any opportunity that presented itself on the Tuesday to do the murder. He had deliberately decided on a crowded place. The silenced automatic would not make sufficient noise to draw attention to himself and, as long as he kept his head, he would not be identified in the ensuing panic. It would be an easy matter to disappear into the crowd. From his observations he was sure that it would be in the evening when she left the office. The streets were always busy and she almost sauntered when she was making her way home. Only rarely did anyone accompany her and they generally left her after a block or so. No, it would be quick and he would be back in London either Tuesday night or Wednesday morning.

He had decided to give up until the morning when he saw the black Merc AMG pull up at the door and she got out. Well, there was a surprise, he thought as he saw a tall man join her on the sidewalk. He saw her slip her arm through his as they walked past the doorman. A boyfriend? He felt he could leave now, they looked comfortable with each other. He didn't think there would be any point in hanging around.

When he arrived back his hotel he phoned Anatoly and checked in, telling him he was ready to go, as they had discussed. He had a drink at the bar and noticed a couple of American girls, obviously tourists, looking at him. He smiled at them, disinterested, part of the discipline that Anatoly had drummed into them. No distractions when on a job. It was too easy to slip up, they could find his gun and then there would be hell to pay; all sorts of unwanted complications could arise when discipline was not adhered to. A pity, he thought, they could have provided a pleasant distraction for a few hours.

Early on Monday morning he had checked her progress to work. He knew that it was unlikely she would reappear for the rest of the day, unless to attend some meeting or other. He would have no chance of taking her then as she was picked up at the door by a car and dropped off, not spending any time in the open. To fill in the time he walked the streets, stopping for a coffee, acting very much like the thousands of tourists who thronged the streets. He had checked the weather forecast that morning and was disappointed to find that the fine summer weather would continue well into the week. Rain was always a good cover; umbrellas and coats made the concealment of a weapon far simpler and decreased the risk of recognition from the countless CCTV cameras.

On the Tuesday morning he decided that this would be the day. He was bored walking around and longed to get back to London where the main action would be. This kind of hit was mundane, routine, requiring little skill, whereas the shooting they planned required all his skills. Prior to leaving the hotel room he cleaned his Walther, adding the sound suppressor and working a round into the breech. He stuck the weapon in the waist band of his trousers in the small of his back. He parked in a multi storey car park close to the offices and waited somewhat impatiently for the lunch break to see if she would come out. He was prepared to wait until the evening if necessary, but fervently hoped she would take a lunch break out of the office. That would mean he could catch an afternoon train across the Channel.

At twelve thirty he recognised the tall man he had seen with her on the Sunday. He was waiting outside the building, checking his watch as he arrived. He thought he was a bit old to be her boyfriend, but there was no accounting for taste. He was well dressed in an expensive suit and shoes. Maybe that was it. Money; he scorned these Western woman, whose priorities seemed to focus primarily on the wealth of suitors. Watching the man as he waited, he did not think he would pose any problems. He would, if necessary, take him down if he interfered, it would not cause any extra fuss for him. A middle aged businessman would be too stunned and shocked at the sight of his girlfriend lying dead at his feet for any immediate reaction. He fully expected he would drop to her side and try to help, all the while screaming for help, when he saw she had been shot.

She came out of the entrance after a few minutes, looking around and breaking into a broad smile as she saw her escort waiting. She moved to him and gave him a kiss on the cheek, taking his arm and moving off. He crossed the street and fell in behind them, starting thirty feet behind then closing the gap. He reached to his back and, using a crowd as cover, drew his weapon, covering it with a folded edition of Le Figaro. He had closed in on them and was now only six feet away. He prepared to take his shot.

At the moment when he was taking up the pressure on the trigger, the couple swung sharply to the left. His first thought was that he had been seen, but when he looked he saw they were turning into the George Cinq Hotel. Damn. For the sake of a couple of seconds, it could all have been over. Now he would have to wait for them exit.

He kept moving, hiding the weapon again in the small of his back. He crossed the street and lifted the camera slung around his neck to take a photograph of the front of the world renowned hotel.

He moved along the sidewalk in the direction of the Champs Elysee, finding a cafe and taking a seat on the sidewalk where he could observe the hotel entrance. As he thought he had plenty of time, he ordered some food, more to be able to keep the table than because he was hungry. If they were eating lunch, it could be an hour or longer before they reappeared. He listened to the conversations going on around him as he ate. There were at least four different languages he could make out, not one of them French. He ate slowly, always maintaining a look out on the entrance. He had finished his meal and was having a second cup of coffee when he saw them standing on the steps discussing something. He glanced at his watch as he stood and paid the bill. One hour twenty minutes they had taken. She was obviously in no hurry to return to her office, a fact confirmed as they came down the steps and turned in his direction. He quickly crossed the street behind them, trying to close the gap as quickly as possible. Turning left on the Champs Elysee he was back within a few feet. Again he retrieved his weapon from his belt and placed it under the newspaper, his thumb finding the safety catch and ensuring it was in the off position.

They were approaching a group of tourists standing taking photographs and the man leaned down to say something to the woman. They slowed next to the group as she rummaged in her hand bag for something. This brought the gap to about four feet; he could almost reach out and touch her. He tightened his finger on the trigger, feeling the tension, requiring the slightest pressure which would end her life with a bullet through the heart.

He started to squeeze the trigger. As he felt the small kick in the palm of his hand he saw that the woman was being pulled in front of the man. His round hit a skateboarder in the centre of the chest, knocking him backward onto the sidewalk.

He tried to catch up the few feet that widened between them, but was hampered by the tourists. He could see the two of them stop at the side of the road and she turned to kiss him. That was when the first scream sounded, as someone realised what had happened. The woman looked over her shoulder, before continuing across the road. He tried to disentangle himself from the crowd now milling on the sidewalk, not sure whether to move on or stand and gawk at the fallen skateboarder. Over their heads he could see them reach the other side of the road and continue past the cinema and night club entrance. He rushed to cross the road, ignoring the red pedestrian lights and dodging cars. He hurried to the top of the Champs Elysee, and turned where he had seen them turn. There was no sign of them. He forced himself to walk at a normal pace down the street. Arriving at a corner he saw a black Mercedes pull away, just a bit too fast, he thought. He made out the number plate and made a note. It may not have been them, but it would do no harm to check.

Was it possible they had known? He ran over the events immediately after the shooting. No, he did not think they were aware of what had happened behind them. The actions as they waited to cross the road were too casual, the kiss too spontaneous and the look of curiosity at the cause of the first scream did not indicate any alarm. He was sure he would soon pick them up again. This time he would not make any mistakes.

He hurried back to the office but did not see her return. After waiting for fifteen minutes he decided to phone. The receptionist was very helpful when he asked to speak to her. No, she would not be returning to the office for the rest of the day, but she could ask him to return his call the next morning. He retrieved his car and drove to the apartment building. At six in the evening, when she had still not returned, he decided to phone Anatoly.

When he got through he was brief and to the point. "I missed. It was bad luck, a combination of events. The problem is now I have lost her.

She won't be back in the office till tomorrow. I don't think she is aware of me, but I would like you to check her location for me. I have a car registration, it's a new Mercedes and should have GPS tracking. Can you do it?"

Anatoly did not ask questions. The explanation was enough. He said he would call back, and, after taking the car details, he hung up. Alexei felt only frustration that he had missed his shot. The skateboarder was an unfortunate, who happened to be in the wrong place at the wrong time. These things happened. It did not take Anatoly long to get back to him. He gave him the location of the phone and told him the car was currently stationary in car park in Bievres.

"Shit, that means I've been clocked. The location of the phone is near to where I lost them. They must have dumped it. I'll go to Bievres and see what I can find. I think we have to use some people to cover the usual places, in case they try to get back to London."

"I'll phone Gregori's man in Paris and get some watchers out. If you turn up nothing in Bievres I think they will head north, and try to cross the channel. If they have clocked you they will know to avoid the railway stations and airports. If it were me, I would try for the ferries. I'll see what I can do. Let me know when you're in Bievres."

It was late evening before he had made it to the car park and located the Mercedes. He settled back to wait, telling Anatoly where he was and what he was doing. He was told that all the railway stations and the airports were covered.

"It isn't serious if they manage to get back. It only means we have one more to deal with here. It would be better if we could get her before she makes it to the house. I'll step up the surveillance on the house, see if anyone tries to help her. It's what I would do. In the meantime I think you should go back to Paris and wait in your hotel until I call you."

Driving back to Paris in the dusk light Alexei was furious with himself. He had assumed too much. They had outwitted him. It had all been an act to buy time to elude him. Of that, he was now sure. It would not happen again. He spent a long time wondering who the unknown boyfriend was. He was not as harmless and ineffectual as he first appeared if the act was his idea. The only comfort he had was that he believed Anatoly's assessment was correct. They would try and head for England. It would be easy to find her if her father sent someone across to assist in her evasion. He hated failing, it was rare for him to do so and he looked forward to taking care of the strange man as soon as he had dispatched the woman. It was only a matter of time before he found them. Gregori's assets were numerous.

CHAPTER TWENTY

They turned left onto the Champs Elysee. The wide boulevard was busy with a never-ending stream of cars and motorcycles, stopping and starting as the traffic lights changed. The broad, tree lined sidewalks teemed with tourists and Parisians alike, the tourists dressed in the long legged baggy trousers so many found comfortable. Americans were noticeable by their somewhat gaudy dress sense, the men in brash trousers more suited to the golf course and the women in an assortment of baggy, unflattering fashion styles. All contrasting with the business men and women in their suits, speaking fervently into their mobile phones, free hand gesticulating wildly as only the French can do. The sidewalk cafes were doing a lively trade, most of their tables full. The incongruity of the yellow and red MacDonalds sign was completely out of place among the designer boutiques. James had always enjoyed this aspect of Paris, the contrasts and the bustle, but preferred the quiet back streets where the locals gathered for their coffee and aperitifs.

"We'll meet Etienne outside the Chat d'Or and head back to the office." He slid open his mobile phone and saw that the battery was dead. "May I borrow your phone? Mine's dead."

Monique started to dig around in her handbag. He smiled, "I don't know how you women can ever find anything in there, you carry everything but the kitchen sink."

She laughed as held her phone to him in triumph. "See, there's method in there."

They moved closer to the shop fronts to pass a group of tourists taking photographs of the Arc de Triomphe, the huge French tricolour moving slowly in the light breeze, and he started to dial Etienne's number. He saw the skateboarder heading straight for them and pulled Monique to his side, the crowd forcing her in front of him. As she moved and the skateboarder drew level he was jerked backward, a hole appearing in the centre of his white T-shirt, a red circle slowly increasing in circumference. He flopped onto his back, the skateboard rolling past them. It took a second for the sight to register on James' brain before he started acting.

"Shit." He kept her in front of him, silently pushing her forward, dodging around the tourists. "Don't look down, keep calm and head towards the crossing just like we were doing." As they rounded the tourists he put an arm around her waist and whispered in her ear, trying to look as though they were oblivious to all else. "Put your arm around my waist and look directly at me, laugh and give me a kiss on the lips." She did as he instructed, although he could see she had been shaken by the sight of the skateboarder.

After she had kissed him, he continued guiding her to the crossing. She went along with him but managed to ask "Was that guy shot? Do you think it was meant for me? Tell me James."

"I will, I promise, just as soon as we're on the other side and have a bit of time. All you need to do now is to try act naturally, as if nothing happened. Please do that for me, all right?"

She nodded as the first scream pierced the air. As an ordinary person would do he turned to look and see what the fuss was about and indicated that she do the same. Nothing could be seen of the skateboarder through the crowd and he used the opportunity to briefly scan the pedestrians to try and spot the shooter. But there were just too many people milling about and no one stood out or appeared to paying them too much attention. He had to hope that, after the failed attempt, whoever it was had pulled back into the crowd and was now being held up by the press of bodies as a pedestrian traffic jam formed.

A break in the traffic allowed them to start crossing the road. He was eager to get to the other side and ignored the stop signs, stepping directly into the traffic heading up the boulevard, weaving and dodging cars and motor cycles, ignoring the shouts of drivers as they hurriedly braked. Almost dragging her they managed to gain the centre island and then start the same process across to the other sidewalk. With a great deal of luck they stepped onto the pavement, the shouts and obscene gestures of the drivers in their wake following them as they passed the cinema entrance and made it to a turn off into the Rue Tivoli. Turning down the street he dialed Etienne's number. It was answered after only one ring.

"Etienne we're going down the Rue Tivoli." He glanced around. "Just passing the Tivoli Etoile. We might have a shooter on our tail. We need to be picked up right now."

"Oui, I know the place. Take the first right and half way down the block on the left you will see a Vietnamese restaurant. I should be there the same time as you. I'm on my way."

"Come Monique, we have to keep moving." He glanced behind them as they turned a corner, but still could not see anyone he could identify as the shooter. Everyone on the street either looked like tourists or office workers on their lunch break. It only took a couple of minutes to reach the restaurant, and as they did there was a screech of tyres as the Mercedes rounded a corner at speed and pulled up next to them. Before it even stopped the back door swung open and James bundled Monique into the back seat, quickly following her. The speed of Etienne accelerating away closed the door just as his ankles cleared the door. He pushed Monique flat, and tried to watch the passers by as they sped up the street, before turning right into the Rue Tivoli. He did not see anyone taking any undue interest in the car or its occupants before they turned again. With no obvious threat, he allowed Monique to straighten in the seat.

He held up his hand to stop the questions forming on her lips. "Etienne, drive around, moving us into the suburbs, and see if you can spot any obvious tail." At Etienne's nod of understanding he turned back to Monique. "Did you see what happened to the skateboarder?"

"Only a glimpse, you were pulling me away too fast. Was he shot? What happened?"

He could see her hand was shaking as she tried to gather up the contents of her purse, which had spilled on the floor. "Yes, he was. I think if I hadn't pulled you out of his way it might have been you. He saved your life, poor chap. You going to be all right? Can you hold on for a few more minutes?"

"Yes, what are we going to do?"

"I'll tell you in a minute, let me make a call first."

He dialled Mike's number, willing him to pick up. When he did he cut short the pleasantries. "Hello Mike. Look, I don't have much time. I'm using Monique's phone." This so Mike would understand it was not a secure line. "I have to get to another meeting. I thought I had better let you know that the deal has gone bad on me and I'll have to try and figure out a new approach. How's the technology at your end, I need to send you confidential stuff?" It was cryptic, and he had taken that approach in case anyone was listening, and he wanted to remain anonymous - just a business man and friend of Monique.

Thankfully Mike got the drift of the conversation straight away and replied. "I'm not in my office now, so you will have to call me back, but to answer your question the equipment I have there will be more than adequate for your documents. How about the other parties? Are they out of it altogether or can we salvage the deal?"

"No they are all fine, it's a third party that has just entered the game. I'll send everything to you in order that we can restructure our offer. Give you a call in an hour or so, if that's all right."

"That's good James. I'll start working on it while I wait for your call and should have some ideas for you." He hung up and James felt Monique's eyes on him as he closed her phone.

"Etienne, we need to dump the car and get another, just in case they saw the number plate. This model will have GPS tracking, and we cannot afford to take any chances." He looked at Monique; she looked exhausted and on the verge of shock. "Also we need some place to rest up for a couple of hours. Any ideas?"

"Oui m'sieur, I have a friend who is working in Marseilles for the week. We will go to his place and I will call and borrow his car. I do not think we are being followed."

"Good, pull over and give me your phone Etienne, I'll throw these phones into that garbage can." He took the phones, switched them off, removing the SIM cards and burning them with a lighter, and wrapped them in a newspaper he found on the front seat. Then he reached out of the window to throw them into the litter bin. "Right, let's get to your friend's place. No, on second thoughts I don't want to put your friend in danger if they trace the car to his place. Do you know of a parking garage nearby?" At the nod he continued. "All right, drive there and we'll walk to the apartment." He knew it was time for an explanation to the visibly shaken Monique. He put an arm around her shoulders and she moved closer to him, seeming to relax with her head resting back on his arm. He could feel that she was still trembling, and gave her a quick squeeze to try and reassure her.

"Is that holder a charger as well?" It was, and he put his phone in it to charge. He was thinking all the time, trying to work out what their next move should be. "Etienne, your passport. Where is it?"
"Right here m'sieur, I always carry it and a bag with a change of clothes when I have a job."

"Great." Lifting Monique's chin with his hand he gently asked her. "And you, I suppose your passport's at your apartment?"

She managed a wan smile. "No actually, I always carry it. It's the best ID in case I'm ever asked, you know banks, that sort of thing."

One problem out of the way, he thought. At least they could cross borders and, ultimately, the Channel. "One more question, Monique. Do you have any cash on you? I've got about two hundred Euros."

She rummaged around in her bag coming up with her purse. Checking, she showed him seventy Euros in bills and some change.

He knew they would need cash. He did not want to use his bank account or credit cards. With the right connections, they could be too easily traced. Assuming the worst case scenario had worked well for him in the past and there was no point in changing tactics now. He had not been giving any attention to where they heading but now noticed that they had crossed the Seine. This part of Paris was unfamiliar and he had to trust that Etienne knew what he was doing. What to do with him was another problem. He decided he would discuss it with him after he had settled Monique in the apartment. James dimly registered the fact that they had driven through the 14th Arrondissement and were passing through the outer suburbs of Paris.

His thoughts were interrupted by Monique, who stirred and lifted her head from its resting place on his arm. "What are we going to do James?"

"Let's wait until we arrive wherever we're going to and then I'll tell you both. How much further Etienne?"

"Maybe twenty minutes."

"We'll go to your friend's apartment, let Monique get some rest and then the two of us will get some supplies and make a phone call." To Monique he said, "You need some rest, get over what happened. I know it will be hard but you have to try and chase it out of your mind. I need you strong and rested for the next leg, all right?"

She only nodded her assent and rested her back on his arm. He resumed his absent minded gaze through the window. At least, he thought, I have the next two moves planned. A lot depended on what Mike was able to tell him when he called. It had been fortunate that he had taken his guns and documents with him when he had left that morning. That decision had only been to prevent having to give an awkward explanation to Monique if she had accidentally stumbled across them. He sighed to himself; that appeared to have been the only good decision he had made today. The shooting had caught him totally off guard. The fact that the shooter had the confidence to make the attempt on the busiest street in Paris was worrying. Whoever it was had no qualms about innocent bystanders getting injured.

"We're almost there." Etienne interrupted his thought process and he glimpsed a sign that told him they were entering Bievres. They skirted the market place, where the stall holders were in the process of packing away unsold items and tidying their stalls. A couple of minutes and they were pulling into a four-level parking garage. They left the car on the top floor and walked a short distance, ending up in front of an old house which had obviously been converted into several apartments. In its day it must have been owned by an affluent merchant but now, worn by the passage of time, it lacked the grandiose feel although efforts had been made to restore the facade to something like its original state.

Etienne led the way, using a key to gain entrance through the front door and setting off up a wide sweeping staircase to the second floor. There were only two doors on the landing, and he showed them into an entrance hall pointing through to the lounge, before locking the door behind them. James guided Monique to a long settee and sat her down. Glancing around, he saw that the room was clean and neat. Not what he had expected from a bachelor's flat. He opened some cupboards and saw crockery stacked, books arrayed on shelves in alphabetical order. He went through to the kitchen and checked the shelves there, eventually finding what he was looking for. A bottle of Courvoisier brandy. He took a tumbler and the bottle back into the lounge and poured a generous measure, handing it Monique. She cupped the tumbler in both hands and lifted it to her nose.

"Drink," he urged her gently. She sipped and he noticed that her hands were steady as they lifted the glass to her lips. He went into the bedroom and found a blanket in a cupboard, returning to her and pushing her down on the settee, covering her with the blanket. "Try and get some rest, sleep if you can. We'll be back in half an hour at the most. Wait," he stopped her question as it formed, "I need to speak with Mike then I'll give you the whole picture. Come on, relax now." He stopped and smiled at her, "ET has to phone home." Trying and failing to imitate the voice. At least it raised a smile.

James and Etienne left the apartment, locking the door behind them. On the street Etienne led to a grocer where James left him with some money and instructions to buy bottles of water and some items that they could eat on the road. He had seen a bistro across the road and arranged to meet him after he had made a call.

Inside the bistro he sat at the counter and ordered a beer. It tasted good, sliding down his throat, a nectar of the gods. Ordering another, he took his beer with him to a table near the window. His phone was almost fully charged and he pushed the speed dial. The phone rang only twice before Mike picked up.

"Mike, how secure are we?"

"Got your phone, I see. We should be fine, but let's play on the safe side. Listen, I have made some arrangements since we spoke. Do you remember the young feller you helped in Rwanda?" James told him he did. "Right, he's going to meet up with you, give you some stuff which will make the arrangements more convenient. You need anything in particular?"

James had thought about this during the drive. "Cash; I have close contact with the Browning brothers but I might have to feed them if negotiations drag on. A secure means of transmitting documents. And information about the third party, as much as you can give. I'm blind Mike and I don't like it."

"Gotcha, all those things will be coming with the young feller. Where do you want to rendezvous?" This caused James to stop for a moment.

"Speaking of Rwanda, remember where we landed afterwards and how we got home?" When Mike said he did, he continued. "OK, there, tomorrow at the time we got our transport home. I'll find him, but that cafe might be a good place. And Mike, we need anonymity."

"Understood James. I'll take care of everything. By the way, how many packages of documents are you thinking of sending?"

"Three. Thanks, Mike I'll speak with you tomorrow." He hung up and went back to the bar to finish his beer, watching through the window for Etienne to come out of the shop with two brown bags, before leaving the bistro and joining him. Before they entered the apartment building

I, Plague

James stopped him. "Etienne, I think it's better if you come all the way with us. It might not be safe for you to return to Paris on your own, even if you know nothing. These are not nice people. Don't worry, you'll be well paid and looked after until this business is finished. Is that all right with you?"

"Oui m'sieur, it is what I wanted anyway, and was going to ask you before we saw the mam'selle. I will go with you wherever you want, but I am only a driver, I have never been involved in anything else."

"Leave that side to me. I wouldn't want you to get involved in that side anyway. Let's get some rest."

Monique was still lying on the settee when they entered, but she had not fallen asleep. She stood up and took the bags to the kitchen, telling them to sit and she would prepare something to eat. Etienee poured them all some brandy and they sipped at it in silence until Monique returned with a plate heaped with bread, hams and cheese.

"Right guys, this is what is happening. Monique, there is a contract out on the whole of your family. Some Russian who your father upset a long time age. It's also to do with his old business." He had to stop as she started cursing her father and his antecedents. He leaned across and gently squeezed her arm. stopping the tirade. "What's done is done, now we deal with the present. The only plan I have is that we are going to Brussels tonight, we need to be there for six in the morning. Etienne, I'll leave it to you as to what time we need, I assume it'll be up the Periphique onto the A1." Etienne just nodded. "Tomorrow about eight I'll meet a young chap called Ethan. Mike's sending him with all the stuff we need. Apart from that I have no plan. The reason I have no plan is that I'll be tempted to follow it, without it I'll deal with any situation as my gut tells me at the time. Besides, if I can think of a plan then someone else can think of the same plan and then we have all sorts of trouble."

He let his word sink in for a couple of minutes, as he took some bread and cheese from the plate. "What we need now, especially you Etienne, is rest. It will be a long night and there's no guarantee that there will be time tomorrow for a prolonged break. Etienne, you take the bedroom, we'll stay in here."

After he had left, James took off his jacket and took his two automatics from their respective holsters, placing them on the coffee table near his right hand. Monique looked at them, then at him. "That's why you came to Paris, to look after me? Why didn't you tell me?"

He tried to explain that he had come to Paris because of a rumour, nothing more substantial than that. He gave her all the information that Mike had given him and eventually managed to calm her enough that she lay down. He lifted the brandy to her lips and held it there until she had finished it, pulling the blanket up to cover her shoulders, remaining kneeling on the floor at her side, stroking her hair as he would a child until she closed her eyes and her breathing evened.

Once he was sure she had drifted into sleep he stood and went into the kitchen. Checking the washing machine, he saw it incorporated a tumble dry cycle. He undressed and put his underwear and shirt into the machine, selecting the shorter programme, then, with a bath towel wrapped around his waist, he took a leisurely shower. Feeling better and fresher, he applied some of the occupant's deodorant and after shave before quietly going back into the kitchen to check on his wash. As he waited he took a bottle of water and sat at the table, trying to think of all the eventualities which he had to cover. His thinking continued as he ironed his shirt and pressed his trousers, letting them air as he sat back in the lounge.

He was surprised by the hand softly shaking him by the shoulder. He had fallen asleep. He decided that it must have been the two beers and large brandy, but he did feel better. He dressed quickly in the kitchen as Etienne woke Monique and he heard her stir and move to the bathroom. A strong black coffee for him and Etienne and Monique came in, hair still wet from the shower. "God, I need one of those" - helping herself to a mug. "Jeez James, you look the same as you did this morning, how do you do it?"

"Old habits. Right, we set to go?" The others nodded their affirmative.

CHAPTER TWENTY ONE

They were driving into Brussels city centre as dawn was breaking. The drive had been uneventful, boring. The time had been spent trying to reassure Monique that everything was going to work and that nothing was going to happen to her mother or sister. Although she appeared to have accepted her lot for the time being, he had a feeling that her father was going to get hell when she eventually saw him.

As Etienne pulled up in front of the central railway station, James tried to get his bearings. He instructed Etienne to drive past the front, and then take the second left. They completed a drive around the blocks surrounding the station, before James made up his mind. At the front of the station again, he told Etienne to take the second left and immediately the first right. Asking him to park in the first available space, he told them his intentions.

"OK, here's the plan so far. Ethan should be in the station cafe at eight. I'll go and meet him, he'll come here alone. Once he's here, drive away and follow the same route around to the bridge we went under. Once there, take the first right and wait for me. Got it? It's important that you drive as soon as Ethan gets in the car. If he is being followed I want to minimise the risk of someone getting the make or plates of this car." They both nodded that they understood. "Right, Ethan, you don't know him, Monique. He's about 6 feet tall, slim with light blond hair. If he hasn't changed too much you could mistake him for about eighteen years old. I'll make sure he knows the make of the car and what to do. Etienne, you stand outside, leaning against the wall there so he can see you when he comes around the corner."

"One other thing, Etienne, let me borrow your jacket and cap, please." They were duly passed back and James tried them on. The blouson leather jacket was a bit tight across the shoulders, but otherwise not too bad. He stepped out of the car and asked if they could see any noticeable bulges where his shoulder holsters hung. Satisfied that there was nothing obvious, he sat back down to wait.

They each had some coffee from a flask.

"Who is this Ethan? I thought I had met most of Mike's friends."

"A young feller Mike and I met in Africa. He was on his first job and I sort of helped him out. Taught him a few tricks, if you like. Good young guy, you'll like him." He looked at her, "Not too much, I hope, got enough on my plate without having a jealous Mike around as well." He smiled to show he was teasing her. A blush appeared on her cheeks, "There's nothing like that between Mike and I."

A bit too quick to deny it, he thought, laughing out loud at her discomfort. If nothing else it eased the palpable tension in the car.

"Right, it's time. Take care and I'll see you shortly." He left them and walked slowly back to the station entrance. The building was disgorging a mass of commuters clutching briefcase and mobile phones as they scurried in different directions to the comfort and safety of their routine and habits, probably looking forward to the first cup of coffee. Because he was going against the stream, he could easily check to see that there was no one behind him, a good start, he thought.

Inside the concourse, he wandered slowly to the departures board and looked at it for a minute, checking his watch. He looked around and saw that things had changed since his last visit. There were now three outlets, a Burger King, Starbucks and the older cafe he remembered. He stopped to buy a newspaper, to any casual observer another traveller passing the time until his train was due. He sauntered to the older cafe and saw that Mike had briefed Ethan well. He was sitting against the back wall, a large cup of coffee in front of him. He did not look directly at James except when he lifted his cup to his lips. When their eyes met James lifted a clenched fist to his face and then rubbed his eyes. A clenched fist meaning freeze which is just what Ethan did, dropping his eyes back down to the table.

James bought a cup of coffee and looked for a place to sit, deciding on a table adjacent to Ethan's. Once seated he opened his newspaper and held it up to read the headlines. Behind the cover of the paper he almost whispered.

"Good to see you young feller. I want you to finish your coffee and leave through the main entrance. Turn left and then take the second street on the left. Then first right, you'll see a dark blue Renault Megane, French plates, and a guy leaning against the wall. Monique's inside. Get straight in and duck down. Etienne, the driver, knows what to do."

He glanced at Ethan as he turned the page of his paper and lifted his own coffee. Out of the corner of his eye, he saw Ethan glance at his watch, finish his coffee and stand to leave. Over the rim of his cup, he watched a man in a gray pinstripe suit, sitting at the counter, overlooking the concourse, bend to stand, leaving his stool to the right. As he straightened, James saw a bulge in his jacket at waist level.

"Bugger it," he muttered. Ethan had been tagged in London and followed here. The bulge was almost certainly a handgun in a belt rig. That tell-tale type of mistake was why James favoured the twin shoulder holsters. They also allowed him to wear a short jacket, such as the one he had borrowed from Etienne.

He let the tail leave the café, and then stood and followed. When he left the station he took a minute to identify him again amidst all the others in similar suits. He sped up and was within one metre as they approached the first corner. Halfway down the block there was a service alley and it was here he made his move. He moved alongside and stopped, turning slightly in front of him, lifting the newspaper. The tail looked annoyed at the nuisance and stepped slightly into the alley to skirt James. As he moved, James struck with the knuckles of his right hand, the blow landing on the exposed neck. It had sufficient force behind it that James could feel the larynx and surrounding tissues collapsing.

Generally, with this type of blow, the first reaction is to raise hand to the throat and this was no exception to that rule. He was gasping in vain for the air that his lungs were craving for, clawing at his throat as if to open the air passage. He took the suit by the left arm and propelled him quickly into the alley, hoping that any passers by would think he was assisting a man suddenly feeling unwell, unsteady on his feet. He pushed him between two dumpsters, glanced quickly to his left and saw that there was no interest being taken in them and, with the heel of his hand hit him on the nose, forcing the bone back into the brain. The second blow was hardly necessary, as the tail's eyes glazed over and life drained out of them. James lowered the body to the ground, sitting him between the dumpsters, hidden from view except to those who passed down the alley.

He straightened and, not moving too fast, walked down the alley. As he walked to the pickup point he could only hope that they had only had time to put one man on Ethan and that he hadn't missed any back up in the crush of the station. Still, he reasoned, what's done is done, take it as it comes. They would know soon enough.
There was no alarm raised by the time he reached the end of the alley

and turned to his left, passing under the bridge. The Renault passed him and turned into the rendezvous point. He reached it in minutes and waved Etienne on. "Change of plan, Etienne, head for Ghent, keep an eye on the mirror, see if you can pick up a tail."

Turning to face the two in the back seat he reached out and warmly shook Ethan by the hand. "It really is good to see you again, son. How you been doing?"

"Real good, thanks James. Good to see you too. Got all the stuff you asked for here. Mike gave me a briefing, said I was to stick with you until you got back. Wherever you go I go."

"Good to have you along." James did not argue. "You had a tail from the station, did you know?"

"Yes, I picked him out on the train. Nothing I could do to tell you, sorry."

"Nothing to be sorry about, you did just great back there. Anyway, he's out of the picture now. You sure there was only the one?"

"As sure as I can be. I know Mike had his people watching me until I boarded the train. They were supposed to deal with anyone trying to follow. That one must have slipped through the net."

James looked at the holdall on Ethan's lap and held out his hand. He opened it and saw magazines for his 9mm's, fully loaded, two mobile phones and wads of cash. "Ethan, are these two of the secure phones?" He gave one to Ethan and the other to Monique.

A quick reply told him that they were the most up to date encrypted phones, as good as the police used, if not better. "I dare say Mike's been standing by for the last couple of hours." He turned to Monique. "Hello Miss, good to meet you. Your father's been worried sick since yesterday. He'll be waiting by the phone with Mike."

Monique just nodded as James pushed the speed dial. As Ethan had guessed, it had barely rung when Mike answered. "James, Thank God, you all right?"

"Just fine Mike, the boy did real good. Everything went as planned. He did have a tail on him. He's been neutralised." He could almost feel Monique stiffen at this. "Taking a good long nap. These phones as good as Ethan says?"

"The best money can buy, private or government. What are you thinking about doing now?"

"First things first, Mike. A couple of questions; first, are the opposition as good and well organised as you first thought? Second, if they are, do they have the technology and ability to do anything you or your friends could do? You know, access credit cards, files all that sort of thing? Third, what sort of manpower can they put in the field? And last, but not least, what is the threat level against us?"

"Right, they are as good as the security services, they have all the gear and can do just about anything with it. I take it that's why you wanted cash, not to use credit cards, etc. As for manpower, this group has been taking over Western Europe for the past ten years, so yes they have manpower in abundance, in every city you can think of. Also, James, this is a really bad bunch. We've all heard the stories about their methods, particularly in the U.S., they are as brutal and merciless as they come, make the Colombian cartels look like a Sunday School outing. Listen, I want to give the old man a chance on the phone, but before I do I want you to know that I will do everything in my power to bring you all home safe. Tell Etienne that, will you, I'll take good care of him. OK, here's the old man."

"Mike, before you go, I am not working to any plan, we are going to have to improvise as we go. Make sure the old man understands that, we could be out of touch for long stretches at a time, it all depends on the opposition. I hate running, you know that for yourself, maybe when we team up we can go on the offensive. One last thing, anything on the wires about the shooting in Paris and our possible involvement?"

He was assured that, at least as far as that was concerned, they were in the clear. James handed the phone back to Monique, who took it wordlessly. She surprised him by staying calm and assuring her father that she was fine and in good hands. With this she managed a smile at James. She asked after her mother and sister, and then listened for a few minutes before handing the phone back to James. "He wants to talk to you."

"James, please look after her, I don't know what I would do if anything happened to her."

Assuring him that he would, James closed the phone and turned to Etienne. "See if you can find a Travel Lodge or something. We need to sit down and have a chat."

He turned back and looked behind them as Etienne sped up, slowed down and constantly changed lanes on the freeway. There was no sign of a following vehicle. James saw they had passed one of those large shopping malls, and told Etienne to turn in. He dug in the bag and pulled out a wad of notes, handing them to Monique.

"Ethan, you take Monique in there, we need some fresh clothes. Don't hang about, browsing, or trying anything on. In and out, as fast you can, please. Get enough to last a couple of days at least. Nondescript, ordinary, you know what I mean." He gave her his measurements and Etienne dropped them at the main door and pointed to where he would park. James left the car as soon as it was parked, and watched the other vehicles entering the car park. When he was satisfied that there appeared to be nothing untoward with any of the occupants, he sat next to Etienne and told him what Mike had said. Then they waited.

It took them 45 minutes before they returned, weighed down with shopping bags. As they climbed in he couldn't help joking "Send a woman into a shop with enough money and she'll buy it out." She managed a broad grin back.

"That'll teach you, besides it felt good to spend so much of Dad's money. Boy, I'm looking forward to a shower and a change of clothing. I feel like I've been wearing these for weeks."

They were nearing Ghent before they found the hotel they were looking for, a glass and concrete structure that catered mainly for travellers, one night stays only and no frills. They would not be remembered. James sent Ethan to the desk to register them for two twin rooms and they made their way to them, arranging to meet in James and Monique's room after an hour.

While Monique was in the shower he took the tags off the suitcase and unpacked what she had bought. It was plain, nothing showy, and very practical. He ordered some beer and sandwiches to be brought to the room. With any luck they should be able to go out and eat a proper meal later in the day.

When he came out of the bathroom he found that Monique had packed the bags and tidied the room. "They're in the drawer," she told him when she saw his searching look around the room. "Couldn't let the waiter see them lying on the bed, now, could I?"

He cursed himself. That had been sloppy. He would have to pull himself together and start thinking about small things like that. A knock at the door stopped him, and he let the two others into the room. Gesturing to the beer and sandwiches, he told them they would eat later.

"Let's see where we are. I don't want to sound melodramatic. We're up against a powerful organisation. We don't know who the opposition are. Ergo, we treat every situation and everyone as a threat. Ethan, you're very much like me, this isn't the plains of Africa. It's a whole new ball game. The best I can say is to stay close to me and follow my lead. We do know that they don't mind civilian casualties." He briefly recounted the events in Paris for Ethan. "Our first priority is to get Monique and Etienne safely back in the good old UK. In the event we get split up, Ethan you stick like glue to Etienne. I know it's asking a lot for two people you don't know, but as far as I'm concerned they will both be safe as long as I can draw breath. They are my friends, and I will do whatever it takes. Ethan, if you're lucky, they will become your friends too, over the next day or two."

He paused and looked around; they made for a very sombre group. "On the plus side, the opposition does not know our next move, if for no other reason than we don't know our next move ourselves. We also have enough munitions here to start a small war. We have plenty of money, and Mike will be putting together resources, whatever we need to get home. Also, I am counting on the fact that it is likely that Etienne and me are, for now, at least, unknown faces. I don't know how long that will last, my ugly mug, and probably yours Ethan, is all over files in Special Branch, MI6 and MI5, after Rwanda.

He took a long sip of his beer. "The next order of business is to have a proper meal. We should be all right for the time being." As he said it, he hoped that he was correct in that assumption. "Then a good night's sleep for everyone. No, that's not quite true. Ethan, you and I will go walkabout, have a look around and figure out our next move." He stopped and split the money into four piles, telling each to pocket it. "That is in case we do get separated, you hide up and contact Mike, or me. Ethan, you take one of the phones. Good, questions?"

There was nothing said for a few minutes, enough time to finish one beer and open another, before Ethan hesitantly started. James had to push him. "Spit it out, kid."

"Well, I just want you all to know that I will do everything I can to help. James, I owe you and I want you to know that you can count on me. Well, you know what I mean."

"I do, kid. Mike trusted you to come here, and believe me when I say that you are one of a handful of people I would want with me here." He could see his words had the desired effect of boosting Ethan's confidence.

Monique stretched out her hand and put it in Ethan's forearm. "That goes for me too. And that's based on the little James has told us about you – the very little I might add." She threw a meaningful look at James.

From the information at reception, they found a small restaurant near the hotel and enjoyed a relaxing meal. Afterwards, James and Ethan left the others in their rooms and walked onto the street.

"Right kid, remember anything I taught you?"

"I remember it all, we're going to have a look at the terrain in case we have to make a stand. Always better to have the choice of ground, also to establish escape routes if we have to run. Although I figure, in this case, it's more about escape. Right?"

"Spot on. Now tell me what's going on back home. By the way, I appreciate your not mentioning anything earlier in front of Monique."

"Mike briefed me well on what to say, and how much. Well you know there's been five killings so far. The regional guys of the old man's old outfit. It's a well organised, almost military operation. They had people ready to step in and fill the gaps. No arguments, anyone unhappy takes a beating or disappears. Word is that there's been a few of them already. What you said earlier about them being brutal and ruthless is only too accurate. Got the police spooked; Mike's contact says they are setting up a nationwide task force to try and knock this on head before it begins. But he also says they've never experienced anything like it before. They are taking advice from the FBI because they have experience of this situation over there. As far as the old man and his family go, well, that's personal. Seems the old man really pissed off this Gregori some years ago when he refused to let him in on the UK operation. He took it personally and his reputation is that he doesn't only take the man down, he also does the whole family before killing the man."

They walked a bit in silence. "Mike said it might be something like that. How sure is he now that's the case?"

"100 per cent. Information from both the police and the street." Ethan paused and stopped to look at James. "There's more. The shooter is a professional, ex Russian military, suspected KGB and *Stasi*. He's good, never been identified, never leaves anything at the scene. The first two murders were up close and personal, but then he switched to long range sniping. Probably figured all his targets would have the wind up and tighten their security. Also, he is believed to have his own team, which would explain the attempt in Paris. Mike thinks he thought Monique would be a soft target, and sent one of his team to do the job. Mike also thinks he had a specific order for the family, children, oldest first, then wife and finally the old man."

"Shit, all this for a perceived insult." They walked on until James stopped them at a bar. "Come on, kid, let's have a drink."

Once seated with their drinks, James made up his mind. "Look Ethan, this is a major cock up. I have no right, neither does Mike, to ask you to stay."

"The way things are shaping up, it could get more than a little hairy around here. Make Rwanda seem like a picnic. If you want to pull out, I won't hold it against you. In fact, I want you to pull out." He held up his hand, stopping Ethan speaking. "You have done what you were sent to do. No need for you to stick your neck out any further."

"No way am I leaving you. No arguments, I appreciate what you're doing, but I'm not that green kid anymore. No! Let me finish. I owe you and Mike and that's part of it. But the biggest thing for me is finishing this. I started and I *will* finish, however it works out. Want another drink?" He stood and went to the bar without waiting for a reply. James had to smile as he thought how much he had grown up in the years since their first meeting.

When Ethan came back, all James did was hold out his hand, "Thanks." That was enough between two men.

"By the way, James, when are you going to stop calling me kid?"

James laughed. "When you turn thirty, or hell freezes over, whichever comes first. OK, how are we going to get back across the channel? I'd say the Eurostar is definitely out. The ferry might be a better bet; more space to move if there was a threat. Problem there is that there is too much potential for civilian casualties." James knew he was thinking out loud, but it was good to be able to do it, with someone listening who could contribute. "Still, the problem of them watching the terminals, the same applies to flying. Although flying might be better; even if they spotted us they would be suicidal to try anything in an airport. That would mean we would lose our firepower, which could be bad if we had to turn around. What do you think?"

"I don't know. You've about covered it. I wish we had a plane." Ethan smiled at his joke.

"No, you're right. Private transport, plane, or boat. Shit, I'm getting slow, why didn't I think of that? Well done, kid."

"Hell, James, they don't come cheap. I don't think we have money for something like that."

"I know, but it's something to think about if we have no other choice. I'm sure that it wouldn't take too much effort to organise. We choose an airfield or port, get picked up, and then we're home free."

"Sounds too easy, and remember what you told me about things that sound or look easy? There's always a complication. Something you cannot plan for, Murphy's Law you called it."

"You're absolutely right, Ethan, but it's an idea that we can throw in the pot. Anyway, we'd better get back. We've both had a long day, we might think better in the morning after a good sleep."

They strolled back to the hotel, both alert to anything that might be unusual. As they approached the entrance, James stopped Ethan. "If we have to leave unexpectedly we meet round the corner from that bar, at the side of the supermarket, where it was a bit darker. Did you see it?"

"I know exactly where you mean."
"Ok, kid, you know the routine, ready to go at the drop of a hat. Make sure Etienne does the same, remember he's only a driver, he's never been involved in anything like this. Good night, kid, sleep well."

James watched Ethan take the stairs, and was inordinately pleased at the sight. The kid had really learned his trade well. A lift was confining; if the door opened and someone was waiting for you, there was nowhere to go. He went into the lounge and found a quiet corner where he could see the lobby and, after ordering coffee, hit the speed dial.

"James, what's wrong?"

"It's all right Mike, just a social call, checking in. Everything is going fine. The others are sleeping, I hope."

"You come up with any ideas?"

"I have. But first, why don't you just ask? I know you've been dying to since we first spoke."

There was a silence, James grinned as he imagined Mike's embarrassment. "You know me too well. All right I'll play – how is she?"

"Who's she Mike?" They had often played this game when in a tight situation. It helped relieve the tension, relaxed them.

"OK, OK, Monique, how is she? Is she holding up, not too scared?"

"She's doing great, Mike. I'll tell her I spoke to you and you sent your love."

"Don't you bloody dare, you hear me?"

"I hear you. Listen, Ethan's turned out to be really good. He's grown up and shows some sense. I haven't had a chance to gossip, but I'm sure he'll be a good man in a corner." He continued. "Mike, we figure all the ferry ports, train stations and airports will be watched. How about a boat across the channel? Maybe a pick up from some small fishing village and the same on your end. That way we could bring all our gear with us. No customs and all that. That would remove the threat until we actually hit London. Provided, of course, that you could get someone down to meet us without being followed. Ethan's idea, not mine."

"Now, why didn't I think of that? It's possible, I'll get right on it and speak to you in the morning. Anything else?"

"Funny, that's exactly what I said to the kid, why didn't I think of that. We must be getting too old for this Mike. Good night, old friend. Stay safe."

Entering the room, James saw that Monique was sound asleep, lying curled on her side. Like that she looked far younger than her twenty six years. Her dark hair was a contrast against the white of the pillow. He propped himself up against the pillows and sat up on the bed. He was prepared to doze the night away, but knew that sleep would not come easily.

CHAPTER TWENTY TWO

As dawn broke, slivers of light creeping through cracks in the curtains, he stood and went to have a shower. It had been a long night. He had checked the corridors a few times and tried to relax, sometimes lightly dozing, but some sound always had him alert.

Monique was awake when he entered the room, feeling fresher but still slightly weary.

"You've been up all night, haven't you?" She propped herself on one elbow, trying to straighten her sleep tousled hair.

"It was necessary. Why don't you get cleaned up and ready to move out? I'm just going to check on the others."

Ethan answered the knock on the door straight away, and James saw that Etienne's bed was empty, the sound of the shower confirming where he was.

"Morning. Let's have a look around before we do anything else. Check the car park and the lobby, see if we have anyone out of the ordinary. You take the fire escape. I'll take the main entrance, meet back in my room in ten minutes."

Ethan headed to the end of the corridor to the fire escape stairs, and James went in the opposite direction to the stairs to the reception area. He looked around and saw that, despite the early hour, there were groups of guests heading for breakfast, and checking out. Most of them were businessmen with early appointments, he assumed, but none were out of place. He walked to the glass doors and looked out. The car park was almost full but devoid of any guests. The cars he could see appeared to be empty. He moved through to the breakfast room and looked through the windows. Again, he could not pick up anything out of the ordinary.

Ethan was waiting for him when he arrived back at the room.

"Bad news. I used the windows on the fire escape to give a better view, and picked up two men in a Ford Focus parked at the far corner of the car park. From there they can see both exits. Fas far as I could make out, it has local plates. I saw quite a few cigarette butts on the ground next to the driver's door. Could be they have been there for most of the night. They certainly weren't there when we got back last night. I would have noticed a car parked so far from the entrance. It's a good position, though, they are pretty isolated, nothing close to them. It would be hard to approach without being seen."

"Shit, buggery and corruption." Despite the bad news, James was impressed by the report. He was about to speak when there was a knock at the door, and they heard Etienne's voice. Ethan went to answer it, drawing his gun on the way, standing to one side of the door before turning the handle. Etienne looked mildly alarmed when he saw the precautions and, looking at their faces, immediately asked. "What's wrong?"

James gestured for them to sit on the beds and thought for a couple of minutes. "What do we have? Two men sitting in a car, a good position to observe anyone leaving the building. Indications that they have been there some time. Conclusion: they are only staking out the place, might be part of a team that are watching all the obvious places where we might have stopped for the night. We know they have the manpower to do this, hell, they have every crack-head and dealer at their disposal. They don't know for sure we are here – this we have to assume, because no move was made during the night. Chances are, I hope, that they are only to observe and report movement. Any comments so far?"

Nothing was said. "So we can reasonably assume that they are low-level, not part of the murder team. That doesn't mean they're not dangerous. They might have weapons. We have two options, as I see it. We try to get out of here without being spotted, difficult but not impossible; again we have to make an assumption and that is that they have a good idea of what we look like. I know, I know, it's hard to imagine. We could have been photographed in Paris, or Ethan, you on your way here. The only one who might be unknown to them is Etienne. If that is the case, I want to keep Etienne unknown, we never know when we might need an ace up our sleeve. Option two, we take them out of the picture." He smiled at Ethan. "I wish we had some of the tools we used in Africa."

Before he could continue, Ethan reached into his bag and pulled out a sheathed dagger. "Like this." James knew that the double-edged nine inch blade would be sharp enough to shave with, deadly efficient in the right hands. But he saw the look of shock on Monique's face and glared at Ethan. "Not quite what I had in mind."
Ethan interpreted the look correctly; "Sorry"; and put it away.

I, Plague

James made up his mind. "Here's what we do. Etienne, you go down for breakfast. Get a table near the window and watch the car park. It should be guests leaving, maybe a car or taxi doing a pick up. Watch for anyone arriving and sitting in their car. While you're there, and take your time over breakfast, see who is working. You're looking for a youngster who will do a job for a bit of money. How much is up to you. What I want is for someone to take our bags to the car and then drive it to the supermarket down the street on the left. Use your imagination, any story that's half believable, wife following you, running from your mistress, anything. Don't push too hard, that would make them suspicious, think that you might be a criminal and that might stop them from helping. Tell us before you finalise anything. We will have to be able to observe our two friends as the car leaves. If they follow, then we have a problem, if they don't, all well and good. Can you do that?"

"No problemo, m'sieu. I am hungry anyway." He left the three sitting on the beds.

"Monique, I need to ask you to do something as well. They have bedrooms on the ground floor. The ones at the back are the same as this one, if you look out you can see a grassed area, and the warehouses on the other side of a low wall. It would be good if we could gain access to one of those rooms and make our way out through a window. The closer we are to the reception area end of the building the better, we'll be hidden from view. All the windows are the same, look." He stood and pulled the window open. "Bags of room to climb through. Where you come in is getting us into one of those rooms. The chamber maids are more likely to trust a woman, we may have to hang around reception in order to pick out a woman checking out of one of those rooms. Then you say you've already checked out. The key card won't work after you're out of the system and that's where the maid comes in. You claim to have forgotten something in your room. The chances are she'll leave you alone, you don't wait too long but when you leave you tape back the lock. This will allow us to push it open and Bob's your uncle." He looked at them. "Now would be a good time for any suggestions."

Monique was the first to speak. "What if they follow the car? That will mean they know where we are."

"Correct. In that case, if you'll pardon the French, we're up shit creek without a paddle. In fact we won't even have a canoe. We'll be wading through it for some time. Seriously, we'll deal with that if and when it happens." He watched her face, she was putting on a brave front for a corporate lawyer running for her life. He decided it was time to be brutally honest. He leaned across and took her hands in his his, holding them tight. "Look Monique, if the worst happens and we cannot get clean away, then we," indicating Ethan, "just might have to do things that you won't like. You have to understand that anything we do is to protect you, you and Etienne. Do you understand that?"

She looked up from his hands, straight into his eyes, holding the look before looking back down and murmuring, "I understand." Then she stared directly at him again. "I presume you mean you might have to kill someone. Just promise me you won't do anything unless it is really necessary." The tears were welling up and James knelt in front of her, now pulling her into a hug, holding her as the crying started. "My bloody father and his bloody business. It's not fair, it's just not fair."

He tried to reassure her and she had stopped sobbing when Etienne returned, entering the room with a triumphant grin, which disappeared when he saw the tear streaked face of Monique.

"It's all right Etienne, the strain is getting to all of us. You look pleased with yourself. Did you manage to find someone?"

"Qui m'sieu, mais certainement. There is a young waiter who is working his way through college and needs all the money he can get. I have to pay him one hundred Euros but he will do as we ask. I told him I am trying to hide from my ex wife, who is chasing me for money. A simple deception I told him, with no implications for him. He will take a break when we are ready, leave the car at the supermarket car park and come back here."

"Bloody well done, Etienne. Well," trying to lighten the mood, "as the guy who threw himself off a tall building was heard to say, as he passed each floor, so far so good, so far so good." He was pleased to see a small smile from Monique. "No point in hanging around. Get your stuff out of the room, Etienne, go down and check out, give the boy your overnight bag and then watch him leave. Ethan, you head along to where you can watch our friends. We'll wait here for you."

After they had left he told Monique to freshen up, apply some make up and be ready to leave, telling her that he was going to check on Ethan. He found him one floor up looking through a window. He indicated the parked car and the two occupants, obviously watching the front entrance of the hotel. The driver had his window rolled fully down and was smoking. As they watched there was no change in their attitude. After ten minutes James told Ethan he was going to check if Etienne was back.

He had to wait another ten minutes before Etienne returned and informed them that the car had left the car park. He went back to Ethan; the watchers were still in place. "Good, that means they haven't clocked our car." Ethan turned to start back to the room when James stopped him. "Ethan, I don't want to leave someone behind, we have to make sure we get clean away. Buy some time. You don't have to come, you up for it?"

"Sure, what's the plan?"

"Same as before, get out through the back, send the others on their way, we go around the building. You take the frontal approach, I'll go round the back to the passenger. They'll probably watch you approach, you go to the driver, use that toothpick to take him down. I'll take care of the passenger."

"Got it, I'll try for the back of the neck, spine. With a bit of luck it'll look as if I'm talking to him."

They moved down to reception, where Ethan checked them out. Monique stood at the end of the ground floor corridor and watched. Fortunately, it didn't take too long for a couple to leave one of the rooms and check out. She waited until they had exited the building before moving down the corridor. James moved to where he could watch her. He saw her move past the housekeeping trolley, enter a room and come out with the maid. Sure enough, she was let into a room and the maid went back to her chores. James indicated to the others to follow and quickly made his way to the room.

"No need for the tape, we'll go now, open the window will you." He peered round the door and let the others into the room. He applied the door lock.

"James, I can't get the window open." He had a sinking feeling that it might have restricted movement to prevent break ins and went straight over. He looked and saw there was no mechanism to block the opening. He moved Monique to one side and gave it an almighty tug. It sprang free and slid all the way open. He climbed out first and checked in both directions, before helping Monique over the sill. When they were all outside, he gave Etienne directions to the supermarket, warning him to stay off the main street and telling him they would join them in a couple of minutes. He warned them to stay away from the car until he arrived.

Without a word he and Ethan separated and walked around the building. As James turned the corner he spotted the car. Both occupants were still inside, the driver smoking yet another cigarette. He started slowly towards it, knowing that Ethan had more ground to cover. As he walked across the car park he saw Ethan making his way directly to the car, adjusting his pace to ensure he arrived at the same time as James. James watched closely but neither watcher made a move that might mean they were going for a phone or weapons. Ethan was a few paces from the driver's window when James reached the rear. He paused briefly, allowing Ethan time to reach and greet the driver. He slid forward, shit, the passenger window was closed. He hoped the door was unlocked. He glanced across the roof and saw the sudden movement as Ethan plunged the dagger into the driver. He grabbed and swung open the passenger door, reaching in taking a hold on his head with both hands. A swift, hard twist and there was the loud snap as his neck broke. It had all taken less than fifteen seconds. James straightened the passenger, moving his head slightly from the obviously unnatural angle. He looked across and saw that Ethan had managed a clean kill; there was blood at the base of the man's skull but that would be covered by the head rest against which Ethan was placing him. He closed the door, quickly used his handkerchief to wipe the door handle and the area above it where his fingers or thumb might have touched and they walked away.

Strange, thought James, so often he had heard that people said that time spent in action always slowed down, that things moved as if in slow motion. He had never experienced that, maybe it was the adrenalin but things seemed to move quicker, probably poetic license on the part of some authors or people who had never been in close contact action. Still, he told himself, you have to stop leaving bodies behind. That made the body count three, only two by his own hand admittedly, but enough to make the police sit up and take notice. It would be of interest to them that the methods of the kills were not normal for street violence. They would put the deaths down to professionals. As the man said – it was time to get out of Dodge!

They located the others standing outside the supermarket drinking coffee, holding spares for them. Monique looked at him, "James?" The rest of the question was unspoken. He smiled at her. "It's OK, they're just having an unscheduled and long nap. Long enough for us to get out of here."

Once in the car he told Etienne to head for the coast, to stick to back roads as much as possible. To do this they had to buy a map, and, as they needed petrol anyway, found a small garage in the village.

Once they were on the back roads James dialled Mike. "We had a spot of bother back at the hotel. They had spotters out, but they didn't have a description of the car. We're on the move again, the spotters have been put out of action."

"Understood James. We've been working most of the night on getting you out. Your idea with the boat is good, I'll have it ready to go late this afternoon, a long time but we've had to find the skipper, fuel and provision for it. Also it has to come down the Thames from its berth, so will be longer getting to your side. All things being equal it should be there early tomorrow. Now where will you meet it?"

"Hold on," he indicated to Etienne that he should pull over. As he waited. "Mike, we really need this extraction, things will be hotting up from all sides any hour now."

Mike got the drift. "Jesus, James, what's the body count?"

"Three."

They pulled off the road into a farm gate entrance. James spread the road map on the bonnet. "Mike, we've left Evergem outside Ghent and are now on the N9 heading towards Brugge. We can take the N371 to a place called Blankenberge. On the map it looks like a small resort type of place. Might be all right, one thing for sure it looks like an unlikely place for us to go. We can't afford to use a hotel again though, we'll have to rough it for the rest of today and tonight. You want to put it to your skipper?"

"Will do, can I call you back?"

"Of course, old man, you know I'll be eagerly waiting to hear your dulcet tones again. One thing Mike – you trust this skipper? We won't tell him where we'll land until we're almost at the English coast."
"Sarcastic old fart. Yes I trust him, the owner is an old friend of the family. All we'll tell him is that he's coming to pick up Monique and some friends. Speak soon. No, wait. The old man wants a word with

Monique."

"I'll put her on," he waved Monique over. "By the way Mike, I passed on your love."

"You know you are one of the most evil men I have ever had the displeasure of knowing. Here's the old man."

James handed the phone across to Monique, almost laughing at her expression. He absently listened to her assuring her father that she was well and safe. It was a short conversation, and they were soon on their way, James filling the rest in on the plan of action, adding "The thing we have to do once we get there is to find a wood, disused barn, building, anywhere we can hide up until we meet the boat. Etienne, I haven't forgotten about your friend. We'll put the car somewhere safe, send him enough money to cover his expenses and tell him where his car is. By that time it should be safe enough for him to collect it. You can phone him tomorrow."

They all settled back for the drive. "What did you mean when you told Mike you had passed on his love?"

"Just teasing him. You know how easily embarrassed he gets."

She was not going to give up that easily. "Is there something I should know? Come on, you can't keep it from me. You did promise, a long time ago, that you'd always be honest with me."

Women, he thought, never forget. To her he said, "No. I was just teasing him." Even as he spoke, he knew that he had not heard the end of the matter.

He was becoming impatient. It was time to hide the car; they could not hope that the bodies would remain undiscovered forever. Or that the police would not soon find out about the business with the car from the waiter. They were now past Brugge and on the N371. "Time to keep an eye open for someplace to stop" he reminded the others. They saw one small wood but it was 5 kilometres from Blankenberg, too far to walk without arousing suspicion. They were in the town centre, and moved out along the coast road. It was one kilometre out when they saw a house fronting onto the beach. It was secluded and had a garage. He told Etienne to turn and drive down, telling him to knock on the door. If there was someone home he would ask for directions to Antwerp. If not they would break in and wait out the night. God, he was really notching up the number of crimes, he could spend two or three lifetimes in jail if they got caught. Not exactly what his friends back home would think a country gentleman to be capable of. He missed his home, it felt like he had been on the run for ages. He stopped and remembered this was only the fourth day. It had only been five days since he left for London.

They watched Etienne knock on the door, wait and knock again. Then he disappeared around the corner, reappearing after he circled the building. James got out and joined him. They all gathered at the front door. "Ethan, come with me. You two wait in the car."

He moved to the front of the house, out of sight of the road and, borrowing Ethan's knife, forced a window. They climbed through and James went straight to the kitchen. He checked the fridge; it was empty. He flicked the light switch; nothing. "Good," he told Ethan. "Means there's no one staying here, they probably only use it on weekends. Check upstairs for clothes, that sort of thing, I'll get the others." He opened one of two doors. Stairs led down to the darkness of a cellar. The second door opened into the garage. He opened the garage door from the inside, checking the distant road for traffic, and motioned that Etienne should drive in. He quickly closed the door behind them and led them into the kitchen.

Leaving them there, he returned to the window through which he had entered and repaired it as best he could. To the casual observer it would at least appear secure. Ethan returned and informed them that there were very few clothes in the bedrooms. Mainly clothes that would be worn for outdoors.

They returned to the kitchen. "Good, it looks like we'll be all right here for the night. No electricity. Can't have a light on when there shouldn't be one. On the bright side, we have some place warm to spend the next few hours. OK guys, make yourselves comfortable."

He took Etienne to one side. "There's one more thing for you to do. We need to take the car out at night and park it somewhere your friend can find it. Also, before we do that, it needs to be thoroughly cleaned. No trace of us can be found, no hair, no wrappers, absolutely nothing. We'll all help with that. I know you have gloves, I saw them earlier, so when you take the car tonight, make sure you wear them, and your cap, tucking all your hair under it. Brush the seat down before you leave it. Can you do that one last thing?"

"Mais oui m'sieur. I have been thinking about that. I could try a garage, put it in for a service and valet clean, tell them my friend will collect it. Pay in advance. That way it will be out of sight and doubly clean. I will try find a garage that has a yard or some place to keep it."

"That's very good thinking, Etienne. Let's get the others and get started."

Ethan found the power panel and switched it on. They located some cleaning material and assembled in the garage, now well lit by ceiling fluorescent lighting. "Right everyone, we scrub every inch of the car inside and out. We cannot afford to leave anything behind that may identify us. Make sure you clean behind door handles, vacuum only after the washing down of every surface is complete." They started on the job and were making good progress when Mike called. He had good news.

"They've left and are now well down the Thames. ETA on your side is four in the morning. Have you decided on a pick up point?"

James had. "We're in a beach house about one kilometre east of Blankenberge. The house faces the sea with a road 200 metres behind us. We're nicely isolated, the nearest habitation is another kilometre in each direction. Does the boat have a tender that can come into shore and pick us up?" He was told it did. "Right, we'll signal with a flashlight at five minute intervals from four am onwards. Tell him not to signal back, it could be picked up and we don't know if our friends will be in this vicinity. If push comes to shove, we'll wait until daybreak, then we'll improvise something to draw his attention. How does that grab you?"

"Sounds good. Got some paper handy? I'll give you the number of the satellite phone on board in case you need it." James took down the number.

"Hang on a second." He gestured to Ethan to follow him and went into the kitchen. "I know you've got the pickup covered but there's something else."

"You're right, it's already in motion. I'll be there myself to meet you. You going to call me with a site when you're on board, right?"

"Correct. Now, are we on speaker, and is Lou there?" He was told yes to both questions. "I would like a couple of things. It'll be expensive, but I believe we have to end this once and for all." A short pause and he was told anything he wanted he would get. "Good. First, as I remember there are small windows set into the roof, effectively a fourth floor to the house. Tonight I would like you to remove the glass from two adjacent ones. The ones with the best view over the common, in particular any wooded areas. You can guess where I'm going with that. Next, two M40A1's, preferably with silent capability, along with two Swarovski 12x50 dual range finder scopes. Better yet, if you can get hold of some 458 Whisper from KSK Technology. I doubt you'll manage that, but you never know what's on the market. If there's a problem with that then the Israeli Galil 7.62. A night vision capability, thermal imaging scopes, anything along those lines. Lou, I'll explain. If it were me, I would place two snipers where I could take out targets in your house or grounds. If that is the case they will have shooting platforms and be established, ready for any sighting. If not, then we will need the weapons to take them on at their own game. Besides, just think what you could do with those weapons if you took up grouse shooting. Oh yes. One more thing, two actually, sound suppressors for my Berettas. Think you can do that?"

"Hell, James, not asking for much are you? That's high end gear, the only people I know who use it are the CIA, but yes I'll get you something. We agree, by the way, it is time to go on the offensive. You all leaving the area clean?"

"As a whistle, there may be some vague descriptions from the hotel, but nothing definitive, I've tried to cover all the bases as we went along. Well, old friend, I hope we'll be seeing you sometime tomorrow. Bye."

Hanging up, he turned to Ethan. "Well kid, I hope your skills with a long gun have improved since the last time I saw you shoot." It was only said as a joke; Ethan was in fact very good with a rifle, one of the best he had seen. He had a sniper's infinite patience, he was capable of performing the necessary calculations for velocity and range, which would tax the mind of a maths major, and an uncanny knack for predicting movements of the target, almost seeing them before they happened and timing his shot to factor that into the equation.

Back in the garage, they bent to the task of cleaning the car. As they worked James told them of Etienne's idea, asking Ethan to go with him into the village, saying they would bring the time forward to five o'clock, to make sure they caught a garage still open. He asked them to buy two flashlights and then told Monique that she and he would clean down the house, wiping any surfaces they may have touched, turning the power off and replacing the items they had used; then all they could do was wait.

James had not felt so exhausted for quite a few years. His eyelids felt like sandpaper as they brushed over the pupils. His neck and shoulder muscles ached and his mind felt as if it were closing down, screaming in protest every time he tried to think. He knew this was dangerous. He could not afford to lose his edge, but it would take a huge amount of adrenalin injected into his system to spur him into action. Wearily he sat on the long couch, the sound of the waves breaking on the beach muted by the double glazing of the windows. He tried to think, worrying that he had forgotten something, but could not. He gave up and tried to relax without falling asleep. The next fourteen hours would be a strain, if only because of the enforced inactivity.

Waiting. There was always a waiting period. It was the worst part of any operation.

James and Monique had cleaned down the house while they waited for for the others to return from the village. Any activity was now an effort for James, but he knew if he sat down he would fall asleep. While they worked Monique asked about Ethan.

"It was his first job. We were going in to deal with a really bad gang who were trying to corner the market in blood diamonds, conflict diamonds. Anyway they were really messing up the locals and the government and mining companies needed some help for which they would be unaccountable if something went wrong. To cut a long story short there were a few problems and Ethan was too raw to deal with them in the same way as Mike and me. I sort of helped him out. And that, as they say, is that. Simple really, he's a good kid."

"I'm sure there's a lot more to it than that. I suppose I'll have to use my charms on Ethan to get the full story."

They were sitting in the kitchen, watching the road and drive when the others returned. They had been successful in booking the car into a garage, and they had brought back some food, which could be prepared cold, and a couple of flashlights. James told them that after dark they would stay in the front room, using the flashlight sparingly. He and Ethan would take turns watching the drive. Some food was prepared, but James could not bring himself to eat. He knew that this could be the most dangerous time. So close to extraction it was natural to relax a little.

It seemed to take forever for darkness to fall. Ethan took the first watch, but James could not relax. He joined him outside. They sat in silence, watching and listening. There were very few cars passing on the road. None slowed down. At one in the morning, James told Ethan to go inside and get some sleep. He refused. "I couldn't sleep anyway. Remember what you told me? Anyway, it's only a few hours till we start signalling. How do you want to play it?"

"When it's time, we'll all wait outside, on the beach. Leave the place as we found it. With nothing disturbed or missing, the owners should not have any cause for alarm. I hope they will think they forgot about the window when they left and thank their lucky stars that no one had broken in. That's another lesson for you – sometimes we forget that civilians don't think the same as us. We look for complications, they tend to accept things at face value. Anyway, we'll all wait on the beach, except for you. You will stay here until the last minute, just in case. I wouldn't want to be caught up to my knees in water."

"Sounds good. How about some coffee? I could use a cup, I'm getting a bit chilly."

Just before three, James took the cups back inside and checked on the others. He carefully put the cups away, making sure the kettle was empty, as they had found it. He shook the others awake and told them to get ready. If they wanted to use the toilet he asked them to go outside. It would be too hard to check the facilities in the dark. Before going outside to join them he had a quick check, climbing through the window and closing it behind him, using the dagger to try and flick the catch as closed as possible. He wiped down the parts he had touched, and then sat on the veranda to let his eyes readjust to the dark. He could make out the white of the waves breaking on the shore. Apart from the crash and hiss of the waves, the night was quiet. Any light from the night sky was obscured by clouds. He could not see a single star.

At four am he walked to the sand and, checking around, switched the flashlight on for a count of ten. He could not make out any shapes or lights on the sea in front of him. He sat back down and waited. He was about to stand up again when Etienne pointed to their right, west. There was a ship moving along the coast.

It was brightly lit and looked bigger than a fishing vessel. James cursed under his breath. He would have to wait until it passed before signalling again.

He went round to check on Ethan and tell him about the delay. Etienne joined them. "That ship, it's slowed and looks as if it's stopped. Do you think it might be the one?"

James went to look and saw that it was quite close inshore and had indeed stopped. Here goes nothing, he thought as he lifted the flashlight and switched it on for another ten seconds. He thought he could make out some movement at the stern of the ship. They waited and were rewarded with the low murmur of an outboard motor approaching the beach. After a few minutes a tender came into sight, surfing the low waves to beach itself.

"James Hawk?" A whispered question. James sent Monique and Ethan to the water's edge and went to collect Ethan. There had been no movement from the road, he was informed. By the time they rounded the house, they saw that the others were aboard the dinghy and wasted no time in joining them. A quick push, a turn of the throttle, and they were bouncing their way over the breakers. Only when they were safely past the surf line did James permit himself to relax. He was going to reassure the others that it looked like they were in the clear, but stopped himself. No point in pushing fate. As they approached the vessel, they saw that it was big. James guessed it at ninety feet in length. There was a ladder hanging down the side and it was there the dinghy stopped to allow them off. It then made its way to the stern where they could hear it being winched aboard. A big man with a white beard met them at the top of the ladder. He epitomised the Hollywood version of what every skipper should look like - Captain Birdseye in the flesh!

"Hello miss, good to see you again. Jim here will show you and your party to some cabins."

"Mind if I come with you to the bridge?" James asked.

"Me too," piped up Ethan.
All they received was a nod of the head. Once on the bridge the skipper spoke. "I've been told this is nothing illegal, but I want to hear it from you."

"It's nothing illegal. We had to get Monique out of the country, for her safety. Problems with clients who were unhappy."

I, Plague

"Good, I've known Monique a while, but I wanted to hear it from you. That's what my boss told me. I'm glad to be able to help. I heard all about you from Mona, by the way, she couldn't stop talking about the horses the whole trip. Can I get you something to drink?"

They were well under way by the time the coffee accompanied by a bottle of Bells whiskey arrived. They laced their coffee with the whiskey and felt a warm glow spread down their throats into their stomachs.

The drink and the warm red glow, the only lighting on the bridge, suffused them with warmth. Already, to the east, there was a low lighting of the sky. Dawn would follow soon. There was a feeling of isolation, the busy blips on the radar screen the only indication that they were not alone on the sea.

"You know of a place to land us?"

The skipper headed for a map table. "Here, I discussed it with Mike and thought this would be the best place." He indicated an inlet on the map, midway between Ramsgate and Herne Bay. "It's a popular stop off point, but there shouldn't be anyone anchored there this time of day. Before you ask, we should arrive in another four hours or so."

James went back to a chair anchored to the deck and sat in it. God, he was tired. Ethan did not look much better. He dialled Mike's number and was surprised when it was answered quickly.

"Morning, didn't expect to catch you up. I know you executives like your bed."

"Cheeky bugger. I'll have you know I've been up since two this morning. Are you on board?" James told him that it had gone well. "Thank God for that. I'm almost at the pickup point. I've got cars heading all over the place to act as decoys. Heathrow, Gatwick, Stanstead and Dover. I'm sure we haven't been followed, but I have contingency plans ready, just in case. I'll be glad to see you all back in London."

"Not nearly as much as us. It'll be good to get out of these clothes. You didn't tell me you were sending the QE2 to pick us up. Talk about luxury. The skipper says we'll be there in about four hours, that'll be," he tried to focus on the watch face. "Around eight. Look forward to seeing you then."

He could see Ethan was having trouble staying awake and suggested he go below and lie down. "I'd rather stay here with you. You've had less sleep than me, not too bad for an old man. I'd like to see this through to the end."

When the sun rose over the Channel, James could make out several large tankers and container ships in close proximity, some heading to Rotterdam and about half heading down the Channel, so the skipper informed him. At seven they could make out the coast of England. James had never been so glad to see the country before. Another couple of hours and this phase would hopefully be over.

As they sipped another cup of coffee, more whiskey than coffee, the land mass steadily grew. The skipper moved between the GPS and the front of the bridge, apparently trying to pick out the landing area. With a grunt he indicated to the two that it was in sight. James looked through his binoculars and could make out an inlet in a small cove.

On the headland he could see some cars and a van. He hoped they belonged to Mike.

Monique and Etienne came onto the bridge. Monique gave the skipper a hug and thanked him for taking the trouble. He made some gruff reply, before starting to give orders, to bring them as close to shore as he could. They could hear the winch as the dinghy was prepared, then the boat slowed.

"Good luck to you all." He offered his hand and James shook it, thanking him again.

It was only a couple of hundred metres to the shore. There were no other boats in sight and they could see a cluster of men on the beach, waiting. Several more men were stationed around the headland. James and Ethan leaped out of the boat and half carried Monique through the surf to the shore. With relief that was palpable, James saw Mike was one of the group walking rapidly towards him.

It was a quick and subdued greeting. Mike was anxious to get them off the beach and into the vehicles. He guided them to a Chrysler van, showing them in. What a surprise; it had been converted, with the walls well padded in a dark red upholstery. There were upholstered seats in the same colour affixed to the walls and the floor was covered with a lush carpet. As soon as they were seated the driver started off. Through the tinted windows James could see another car dropping in behind them.

"To be brutally honest, James," Mike grinned to take the sting out of his words, "you look like shit. When was the last time you were in a bed?"

James was surprised to find he could not remember. "I don't know, three or four nights ago. We going to get into the house all right?"

Mike was busying himself in a cupboard they had not noticed before. He straightened and handed out steaming mugs of coffee. "How are you Monique? Your father's been worried sick." She assured him she was fine, a bit tired but fine. "You must be Etienne? Good to meet you. Thanks for all your help."

"My pleasure m'sieur. But I am worried about my friend. Can I phone him and tell him what has happened to his car?"

"Of course, my boy. As soon as we get back you can phone. Tell him we will make sure he is well looked after for his help."

James left Mike to continue talking to Monique and Etienne, paying little attention as he closed his eyes and allowed himself to relax. He did not fall asleep, as much as he would have liked to; the job would not be over until they were safely indoors. With his eyes closed he planned what he was going to say to Mike when they had the time.

His only wish was that the journey would end. He did not know how long he stayed like that, but he became aware that the vehicle was stopping and starting much more. He opened his eyes and looked out of the window. They were in heavy traffic, they must have made it into London. He did recognise the streets but that was cleared up by Mike. "Almost there, maybe another ten minutes." Then he busied himself on his phone. From the one side he could hear he knew that Mike was checking on the arrangements. He also called in other cars to form around them as they approached the house. He saw James watching and explained. "Decoys coming from all the place at the same time. Hopefully muddy the waters and allow us in without any problems. It's going to cost a bloody fortune in petrol, all this running around all over the South East." The vehicle sped up and made a sharp left. They had pulled into the drive and went immediately to the rear of the house. A pause, and they reversed right up to the back door. The van's doors swung open and they were ushered through the kitchen door.

As they entered the kitchen Monique was enveloped in the arms of her parents and sister. James whispered one word to Mike. "Beer!" He put his arm around Ethan's shoulder and guided him into the family room, taking off his jacket and shoulder holster, dropping them on an armchair, and throwing himself into a couch, feeling the softness fold around him. God, it was good to relax, He took a beer from Mike and lifted it to Ethan. "Thanks for your help, kid. You've done real good."

"I didn't do anything" he protested. "Yes, you did, more than you know. You backed me up. I appreciate it." He swung his legs onto the couch and laid his head against the arm rest. A sip of beer and a huge sigh of contentment. He could feel the fatigue seeping through every muscle, through every part of his brain. Unfortunately, Mike and Lou chose that moment to come into the room. Lou's first words were. "God, you two look like you're all in. You'd better get off to bed. I just wanted to thank you for bringing Monique home."

"We couldn't have done it without help from you and Mike." James dismissed the thanks. "One thing, though, any news about the guys we left behind?"

"Not much." Mike stepped in. "Seems the police are a bit baffled. They think it might be turf related. As far as we can tell there are no witnesses and no descriptions of you guys. Was it necessary to take them out?" He saw Ethan start to react defensively and stopped him. "Not a criticism, only a question."

James replied for both of them. "Yes. The first one, in Brussels was carrying a belt rig. He had been picked up on the train by Ethan and would have followed us to the pickup point, then we would have been tagged straight away. The other two in the hotel car park. Well, I suppose we could have made it clear, but I didn't want to take any chances. It bought us the time to make it to the coast. Unfortunate, but, as you know, sometimes it's necessary." He thought for a minute, trying to marshal his tired thoughts.

"If we had been followed to the beach we would have been sitting ducks for anyone to pick off."

Lou jumped in before Mike could say anything. "We know that, boys. You have done a good job of looking after my daughter. I am indebted to you Ethan and getting deeper in debt all the time to you James. I'll never be able to repay you, either of you."

James could see that Ethan was almost asleep and knew that he was on the verge of falling asleep where he sat. It was always the same. Remove the tension, the potential need for action, and the fatigue came on very quickly. He took another sip of his beer and stood. "Can we talk more later? I need to get horizontal in the next few minutes, and by the look of it, so does Ethan."

Mike showed them to their rooms. James climbed into the bed, the cool, clean sheets and pillows caressing his skin, gently covering him. That was his last waking thought – how good it felt to lie in a bed again.

CHAPTER TWENTY THREE

Anatoly was very frustrated. It was already Friday morning, and the first part of the contract had not been completed. Which in turn meant that Piotr and Alexander had not even started the operation against the house. The delay had allowed his opposition to get organised. He had been to the site and seen the men in the grounds, the drawn curtains and the way they kept vehicles out of the grounds. It would make things awkward, not impossible, just more awkward and time consuming. In his original plan he should be making his way home by now. He accepted that, in any game, both sides have both bad and good luck. Alexei had been unlucky, there were some things you could not plan for. He knew he would be blaming himself, but also, that he was experienced enough to put it behind him, accept that it was in the past.

Bloody amateurs. He hated using them. They were all well and good in the environment they were accustomed to working in, but, when it came to his line of work, they were next to useless. He had asked for the most reliable and had been given rubbish. Only one man had made it through the interference to follow the young boy onto the train to Brussels. And now he was dead. To make matters worse, he had been found with his pistol strapped to his belt. The bloody fools could not even follow the simplest orders. Then the two in the car park. How could they have been taken so easily? Bloody amateurs, he thought again.

He had called Alexei back from France and he was due to arrive that morning. No point in wasting any more time there. The woman was in all likelihood safely ensconced in the house by now. It didn't matter how they had eluded him, it was done with, now he had to repair the damage and finish the job.

One of the main reasons for his frustration, he knew, was that it was his own fault that things had gone so wrong. The only blame for having to resort to those bloody amateurs was his. He had committed the cardinal sin of underestimating the enemy. He should have realised they would have access to manpower. He had to admit that their manpower was of a higher calibre than his own. The way they had blocked the followers from boarding the train had been professional. It had been sheer good luck, which he reckoned he deserved, that one had made it. And then there was the manner in which he had been taken out; by all accounts, that was the work of a fellow professional. Quick and silent. Lethal blows. Same with the others, it must have taken two of them. The knife and the broken neck, they knew what they were doing. He could only conclude that the boy had teamed up with the older man Alexei had described. Alexei had been very wrong about the so-called boyfriend. He was being very effective in looking after the woman. Too effective, he had outguessed them all the way. Yes, he decided, somehow they had professional help. He would have to see if they could find out more about the opposition.

The phone rang and he grabbed it, eager for some good news. It was not to be. It was the coordinator for the watchers he had deployed around the house for the last two days. They were instructed to follow every vehicle. It was an attempt to ascertain if the woman was being picked up. Thursday had been uneventful, however, early that morning, seven vehicles had left the house, each heading in a different direction. He did not have enough manpower or vehicles to follow them all and this angered him further. He knew it was almost certain that one of them was going to pick up the woman and her party. They had now all returned after leading his men on a wild goose chase around the south of England.

CHAPTER TWENTY FOUR

Daylight was seeping through the edge of the curtains when James opened his eyes. He looked at his watch; it was just after seven. He felt relaxed. Pushing himself up, he saw that he had hardly moved in his sleep. It must have been a good five or six hours, he thought. He was ravenous and moved to shower and shave, hoping that he would not be too late for dinner. The jets of warm water brought a glow to his skin as the blood was awakened from its sluggish sleep and started flowing as a fast river instead.

He walked into the lounge and found it empty, as was the dining room. Strange, they must have eaten early to allow Monique an early night. No matter, he would go through to the kitchen and see what he could find in the fridge.

Mike and Monique were sitting at the table and looked up when he entered. "Good morning," was the bright and cheery greeting.

"Morning? I thought it was seven in the evening. I have been asleep all this time?"

"Sure have." Mike smiled at Monique. "You said it – you're too old for all this gallivanting around the continent, not sleeping or eating properly. Too used to the easy life. How someone can sleep for fifteen hours is beyond me."

"I need coffee, that fresh? I presume I'm correct in thinking it's Saturday?" He moved to the pot and poured himself some. "How about you, Monique, you get a good sleep?" She said she had and added that as far as she knew Ethan was still in bed, telling him that they had thought they would let them both sleep as long as they needed. "Like Mike says, you're both getting too old for this."

After finishing off some eggs and toast, James asked if she would excuse them as he needed to speak with Mike. He caught her look, almost sad. "Not over yet, is it?"

"Not yet, but it soon will be, promise."

He and Mike went into a front room. "Lou's office" Mike explained. They sat on a leather couch. James looked through the window at a view of a wall covered in ivy. "Did you manage to get the stuff I asked for?"

"I did, it won't arrive until Monday morning. Not exactly normal wares for the British shops to carry. Had to go far afield to lay my hands on it. Not exactly cheap, either. But, as the old man says, you want it, you get it, you must have something in mind. Is he right?"

"He is, although all I have are ideas. I think we should probably put it to him as well. It is, after all, his house and family. I wouldn't want to do something without him knowing."

"I'll get him, he's around somewhere. Back in a tick." He was as good as his word. They both returned in a couple of minutes. "I met Ethan on the way, he's just grabbing a bite and some coffee then he'll join us." Ethan and Monique came in bearing mugs of coffee.

"You look a bit better this morning, kid. Sleep well?" There was a moment's repetition about James' age before he could get started.

"As I said, this is just an idea, Lou. We will need your go ahead before we do anything." He waited for the nod and continued. "The way I figure it, we have at least two, maybe more, waiting to fill the contract. Makes sense, one in Paris and one here. If it were me I would set up shooting positions on the Common. There are a couple of stands of trees with some undergrowth which could be used. That's the reason I asked for you to take out the window panes in the attic. When we get the scopes and range finder, we can have a look and see if that is indeed the case." He saw the puzzled look on Lou's face and explained. "We sit back in the room, in the dark and look out. We're virtually hidden from view unless there is back light or light, like the sun shining directly into the room. If we do find that there are shooters out there, then we," indicating Ethan and himself, "will take them out. OK so far?" Nods again. "Now if we do that, we can't leave them in situ, it's possible they may be knocked off the platforms, but maybe not. It's not Africa, we can't leave dead bodies lying around. To that end, what I thought was, we station a couple of transit vans and men, both disguised to blend in, something like the parks department. That would also provide the necessary cover for them to carry ladders, in case we have to go up the tree. It will also be seen as non-threatening by the shooters. You know, the guys potter about with rakes and such." He stopped and waited for a reaction.

Mike was the first to speak, practical as always. "That's some shot, each of these sites must be a good thousand, twelve hundred metres. I know you can make that kind of shot but what about you Ethan, you happy to do that, if necessary?" Ethan said he was. Then it was Lou's turn to speak.

"You think this is necessary, no other way?"

"From the little I know of these type of guys, they take a contract and they finish it. It's not good for future business if they don't finish what they contracted to do. Also, it doesn't sound like this guy, Gregor," he looked at Mike. "Yes Gregori." He went on. "OK Gregori, doesn't sound like he's a quitter. He probably also has his reputation to protect. Having put out the word, it wouldn't do for him to stop, show weakness."

"You're right, of course. I guess I was hoping it might end when you got back. Go on James."

"I don't think we should wait. We have to take it out to them. The first order is to get rid of the shooters. Then, and this is the hard part, we have to go after Gregori, end it once and for all."

He heard a quiet, "Holy Shit," from Mike, a low whistle from Ethan, and a gasp from the old man.

"Wait, before you say anything, think about it. We would have the element of surprise, provided we can account for all the shooters here. I would imagine that not too many people, apart from the Law, have gone after him, so it would be the last thing on his mind. Do we know anything about him that would help us do this?"

"Jesus, James. You can still surprise me. Shit." Mike thought about what he was going to say. "First off, he hasn't left Russia or the Ukraine in years. He's too high profile, the police would be all over him like a bad rash if he turned up in Western Europe. I don't know where is he is now, not even where he has his headquarters, or where he lives. I don't know if it can be done. Double shit, taking him on in his home turf, that's some task."

"Russia, Ukraine, England, Scotland, France, what's the difference? Might be easier doing it over there. But the whole idea is a non-starter if we can't get the intelligence. But, again, think about it. You, Lou, need him out of the way. Otherwise you'll be looking over your shoulder, and the shoulders of your family, for the rest of your life."

Lou was very thoughtful when he replied. "I take your point. What you say is both true and logical. But, Christ, James, taking the fight to him is either one of the most stupid or brilliantly audacious things I've ever heard. What do you think Mike, Ethan?"

Ethan had been watching James face closely as he had talked. "I take it I would be invited? Young man to help carry the bags?" A cheeky grin at James. "Seriously, I think James is right. We should finish it, wherever. You think the two of us could really do it?"

"Yes, it will be a tad risky, too many things could go wrong, but yes, I think with good intelligence and a bit of daring, and a lot of luck, we could pull it off. I was rather hoping there might be three of us." He looked at Mike.

"Of course, I would be in, I wouldn't let you go off on your own. On that point though, we should be four, two teams of two." As soon as Mike said that James knew he had him hooked. He was already thinking about the logistics, and not the many problems that would beset them.

"You guys are crazy. I can't let you do this, even for the sake of my children. Rather, for the sake of my children, I think I should stop you. You'll never get away with it."

"All right, Lou, it's just an idea. As Mike rightly said, we don't even know what country he's in. We have to deal with the immediate threat first. Are you in agreement with that? We'll discuss the other thing later when we have some more facts."

Lou agreed to the initial idea. All they had to do was wait for the equipment to arrive. He stood up. "I'm going to talk to some sane people."

James stood up and stretched, taking another mug of coffee, turning to look at Mike. "Well, this is another fine mess you've got me into, a relaxing break in Paris with a beautiful woman. Some break!"

"Seriously, for a moment, Ethan. Indulge an old man, will you?" Ethan waited. "Now is the time to get out and run. I said it before, but I'll say it again. No-one is going to hold it against you. You haven't contracted for this, you have no obligation to me or Mike, certainly not to Lou and his family. You're in the clear as far as I'm concerned. Hell, we haven't even asked if you were in or not. I suppose this is the time to ask, and think very carefully about your answer. Despite what I said to Lou, and I think Mike will agree with me, the chances of our pulling this off are remote to say the least. We could all be killed if we go ahead and hunt this Gregori down."

He didn't take long to come back with an answer. "You have asked me and I said yes. You two were good to me, I owe you. No arguments, I'm in. Besides, I haven't heard anyone giving you two the chance to back down."

He had a point, the only snag was that there was no-one around who was in a position to ask that question. "How about it Mike, you in for the long haul?" He knew the answer before he agreed. "As for me, kid, I figure this guy won't stop and sooner or later he's going to find out about me. Then, who knows, maybe by then I'll have pissed him off so much he'll come after me. Either way, I still think he'll keep coming. Mike?"

"I have to agree. I am worn out trying to get good information for us to work on, though. Could take some time." He looked at James. "One question; why snipers?"

"Well, first off it's what I would do. Look at it this way. He's made sure that word has reached Lou about what he intends to do. Possibly, just possibly, that was a mistake. I think he's over confident, and we know what that can do. He would then know that the hatches would be battened down against a close encounter. That only leaves a distance kill. You told me that's the latest method, remember. The numbers – well that's pure guesswork. But apply some logic. Good snipers operate in pairs, the shooting in Paris and the shooting here last Friday. I'm guessing, but I would say that there was already at least one in Paris, watching Monique's movements. Who knows? I could be wrong on all of the above. But why take the chance? Also, think about the location. An assault on the house would be too conspicuous, no matter how hard they tried. Too many guys in and around the place. Neighbours nearby. No, he would be taking too many risks for that approach, and, again if I'm right, he doesn't have the manpower. Let's deal with the immediate threat first and worry about Gregori himself later."

"There's a lot of ifs and buts in there. But I see the logic of it. Ethan, any thoughts?" Mike asked.

"Nope, one observation only. If there are shooters out there, it's a hell of a shot, for both sides. They have the advantage of knowing exactly where we are, we will only get one chance. We screw it up, they'll draw down on us pretty fast."

James now knew they were both thinking hard about the proposals. "You're 100% correct. What I'm counting on is the surprise element. If I'm right, they will be scanning the grounds and lower floor windows, looking for a target. They won't be paying too much attention to the attic. I'm hoping they will have ruled that out. I know, still a lot of ifs. We'll have a better idea once the gear is here and we can see for ourselves. By the way, where did you manage to get your hands on it?"

Mike reminded him about an arms dealer in Amsterdam they had used regularly in the old days. "The only thing I couldn't get was the rounds you asked for. We have to settle for sound suppressors."

Again the wait. They tried to relax and talk about anything but the job on hand.

What seemed like endless mugs of coffee later, Lou brought his family into the room. Shit, was James' first thought. "He's told them everything." He looked at Mike who only shrugged his shoulders, as if to say, what can I do, I just work here.

Mona came and sat next to James, Monique sat next to Mike and Carmen stayed with her husband. "I've told them the whole story. Right up to when I left the room. We have all agreed that we are all in this together. We want to be involved in whatever you are going to do. None of us is very sure about letting you three become embroiled in this, but we don't think we have any choice."

James looked at Mike, encouraging him to say something. All he came up with was. "And now?"

Laughing, he joked. "Jeez Mike, that was really constructive."

It was Monique who jumped at the sound of their laughter. "How can you sit, joke and laugh? You're talking about killing two men, and going after another." Mike looked down, embarrassed. James was going to reply when Lou spoke first.

"Come on Monique, we talked about this. These guys have done us a hell of a favour so far. They're here to protect us, remember. We agreed there would no judgements. Please."

"I'm sorry. It all seems so unfair. I suppose I should be thanking you, all of you. I guess we're scared." She took her sister's hand.

"OK, something constructive. No jokes." Mike took her other hand and forced her to look at him. "Something I, we, don't want to think about is what if we do nothing. Then one day you're out in Paris, in your office, at home. One week, one month, one year from now and someone walks up to you and shoots you. Same applies to Mona, school, movies, whatever. Then there's your parents, same scenario. To be selfish, there are the three of us. James pointed out earlier that, sooner or later, we'll all be identified and then we'll be in the firing line as well. Think about all the people who work for James. They could be involved. We know they don't mind who gets in the way. We can't stay locked up in here for the rest of our lives."

James looked down at Mona and saw she was terrified. She was still young, she was capable of thinking like an adult, but this was beyond her scope. Hell, he thought, it's almost beyond my scope. He reached an arm around her shoulder and pulled her close. Leaning down he whispered in her ear. "It'll be all right. I'm not going to let anything bad happen. I promise. You believe that?" She looked up and he saw that the tears were streaming down her face. She sniffed and tried to brush the tears away, nodding. He held her close.

After a silence, during which James noted that Monique and Mike were still holding hands, Lou spoke again. "I want to make sure you guys want to do this. I, no, we, have no right to ask this of you."

James answered first. "You're friends, too late to turn back now."

"Likewise." From Mike.

"Nothing better to do." From Ethan. This brought roars of laughter from the other two. "Nothing better to do. Kid, you've been watching too many movies. Nothing better to do!"

The laughter spread to all of them and the tension in the room eased palpably. With an effort, James put on a serious face and waited for the laughter to die down. "We really have something we have to do right now. Is everyone ready to do their bit?" Serious now they all nodded, waiting to see what was coming. "First order of business is," he paused, looking at each in turn, "to rent some movies for the kid here to watch." The laughter erupted again. It was almost hysterical, a sign that the tension and stress had been getting to them.

James had a flash of inspiration, he hoped it was inspirational, anyway. "I've had an idea. Tell me what you think. Two can play mind games. How about when we have finished with these guys, we send a message to this Gregori. Put him on the defensive." He immediately saw the concerned looks. "No, hold on, I don't mean we actually turn round and say that four of us are on our way, I mean a cryptic message. Thoughts?"

Ethan with his imagination was the first to grasp the idea. "Mike told me about something you said once. Something from the Bible, Mike?"

Then Lou picked it up. "Yes the quote you used on Marcus, about the pale horse and the plague." Mike finished the quote. *"there came a pale horse, whose rider was called Plague, and Hell followed at his heels."*

The Four Horsemen of the Apocalypse, James remembered. "I've got a better one than that, it might have been written for just a situation as this. Do you have a Bible? Let's see if I can find it. *"And there went out another horse that was red: and power was given to him that sat thereon to take peace from the earth, and that they should kill one another: and there was given unto him a great sword."*

"Wow," Ethan almost breathed the word.

"Not the most eloquent of critiques I've heard. But he's right, it's perfect. Provided, of course, that the Russuain Orthodox religion has that quote and he can understand the context."

It was Mona who asked the question. "How will you get the message to him? You don't know where he is. You can't phone him."

A few smiles. "What?" she demanded. Mike explained. "No phone call, Mona. We'll get hold of someone, who will tell someone else, who will tell someone else, and so on until the message reaches him."

"How can you know it will be passed on?"

Mike again explained. "Oh, don't worry about that, we know it will be passed on to him. Enough of this subject for now, we've plenty of time to fill in the blanks. We've got all of tomorrow to talk, but Mike, can you get your contacts on it right away? After all, the sooner we have the information the sooner we can stop speculating."

CHAPTER TWENTY FIVE

It was close to three on the Monday afternoon when a DHL van delivered the three boxes. Once Mike had brought them inside they took them to the attic and unpacked them. Everything was brand new.

"DHL delivery? Talk about taking a chance." James was astounded at the brazeness of it.

"Hidden in plain view" replied Mike. "Anton knows what he's doing. They didn't come all the way by DHL, though. That was just the final stage. Having them delivered here it was the best way to lessen any suspicion. It is good though; imagine the driver's face if he knew what he had been carrying."

They would have to spend an hour cleaning the packing grease and oil from them before they were serviceable. The M40A1 weighed around thirteen and a half pounds, was easy to assemble and ideal for the job of sniper. The sound suppressor added to the length, but did not detract from the balance. In the right hands it was as lethal as any firearm could be.

They worked quietly, using latex gloves from the moment they opened the boxes, through the cleaning process and while handling the rounds, which were also cleaned.

After an hour they were set and Ethan and James each took up a position at the rear of the room, arranging packing cases in front of them, as much for a resting place as for cover. They would not protect them, but could give them precious seconds in the event of something going wrong, a shot missed, an alert sniper in the trees making a sweep of all the house windows. The sun was now well over the house and would be shining in the eyes of anyone looking at the house from the Common. It wouldn't blind them, although they hoped it would limit their line of sight into the darkness of the attic.

James checked with Ethan that he was ready, reminding him that all they wanted to do at this stage was to gain any visuals they could and mark the positions. They had decided that they could not show their hand at this early stage. There were still too many things to sort out.

They took up their positions, sighting down the barrels and starting a sweep of the stands of trees they had identified as the most likely places someone would lie in wait. Mike would handle the range finder once they had located a target.

James found the trees he wanted to sweep first and started slowly examining each from top to bottom. There was a lot of foliage on every tree and it was difficult to try and pinpoint any anomaly. As long as anyone there remained still, he would be extremely difficult to spot. Patience was the key. The sharp clarity the scope offered brought the branches and leaves into focus.

It took fifteen minutes before James saw a branch move where no others did. He concentrated on the branch, adjusting the scope for greater focus and slowly began to discern an indistinct shape against the trunk of the tree. He had to move his eyes away from the scope for a couple of minutes to rest them. Looking again, he could see that the shape did not fit in with the trunk or branches. He was very well camouflaged. So good that James had difficulty making out the shape of the rifle barrel and following it back to the head. He indicated to Mike that he had seen something, and quietly described the location. As he spoke he was aware that he was whispering, incongruous, he knew, but it felt right. They were all adopting the old habits. Out of the corner of his eye he saw Mike adjusting the range finder and searched for the target.

"Bugger it, I can't see him."

James started counting, first to identify the tree and then to identify the fork where the branch met the trunk. Eventually Mike stated. "Got him." A short wait and then. "One thousand and sixty four metres. That's a hell of a shot. Pity you can't take it now, perfect conditions." Adding, "That's good cover, really professional. You could be right in front of the bugger and not see him."

James marked the tree and put down the rifle, rubbing his eyes which were starting to ache from the strain. They both sat back and watched as Ethan continued his sweep. He had moved back to his original target area and was sweeping again, he informed them. He sat up to rest his eyes and then took a look, locating the first position. "Right, let's try again," he said, this time lying on his belly to start the scan.

It was another long twenty minutes before there was a satisfied grunt. "Got him, he's good. I've been over that position twice." He did the same as James, guiding James onto the spot. "Nine hundred and thirteen meters." They used the tops of the packing cases to mark down the angles and range, ensuring they would be able to relocate the targets without any searching when the time was right. Before he finished, Ethan reiterated Mike's comment. "It's a bloody shame we can't do it now. Atmosphere, wind, light, just about as perfect as they could be. It could all change by tomorrow or the next day."

James felt he had to remind them of a salient fact. "It's not only perfect for us. Remember, it's just as perfect for them."

"Wonder how they move in and out. These long days must be a swine for them." They speculated on Ethan's question. Mike had a possible answer. "See the undergrowth around each tree? The council leaves it like that to encourage wildlife, birds, insects and all that. Anyway, it's quite thick, they could climb down there, stow the camouflage gear and step out when no-one's around. Or, they could be leaving their gear in situ. If they're wearing coveralls, I suppose they could slip into them once they've climbed up." He paused for a minute. "One thing we never thought of; why don't we take them when they come down, on the way to their vehicle? We could find the vehicle quite easily."

James did not have to think about it. "The trouble with these long days is that there's always someone walking their dog, jogging, or just lying around. Look at the number of people out there now, and it's only just before five. It should get busier as they arrive home from work. Also, they may not leave a vehicle, it might attract unwanted attention, get towed, for example, and then they would be on foot. Let's stick to the original idea."

"You're right. OK, let's get downstairs and have a drink. I have to start putting things together. Also, we'd better give the old man the bad news. I think he was kind of hoping for the all clear. I know I was." He gave a quick, almost bitter laugh. "Oh, for the quiet life, eh James?"

"I'll drink to that."

They found the family sitting in the lounge, the room darkened by the heavy curtains pulled across the windows. It was the same in every room. Sit inside long enough, thought James as he sat down, and it would soon become very depressing. No sunlight, no fresh air. They would have to act sooner rather than later, before one of them made a stupid mistake; just poking a head out of a door for a look around, pulling aside a curtain for a glimpse of the outside world, could prove fatal. It was all very melodramatic; it would make for a good TV show.

They had eaten a quiet dinner. The conversation was subdued and they were now sitting back in the lounge. James watched Mike and Monique talking and wondered if there was actually something beginning to blossom. Mona was playing some video game with Etienne, and Lou and Carmen were watching. Sitting alone in an armchair in the corner, James found his mind going back to his home. Would he be here if Marie had still been alive? Just watching Mike and Monique brought twinges of pain, of loneliness. Inevitably, his thoughts turned to Jean. He didn't know how to feel about her. He didn't really know that much about her, her likes or dislikes. It had always been a very proper working relationship. She was very attractive and he almost wished she was here tonight. He was always maudlin before any action and assumed that this was exacerbated because he missed his wife. He felt someone sitting on the arm of his chair and a hand on his shoulder. "Penny for them?" He looked up; it was Monique. Mike had left the room.

"Oh, nothing worth a penny." He forced himself to smile. She leaned down and took his hand. "Come on, let's go and get a beer." He allowed himself to be led into the kitchen, where she took two bottles from the fridge. Leaning back, she offered him one. "Can I ask you something?" At his nod she continued. "I've never been able to work out why I like you and Mike so much, now Ethan as well. It's just that you're like a lot of guys, nicer than most, actually. Yet you can kill people and not think twice about it. I don't get it. I would have thought you'd be all hard, bitter and twisted. Why do you do it?"

It was a question he had asked himself. He had, in fact, discussed with Mike on a few occasions. "I don't know the answer to that. I fell into the soldiering game and was good at it, liked it. Then the mercenary side was a sort of natural progression. I could never imagine myself in an office. Again I was good at it, I seemed to have developed a talent for planning. The rest you know. As for this business, I assume that's what you're thinking of, well, you're friends, all of you. Mike asked and I came. I have to admit, I didn't think it was going to develop the way it has. I thought I'd spend a few days in Paris, looking around, eating and drinking. Just the way it goes" he ended lamely.

"But if you do the things we were talking about, you could all be killed. I love my family and would do anything for them, but the three of you, well I don't understand why you would risk everything for us. No, wait, I appreciate what you're doing for us, don't get me wrong."

I, Plague

"Like I said, you're friends. I don't think any of us could stand by and watch if someone we knew needed help. That's about the whole of it, I'm afraid." He smiled at her. "Anyway, I've nothing better to do." That did the trick, raising a smile of sorts from her.

"OK, I asked for that. One more thing. When you were sitting there, were you thinking about Marie, how things may have been different if she were still alive?"

He looked at her and made up his mind. He knew he could trust her and maybe, just maybe, get some good advice. "Yes and no, to that. I was thinking about her, what she would have said. But there's something else." He went on to tell about the night when he and Jean had kissed and then the conversation in the pub when they had agreed to be friends. She listened carefully, nodding occasionally, saying nothing until he had finished.

"I'm not going to tell you to forget her, if that's what you think. You men, especially you, you are so good at seeing some things, but other things can be staring you in the face, sitting there as plain as day and you just don't see them. You don't know, or don't believe that there are at least ten women I know of who are in love with you. Don't you dare speak." She saw the automatic protest forming on his lips. "All right, three or four of them are only girls and they love you like an uncle or something. But the rest are full grown women. A couple you will never know about, because they are happy in their marriages and love their husbands as well. Then there's the kind of love a woman feels, like Marie felt, I would imagine, and you just don't see it. Jean is the perfect example. You hold people at bay, the only person who ever broke through was Marie. You just will not allow yourself to let anyone in. Well, I have news for you, you have to. It's just not good enough, and if it bloody well kills me I'll make you." She stopped, taking a deep breath, watching him. "Christ, you don't have the first idea about what I'm trying to say, do you?"

He had to confess that he didn't. He felt he was swimming in waters way beyond his depth.

"Bloody hell, I swear, if you make me cry you'll look forward to going to Russia. Shit, too late. Bloody men!" She was dabbing at her eyes with a tissue when the door opened and Mike came in. He looked at the crying Monique and then at James who held up his hands. "I swear, I said nothing."

"I take it things are not going quite according to plan then. I think I'll take a beer and get the hell out of Dodge. James, why don't you do something constructive, as I remember you saying to me? Hold the bloody woman, before she sobs her heart out."

Now he was really skating on thin ice he thought, but with a shove in the back from Mike she came into his arms. He held her gently till she finished crying and pulled back from him to dry her eyes and cheeks.

"Sorry. I'm probably not making too good a job of this. Mike's right, it's not going according to plan." She looked up at him and then gestured that they should sit. "I think I get it now, stupid of me not have seen it before. Don't say anything, just nod if I'm correct, ok?" He nodded, wondering what was coming next. "After dinner, when Mike and I were sitting talking, and before he held my hand, you were thinking – good that's the start of something. True?" He nodded. "How wrong you were. Truth is we were talking about you. Yes, Mike and I like each other, but it will never go further than that. I know he had a crush on me, but we've outgrown that. We'll be close friends forever, but romance, no that's not on the cards. Talking about you – yes – your belief that Mike and I were suited, your hurt over Marie, how you looked alone and needed to be held. It was Mike who suggested that I bring you in here for a beer and a talk. Rightly, he reminded me that the best way to deal with things was head on. Make the most of now, he said. So that's what I'm doing; things any clearer yet?" He shook his head. "I didn't think so."

Mike chose that moment to stick his head around the door. "I've put a bottle and two glasses in the office. Thought you'd be more comfortable in there." He promptly disappeared. Monique stood and led him through, sitting him down and pouring two stiff drinks.

It was dim in the room, the only light coming from the desk lamp. It cast half her face in shadows and oddly lit the streaks on her cheeks where the tears had fallen. He felt close to her at that moment, with an overwhelming urge to hold her and prevent a return of whatever it was that had upset her before. He also supposed that this urge was partly that he wanted to be held. He resisted it, settling back in the sofa. "It appears that Mike knows what this is all about." A statement needing no reply. "Anyone else? Your mother?" This time a nod. "That means your father knows?" Again a nod. "I suppose that means Mona knows, how about Etienne?" This time a shake of the head. "Well, I appear to be the last person to find out. Why not just spit it out?"

"OK. You know how I feel about dad's old life. You know also how I hate violence. By my standards I should hate you and Mike for what you've done and what you're about to do. But, as I said earlier, I can't think of two nicer blokes. Dad says that the world needs guys like you. I suppose I have to accept that. But you have to agree that there is only one difference between the men out there and you – they are paid for what they do, and this time you aren't being paid. Apart from that, you're the same."

The only reply James had was "There but for the grace of God, etc, etc."

"Another thing in your favour is that Mike told me you never hurt women and children, whereas they are looking to kill us all.

"You once said something that's been stuck in my brain. It was a long time ago and I wasn't there, but Pippa was and she told Mona, who told me. You said that in all the time you had been going away, leaving on some posting or job, you never had anyone to say goodbye to, never had anyone to go the station, airport, whatever. Mona told me this because she thought it was sad, her words, not mine, and she wanted me to understand a bit more about you. Well, anyway, now you have someone. I know you had Marie, but you never left her. I think what I'm trying to say is that I would like to be the person now who will be there when you leave and when you get back. God, I'm not doing a very good job of this. Just bear with me, will you? Oh, I don't know what I'm trying to say. It boils down to this." Good, James thought, we're getting to the crux of the matter, at last. "We...I love you." She stopped dead.

"I know that, you already said that we're like best friends. And Mona always says that she loves me. It's good to know." Lame, he thought, corny in the extreme and lame, bloody lame, but he didn't know what was required of him.

"Christ, do I have to spell it out. *I.L.O.V.E.Y.O.U.* Not like Mona or Pippa. Me, the person - I Love You. Always have, always will. There, I've said it. Now do you understand, you frustrating, bloody man?" She promptly started crying again. "Shit, you've made me cry again. I don't remember ever having cried so much in one day."

He was struck dumb. He did not have the slightest idea what to do. He wanted the couch to open up and swallow him. The only thing on his mind was that a trip to visit Gregori would be far more preferable to this. "I'm sorry, I didn't know."

"Of course you didn't know. I only found out myself during the last few days. I'm as good at hiding thing from myself and others as you are." She wiped her eyes with the back of her hand. "When we were in Brussels and you went to meet Ethan, that was when I first thought about it. I didn't want you to go. Then, when I started being honest with myself, I knew. I truly think I began loving you that very first time we met. Even though I thought you were just another hired gun, working for my father." She gathered her thoughts.

"Then I couldn't do anything about it. You were so much in love with Marie. I was happy for you, I worked hard at burying my feelings and damned near succeeded as well. I would have been fine if it hadn't been for this business. Mike saw it when he met us. I don't know how, but he picked up on it straight away. So did Mum. I think the giveaway for her was my going to your room after you were asleep, just to check that you were all right." She stopped to take a drink and wipe the rest of her tears away. "Then when you told me about Jean, it just about broke my resolve to tell you this. There, I've said it, now I think we'd better get back to the others. I've also had too much to drink."

CHAPTER TWENTY SIX

Tuesday started as a bright, warm sunny day. It was a good spell of weather for the UK, as the news casts and newspaper were quick to point out. Front pages were covered with photographs of girls lying on beaches and in parks sunbathing. No-one doubted that rain would soon come; Wimbledon tennis was due to start in the next couple of weeks.

The morning had been spent with Mike, checking that his men were busy working on the Common in the guise of parks officers. It was one job they joked they were glad not to be doing. It was warming up more each hour, and they would be at it until at least one o' clock. There was no way they could take a shot while the sun shone on the front of the house. It would have been in their eyes, and there was too much chance of a reflection from the scopes catching the eye of those hidden in the trees.

As soon as the sun had passed over the roof of the house, however, James and Ethan made their way to the attic. Nothing was said as they passed Lou on the stairs, and they quickly took up their positions. James called Mike on the radio, while scanning the ground to locate his men.

"Good to go down here, James." He double clicked the mike in acknowledgement.

"Ethan?" A whispered OK and he settled down to find his target. If it hadn't been for the markings on the case before him he would have had to search for a long time. He made out the rifle barrel first, then the scope came into focus. He shifted his aim slightly to the right of the scope, hoping he would be drawing down on the centre of the forehead. Mike came back on the radio to tell them that it was still, there was no noticeable breeze. The atmosphere was moderately heavy, something to be expected at that time of day, and they made the necessary calculations, adjusting their aim accordingly. At a grunt from Ethan, indicating he was ready, James tapped the transmition button.

Mike counted down from three to ensure they both fired simultaneously. On the count of two, James eased back on the trigger, and took a breath, holding it as the barrel lowered onto his target. "One" and he squeezed against the resistance of the trigger, feeling the kick into his shoulder and the round sped from the barrel. There was loud *phut* of escaping gases and a fraction of a second later he heard the same from his left side. Through the scope he could make out movement among the leaves and smaller branches. He saw the rifle fall to the ground, bouncing off the lower branches of the tree, the scope being knocked from its bracket and shattering as it fell. He saw an arm fall dangling over the branch, then, in slow motion a shoulder, a head and then the neck. The target appeared to be held in that position before gravity kicked in and he slowly tumbled from his perch. As with the rifle, he hit every branch on the way down, before hitting the ground in an array of loose limbs and torso. The birds were rising from the surrounding trees and bushes, disturbed by the unaccustomed sounds and movements.

As James swung the scope to find Mike's men he felt more than heard a round buzzing over his head, embedding itself in the wooden beam behind him.

"Shit, I missed." As another round flew past James six inches to his left.

"Down, Ethan. He's shooting blind. Bloody good." Another round another six inches to the left. "He's probing. What happened?"

"Aimed to the right of the scope. Must be left handed. Must have been mighty close though."

James grabbed the radio. "Mike, hold, I say again, hold. Number two is still active." Turning to Ethan, he started to slide across the floor. "Right kid, we'll both take him. Let's see what the next round he fires does. See where he's going." They waited. Another two rounds came through the attic, this time directly over Ethan's firing position. Then nothing. "You stay down, I'll take an oblique angle and see if I can take a shot from there." He moved to the corner of the attic, at the extreme limit of visibility for the tree. He sighted and managed to locate a shudder of leaves and then the barrel. "Got him, he's making some movement, maybe reloading. You take up your position and we'll both try again. Take your time."

Through the scope, he could see the barrel steady and swing in his direction. "Wait, down, he's trying for another shot." Sure enough, there were two shots in rapid succession, each whistling above James' head and burying themselves in the beams. A third further over and he risked another look over the case. "Hang on a sec, kid." He focused. "Right let's do it." He was nestled with the stock comfortable against his cheek and about to apply the initial trigger pressure when he heard a sound behind him. He swung round the rifle barrel leveled. "Hold" he cried as he made out the figure of Monique coming through the trap door, her smile freezing as she saw the black hole swinging towards her. He desperately forced his left hand high and wide as his finger involuntarily tightened on the trigger. The shot went into the rafters. He threw the rifle on the floor and dragged her through the trap door and onto the floor. Evenly spaced rounds were still flying through the attic above their heads, silently embedding themselves with a solid *thwack*.

"For Christ's sake stay there until I tell you to move. Understand?" He knew he was shouting at her and stared hard at her until she nodded. "Ethan, how does it look?" Ethan had resumed his firing position and did not reply or move. James saw the knuckles whiten on his right hand and then heard the gas escaping. A second passed. "Got him."

James was on the radio straight away. "Mike, move in." Then he turned to Monique.

"Jesus, what the hell did you think you were doing bursting in like that? You could have been killed. Christ, I could have shot you. Stay there."

He turned back to look out of the window, picking up his rifle and sighting in on the trees. He checked his own target area first, and saw a group of three men at the foot of the tree with what looked like black bin bags, but which was actually a body bag. They had almost concealed the first corpse. Swinging to the next site he could again make out activity in the undergrowth, but then with dismay saw a ladder being moved into place. He lifted his gaze up the tree and saw the second body entangled in some branches, thankfully almost at ground level. He swung the scope around and did not see anyone close to the site. He checked on the radio.

"Everything's under control James. Just about to recover number two. No-one around and the area will be clear in two minutes. See you back at the house."

James sat down, leaning back against the packing cases. "Ethan, are you all right?" He saw him relaxing against the wall.

"Yep, I'm fine. That was bloody good shooting. Came bloody close there when the door opened."

Next he looked down at Monique, almost lying at his feet. She was as white as a sheet and trembling uncontrollably.

James didn't trust himself to say anything. He stood and went to the stairs, sitting down at the bottom. He lifted his hands and saw they were shaking. That had been too close, a fraction of a second and he would have done their job for them. He leaned forward and put his head in his hands, trying to compose himself. He knew he would have to say something to Monique, but he needed to calm himself before he did.

He heard movement above him and then Ethan's voice. "You all right? Here, sit here with me." He could imagine Ethan cradling her, trying to soothe her.

"Shit, I thought you were dead back there."

Good start, kid. That'll really quieten her.

"You know what happened?" He didn't hear a reply, but Ethan went on. "Well, you see we were just about to take a shot and were at the point where the slack on the trigger is taken up. All it needs then is just a little squeeze and bang. Well, when you popped up like that, it was an instinctive reaction, it was because our minds are tuned into what we're doing and a noise or movement is seen by our mind as a threat. When James turned on you, it was because everything told him you were a threat. He could no more have stopped himself pulling that trigger than he could stop his heart beating. Thank God, he had enough time to fire into the roof." There was a pause and James could hear her sobbing now. "There's something else. When he left just now, it wasn't because he didn't want to speak to you, shout at you or anything like that. It was something I've never seen in James before. He was scared. I don't mean about the bullets flying around in here. It was because of what could have happened." James could almost see Ethan smiling at her. "There, you've managed to do what no other man has done before. In the words of Captain Kirk - *"you've boldly gone where no man has gone before."* Him and his bloody movies. At least he heard a bit of a laugh. Well done, kid, when did you get so wise?

As he stood, seeing that his hands had stopped shaking, he heard the final question. "You feeling a bit better now?" He had to admit he was feeling better himself, having heard Ethan's version of events. He started to climb the stairs.

Coming through the hatch, he caught Ethan's eye and nodded.
"I think I'll go and get us some coffee." He stood to leave. James touched him lightly on the shoulder as he passed in acknowledgement,

before sitting down next to Monique.

He didn't know what to do, so put an arm around her shoulders, saying nothing. She had stopped trembling. He knew from the past week that she was tougher than she looked and had an amazing resilience. It didn't take her long to say something.

"I'm sorry James, I only wanted to check that you were all right, maybe see if you wanted something to drink or eat. I didn't think about it. Just came straight up."

"Don't worry about it. Really. No harm done, thank God. But, Ethan was right, it was close."

She pulled her head away and looked him in the eye. "Tell me the truth. I could have got Ethan killed, you too, distracting you like that?"

"Yes." He had no choice but to admit it. "But you didn't. You couldn't know we were taking fire when you came up. But you really have to listen to us when we ask you to do something. Promise?" After she had nodded her agreement he continued. "The worst part of the business is that you could have been killed. Do you understand that? That's one of the biggest problems in situations like this. There can be a terrible accident and, to be honest with you, I don't know how I could have lived with myself if anything had happened to you." As he said it he knew that he could have phrased that better.

She managed a smile, her old self beginning to shine through. "It would have been ironic in the extreme – killed by the man I love. It gives new meaning to breaking my heart." They laughed at that, maybe a bit forced, but laughter all the same. He could feel her relaxing even more. He waited until he heard steps on the ladder before suggesting she go downstairs and leave them to clean up. She waited for Ethan to climb into the attic and took the stairs.

They were sitting in silence when Mike joined them, gratefully taking a mug and sitting on a case.

"All packed away and secure. You would never know they had been there. We've got the photographs as well." They had agreed that photographs of the bodies with their rifles would be a good way of delivering the message to Gregori.

"Any indication that they had a coms link or mobile phone, that number two could have passed a message?" James didn't think that he had the time to make a call. The return of fire had been too quick.

"Nothing, they both had phones but I checked the call log and there were no calls made all morning. What happened up here?" Indicating the pockmarked walls. "And what was Monique doing here?"

James left it to Ethan to explain.

The atmosphere in the attic was heavy, almost oppressive. The anticlimax of the shooting was affecting each of them differently. The only sound was the clicking of parts as they stripped and cleaned their weapons. Ethan was the first to speak.

"I've never done anything like that before. It's not how I thought it would be. I don't know, I guess I don't feel good about it."

James and Mike looked at each other. It was silently agreed that James should answer. "Ethan, there are a couple of things you have to remember. One is that we are in the middle of a rich suburb in one of the biggest cities in the world. This is not a normal situation, it's not a war zone. Two, this isn't a movie where the hero walks away and displays no emotion. We all have emotions about what we do, even in the field. It's permitted to feel bad, guilty even, but remember those guys were going to wipe out a family. They may, or may not, have had any feelings about that, we'll never know, but they were going to do it. When Monique and I were talking last night, she told me that the only difference between us and them is that they get paid for what they do. She was right. It's no use thinking we are any different. The one thing is that if we hadn't taken them down, they would have done the same to us and to Lou and his family. But yes, in the eyes of the law we have just murdered two men. We never saw their faces, we don't know how old they were, what type of people they were. I suppose what I'm trying to say is that it makes a difference. It's easy when you have a definite enemy, when you know what is required of you and of them, but this fight is not the same as the ones you've known. Take that guy in the car park. You didn't know him, yet you killed him. What's the difference?"

"I suppose the fact that he was there and was a threat to us; it was necessary."
"Correct. Those two were more of a threat; it's only that the threat was more implied. It would only have become reality when they opened fire, that, and that alone, would have made them an obvious enemy, and

you would not have thought twice about shooting back. I'm not going to lecture you, but do not try and put a face or personality on your target."

"I'm sorry, guys. I just don't know what to feel." He looked at each in turn. "One thing; did we do the right thing?"

They both agreed and Mike continued. "Look, kid, it's still not too late to back out. Wait." He stopped the interruption. "I'm not saying that because of what you said. I, we, don't want to drag you into something you're not comfortable with, and there might be more of the same thing coming our way. That's all I'm saying; think about it."

"No, I'm still in. They wouldn't have hesitated to shoot the girls or Carmen. I guess I was in that low. You know the kind we all get after a fight?"

"I remember when I was in Angola once." James said. "We came up against some guys hired by a Micky Mouse outfit. Most of them had no combat experience, they were working for low wages. A couple of the younger ones had deserted from the Army to do the job. Turns out the ones who made it out were never paid a penny. Anyway, during the firefight I had this one guy coming straight at me. I didn't pick up on him till he was almost on me. I was looking straight down the barrel, I knew there was hardly time to swing myself around but I tried. I made it and shot him. After it was all over, I went to the body and had a look. I wanted to know why he never pulled the trigger and why he wore such a terror stricken look on his face when he realised he was about to die. I'll tell you, it changed my outlook forever. He was a boy, he couldn't have been more than eighteen or nineteen. I checked his rifle, an FN, he had a blockage, his weapon was filthy, he could have cleared it in a second or two. We've all done it. The point is that he didn't have the experience and the training to do it under fire. The object of my telling you this is that I felt exactly the same as you do now. I know we can justify to ourselves and to others that whatever we do has a reason, but the cold hard fact remains, we killed someone. It's that simple. We have to live with it."

There was a prolonged silence, which Mike broke when the cleaning had been done. "I think we all need a stiff drink. Come on you two, let's go downstairs."
Ethan excused himself and left James and Mike in the study. They were sitting in silence, nursing their drinks when Lou came in. "I'm sorry, I should have kept an eye on Monique. Thank God she wasn't hurt. I

passed Ethan on the stairs, is he all right? It seemed like something was on his mind."

"He'll be fine, he just needs to have some time on his own." James filled Lou in on what had happened and been said. "It happens to us all at some point."

"It's a bit early in the day for this, but what the hell, it's not exactly normal times." Mike got up and poured them another drink. Nothing was said as each sat with their own thoughts. James had time to wonder what the others were thinking about. He was thinking about how he wanted this to end so he could go home and resume his normal life.

Ethan came quietly into the study and looked at the others as he sat down. "I've been thinking," he started. "Do we think it was only the two? What if there are others out there? How will we know?"

"That's the million dollar question, kid. Any ideas? My mind isn't working at full speed yet."

Nothing. Silence as each absorbed the implications that there might be another killer waiting for them to make a mistake.

James had to break the silence. He could feel it dragging them down. "How about we put a man in the attic with a pair of binoculars. If it were me out there and I was missing two men, I would come looking sooner or later. We know they must have the means for egress from the site. That implies a driver. Again, if it were me, I'd come to have a look either tonight or tomorrow morning. It depends what back up plans they had for a rendezvous or extraction. Can't do any harm."

"You're right, I'll organise it now. But what if there are more? I doubt they'd try those positions again." Mike stood and left to place his man. When he returned they were all still silent. "Any thoughts?"

It was Ethan who spoke, slowly and thoughtfully. "Well, if there are one or two more then we would have to draw them out. Seems to me that the only option, while we're locked down in here, is to come to us. A frontal assault, if you like. We all know how easy it is to penetrate a place like this. The guys outside wouldn't have much of a chance."

"He's spot on" agreed Mike. "Remember the times we've used things like crossbows to take out sentries silently? They could be in the house before we knew it. Shit, bugger, that's a big headache."

"OK." James could see the alarm on Lou's face. "First things first. Let's see what the observation turns up. Could be no-one shows. If they do, then we'll work something out. Remember, they have to come to us. We have the high ground, home turf. I figure we've got time before they're missed and then they work out what happened. If that's the case then they have to put together a plan to get at us. So let's wait and see what the morning brings."

"One thing we might consider is a camera instead of binoculars. Could enhance the picture on the computer. At least then we'd have an idea of what they looked like. Make an ID we could give to the guys."

"Ethan, you're a genius. What do you say, Mike, are we getting too old for this or what?"

"Could well be, James. Never thought about using a computer to enhance a photograph. I've seen it on TV. Can you really do that kind of stuff, kid?"

"No problem, it would be handy if there's some type of zoom lens, make it clearer."

Lou said he had just the thing and returned with a camera and huge lense. "Mona was into photography last year some time. This should do the trick." He handed it to Ethan.

"Perfect. Mike, who are you putting upstairs?" Mike told him. "Right, I'll go and see George, tell him what we want."

"What's on your mind James?"

"Nothing, Lou." He paused and decided to be honest. "Well, I can't help thinking I've missed something. We can't afford a mistake, no matter how small it might seem. I hope I'm up to this. It's been a hell of long time since I've done this. Sorry, I'm becoming a worrier in my dotage."

"I feel exactly the same, old friend. I thought we'd left this behind us. Remember when we talked at your place? The quiet life, eh?"
"I'm sorry you guys have been dragged into this. I really am." Now Lou was the one who was looking worried. "I think we forget that you three are doing all the worrying for us; we just assume that you'll sort something out, take care of things. I forgot you're used to looking after

each other and yourselves, not the excess baggage you have now. You've taken on a tremendous responsibility, which should be mine. The safety of my family. I'm truly sorry that I lost sight of it, but I, God, I don't know what to say."

"Don't say anything Lou. Let's have another drink. I don't think we'll be needed tonight. Hell, the sun's over the yardarm somewhere in the world. So sundowners all round." James stood and poured the drinks. "Besides, we're being maudlin enough without being drunk, imagine how maudlin we'll be with a few belts inside us." A weak attempt at humour, but enough to lighten the mood.

Ethan came back in with the whole family in tow. It was Carmen who told them to move into the lounge, where they could all sit together more comfortably.

This time Monique sat close to James. She made no attempt to touch him, but was close enough for their sides and elbows to touch. As usual it was the innocence of youth who broached the subject everyone studiously avoided.

"Those two men, did you have to shoot them? Are they dead? Is it over?" Mona asked. Mike and James looked to Lou to answer.

"Yes and no, it's not over just yet. We have to wait and see, at least until tomorrow."

But she wasn't finished yet. "Ethan, is it true, what Monique says, that you were almost shot because of her?"

Ethan forced a laugh at her directness. "No, he missed by a mile. Besides, you shouldn't be talking like this. You're too young."

Mike burst out laughing.

"That was the biggest mistake you're ever likely to make, kid." He watched the reaction and the retort rise immediately to Mona's lips, her indignation at being told she was too young evident in the posture of her body.

"I am not too young. I understand everything. OK, maybe I ask too many questions, that's what Mum's always telling me, it's only that I want to know."

I, Plague

They all had to laugh at this, and she lost her indignant expression and smiled back at them, promptly changing her position and plopping herself down next to Ethan and threading her arm through his, much to his embarrassment. His blushes caused another round of laughter. It was when they were laughing that James felt Monique's hand resting lightly on his forearm. She made no move to lift it when the laughter subsided and he was acutely aware of Mike's grin and the way the others avoided looking at them.

CHAPTER TWENTY SEVEN

It was the second (this time unscheduled) visit, to the dead letter drop for Steve. He had increased the frequency of his visits to the fountain after sending off the first message, warning of impending arms and drugs shipments. Unusually, he had received a message back, briefing him on the events in the UK. It was unusual in that confirmation of the information received was only rarely passed on. He could only think that, if the next information proved accurate, then it would become extremely urgent to pull the agent out of Kiev. He had been informed of the nationwide operation which would be swinging into place on his word. He realised it was an awesome responsibility, but he trusted his agent; he had never given them a bad lead in the years he had been working.

That was why he found himself strolling through the park. This time he brought some sandwiches and a couple of bottles of beer, planning to sit and enjoy them while watching the young families at play. At the back of his mind, though, he recognised the fact that he was hoping for a glimpse of the man who would drop off a message. All the better to deal with his extraction if he knew what he looked like. This, he knew, was a forlorn hope; he would never have lasted this long had he been careless in the protection of his identity. Still, it was a nice day for a stroll and a small picnic.

He would be sorry to leave the Ukraine; it had been a good posting despite the lack of activity. Once he had become accustomed to the people, he had enjoyed their company. They had struck him, initially, as an unfriendly lot, unsmiling and serious in countenance. He supposed that to be a throwback to the old days. Now there were fashionable shops and sidewalk cafes which only the well off could afford to frequent. The locals far preferred to entertain at home, as he had found on numerous visits he had made to friends he had made in the area. The one drawback he had found was the cold winters; his old body, he often joked, had too many broken bones and stiff joints for the cold to be pleasant. There were too many aches and pains when the cold seeped through to his bones. Things had not been made easier the last winter when Russia had cut off the gas supplies because of a pricing dispute. Not even the diplomatic service was exempt from the discomfort felt by the Ukrainian people.

He looked around as if trying to make up his mind where to sit, and moved to the fountain. Once seated he opened his bag and took out a bottle of beer and the sandwiches. He placed them to his side and dropped his hand inside the fountain and found the loose brick. He felt the paper and palmed it, replacing the brick and picking up his beer to take a swallow. Taking his paper out, he opened it and under its cover glanced at the message. This time it was detailed. There were ship's names, container numbers, dates of departure and estimated times of arrival and the location of the drugs haul within the hold of a ship.

This was definitely it, he knew it, this was going to hurt the organisation if both shipments could be stopped and seized. At the same time he knew that his agent would be at great risk as soon as the operation started. From the message he knew the time scale, and could guess with reasonable accuracy what would happen in the UK once this information was received. The sooner he extracted his agent the better.

He suppressed his excitement and sipped slowly at his beer while eating his sandwiches. The temptation to scribble a note and leave it had to be strongly resisted. He knew that such hurried decisions and action had often, in the past, blown the whole operation. He decided that he would leave it until the next day before returning and leaving the final message. He hoped that London would have got back to him by then and, if necessary, they would have a plan in place to remove his man from the Ukraine.

He replaced his paper in the bag and sat watching the mothers and children play in the sunshine. He smiled at the falls and concerned mothers rushing to the side of their infants to comfort them. Ruefully, he regretted that he had never had children to look after and then, in his retirement, to look after him. He had not even spoken to his ex wife for fourteen years. He idly wondered if life had been kind to her and she had found the man she had been looking for, someone with a regular job who returned home every night and spent his weekends with her.

He finished his second beer, sighed and stood to make his way back to his office. At least the end was in sight; maybe, just maybe, he could start planning the future.

CHAPTER TWENTY EIGHT

Tuesday morning, and the whole group was sitting in the incident room. Andy had arrived back from Scotland with Stewart on the Monday afternoon. When they had met the others at the hotel there was a rumour circulating that something had broke and they would hear in the morning. So the air of expectancy was palpable as they sat and waited for Commander Bond to join them.

They had been given the weekend off after all the planning that could be accomplished was completed. There was, after all, she had said, only so much that could be done until they had definite times and dates. It had appeased Andy's wife to have him home for the weekend and he had spoiled her by taking her to dinner and spending all his time with her.

A few minutes after eight and Jane Bond entered the room, flanked by an Assistant Commissioner and two men in plain clothes.

"I hope you all had a good rest over the weekend. No divorces looming, I hope? All the brains in full working mode? Good. These two gentlemen are from Customs. The reason for their presence will become clear in the next few minutes. Before I go on, I would like to thank you for the hard work you put in over the last week. All the contingency plans have been reviewed and passed. Well done." Praise indeed, thought Andy, as he smiled at Stewart, whispering.

"Wonder what's coming next?"

"To business." He did not have long to wait as she continued. "We have reliable information on two fronts. One. A freighter is bound for East Africa, via Southampton and the Middle East. It is registered to one of Gregori's companies, and, along with perfectly legitimate cargo, is carrying three containers of arms bound for these two countries. This represents a big investment, millions of dollars, and consists of small arms, the usual AK47's, RPGs and some high tech stuff that could inflict a lot of damage. We have a report that it also contains Stinger missiles, but this is, as yet, unconfirmed. Before you ask, our source is well placed and his information has always been reliable. And, yes, he is one of us." Everyone in the room appreciated what this meant; a deep cover undercover agent working within the organisation. "Needless to say, this information is highly confidential, top secret, and not to be discussed outside this room. With regard to this shipment; we know that the paperwork for the arms is false, end user certificates and such. We intend to seize that shipment. Not only for reasons of not arming contentious factions who our government do not support, but more for the practical reason that it will hit our friend Gregori where it hurts most. In his pocket. I will come back to that operation later."

She took a sip of water and looked around the room, her eyes lingering on each individual, almost as if she were evaluating them. "The second piece of information is why we are all here." The was an audible, collective movement, a scraping of chairs, a movement of everyone sitting up and leaning forward. "As expected, or more likely as we hoped, there is a large shipment of drugs leaving Russia today. It has been tracked from Afghanistan and into Russia, where we lost it. We don't know where his factories are. However, we do know that it will be hidden on board a motor yacht sailing for the east coast of Scotland. Our source tells us that it will land on the Fife coast, somewhere in the region of St Andrews. The estimated street value of this consignment is ten million pounds. As if that wasn't enough, the shipment which was hijacked a week ago will go on the market in the South and the Midlands towards the end of this week. This has obviously been well timed. The supply has been drying up and the price has almost doubled. We have a lot of hungry addicts out there craving for a fix. Let me add, at this point, that our source will be leaving Russia, hopefully, in the next day or two. Our operation will blow his cover further out of the water than an A bomb going off. Right, now is the time to start setting in motion your plans. I'll hand over to George Forson now."

"Good morning. The container ship is due to arrive in Southampton to take on containers on Wednesday. The yacht with the drugs won't reach the Scottish coast until some time on Thursday or Friday. It is our intention to hold the ship off Southampton until we know that the yacht is in our waters. This is not too unusual. We will cite the reason as a vessel being delayed in getting underway. Once the ship is docked we will do our thing. Again we won't depart from the norm, tying in with your timing, finding the false paperwork at the last possible minute. We will then seize the cargo. This will be a time consuming operation as we do not expect to find the suspect containers easily. They will, in all likelihood, be at the bottom of the pile and it will be quite a task to off load them. Hopefully by the time we get to the paperwork your side will be in full swing."

Next to Andy, Stewart gave a visible shudder, causing all in the room to look at him.

"I just had a vision of my future career" he explained. "Saw myself checking fishing boats off the Outer Hebrides." Another shudder and he had the room laughing.

"How about your side Casper, ready to go?" This from Cecil Farrington. When he saw the quizzical look from Jane Bond, he explained. "Casper the Friendly Ghost, or in this case, Spook."

The MI5 officer grinned widely; he had been given the nickname at the very start and was secretly pleased with it. It had shown that he was accepted by the police element and not viewed as an outsider, which was so often the case. "When we have the times we'll have everything that was promised." He spoke directly to the three at the top table. "Can you give me everything on the two ships so I can get started with the satellite tracking? We can also start finding out what communications they have, ready to start jamming."

They were all given the information before Bond continued. "As you can see from the information sheets, the yacht's name is "Alexander III", a touch of the grandoise, don't you think? Anyway, HMS Norfolk is en route to the East Coast to standby for the interception. The spot is ideal for onward transportation, it has access to all the main routes, both North and South. That works in our favour in so far as it will be easier to follow them on busy roads and not country lanes. Andy and Stewart, leave tonight for Edinburgh, flights are already booked, I'm sorry you had to come down again, but this information only reached us late last night. Cecil, you go back to Manchester. Each of you will have duplicates of this room, it's being set up as we speak. The rest of us will stay here and co-ordinate any action as and when they move further south. Your Chief Constables have already been briefed as far as we have seen fit. You will receive every co-operation from Air Support down to the copper on the beat. Remember people, this is a rolling operation and security right down the line is important. Andy, Stewart, that is the most important aspect of your end. You are the beginning, if it goes wrong there we're screwed. Trust no-one." She paused and smiled at them. "We might end up thinking the Outer Hebrides is a holiday camp."

"Well, this is it, good luck to us all. And to coin a phrase from my favourite TV show - *"be careful out there"*."

There was an excited, electric buzz in the air as Andy, Stewart and Cecil gathered their stuff and made their farewells. They discussed their concerns on the way to the airport. Each had different worries, but the security of the whole affair was paramount in each of their minds. Add anticipation to the worry and Andy, for one, knew that the adrenalin rush would last him through the next few days.

"One step at a time" he reminded the others. "That's the easiest way to handle it, just one step at a time."

Cecil laughed dryly. "I know that my Chief Constable's going to have kittens over the overtime and support staff on this. He never was the biggest spender in town, at the best of times. I can almost see him in his office, calculating the costs against the chances of his move to the Met."

After a quick drink to their success, they parted to catch their flights.

CHAPTER TWENTY NINE

Anatoly waited for thirty minutes past the pick up time before starting up the Vauxhall and driving out of the parking area. He was not too concerned; it was possible that they could not descend from their hideouts because of strollers in the park, a hundred reasons, and a backup point was prearranged. He would drive past the house and take a look on his way to the alternative pick up point.

Driving slowly, he saw that the gates were open and a Tesco van was blocking the drive. It was being checked by one man with another standing at the front talking to the driver. He did not see anyone else, but could imagine that there would be at least one back up in the near vicinity.

"Yes," he thought. "This was being run by a professional. Pity Alexei had missed." It would have been so much easier if the family had to leave for a funeral, or to meet the casket. But, the best laid plans always had a back up.

He arrived at the alternative pick up point after driving around for forty minutes. There was no sign of the others. He waited for another thirty minutes and then started to worry. It was well into the evening, and there was not much light left. He decided to leave and hope they made their own way back. If they did not show he would have a look around the hideouts in the morning.

The thought that he had somehow lost two men nagged at him during the drive into the centre of London. He decided to stop at a pub and have a drink. It was no good trying to think and drive at the same time.

Sitting with his pint of cold lager he stared at the table top. His men were the best. The hideouts could not be seen unless someone knew what they were looking for. He had personally checked them. They were not stupid enough to sight into the sun and give away their position by a chance reflection. They knew to scan the area around them and one was in a position to cover the other. No, he decided, they were as well prepared as could be expected. If something had happened and they had been taken out then the person who was organising the house security was very good. He was thinking as he would, and that was dangerous. Also they had the advantage that Anatoly would have to come to them, could sit and wait. His mind was working fast; if his men had been taken, would they then believe that the threat had been eliminated, that there were only the two? That was possible. They would know one had been in Paris and one had been in London, he could only hope that they believed it was a team of two. That just might give him an edge when he made his next move. And that was the big question – what was the next move? If his men had been taken then using sniper positions again was out of the question. It would have to be up close. They might have to breach the security and get into the house. That might also be the last thing they would expect.

He absently looked at his glass and saw that he had finished the beer. He stood and left, making his way back to the hotel.

In his room he briefed Alexei on what he thought might have happened and they agreed to wait until the morning to return to the site and see what they could find. Neither of them said it, but it was accepted that the others would not be returning.

They walked across the Common, through the light ground mist, their footsteps marking their passage in the dew covered grass. The sun was warming the air despite the early hour. They moved into the shadows of the trees and separated, each moving to the hideouts. Anatoly stood under the tree and gazed up. He could see two freshly snapped branches, the whiteness of the bark stark against the darkness of the trunk. It looked as if something heavy had fallen. He examined the ground under the broken branches and saw, firstly, some dark spots on the dried leaves. Moving in a tight circle he saw a larger dark stain. Just the type that might form from a body lying on the ground after having been shot. It was a large stain so he must have lain there for a few minutes. He also guessed that it must have been a head shot for so much blood to have formed.

With a sigh he stood and looked at the house. It was bathed in the sunlight and as he looked he caught a flash of the sun on glass. He turned his head and watched from the periphery of his vision. Sure enough there it was again. It was not a steady glint of sun reflecting off a window. He was sure it was either a scope or binoculars. He moved suddenly to his left and retreated further into undergrowth, constantly changing his direction. He manage to catch the attention of Alexei was straightening up from looking at the ground. He signalled him to leave the area. Still walking and making sudden directional changes, he retreated. The point midway between his shoulder blades tingled and the small hairs on the back of neck seemed to be standing on end. So this is what it felt like to be a target.

When he had met with Alexei they compared notes.

"I found broken branches and blood on the ground." Anatoly was thinking as he was talking. "Must have been knocked from the platform. Same with you?" Alexei nodded. "Then it must have been a shot from the house, head shot as well, the attic would be the place. Whoever made that shot is good, as good as us. Maybe better; he had to spot them first. Yes, they're good. I'm thinking they must be ex-military, like us. They had luck with you in Paris, but the way you described it shows how professional they are, quick thinking too. Now this. Alexei, my friend, I have made the mistake of underestimating them, but not again, no, not again."

During the drive Alexei asked Anatoly to drop him off in the West End. He only said he had an idea and that he would explain fully when he returned to the hotel.

CHAPTER THIRTY

Mike woke James up at seven thirty on a bright Wednesday with the news that two men had been seen and photographed at the sniper sites. He quickly showered and dressed, arriving in the study as Ethan was triumphantly printing off the photos.

"There, it's a good picture. At least now we know."

"Unfortunately, yes. Another two, no doubt about it, is there? They knew where to look and what to look for, they've probably seen enough to tell the story. Bugger, now what do we do?" Mike and Ethan knew it was a rhetorical question and said nothing. Mike was interrupted by a phone call. "Anton," he explained. They listened to his side of the conversation. He was asking that arms be delivered to Kiev, asking for two of the same rifles and handguns, specifying Berettas and Glock, with spare magazines and ammunition. He agreed to the price and, after a pause, hung up.

"Well, that's done. The stuff will be there by Saturday. Anton is going to e-mail an address where we can pick them up. Sorry." He picked up the phone again as it rang. "Christ, I had forgotten all about her. Send her in to the study." That was all. He waited until the door opened and a young woman walked in. As James watched her he saw that she moved with a fluid grace. She was strikingly tall, nearly as tall as him, slim built with obvious muscles rippling under her tee shirt. She stood for a moment, looking at each of them in turn. When her eyes met James' he could read nothing in them. The light blue was glacial.

Mike broke her appraisal. "Guys, this is Lizelle Fourie. I asked her to come and see us, as I thought she might make the fourth member of our team. Don't look so surprised, Ethan, it's rude to stare with your mouth open." Ethan immediately was subjected to one of his blushes, murmuring what sounded like an apology.

Mike sat her down and gave her a cup of coffee. "Lizelle is well qualified for the job. She's good with a long gun, handgun and can handle herself in most situations."

"I asked Jannie about you after Mike called me. I was told you were good guys and I could do worse than teaming up with you." She waited for their reaction.

"Jannie called me and vouched for her, if I needed confirmation then that was it." They all knew who she was talking about. James and Mike had worked with him on three occasions, Ethan the once.

"Good enough for me." James looked at her. "Do you have any idea what this is all about?"

She didn't. "OK, I'll bring you up to date on what we're thinking about and then you can make up your mind. One thing I'll say right off, it's hazardous, no that's not right, it's downright dangerous. No guarantee any of us will walk away from this." She nodded, no emotion showing on her face, her body posture unchanged and relaxed. A good sign, he thought. He continued to watch her closely as he gave her the background and described what they intended to do. When he finished she said nothing, her eyes examining each of them in turn.

"I'm in. I've never been to Kiev." That was all. What an easy way to commit to something that could get you killed, James thought. He took a sip from his now almost cold coffee.

"Good, now we have to deal with the immediate problem. How are we going to draw these guys out? I have a couple of ideas. Tell me what you think. One, we offer them bait; I go out in the car in Lou's clothes. We'll have to do something with my hair." There were protests as soon as he said it. "Hold on, that's the riskier option, but it also has too many holes in it. Second. We use the house as a trap, the unprotected family as the bait." Again he had to hold up his hand to quieten them. "We make a show of sending the guys home. Make them think the protection has been reduced. What I thought was that we bring everyone into the house, then we bring a delivery van in with six or seven hidden in the back. We use them to drive off. With any luck they'll be seen leaving. Then we set up an ambush inside the house."

Mike thought before speaking. "Sounds good. If we left the guys outside they would be taken out during the infiltration. Being inside would give them a better chance. What about the van to bring them in the decoys?"

"Something like a Tesco van would be big enough. I reckon if we give the driver enough money he would do it. Also, if they were watching, they would see the van drive straight through without the checks we've had in place. That could allay their suspicions somewhat."

"All right James, we've got the guys inside, then what? Do we have enough weapons for them?"

"Good, Ethan, you're thinking. Mike, apart from the rifles, my two handguns and Ethan's, what else do we have?"

"I've got another two Glocks stashed away, plus a 30.30. Lizelle, I don't suppose you've brought along a Mother's Little Helper?"

"As a matter of fact, yes." She dug into her cavernous handbag and pulled out a Browning 9mm. "You told me that I would be starting straight away, so I brought most of what I would need in here."

"I wonder if the police know there are this many firearms floating around the country? I suppose they do; every gang in the country has access to guns of some shape or another."

"All right, are we agreed on the principal?" Mike waited for them to nod their agreement. "Let's get the family and run it past them, they have a right to know we're using them as bait. Christ, that's scary. I'll make a quick call and join you in the lounge in a couple of minutes."

"How about bringing in the guys, it would save having to go through the whole thing twice?" Ethan volunteered to bring them in.

In the hall Lizelle stopped James. "Jannie told me good things about you, especially that Rwanda gig. But are you really going to tell the family everything?" Now she'd spoken a full sentence, James could hear the strong South African accent and guessed that she was Afrikaans.

"Yes. They insisted from the start that they be kept informed of everything, absolutely everything. Anyway, they have a right to know, we're risking their lives."

"And ours" was the dry comment. She smiled to show that she was unconcerned. "Lead on, master."

He asked Lou to gather everyone together and, when they were seated, introduced Lizelle as the new member of the team. He watched them as they spoke with her. The contrast between the fair Lizelle and the darker girls could not have been greater. He wondered about her age. She, like Ethan, he guessed, looked younger than her actual years. He would put her in her late twenties or early thirties. He half listened to the chat as they waited for Mike to join them.

When he came in he spoke to James and the other two. "Right, the wheels are in motion, it shouldn't take too long. I'll give them a call for the go ahead when we finish here."

James pulled an upright chair into a position where he was facing them all. "We now know that there are another two out there. They were seen and photographed this morning. Before you ask if we're sure – the answer is yes. As sure as we can be. We only had two options on this." He thought for a moment before continuing, better to give them both he decided. "The first was that one of us dress up like Lou and draw them into taking a shot." As expected the protests were loud and vociferous. "Wait," he quieted them, "we're not going to do that, unless someone has any thoughts or reasons why we should." Nothing was said and he continued. "The only other thing we've got is that we draw them into the house. To do this we have to pull a Trojan Horse stunt in reverse, in other words make them think that all the protection has left and that we're vulnerable." He waited for a reaction but there was none.

They were all watching him intently. "What we plan is to deliver seven guys in a van and then have them leave openly so that anyone watching would see them. The guys we already have here we will bring into the house and keep them here. The van won't be checked, all to further the illusion that we think the threat is over. All this means that you will all be confined to one room upstairs."

He looked at the seven men. "As for you guys, we'll run through positions and all that when we're finished here. Now, however, is the time for you to pull out if you want."

George spoke after the others looked to him. "Ethan told us briefly about this, said you were pulling us indoors to try and protect us. We appreciate that, we can all see how vulnerable we would be to a determined infiltration." He looked at the other six. "We're in, just tell us what to do. By the way, Mrs Carter, we've never had a chance to say thanks for all the good food, so we're saying it now." Carmen gave each of them her warmest smile.

"OK, that's the idea, Lou it's up to you and the girls to accept or reject. But I want to add one more thing." This he addressed to the seven men, Mike, Ethan and Lizelle. "If we do this I want a two layer ring of steel around them. Nothing less is acceptable. The only way they get into that room is through us."

Everyone silently nodded. Lou, holding Carmen's hand so tightly his knuckles were white eventually spoke. "We agree."

"Is there no other way?" This from Monique. "I know it's a stupid question, but, it's just that I don't want to see any of you hurt."

It was George who piped up. "Don't you worry none about us, Miss. We'll be fine. So will you."

Mike stood. "Let's go outside and have a look around the house, see where we can set up for the maximum coverage."

They stood in the hall. James looked at the stairs and the landing leading to the bedrooms. "Mike, we need a room big enough to hold five people, the family and one of us, with room for two on each side wall. I've never been out back, but I don't suppose there's one that's set back? I'm thinking of crossfire if they come up the wall." He stopped but before Mike could reply he had a thought. "Mario, can someone get me Mario?"

"No, but there's one with a bathroom window which could cover the outside."

"We'll have a look. Mario, go round and open all the front curtains, tell the family to stay in the back. What's normal, the front gate to be open or closed?" He was told open during the day and closed at night. "All right, Mario, open the gate and then come back here." He waited till he left.

"OK guys, and gal, here's my thinking. We've got the family in a room, we have to draw the shooters into the open, that would mean here or on the stairs. I think we should have someone on each side of the landing with the rifles. They have to be set right back in the shadows, which restricts the field of fire until they're almost at the top of the stairs, but concealment is the preferable option, at least until the last possible minute. Then, further along the corridor, two more firing positions, using the rooms on either side of the hall. Two more outside the door and one inside the room. The person inside the room has to cover the window and stop any panic, you know, someone trying to run out when they hear the firing. Lizelle, I think that should be you, you have to keep them calm and against the walls. You're our last line of defence, if it comes down to only you, well, you know what that means. I honestly don't believe that's likely. If we don't stop them out here, we're not very good at our job." He thought that was enough. "Listen, if any of you guys have any ideas, spit them out." No-one said anything. "Right, I also think we should have a back stop, but that's a bit trickier. We don't know how they are going to gain access. The ideal situation would be to have someone in one of these rooms ready to fire from their rear. We'll have a look and see if it's possible to conceal someone down here."

They had reached the back of the house and Mike and James looked in the bathroom. It had a small glazed window which could be swung upwards to open it. It remained open without any prop. "Good, we could put someone in here. Let's go to that room."

They opened the door and James groaned when he saw the amount of furniture in the room. "We'll have to shift all this, put two mattresses down either side."

"Might not be a bad thing, moving all this." Mike gestured to the furniture. "We could use some of it as cover for the guys on the landing. They don't know what the inside looks like, so if we place it properly they will think it's normal."

James saw Mario. "Mario, you and a couple of the guys move all this furniture out of this room. George, you know what to do? When it's empty move four mattresses and blankets in." He looked around. "Leave that table under the window and put a lamp on it. Lizelle, that's the only light they can use, no back drop, silhouette. Get the picture?"

"Mike, Ethan, get all the weapons out and issue them. Work out among yourselves who's best suited to what position. After that I suggest we all get some rest; it could be a long night, and, there's no guarantee that they'll even come tonight." He looked at Mike, who responded; "I'll get that organised."

James left them to it and went downstairs to have a look at the rooms on the ground floor.

CHAPTER THIRTY ONE

Humming quietly to himself, "I'm the Man Who Broke The Bank at Monte Carlo", the elderly MI6 operative walked through the park. He had every reason to be cheerful. He would be going home soon. His work in the Ukraine was almost finished. He had received a message that morning telling him the action was being taken based on the information provided and that he should close down his operation. Yes, he was happy. A couple of years behind a desk in some obscure section and that would be it. Retirement. He hadn't dared to think about it. Maybe he could find a cottage near a river and spend his days fishing. His one regret was that he had no one to spend all that time with. His only marriage had been a disastrous affair. Too many sudden and unexplained trips away, too many lonely nights for her.

He hoped his agent would not take too long picking up the note. It only contained two words - "Call – Urgent". He wondered if he would be as glad to be getting out as he was. He had only begun to think of him as a real person in the last few months. He knew absolutely nothing about him outside of the bare information he had seen from his file. He was not even privy to his full name, or the name he was working under. He only knew him as Peter. It was possible he had passed him in the street, or sat next to him while having his morning coffee.

He had run his share of undercover operations, and had a deep respect for the men who could maintain the deception of living a life that was an utter fabrication. He had seen it all go horribly wrong, and he had seen all the effort pay off. The one thing he did know for sure was that, when he was home, and the debriefings were over, he would have a hard time adjusting. He hoped the psychological help had improved since he had last brought an agent home. That poor fellow still had problems with his identity and coping with a normal everyday life.

He approached the fountain and sat in his usual place, unfolding his newspaper and unobstrusively slipping his message into the hiding place. He sat longer that normal, watching the passers by, watching to see if anyone took an interest in him. He didn't know what made him do it, but thinking, he knew he hoped to see if Peter turned up. It was a silly notion. Peter was too professional to pay him any attention even if he was among the strollers in the park.

He also supposed that it was the urgency of the situation that made him stay and watch. He needed Peter to call as soon as possible. It would not do for him to be in place when the operation started in the UK. If everything went according to plan, it was going to hurt the organisation very badly, and, there was only one way that success could be gained. There would be no doubt in anyone's mind that an informer was working inside the organisation. That would be disastrous for Peter. The amount of information he supplied would have to have come from someone high up and trusted.

He had thought about trying undercover work earlier in his career, and had dismissed it as unsuitable for him. It was not that he lacked the intelligence or quick wits to be successful. He did not even think he lacked the courage, although from what he had seen when things had gone wrong for the agent, they had never had an easy time dying. No, he was better in the planning and back up necessary for someone in the field. He had indulged in forays into the East, behind the Iron Curtain, but they had not been protracted stays and he had always made it back safely, leaving his KGB counterparts at the wire.

It had been a good career, he mused, not particularly distinguished, but a good career nonetheless.

He had given up any pretext of reading the newspaper, and was absently watching a young mother with her two children playing and chasing each other over the grass. How different everything would have been, he thought, if I had chosen a different path from university. That could be me playing with my grandchildren, not a care in world but the security and happiness of the children. He smiled as the picture of him as a father crossed his mind. No, perhaps not, he never had the temperament for that kind of thing. He smiled to himself again as he thought of the reactions of any sons to the news that their father was a secret service man, a spook.

He pushed these thoughts out of his mind and sighed as he folded the newspaper. He suddenly felt old and tired as he patted the stonework.

"Come on Peter, give me a call and let's get the hell out of here."

CHAPTER THIRTY TWO

Alexei kept him waiting for almost two hours, entering the room with a satisfied smile.

"I have an idea, look." He spread plans of a house on the bed. "You can get anything in this country. These are the plans for the Carter house. I thought we could use them to work out how we could get in and out."

They pored over the plans and an idea started to form in Anatoly's head. After twenty minutes, he announced they should drive back and have a look at the house on the ground.

They parked the Vauxhall a couple of hundred yards from the front gate and walked onto the Common. "It doesn't make any difference if they are watching, they will have identified us this morning. We'll soon know. Keep an eye on those attic windows, just in case."

They sat on the grass facing the house. They could see the front and sides and the idea grew firmer. "Look at the west side. The wall is close to the property, in particular the conservatory. We could climb onto the roof. From there we go up the wall to the main house roof. Then we come down the front and in through the attic windows. This morning, when I saw the flash of the sun I didn't see a reflection of any glass. I'm sure they removed the window panes for the shooting and haven't replaced them yet. We'll drive past to make sure. But if that's the case then we have our way in."

"Sounds good, but what about getting out, Anatoly?"

"Through the door, after all, there isn't going to be anyone to see or stop us."

"When?"

"Tonight. Let's finish this. I want to get out of this godforsaken country. We can be home tomorrow, drinking vodka and speaking to Russian women." He allowed himself a smile at the thought. "But first, we have to get some rope, in case we need it to get down the roof. Also, we have to get hold of some dark clothing. Then we'll have something to eat and a rest. Get here at three in the morning. At that time, if there is anyone on watch, they will be easier to take. You agree?" He wasn't in the habit of asking for opinions but as there were only the two of them, it seemed like a good idea.

Alexei had nothing to add, except a request. "When we're done with the family, I want to take out any men left in the house. One of them must have either set up the shooting of our friends or done it himself. Either way, I want him."

They took a slow drive past the house. The attic windows had not been replaced. There was no sign of anyone in the grounds behind the open gate.

All the items they needed were easily obtained and, while they ate, they studied the house plans, memorising the route to the bedrooms on the first floor and the apartment above the garage. They noted the servants quarters set at the back of the house, one more level up, and decided to ignore any of those occupants unless it was necessary.

CHAPTER THIRTY THREE

James was lying on the sofa in the study with his eyes closed. A quick glance and he would seem to be sleeping. He had evened his breathing and would not have minded at all if sleep would come. However, his mind was working furiously, trying to second guess the next moves his opponents would make. Ideally, he thought, it would make things easier and safer if he could somehow manipulate them into following a route of his choosing, but that was easier said than done. They could become suspicious if he made things too easy for them. He also worried that he had covered all the eventualities that might present themselves. He heard the door open, but did not open his eyes.

Mike and Lizelle entered and quietly sat down, conversing in whispers.

"What have you two been up to?" He startled them as he turned on his side, his head resting on the arm rest.

"Just checking the guys on look out, all quiet, but that's to be expected, I suppose." Mike was still speaking quietly and James saw that Ethan was asleep on the other sofa. "Remember the time when we could do that, sleep anywhere at the drop of a hat?"

"I wish I could do that now. Too much running around in the old brain box for that, though." James looked at Lizelle. "Not able to sleep either?"

"No, I've always been the same. Too many things floating around to relax." James had to concede that she looked relaxed, despite her words.

"Heard you took a bullet for your principle on the last job. Have you always been in the close protection business?"

"Ja, after the army and then the police it seemed like the right move to make. That guy was the worst kind of client, though." She paused and smiled at the thought. "A real arse, wouldn't take direction from any of us. His agent and production company hired us, so he thought we were a nuisance, not letting him gallivant around, do all the shit he was used to. That caused the problem, he strayed too far away. He was lucky I was able to get to him. No bloody thanks, nothing. Like I said, the guy was a supreme prick. Anyway, that's when I thought I might try my luck over here. The rest you know."

Maurice Johns

"Good to have you on board, eh Mike?" Mike nodded his agreement.

After a few minutes Lizelle asked. "What makes you think they'll come tonight?"

This was the one thing that James had been thinking hard about. "Well, first it's what I'd do. They can't realistically hope to perform a successful infiltration during daylight, they'd be too obvious. Next, as we know, the worst time for anyone waiting and watching is the hours just before light. That's when we're at our most vulnerable. If we've been successful in making him believe that the bulk of the protection has been pulled out then three or four in the morning would be the logical time to hit. As for tonight, that's a guess, if not tonight then tomorrow. I think they will want to get in quickly, catch everyone in the house. They'll think that the relief, combined with the strain of the last week or so, will take its toll and make the household easy targets. It's all guesswork and conjecture. I hope I'm right."

"Makes sense. Now about Kiev or Russia or wherever. Mike told me he has feelers out, any new thoughts about how we're going to handle it?"

James looked rueful. "None, as yet. Thought we'd get this out of the way first. You know we're going to reciprocate with a message that we're coming. If we manage to take care of these two, then we'll send the photographs of the four of them. But, and it's a big but, if we can tie this up in the next day or two, then we'll move as quickly as possible. Arrive as soon after the message as possible. Sorry I can't tell you more."

She accepted that and stretched her legs, putting her heels on the desk, sinking back into the folds of the armchair.

"Waiting, always the bloody waiting. God, I hate this part."

Mike moaned good naturedly. "It'll be easier when it gets dark."

The four of them remained in the study for the remainder of the afternoon and evening, each trying to relax and control their thoughts about the evening ahead. It was after seven when Ethan woke, saying how good he felt and asking why the others were not sleeping, joking about needing less sleep at an advanced age. This warranted two cushions to be thrown at him and an instruction to check the men.

The sky was still light although the sun had since set when Lou and the family came in bearing trays of food. "We've fed the rest of the guys and thought you might like something before we go upstairs." They put the trays on the desk. "Help yourselves."

James had thought they had left the room and was helping himself to the food when Mike kicked his shin and beckoned to the door. "Go and speak to her you bloody idiot." He turned and saw Monique hovering, looking more like a lost little girl than a confident woman.

He took her elbow and led her into the hall. "You OK?"

"No, I'm scared." There was a tremor to her voice.

"Don't be, you'll all be just fine."

"I'm not scared for me. God, you can be so dense sometimes. I'm scared for you. I've been thinking about it all day. This is one of those times we talked about. Oh, you're not going anywhere, and this isn't an airport or station. But I want to…oh, I don't know what, I only wanted to be here. Will you hold me?"

He took her in his arms and she rested her head on his shoulder. It took a while for him to realise that she was crying, the shaking of her shoulders ever so gentle. He was lost. He did not have a clue as to what to do, so he stroked her head and tried to reassure her that it was all going to be over very soon. She whispered in his ear. "I want you to know that I do really love you. Please be careful." She pulled back. "I wish you were staying in the room with us. Let Mike be the one to stay outside. Please."

"I can't do that. For whatever reason, I seem to have ended up in charge. It's my place to be with them. Don't worry, I'll be fine."

"Promise you'll come and get me when it's over. And that you'll be careful. Promise."

He promised and gently prised himself loose from her grip. "Come on, I'll see you to the room." She took his hand and allowed herself to be led up the stairs. Much to his embarrassment, he saw the rest of the family waiting on the landing, flanked by four of the men. He walked past them saying nothing, opening the bedroom door and stepping aside to let them enter. Lou was the last to pass him and he stopped. "Don't worry about it, James. We've known about Monique for ages. Take care, son." He stepped into the room.

James went around the positions until he was satisfied that they had covered all the angles and then went back to the study to finish his food.

"Right, you three, get into your positions. Good luck to all of us."

There was no banter as they left the room.

CHAPTER THIRTY FOUR

The two Russians parked their car on a grass verge two hundred yards from the front of the house and walked in the shadows of the hedgerows and trees until they reached the gate. It was past midnight and the streets were quiet. The houses they had seen on the journey were, in the main, dark, their occupants secure in their quiet existences.

They did not speak as they observed the surrounding area before slipping into the shadow of an overhanging tree and scaling the wall. They dropped quickly to the ground and remained motionless, each scanning the grounds and listening intently for any sound or movement to indicate they had been seen. Once satisfied that they were undetected they hugged the wall round to a point opposite the conservatory. Each silently checked their equipment before climbing to the top of the wall and then jumping the five foot gap onto the conservatory roof. They landed silently and Alexei immediately started shinning up the drain. It was a climb of only about ten feet but he took his time, constantly stopping, checking the area under him and also the strength of the pipe. It was still only a matter of a couple of minutes before he made it onto the tiled roof, using the guttering to brace his feet as he waited for Anatoly.

They had agreed the next part was the most risky as they negotiated the slope to the apex of the roof. It was possible that it might be slippery and difficult to maintain their footing. Alexei was the lighter of the two and would go first. He set off, using his gloved hands and sneakers to scrabble up the roof. On the apex he quickly shimmied his way to the chimney stacks where he would be hidden from the street below and from where he could secure the rope. Anatoly used the rope to steady himself on his ascent and they were both soon sitting behind the chimney stack.

They gathered themselves and Anatoly whispered. "Right, through the window." He lowered himself down the rope until he was level with the windows. Then he started walking along the roof, feeding himself more rope as he neared them. To the side of the window he stopped. He leaned his torso closer to the frame and listened for two minutes before moving his head to look into the darkness of the attic. He could see nothing, he could hear nothing. Fortunately the road was quiet and he was as sure as he could be that there was no-one hiding in wait. He freed his Glock and moved through the window, releasing the rope and landing lightly on his feet, stooping to a crouch as he scanned the long open space. Now he was inside his eyes adjusted to the small amount of light coming from the street lights. No, he was satisfied, he was alone. He tugged on the rope to indicate that Alexei should join him.

They moved carefully around the attic, stooping to keep as close to the sides as possible to avoid stepping on a loose plank which could make a noise and alert anyone below to their presence. Seeing a larger open space than the rest of the attic, Anatoly made his way slowly in that direction. He was rewarded when he saw the trap door.

He lay on his belly and slithered across the floor until he was next to it, adjusting his position to ensure he was lying next to the handle set into the door. Alexei moved next to him. "We'll wait until three before we move." A very quiet whisper directly into his ear. "Give anyone down there time to settle."

The two settled down to wait, relaxed but alert to any sounds. For a long time there were only the sounds of a house at night. They heard the footsteps at the same time. There was a muffled, brief conversation which seemed to come from directly beneath them. Anatoly glanced at his watch. He was surprised to see that it was almost three. He hadn't realised they had been there so long! His mind had been wondering to the Black Sea and thoughts of retirement. He mentally shook himself; time to concentrate on the job at hand. He put his mouth next to Alexei's ear. "Might be there's someone underneath us. We'll drop through and take care of him, then rush the bedrooms. That corridor will be behind as we land, don't get confused and go in the wrong direction. Ready?" A silent nod.

Anatoly put his left hand on the handle and gently pulled it out of the recess. He applied a bit more pressure and a crack opened. He tried to look downwards but his sight was too limited. He pulled it upwards a bit further and was rewarded with a view of a corridor and the top of a staircase as it reached the landing. He decided there was no point in going slowly and pulled the trapdoor all the way open, quietly laying it against the floor. He stood and straddled the opening, much as he would when parachuting from the hatch of a plane. He pulled out one of his Glocks and, thumbing back the hammer, placed it across his chest, holding it in place with his left hand. He gathered himself, pushing up and then placing his feet together, and dropped through the hatch.

He landed lightly on both feet, knees bent to absorb the impact and to maintain his balance. He saw a prone figure with a rifle pointing down the stairs, slightly to his right and about four feet in front of him. He swung the Glock down and pulled the trigger twice, just as the man was turning to see what the noise had been. He never had a chance to squeeze the trigger or make a sound. He heard Alexei drop down behind him and the shout at the same time as Alexei fired the soft plop and then the sound of rounds hitting flesh.

They moved quickly into the corridor melting into the shadows. As Anatoly turned and dropped to the floor he heard a door softly opening and glanced around to see Alexei disappear into the room. He appeared at the door after a couple of seconds to shake his head. Anatoly gestured for him to stay in the cover of the door, seeing him drop to his belly and peer round the corner to look down the corridor.

Anatoly watched the opposite corridor. He thought he heard the sound of a door handle and concentrated on the shadows. He felt that there was movement; he thought he heard the sound of a whispered question, the sound of someone slithering along the floor. Whoever it was stopped and he couldn't make out anything in the shadows. Not too bad, he thought, it's just as difficult for them as it is for us.

He knew that time was against them. He thought back to the sound he had heard and tried to work out the location. Judging by the noise and then the sound of someone crawling along the floor, he worked out it should be the door at the end. It was also a logical place as they could provide covering fire if someone went at them. That sorted, he started to think about numbers. They had tricked him with the movement of personnel from the property, but that couldn't concern him now. They had taken out two, there was definitely a third, but how many more? Another two, another three? If it was him, he would have another two stationed somewhere along the corridor. They had obviously been expecting them to come through the ground floor. There might be others on the ground level. "Yes", he thought. "That makes sense."

He glanced at his watch; it had been twenty minutes since they had dropped down. He only had one choice as he saw it; he would have to rush them. It had always been said that this was a good form of attack. Firstly, it was generally unexpected and secondly, because it was hard to take a good shot at someone running straight at you firing when he came. There wasn't much room to duck and dive, the corridors were not wide enough for that, but if they bounced off the walls they might create enough confusion to see them through. He slid across to Alexei and outlined his idea, telling him to stay close behind him and lay down covering fire to the sides. When they reached the door he was to watch their backs in case there were men downstairs. They would empty a magazine each along the corridor, he would fire low and Anatoly would fire at waist height. Once agreed he slid back to his original position and freed a spare magazine and his second Glock. He stood and took his aim.

CHAPTER THIRTY FIVE

"Attic, they're in the attic!"

James heard the shout as he was turning the door handle to check the others in the bedroom. "Shit, I forgot about the attic." He forced himself to move, instinct taking over from his recriminations. He pulled the Beretta from the waistband of his trousers and dropped to his knees, hugging the wall. In the dim light from the downstairs hall he could make out the two prone figures of the men placed at the top of the stairs. They were not moving or returning fire. "Shit" he thought again.

He slid slowly down the corridor until he reached the first of the doors on his left. "You OK, in there?" He whispered to the crack in the door. An equally quiet, "Yes," set his mind at ease. Glancing across at the opposite door, he saw the gun barrel move up and down. At least these two were still in place and effective. He retraced his steps to the bedroom door and tapped lightly on it. It opened a fraction. "Two down. Don't know if they're still in the attic. On your toes." The door closed as he finished and he started to make his way back down the hall. It seemed endless. He was vaguely aware that every sense he possessed was running at maximum. As more and more of the attic trapdoor came into view he covered it, at the same time scanning the dark areas of the corridor on the other side of the landing. He paused in his movement and listened. Nothing but the dark quiet, which enveloped a still house. He maintained his position, as still as the shadows on the wall.

A soft shuffle behind him had him swinging his gun hand around, reacting to the thought which immediately flashed across his mind that they had got behind him. It was, however, only George warning him that he was making his way down the corridor to join him on the other side. He moved his attention back to the trapdoor and the landing. Still nothing. He eased himself down onto his belly and, lying prone, took up his shooting position. As he lay there he calculated the risks. The back wall was still covered. There was still one man behind him in the corridor. Mike and Lizelle were in the room with the family. Ethan was somewhere downstairs, hopefully still alive. Where were they? Were they in the house? Were they still in the attic? Had they aborted after seeing that the house was still guarded? Alarm bells rang in his head. He signalled to George to stay, and he slid back to the bedroom door.

Maurice Johns

When the door opened to his tap he saw Lizelle's face above the barrel. "Get them all to move slowly and quietly to lie against this wall. I don't know where they are. It may be that they're still up there, if so, they might shoot down through the ceiling to see if they hit anything. Watch the window as well."

"Got it." No questions, no suggestions. He slid back down the corridor.

As he lay and stared down the corridor into the darkness, his mind started to play tricks on him. He knew this was normal and averted his gaze every few seconds. Shapes started to form in the shadows, then dissipate, only to reappear in another place. He risked a glance at his watch; he thought it had been twenty minutes since the alarm. If they were in the house they would have to move soon. It was perhaps an hour and a half until daylight,;the summer days were against them. The only sounds his straining ears could make out were that of the house settling. All perfectly normal. His mind was still racing. Did he dare try and move forward, exposing himself to the dim light shining up the stair well? Patience, he chided himself. Patience is the only answer. Someone would have to break cover and make the first move and he was determined it would not be him. After all, he reasoned, he still had an element of surprise left. Maybe not, another part of his brain told him. It was possible that they had gained access to the attic early enough to see the placements and numbers. But, his brain argued back, if they had seen that why would they then stay? Because they have a plan to neutralise us, came the answer. He allowed his mind to roam, hoping that one of the random thoughts would provide a solution to resolving the current stalemate.

He found that his eyes were focusing on one point and made a conscious effort to let them roam. He thought he saw a movement in the shadows and stared hard at it, then shifted his eyes to look through the periphery of his vision. Nothing. His eyes were still playing tricks on him. As he looked to his right, the movement dragged his gaze back. Yes, he thought, there had definitely been something, but he couldn't make out any shape against the dark backdrop. This time his eyes were dragged back to the right side, not by a definite change in the shadows, more a perceived change; something had altered. He looked across at George to see if he too had seen something. A nod and slight lifting of his gun confirmed his suspicions.

As he sighted down the barrel the air above his head was filled with buzzing and hissing of rounds, thudding into the floor and walls around him. Any muzzle flashes were disguised by the sound suppressors which only served to make the whistling passage of the bullets all the more weird. In place of a thud he heard a thwack of a round hitting and tearing flesh, accompanied by a grunt of pain. He held his fire and glanced to his right. George indicated his leg and signed that he was all right.

James sighted back down the corridor and heard the sound of a magazine being changed. He was sure that he heard two being slid into place. He took a chance and fired three rounds at the sounds. His only reward was silence, again. It took him a second to realise that two shapes, shadows, had detached from the walls and were moving rapidly towards his position. He led the leading figure, permitting the barrel of his gun to move of its own volition. He squeezed the trigger twice in rapid succession and missed. The figure was jinxing down the corridor, bouncing from wall to wall and was now on the landing. He was lit by the downstairs light. George opened fire at the same time and missed.

A second figure flashed across the landing and they both fired again. It was all too quick and they were on top of James and George before they could change position. James felt a sharp pain explode in his lower left side. He tried to turn onto his back and follow the racing figure of the first man. As he moved his gun his hand erupted in pain, his instinctive reaction to pull it closer to him, loosening his grip on the gun. He dimly saw the sneakered foot coming at his head and tried in vain to pull back. He couldn't move enough, he had pushed himself tightly against the wall in his efforts to turn and the shoe connected on the side of his head just above his ear. He saw stars and felt his grip on consciousness becoming tenuous. As he struggled to tighten his grip on his gun and focus his eyes he could still hear the silenced rounds impacting on walls. George had fallen silent, shots were coming from the door behind James but they fell silent as well. He felt a movement from the direction of the stairs and felt a deep despair. God, there were three of them, it was over. There was nothing between them and the bedroom door. He forced his befuddled brain to move his head to the stairs. It was Ethan. Thank God. "Ethan, shoot," he shouted, his voice a stranger to him. It had sounded more like a croak. He tried again. "Ethan, shoot." Better, and he saw Ethan line up and take a shot. He tried desperately to focus and turn back to look in the direction of the bedroom door, trying to lift his gun hand. He saw the figure in the rear jerk and stagger, reeling against the wall before recovering and moving forward again. The first figure was at the door, raising his foot to kick it in. James willed every muscle in his body to react. Something told him that Ethan did not have a clear shot; the second man was in the line of sight. Nothing he could do would raise his gun hand. He felt a frustration on a level he never experienced before. Two more shots and the figure in the rear fell to the floor. At the same time a well-placed kick sprung the door back on its hinges, banging against the wall. Now he was silhouetted against the window. James could not move, he felt a darkness overwhelming him. He could not focus his vision, even the sound of gunfire abated and faded as the dark covered his eyes.

ooooo....ooooo

Replacing the magazine after the initial fire he ran holding both hands out and firing in a controlled and methodical manner, trying to guess where they would be. Crossing the landing he saw the two lying in the prone position and fired at the them. He was moving so fast he was on top of them as he fired.

He had made it past the two lying on the floor. He knew they had both been hit and in passing had seen one trying to turn to take a shot. He had lashed out with his foot feeling a satisfying, solid connection and feeling the skull crack against the wall. He knew that Alexei was right behind him as he continued his headlong rush to the bedroom door at the end of the corridor where he had seem someone talking earlier.

He heard the shots behind him and Alexei stagger, hitting the wall and grunting in pain. He focused his mind on the door and the place just below the handle where he intended to kick it. He raised his foot and threw his full weight behind the kick. As his foot landed he heard another two shots and the sound of Alexei falling. The door swung inwards, it hit the wall, the impact sending it bouncing back towards him. He moved to his left to stop the door interfering with his shot. He scanned the room; it was bare, they had outwitted him. He knew it was over even as he continued his movement. Sheer survival instinct kicked in, moving his gun hand to sweep the room. As he moved he saw the muzzle flashes from two weapons directly in front of him. He had almost completed his move to the left, scanning the room with his eyes, seeing the two shadows on either side of the window, but no sign of the family.

He was hit from behind. A searing, red hot pain lancing through his right upper back and shoulder. It swung him further to the left and he was looking down at the frightened faces of two women. He wanted desperately to point his gun at them but felt it hanging uselessly in his right hand. He felt another shock, this time in his chest and looked down in disbelief at the two red spots blossoming outwards. He had been knocked back against the door and was still looking at his chest as he slid to the floor. As he sat, his legs folded underneath him. Watching the blood draining from his body, he saw two pairs of feet and willed his head up to look. He saw only the dark, menacing barrels of two guns being pointed at his head. He knew death was coming; there was no more pain, only a difficulty taking a breath and a thirst. He had never felt a thirst like this. He had failed. This thought was suddenly banished by a tremendous regret. He would never see his homeland again, his retirement *dacha* would remain empty. It was his last thought as he closed his eyes. Bloody shame.

CHAPTER THIRTY SIX

Thursday morning brought a warm sun to Edinburgh, the office already heating up with the heat coming through the windows. Andy checked the preparations, making sure there were files in front of the empty places around the table. It had been a hurried affair to collate all the information and get it printed in time for the morning meeting. He knew that it was important that all the information was presented in as concise a way as possible. Time was now beginning to turn against them.

The purpose of the meeting, he rehearsed, was to gain the co-operation of all the Chief Constables in putting together the plan to capture and roll up the chain of drug dealers. He knew that they had been told that their involvement and commitment was required, that was the reason for the delay and his nervous wait. He turned to the screens and checked that the links to Manchester and London were operational. Looking at the satellite imagery, he saw that the yacht was now very close to the Scottish coast. He forced himself to relax, to clear his mind, to be capable of dealing with the changing situation as it occurred.

Filling his mug with coffee he ran through the placements of men he had already made and decided that it was as satisfactory as it could be at this stage. Stewart walking into the room interrupted his reverie.

"Morning, all set?" He was carrying his vest and a small holdall. "Good day for it." He tried to smile, he appeared nervous and on edge.

"What's up? You thought of something we've missed?" Doubt crept into Andy's mind.

"No. Nothing like that." He paused. "You laugh at this and I'll thump you. I don't like flying. To be honest, the thought of the helicopter ride out to the ship is terrifying me."

Andy didn't laugh, he had his own share of phobias, but he felt he had to say something. "It'll be fine, what, maybe half an hour in the air. Then you'll be drinking coffee laced with rum." They both laughed at the idea, stopping when Jane Bond's voice came from the screen behind them.

"Morning, gentlemen, in fine spirits I see. We ready to go?" Andy assured her that everything was ready at his end and Farrington came on to say it was set in Manchester.

I, Plague

At precisely nine Andy's boss led a group of Senior Officers from all around the country into the briefing room. Andy and Stewart watched as they found their name cards and sat, each looking around at the set up.

Andy looked into the camera above the screen and saw Farrington nod that he was ready. It had been decided that Andy take the lead as the commencement of the operation would start in Scotland.

He looked around the room, silently commanding their attention. He introduced himself and Stewart. "Thank you for coming. I know that you want detailed answers to explain the odd requests which have been made of you in the last couple of days. The cancellation of leave and days off for the next few days, the requests for vehicles, all this I will explain to you now. The purpose of this gathering today is to start an operation against an organised crime gang who will be bringing a huge quantity of drugs into the country. The objective is to permit the drugs to be taken from the yacht on which they will arrive, follow them and arrest the groups to which they are delivered. That is the main thrust. We believe there are distribution centres from where the drugs are cut and sent to the street dealers. It is these centres we want. That's it in a nutshell. Before I go into details, I'll hand over to Commander Bond in London." He stood to the side of the screen while Jane Bond explained the full scope of the operation and the level of clearance and involvement of other agencies. As she spoke, Andy watched with interest the reactions on the faces before him. Some were stoical, others leaned forward in anticipation and one or two showed surprise. He could almost hear the calculators ticking over in their minds as they tried to calculate the cost. Jane finished by introducing the Manchester contingent, the camera showing all the occupants of that room, then handed over to Andy.

He pointed to the satellite image. "This vessel is the Alexander. We have reliable information that it is carrying upwards of 200 kilograms of cocaine. Approximate street value 20 million." Here there were some exclamations of shock. "It will be the biggest single shipment to have reached this country. This other ship is HMS Norfolk. Stewart here, along with other DEA officers, will board the Norfolk ready for the interception after the drugs have been offloaded." He stopped as the door opened and a flustered figure bustled into the room. "Sorry, flight was delayed." Finding the only vacant seat he sat.
Andy continued. "Good morning, Mr Carruthers. Mr Carruthers here is

an engineer and represents the phone companies. His role in this will soon become clear. Now, once the drugs have been offloaded, the Norfolk will take over the yacht. The chaps at GCHQ have assured us that they can and will block all radio and telephone communication, ensuring no messages are passed on. Once the drugs have landed, the vehicles will be followed to the distribution points. This, gentlemen, is where you come in. We will require static patrols along the major routes to monitor their progress and general heading. Also, we need teams to be standing by to move immediately we have information as to where they are being dropped. Again, we will block all communication in that area until we have everyone in custody. This is where Mr Carruthers comes into the picture. He will liaise with companies to ensure the phone masts in the areas we designate are closed down. If they can be of help GCHQ will assist in this.

"At this point, I would like to stress that any information passed down to your officers should only be of the nature of their immediate area of responsibility. As this is the start of the operation we are the most vulnerable and if we screw up then the rest of the country remains untouched. I appreciate this is a touchy point but we have to be realistic in facing the possibility of a leak and do everything we can to prevent it." He waited for the message to sink in.

Jane Bond broke in at that point. "I want to reinforce what Andy has said. Every police force in the country is on standby for this operation. If things go wrong up there we will have wasted a lot of time, effort and money for nothing. I will be less tactful than Andy and say that if you have any officers who are suspected of being the slightest bit bent, then they are not to be involved, or their involvement should be kept to the absolute minimum. We can control what the other side do, but we cannot control what our people do. Andy?"

"Thanks Jane," regretting the use of her first name as soon as he said it. "We currently have DEA officers along the Fife coast watching for any movements, which may lead us to the landing site. As soon as that has been identified we will contact your individual operation rooms with the details for the placement of the static patrols. I stress again that their only involvement is to report the vehicles passing. There will be covert surveillance of the suspect vehicles from the time they leave the landing area. When they arrive at a drop off point we will allow them to finish their business before we do anything. Only once the vehicles have left on their next leg will we move in. This should provide enough time for the teams to get into position, and for the communications to be shut down." He saw a question coming and preempted it. "Obviously, this will affect the civilian population in the area. They will lose the signal for their phones, but we hope it will only be for a short time. The vital thing for the success is that the suspects cannot under any circumstances be allowed to communicate with the outside world. Satellite phones? GCHQ will take care of that. Well, that gentlemen, is the overview of the operation. Details of the suggested deployment of your officers and vehicles are in the folders in front of you. But, I have to admit that we will be reacting as the situation develops. Speed and silence are the basics." He stopped talking and looked around the table, catching his own Chief Constable's eye. He nodded and mouthed a 'well done'. There was a raft of questions which he answered. Occasionally, Jane would interrupt to clarify a point, more to stress the amount of autonomy and the authority that had been placed in Andy and Stewart. He heard Farringtone doing the same question and answer session in Manchester.

Half an hour of questions and clarification and he had to interrupt them. "Time is now beginning to run against us. May I suggest that you all return to your forces and start the ball rolling? We will be here until the final whistle. You will have an open line at all times. Thank you for your time and good luck."

His boss asked if Andy minded if he returned to the operations room after he finished the briefing of his senior officers. Andy couldn't object, thinking it might be handy to have the old man there. A bit of extra clout could never go amiss. He and Stewart went over every detail again, trying to spot loopholes. They had to stop when they were interrupted by a constable informing them that Stewart's helicopter was about to land. A shake of the hand and wishes of good luck and he was off, looking distinctly pale at the prospect of his flight.

All he could then was wait. Wait and watch the blips on the screen draw closer and closer to the Scottish coast.

It took two hours of driving and flying to reach the *Norfolk* and be shown onto the bridge. It was Stewart's first time on a warship and the banks of electronics were confusing at first glance. The captain introduced himself as Commander Stephenson, and started his briefing with regards to their position and the position of the target vessel. He told Stewart that they would remain over the horizon until nightfall and then gradually work their way closer, eventually sending over a boarding party after the shipment had reached shore and they had been reassured about the communications blackout. As there was nothing much for Stewart to do, he accepted an offer for one of the junior officers to show him around the ship and make sure he got something to eat in the wardroom.

The junior lieutenant took the Captain at his word and led Stewart through a bewildering array of corridors, up and down ladders and through countless hatches, showing him every inch of the ship in which he obviously had so much pride. It was an exhausted Stewart who was eventually deposited in the wardroom in time for an afternoon snack as the ship's watches changed. He tried to answer the questions thrown at him by the officers as to the full extent of the night's work. He answered as best he could, confident that these men, at least, would not be on the payroll of Gregori.

Darkness had fallen when he was roused from a sleep in one of the armchairs and taken to the bridge. The Captain informed that they were now closing in on the yacht, which was currently sitting a kilometer off the coast. He also saw Andy's face peering from a screen mounted on the bulkhead at the rear of the bridge.

"Evening, Andy. All set to go on your end?"

"Evening, Stewart. You don't look any worse for wear after your trip." Smiling, he continued. "Your feed is going through to London and Manchester, also the tech boys have all the information they need for the jamming of the electronics as soon as we start. Looks good so far. Any problems your end, Captain?"

The Captain assured him that everything was in hand. A contingent of Royal Marines were going to be the boarding party, and they had been briefed that resistance might be encountered. Their officer, however, was confident that things would go smoothly. They had been rehearsing for several days.

Stewart changed the screen to a satellite image of the yacht lying close to shore and was surprised at the clarity of the image.

"That's very good, we'll be able to see the transfer. We should be able to use it as evidence."

He heard Jane Bond's voice and switched the screen back. "Correct, Stewart. I want you to be careful out there. Let the Marines secure the yacht before you go digging around. Better safe than sorry, eh?"

Stewart assured her that he would be careful, adding that he might be too seasick to do anything anyway. This brought laughter from all the men on the bridge. The Captain assured him. "Like a millpond out there tonight, you won't feel a thing."

It certainly looked calm enough from the vantage point of the bridge, but Stewart could feel the motion of the ship under his feet and doubted that the journey across to the yacht would be anything but smooth. He tried to take his mind off the ordeal.

"How are the ground units, Andy?"

"All set and waiting. We have observed four transit vans converging on the beach where the Zodiacs were seen. We have their details, all hired vehicles, but they should be easy enough to follow. The consensus of opinion is that the drugs will be split and the vans will head for Glasgow, Manchester, Birmingham and London. The guys identified as part of the operation have all been observed making for areas where it is possible that the drugs will be delivered and cut before hitting the streets. As they say, so far so good." Andy turned away from the screen and spoke to someone unseen. "Right, I'm going to switch to the satellite, it seems the Zodiacs have left the shore and are heading out. This could be it, good luck Stewart." The same was echoed through the feeds from England. Stewart felt the butterflies flutter in his stomach as he made a final check of his weapon, and was shown down to the forecastle where the seamen and Marines were waiting.

This was, as the Captain had described it, the ticklish part of the operation; to allow the loaded Zodiacs to reach the ship and to apprehend the yacht before it gained too much on the boarding party. Updates were constantly fed down to Stewart as the packages were placed on deck and then the loading into the Zodiacs started. At this point the boarders were lowered onto the sea to float 100 metres from the ship, waiting for the word to move in. There was a lot of nervous anticipation and Stewart could hear weapons being checked and re-checked as they waited for the go ahead.

Stewart endured the gentle movement of the boat as he waited. There was only a gentle swell running and he felt no discomfort, at least, not as much as he had imagined. It was forty-five minutes before the word came over the radio that the off loading was complete and they should start their approach. The tension in the air around Stewart was palpable. They were moving slowly, muffled engines barely discernible above the noise of the water passing under the boats. Eventually he could see the outline of the yacht. It was still stationary with no obvious movement on the decks. It had switched on all the lights now that the clandestine part of their job was over, confident that nothing would be found on board.

After an eternity of barely moving, the radio crackled to life and the order to move in came. It also came with the warning that the yacht appeared to be getting under way. Throttles were opened and the distance closed rapidly. The yacht was gaining speed as they drew alongside in well practised movements. The boats jumped and heaved as they fought the wake thrown back from the bows of the yacht. Lines quickly secured them to the side, and the Marines started to clamber up and over the railings onto the decks.

Stewart was unceremoniously hauled over the railing and landed ungraciously on his backside. His first thought as he righted himself was that the picture on the satellite feed would produce gales of laughter from those watching. However, this thought was immediately banished as a shouted warning went up in Russian. He watched the figure scamper away to the bridge. No shots were fired as the rules of engagement had firmly stated that they were only to fire in self-defense. The Marines moved down each side of the yacht, each to their own preordained points of search. A brief sound of an AK47 being fired and swiftly silenced was the only sound that broke the silence.

Stewart moved in the shadows of a Marine in the direction of the bridge. Once inside he saw that two men were seated in a corner with a brace of Marines looming threateningly over them. The Marine Captain instructed his men to shut down all electronic equipment on the bridge, including the GPS device. As the minutes passed they were joined by the rest of the Marines herding another five men onto the bridge, shepherding them into the captain's cabin. The Sergeant reported one civilian dead, the one who had managed a brief burst of fire, but no casualties on their side. A seaman from the *Norfolk* took over the con and steered the yacht into the seaward side of the warship. The prisoners were quickly and efficiently transferred across and then joined by Stewart who made his way directly to the bridge. It all appeared to have gone smoothly, the whole exercise taking less than fifteen minutes. He felt a sense of anti-climax as he went through the door into the red lighting of the bridge.

On the screen the picture was split between Andy and Jane Bond.

"Good work, Stewart, how's the bum? Must be a bit tender after that landing." He could hear the laughter in the background and stifled laughter from the occupants of the bridge.

He managed a rueful grimace, rubbing his behind. Jane continued, "The Captain says that it went better than expected. No signs from the shore that anything was picked up and there was radio or telephone traffic from the yacht. Andy?"

Andy took over. "They have loaded the vans and they are driving off as we speak. Your part went well, now it's down to us. Captain says he'll put into Rosyth to get rid of the prisoners and the yacht. Expect you'll be having a drop of Navy rum while the rest of us sit here all night."

Stewart was indeed issued with a Navy tot of rum after he signed off. It had all gone so easily. He discussed it with the Captain. They agreed that it was better this way. The planning and the training had paid dividends. Stewart went down to the mess where the Marines were also indulging in a tot of rum and thanked them before going to the wardroom to have a sandwich and coffee to wait for the arrival in port, early that morning, and then it would be back to the operations centre.

As Stewart was beginning to relax, Andy and his team were being kept busy in the Operations Room in Edinburgh. There was a constant stream of radio traffic from the mobile units as the vans were followed to the motorway and then south over the Forth Road Bridge. Andy was glad that the vehicles were all hired and modern. It made the job of tracking them easier. The GPS details of each vehicle had been obtained from the rental company and they were now using them to track them. It permitted the tail vehicles to maintain a good distance. On top of that there were uniformed patrols stationed on the major roads, which they were expected to use, and they radioed in their sightings as the vehicles passed them.

Glasgow, being the nearest city, would be the first drop off point. It would also be the most important, because any breakdown in their communications could alert the rest to the possibility of raids. Andy felt the responsibility weighing down on him and was glad the Chief Constable was still in the room. He was sitting quietly, not interfering, but at least he was available, if needed. He had another hour before they approached the outskirts of the city. He checked that the others were following the routes of the other vehicles. They had split; two looked as if they were heading for the faster West Coast route, and one heading towards the East Coast road. He had time to grab a cup of coffee before starting the operation to close in on the Glasgow vehicle.

He was surprised when he saw that it was almost four on the Friday morning. It hardly seemed possible that so much time had passed since Stewart's departure that morning. Sipping his coffee, he checked around the room; everyone appeared to be alert and ready for whatever might come. He looked at the screen and could see the offices in London and Manchester. They were sitting watching the satellite tracking much as he was, but he knew that would change when the Glasgow part began. This was the crucial first stage.

CHAPTER THIRTY SEVEN

When he looked at the clock, Gregori saw that it was five o' clock. His yacht and its load should be very close to the Scottish coast. He had planned the operation himself, and knew that they would only close on the coast at eleven that evening. Allowing for the one hour time difference that would be midnight his time. He had plenty of time to kill until he received confirmation that the drugs had landed. He intended to pass some of the time trying to find out what the delay was with the ship leaving Southampton for the Middle East. He was not concerned about the delay. It carried hundreds of containers and the ones with the arms were almost at the bottom of the pile. Besides, the false papers would fool most customs officials if they chose to examine goods in transit. There had never been a problem before, and he had no reason to expect problems this time. The delay in the sailing time was more a frustration than a concern.

He picked up his phone and again tried to ring the captain. Still unable to get through, he demanded that his secretary keep trying the satellite link and e-mails. Time was money.

He poured his first Vodka of the day and tilted the glass to his reflection in the window. Anatoly had done a good job. The family should all be dead by now. He expected Anatoly to wait until his return to brief him fully. But that would probably only be on the Friday.

Frustrated by the delay in getting hold of the ship's captain, he started phoning all his lieutenants in Britain to ensure that they were ready to receive the shipment and start the process of supply to the streets. They all assured him they were going to personally oversee the arrival and distribution. Most of the drugs would be on the streets by Saturday and Sunday, in the case of the cities furthest south. At last he had made inroads into the last great bastion of Western Europe; he could feel pleased with himself.

After three vodkas in his now darkened office he opened the bottom drawer of his desk and pulled out an old file. Opening it, he spread the photographs on the desk. They were mainly of hinmself and Anatoly in their Army days. Some were the run of the mill taken in camps and on leave, others were of the two of them posing like big game hunters over their kill. He would miss Anatoly when he retired. He had tried to offer him a job in the organisation, but he had steadfastly refused, saying he was completely finished and wanted to do no more than laze about and fish. Gregori could not blame him; lately he had been thinking along the same lines. It had been many years since he had been able to relax. It was a self-imposed regime, and one which was hard to break with. He supposed he should start thinking about taking a wife and gaining some semblance of normality. He had worked hard to get to his present position and the sacrifices on the way had been many. He thought it dated back to the days in Afghanistan when he had first started out. He had cut out the middleman in all the operations he had built up and then become obsessed with the control of his organisation.

Everything he had ever done had been to tighten his grip, and to make ever increasing amounts of money. But sitting there he reasoned, what was the use of the vast fortune he had accumulated if he could not enjoy the benefits? His whores were all well and good at the time but they were only interested in keeping him happy, they were not interested in him as a person. It was his own fault, he admitted; he had always maintained a distance and instilled a fear in those who worked for him.

He poured another shot of vodka, and decided that, after the British operation was up and running, he would pick a couple of trusted lieutenants and give them more control. He thought over who could do the job and Yuri immediately sprang to mind. He had been with him for several years, joining him on the run from Interpol and most Western police forces. He had adapted well to the environment, and had soon come to the attention of Gregori as a person who could get any job done. It had not been long before he was at the right hand giving advice and gradually becoming the nearest thing he had to a friend. Maybe now was the time to give him more.

He had long since put the folder and thoughts of relaxing away when the phone rang. He could tell it was a satellite call and he received the news that the shipment had been offloaded without a hitch. Checking the clock, he knew that the timetable had been kept to, almost to the minute. Midnight in Kiev meant he could still go to one of the clubs and have a drink. Now, all he had to do was wait for a few days for the distribution down to the streets before he could start raking in the profit.

The only cause for concern, and it had developed into a full blown concern, was that he had been unable to raise the captain of the ship stuck in Southampton. It was unusual for communications to be down so long, and they should have sailed by now, on their way to the Bay of Biscay. He decided to phone his man in the South of England and send him to see what the problem was. After that he would go to the club.

I, Plague

CHAPTER THIRTY EIGHT

Andy, and everyone else in the room, was on edge. There was a building tension in the air, cloudy with forbidden cigarette smoke. It had been agreed to relax the strict no smoking rule on this occasion. No-one could afford to be out of the room for the length of time it took to leave the building and have a break.

The vehicle was now on the outskirts of Glasgow city centre. Andy took control of the microphone and started to direct the following vehicles into positions to parallel the suspects and placed cars behind and in front of it. With the streets being quiet this early in the morning, he knew he had to maintain distance between all the vehicles and keep rotating them just in case they had been seen. He relied heavily on the help of the Strathclyde police officers sitting next to him for the local geography and street layout. He left them to direct the vans containing the armed officers.

As the vehicle moved through the sleeping streets of Glasgow, Andy took a moment to turn to Carruthers. "You guys OK to take down the masts?" A silent nod.

"As soon as we have a location, it'll take about five minutes."

Jane Bond cut in. "Andy, I just heard from GCHQ that there's no unusual chatter in your area. Looks like you're in the clear so far. They're standing by."

"Looks like the target's slowing to make a turn, sir." He turned back to the screen. They had stopped momentarily and moved slowly forward for a short distance before coming to a complete stop.

"We need a close up of that location, now." The screen changed and the image zoomed in on a warehouse. He heard the clicking of the keyboards around him and forced himself to wait.

"Got it." the officer to his right announced. "Warehouse, distributes glassware around the country. Nothing on them, it appears to be a legitimate business." A box appeared on the screen with the name and address of the company. Andy heard Carruthers on the phone and looked to get his nod as he hung up. He started to direct all the mobile units to close in on the building. He watched as they all came to a halt in the streets, surrounding the warehouse. He could almost see, in his mind's eye, the officers moving to cover all sides.

He heard the reports coming in as each unit reached and secured their position. He could hardly contain his impatience as he waited for word that communications had been taken down. He knew impatience was useless. They should have enough time as the drugs were unloaded and checked, but he could not help himself.

Now that everyone was in position the silence was absolute. Everyone jumped at the shrill tone of the phone ringing. Carruthers picked it up said thanks and told Andy, "Masts and exchanges in the area are down, we've gone ultra cautious, can't make a call in a ten square mile area."

"GCHQ reports no traffic" - over the screen from London.

Andy took a breath, looked around the room, finally resting his gaze on his Chief Constable. He gave a reassuring smile and nod.

"Right." He switched to the tactical frequency. "All units, *GO,GO,GO.*"

On the screen he saw two of the vehicles pick up speed and head towards the warehouse. He knew these were to serve as the battering rams for the doors. Controlled instructions and replies flooded the room. One of the microphones picked up the sound of a door being rammed, followed by shouted commands, and identification by the officers as armed police. Then, what everyone in the room had been dreading, the sound of gunfire.

CHAPTER THIRTY NINE

For the men surrounding the warehouse and the Superintendent sitting in his control vehicle, it was a usual surge of adrenalin and nerves that set their bodies tingling as sweat soaked into the material covering them. Scalps felt itchy under the helmets, hair sticking to their scalps.

Superintendent Monaghan was praying fervently that the black out of communications would not affect the dedicated radio frequency they were using. He had been reassured countless times of this fact but had learned that anything could wrong. He was silent as he watched the signal disappear from his mobile phone. Holding his breath involuntarily he pressed the send button and asked for an update. To his relief, he heard the various units respond. Then came the command to go, broadcast to each of his men. Through the microphones he heard the movements and the vehicles starting their drive to burst through the doors.

He was already moving to the front door as the vehicle burst through and he was in time to follow his men into the warehouse. The lights were brighter than he expected. He saw that mobile floodlights had been placed around a series of trestle tables in the middle of the room. Men were standing in a frozen tableau around packages laid out in rows on the table. Another group was frozen in the act of unloading the van. The scene remained static for what felt like an eternity before the group around the table dived to the floor, reaching and scrabbling around on the floor under the tables and coming out with automatic weapons, which started unleashing a virtual hail of bullets around the building. Monaghan dived to one side and took refuge behind some packing cases, quickly looking around to check his men were doing the same. All his officers opened fire simultaneously, a cacophony of sound from all points around the warehouse. He heard sounds of his own men being hit, shouts for the wounded to be pulled clear.

Orders for fire and movement were given, and he listened to the reports coming in about the casualties inflicted. He heard a vehicle start up and an order given to stop it. A burst of heavy firing to his left and the idling of a motor told him all he needed to know about the attempt to drive out.

He squirmed around and joined the unit nearest to him. They were breaking into pairs and moving forward, firing as they went, but the level of fire had decreased significantly, stopping altogether as he stood to move forward.

It was carnage which greeted him as he stepped around the cover of the packing cases. There were bodies strewn around the table, multiple gunshot wounds leaking their bloody contents onto the concrete floor in ever expanding pools. Only a handful of men were standing with their hands raised as high as they could reach above their heads, discarded weapons lying at their feet.

The vehicle which had started up contained more bodies, the insides splattered with impact of rounds hitting and ripping their way through yielding skin and tissue.

The reports kept coming in as each area was secured. External units reported that no-one had left the building. Sweeps were being carried out of every nook and cranny until it was reported that the whole building was clear and secured. He then spoke directly to the operations room and informed them that the operation had been successful. It was an unnecessary act, as he knew that the transmissions and pictures from the head cameras had been fed back to them. Still, protocol had to be observed.

Monaghan walked around the cavernous interior of the warehouse, stopping to talk to a wounded officer, watching the paramedics rush in and aid those who had fallen. By the time he had checked on all the men, he had found that only two had been killed, a surprise for him when he considered the ferocity of the firefight. One he was informed had been unlucky, a fraction of an inch either side and all he would have was a puckered scar. As it was, the bullet had severed the femoral artery and he had bled out before the firefight was over. The other had caught one in the eye, the shattered eyepiece of the visor covering the damage. Again, probably a lucky shot, but that was no consolation. However, there were nine down with varying degrees of gunshot wound, fortunately only one serious. He thought that he should count himself lucky; it could have been far worse.

He heard the sound of his Chief Constable's voice over the radio, congratulating him and all his men on an operation well done. Next came the sound of more vehicles approaching, and squads of both uniformed and plain clothes officers descended on the scene. Monaghan knew that most of these were Narcotics officers and they would be counting and weighing the haul.
It had been a long night and now, with the action finished, he felt weary

as he made his way back to his command vehicle. The day was not over for him. All the paperwork had to be completed. Reports filed on the use of the firearms, detailed accounts from every officer had to be taken. Yes, it would be many hours before he saw his bed.

Back in the control room a stunned silence pervaded the atmosphere. The ferocity of the response had been unexpected. A gun fight of that magnitude was virtually unheard of in the country. Andy broke the silence, addressing the screen. "You get all that, Mike?" He saw the affirmation. "Probably be you next, better pass the word down on what to expect." He turned to Jane. "Still quiet? Did we manage complete surprise?"

"Yes, Andy. All quiet, you and your team seem to have achieved all the goals. Please pass on our sympathies and condolences to the men. Mr Carruthers, thank you for your help. As we get the all clear from the site we can enable the phones again."

Andy knew that even though his part was over, he would stay and monitor the screens, watching as the operation unfolded in the other parts of the country. He was lost in thoughts about the casualties and if they could have been prevented when he heard the Chief Constable clear his throat.

"I just wanted to say that it was a job well done. All of you. I know we have taken a hit among the firearms unit but no-one could have foreseen that kind of firepower. Take a break, have a rest and then we'll start the mop up, get things ship-shape for our friends the prosecutors. Again, well done everyone." When he finished he came and sat down next to Andy. "You know you couldn't have seen that coming, don't you? Mustn't let it get to you. I know, easy to say, but it's true, can't let it get to you." He put a hand on Andy's shoulder as he stood. "I know its useless telling you to go home, so I'll get you a coffee and something to eat."

CHAPTER FORTY

James became aware of two things. His head felt as if it had split open, it throbbed and ached with a vengeance. Then there was a deep seated burning in his side; surely someone was digging a red hot poker into him. Opening his eyes took an effort of will, the light that seeped through his eyelids hurt and he squinted. Even the effort of squinting brought waves of pain from the side of his head. He closed his eyes and listened. At least that didn't hurt. Wherever he was, it was quiet. That it was daytime was obvious from the light. He tore his mind away from the pain and remembered what had happened. The recollection of the door being kicked in, the one man falling, the shots but nothing else.

He had to find out what had happened, and again forced his eyes open. Trying to ignore the pain it caused, he turned his head on the pillow. He was in the room he had been staying in. Sunlight was filtering through the curtains at the window. He remembered that the room was east facing, so that meant that it was some time in the morning. He turned his head to the other side and saw Monique sitting in an armchair close to the bed. Her chin was on her chest and he watched the rise and fall of her chest. How long had he been there was the first question that came to mind. How were the others? He remembered George being hit. Obviously the family was all right, otherwise Monique would not be there. He turned on his left side and pushed his elbow under his torso, trying to lever himself into a more upright position. He thought he was going to be sick, the pain was so great, but he made it into a position where he was sitting leaning back on the pillows. After a few, long moments the pain eased and he wiped his face to clear the sweat which had burst from his pores. An involuntary groan escaped from his mouth as another wave of pain stabbed through his head.

"Don't move." With the words he felt a soothing hand on his forehead, and he opened his eyes again to see Monique leaning over him. "Stay still and I'll go and get the doctor." She left before he could say anything. God, all he wanted was some water. His tongue rasped against the roof of his mouth like sandpaper. He closed his eyes again to wait for someone to come. It felt like a long time before he heard the door open and he opened his eyes to the doctor approaching his bed.

"Getting to be a habit, this fixing you up." He was the same doctor who taken care of his shoulder after the street shooting. "You'll be wanting something to drink?" He didn't wait for a reply, lifting a glass with a straw to his mouth. He drunk thirstily, allowing the water to roll around his mouth before it was absorbed into the blotting paper that coated his throat. The straw was removed too quickly. "That's enough for now, you'll be sick if you drink too quickly. Right, let's have a look." He pulled back the sheet and undid the dressing, ripping the adhesive bandages off quickly, causing as much pain as the wound. "Good, how's the head? Still sore, I'll bet. You took quite a knock there, but nothing you won't get over. I'll give you a shot for the pain, but I'd say you'll be just fine. A bit of bed rest and you'll be on your feet in no time."

As the needle pinched his forearm, James managed a croak. "Thanks, doc. How are the others?"

"George will be good as new in a week or so. Bernie is up and about, a shoulder wound. Mike will tell you about the others. I have to get back to my practice." He turned to Monique as he packed his bag. "You know what to do, try and keep him in bed." He said his goodbyes and left.

As he went out of the door, it remained open and a stream of people entered. Monique was first to the bed and held the straw to his lips. Again it was pulled away before he could quench his thirst. Mike plonked himself on the side of the bed. "Well, my friend, you gave us quite a scare for a while. Looked worse than it was, according to the quack. How are you doing?"

James was about to reply when he was enveloped in a world of pain which left him gasping. Mona was contrite as she pulled herself from his chest. "I'm so sorry, I was so pleased to see you, I didn't think." He managed to gasp that it was all right, taking her hand to reassure her. Once he had got control over his breathing, he asked about the others.

The reply was short and to the point. "Two dead. George and Bernie will be OK. Both gunmen dead. Everyone else is fine. A bit shocked." He turned and looked at the others. "But they'll be fine, given time. It was close. Too close."

James held Mike's gaze. "It's my fault. I forgot about the bloody attic. Should have had someone there, or at the very least, watching. Jesus, those guys are dead because I forgot. Almost came to a bad end for you too." He looked at Lou and his family. "I'm sorry."

Mike tried to dismiss it. "You can't think of everything. Ethan and I didn't think about it either, none of us did. They were good, though. Have to give them that; very good."

"What about the doctor? Is he all right with all this?" He looked to Lou for the answer.

"Of course. He's signed the death certificates as well. I'll make sure they get a decent send off. Make sure something goes to whoever they left behind." He paused and was about to say something else. Monique took over.

"It's not your fault. There's nothing to blame yourself for. We've all talked it through while you were out and we agree on that." She smiled at him. "There is one thing." She watched his confused look. "You broke your promise. You didn't take care of yourself and then you didn't come to get us. We'll have to think up some kind of punishment for that."

He talked with them for a few minutes and then, pleading fatigue, asked to be left alone, motioning for Mike, Ethan and Lizelle to stay.

After the door closed, he asked to be pulled more upright. Once settled, he asked "You got our message on the way? Any sign that there are others? How soon can we get going?"

"Slow down." Mike held up his hand to stop the questions. "Yes, the message is on its way. No, there's no sign of anyone else nosing around. And we can only get going when you've got your strength back. There's plenty of time."

"Who took the guy down, the one who kicked the door?"

Lizelle replied to that. "Both of us, Mike and me. We hit him on the chest. Could have been Ethan, though. He was firing at the same time. Anyway, he went down before he could do anything. Funny thing." She looked at Mike who nodded. "When he burst into the room he had, and I swear it's true, a look on his face, almost as if he knew he had been tricked. Might have been the light, but I swear I saw it. Mike, tell them."

"She's right. It was as though, when he saw the bare room, he knew he had been tricked. Anyway, it's done, finished. The house has even been cleaned. Hardly a sign of what happened. By the way, do you know what day it is?"

"Some time on Thursday. The way the sun is, probably before one. Why?"

"I thought so; it's Friday, you've been out for over twenty six hours. Lazy old bastard."

"Less of the old." James smiled. "But seriously, let's book some flights; we have to allow time for the visas to be processed. Lizelle, is that a problem for you, as a South African passport holder?"

"No" she replied. "My mother was English, so I've got a British passport as well. It helps to get around a bit easier. There won't be any problems there. Are you sure you're going to be fit?"

"Give me a week. Things will move faster once the stitches are out, I'm probably as weak as I am now because of blood loss. Am I right, Mike?" Mike agreed that had been the main source of concern.

"OK, if we're agreed on a week, or a bit longer, depending on visas, you lot can bugger off and let an old man have some rest." They stood to leave and he stopped them. "I could use some more water before you go, maybe something to eat later on. I'm not hungry now, but some food will help the healing process." Ethan gave him some water, grinning at him while he had the straw in his mouth.

"He never stops with the orders, even on his sick bed. He's got us all working like slaves to cater for his every whim."

He managed a wan smile as he closed his eyes. God, he felt tired.

CHAPTER FORTY ONE

Lunchtime on Friday, and Andy's eyelids felt like sandpaper as they dropped over his eyes. He had been able to grab a shower and a change of clothes as they waited for the two vans to near Manchester and Birmingham. The fourth van was well down the M1 when Manchester's suburbs were reached. It had been agreed that the approach to the apprehension, in the other centres, would be different. They would attempt infiltration of the premises before breaching the doors. In that way, it was hoped that casualties among law enforcement would be minimised.

Andy was as tense as he had been when his own operation had been underway, as he listened to the movements of the Manchester vehicles. It followed the same path as before; the net tightening as the target building was identified. The only difference to the whole thing was the wait as teams climbed to the roof and prepared to ab-sail through skylights and enter through the high windows.

When it started there was the babble on the radio and again the sound of gunfire. This time, however, the suppressing fire was heavier and the sound of the doors being rammed was loud in the quiet that followed. Cameras relayed the pictures of men surrendering. A similar layout was revealed. All the drugs were present. There were no casualties from gunfire, although one officer had sprained an ankle landing after his ab-sail. Manchester had been a complete success.

Within an hour an almost identical operation was undertaken in Birmingham with the same success. The fact that there were no warnings sent was relayed through London. Communications remained down.

During the wait for the London end of the operation, Stewart reported from the yacht. He demonstrated how the packets of drugs had been hidden in a false hull. The crew of the yacht had not broken their silence, but the representative of the prosecutor's office confirmed that they had enough evidence from the satellite imagery and the seized drugs to achieve a successful prosecution. Charges of murder would be added to the already long list being faced by the men arrested in the Glasgow raid.

As Andy relaxed again to await the last phase, he felt the fatigue wash over him. He resisted attempts to persuade him to leave and at least lie down for a short time. He knew that if he relaxed to that extent then there was a distinct possibility that he would sleep through the end of the long ordeal. It was now a matter of pride for the Metropolitan Police to emulate the success of their provincial colleagues.

As the van drove into Greater London, Andy could see Jane and her colleagues begin to tense up. They had slightly different problems in that the traffic in London was building towards the afternoon rush hour.

This was playing havoc with the followers, and getting vehicles into the right place at the right time. They did have the advantage of having more manpower and vehicles than the other forces. However, the strain was beginning to tell on the faces of those in the centre of London.

This time it took an hour and a half before the van pulled into a building. Again it was a warehouse, and again there was an interminable wait for communications to be taken out of operation. While they were waiting, the armed units had positioned themselves and reported all ready. One wry comment, that the loss of signal for the mobile phones in the area was going to pay hell in the morning, was heard. The resulting laughter was a release of tension.

The go-ahead was ordered and, after a heavy but thankfully brief firefight, it was reported that the building and suspects were secured. A few brief exchanges and Jane Bond came on the link.

"Well, gentlemen, that's it. It went well, it all seems like a bit of an anti-climax now, doesn't it? We've had a bit of a calculation and figure that we've taken 225 Kilograms. I've no idea of the street value after it's cut, but I'm informed it totals tens of millions. That, plus the arms shipment we've impounded, and a really big hole has been made in Gregori's pocket. I hope this is enough to delay any further action on his part. As an afterthought, we will now have a problem as supply on the streets dries up. However, I'm sure our friends in Narcotics will be glad to take the strain. Well done to all of you, and thank you. We'll meet again after we've sorted through all the bumf."

The screens went blank and Andy knew it was time to go home. There were congratulations and pats on the back as he passed through the building to the car park. As he sat in his car, he realised he had not slept for over thirty six hours. He knew that any explanations to his wife would have to wait until the morning.

I, Plague

CHAPTER FORTY TWO

The next thing James knew was that there was only a little light filtering through his eyelids. He took stock. The headache had gone, and there was only a dull ache in his side. He opened his eyes. The weak light was coming from a reading lamp on the bedside table. Monique was sitting in the same chair but was, this time, reading a book. She looked a treat, her loose hair shining in the light, the skin on her face taking on an alabaster appearance, almost translucent. As he watched her long fingers turning a page he questioned how a woman such as her could possibly fall in love with someone like him. They were worlds apart, maybe not so much now, but psychologically, as far apart as any two people could get. He sighed as he thought he would never understand women. It must have been an audible sigh because she looked up from her book and saw him watching her.

"Awake at last. I thought you were going to sleep for another day. Thirsty?" She stood and put the straw to his mouth. With relief he noticed that she did not draw it away immediately.

As he sipped thirstily at the straw, she told him it was now the Friday night and the time was nine o' clock. He still felt drained, and weak, and satisfied himself watching her, listening to her talk, not really paying too much attention to the content. Letting it wash over him. He had to admit he enjoyed the normality of the scene. Eventually, he came to his senses and interrupted her.

"You and Mona, you really all right? Poor kid, she's seen more than her fair share of killing in the last year or so."

"She'll be fine, she's already asking if this means she can go to your place. If you think it would be safe for her to go, I think it would be a good idea. Anyway, I said I'd ask you."

"Of course it will be all right. I could phone Madge and tell her. They'll take good care of her. There shouldn't be any more risk now. Can I talk to her? No-" - he stopped her before she started - "-I'm fine, and I'd really like to speak to her." She stood but he stopped her at the door. "I'm sorry I didn't keep my promise to you."

She came back to the bed. "Don't be silly, I was only trying to cheer you up. Darling James, you can be such an idiot." She put her head on his shoulder, her words becoming muffled. "I was so scared when I saw you lying there in all that blood, we all were. After they shot him, and you didn't come to the door, that was my first thought. You promised, why weren't you there? I guess I got a bit worked up."

When Mona came into the room he gestured for her to sit on the side of the bed. He thought she looked pale and drawn, not how a young girl should look.

"I wanted to ask you a couple of things, OK?" She nodded. "I've been thinking that I should maybe go home to get over this. I was thinking, if you wanted to, you could come with me. Maybe call the other girls and meet up. They could stay at the house, if they wanted. Then you could exercise Darling for me. How does that sound?" At last her face lit up, enthusiasm spreading and bringing a glow to her cheeks. He could see tears forming in her eyes despite the thought of going away.

She was trying hard to hold them in, but one escaped and rolled down her cheek. She angrily brushed it away. He continued quickly. "The other thing I wanted to ask you is for a favour, a big favour. You don't have to say yes, because I know you'll be busy. The thing is, I think I need some TLC, you know, tender loving care, and someone to look after me, be my nurse, if you like. My head still spins when I move and, well, I hoped you might be my helper. What do you think?"

"Of course I'll help. But what about Mons there? She's been doing it up to now."

"All right, come here." She lay next to him and he put an arm around her shoulder, allowing her head to rest in the crook of his arm. "I think Mons has had enough of me, besides, I think she needs a rest. Think you can handle it? I'm a bad patient. I probably won't do what you tell me, and I get grumpy having to stay in bed." He saw Monique at the door smiling at him.

"You'd better do what I tell you, or there'll be trouble." She nestled closer. "I'm not hurting you am I?"

"No. A big hug is just what I need." They stayed like that, Monique leaving them. He waited a few minutes and quietly said. "How are you doing, really? You've seen too much for someone your age. Probably seen more than a lot of soldiers and policemen." He waited for her to speak.
Eventually she did, but put her arm over his chest before she spoke,

pulling herself closer. "I was really scared when I heard the shooting, and then saw the man in the door. I still am scared. I dream about it, and sometimes I hear myself screaming and that wakes me up. I don't know what to do about it. Daddy says he'll send me to a psychologist. He says it will help."

"Yep, that could be the answer." He thought about what he could say next. "You know, I get scared all the time. And I have bad dreams where I wake up scared. But they get better; I talk to Darling and tell her all about them."

"I bet you don't cry all the time, though."

That was a hard one to answer.

"Just because no-one sees me, doesn't mean I don't cry. You know the movie *"Ghost"?* I use that when I feel like crying. I always cry during it. That's why I watch it on my own." He looked down and saw the doubt on her face. "It's true. If you don't believe me, we'll watch it together. I bet you that I'll cry more than you. But you have to promise not to tell anyone. Deal?"

She giggled. "Not even Mons or Pippa?" He shook his head.

"OK, deal."

Mona was quiet for a long time, and James had been on the verge of sleep himself when he looked down at her to see that she had fallen asleep. He closed his eyes but the door opened before sleep claimed him.

Monique came across to the bed. "Sorry, I didn't mean to wake you. I thought I'd better get her back to her own bed." She made a move to wake the sleeping Mona.

"No, leave her. She's exhausted; a good sleep will do her the world of good." He found himself whispering, not wanting to disturb her. "Did you know about the nightmares?"

She didn't, and James persuaded her to let her sleep in his arms. She pulled the duvet over the two of them, telling him she would stay for a while and pulling a chair to the other side of the bed. "You're really very good with kids. I don't know what it is, I've listened and watched, maybe it's because you treat them like everyone else, as adults, I don't know. Anyway, you are. You'd make a good father." She saw the look of pain that crossed his face, as he thought about Marie and the children they had planned to have. "Sorry, I didn't think." She took his hand. He closed his eyes and Marie's face sprang into focus, laughing as she moved around her beloved horses.

I, Plague

CHAPTER FORTY THREE

It had been a full day since he placed the message in the fountain. He had been living on his nerves and strong cups of coffee ever since. Messages had been coming in from London on a regular basis, and he now knew that the operation had been a tremendous success. The ship carrying the weapons had been impounded and a huge drug haul seized. They didn't say how many arrests had been made but had informed him that the main distribution network had been very badly dented. The news made him all the more anxious about Peter. He did not have much time left to get out.

It was almost eleven in the evening when a call was put through from the communications centre. He heard the code word identifying Peter. He faltered at the sound of the voice. He had almost forgotten the code word, but it was irrelevant, it could only be him.

The voice he heard sounded surprisingly young. The English was overlaid with a Russian accent. Hardly surprising, he thought, if he had only been speaking Russian for so long. But it was the youthfulness which caught his attention. He sounded no older than a teenager.

He started to speak quickly, briefly outlining what had happened as a result of his intelligence. He paused when he had given his resume, and then added;

"It's time to get out. If you come to the Consulate tonight I can have you on a plane home first thing in the morning."

The delay in the reply surprised and worried him. "October, you still there?"

"Yes, but I'm not sure if leaving right now is the best thing. I don't think I am under suspicion, and it could be good to know what his next move is going to be."

"No, October, you leave right now. It's not worth the risk. There's going to be hell to pay for what happened, and a witch hunt to find out who the informer is. It's way too risky to stay any longer. Please, come in tonight and let's finish with this."

Again there was the delay. "No, I think I'll stay for a couple of days.

You never know what's going to turn up. I'll give you a call when I'm ready to pull out. It shouldn't be more than a day or two." The phone went dead.

He slammed the receiver down on his desk in frustration and anger. Not so much directed at Peter or himself, but at his willingness to stay and find out more. He had seen it before with long term deep cover agents.

They began to think themselves invincible, that they could never be suspected of being something other than what they pretended to be. It was a dangerous mind set, which had led to the deaths of quite a few of them. He hoped Peter was not going to end up like that.

God, he had sounded so young.

Damn, now he was going to have explain to London that he was still in place. He was just about to phone his section chief in London when Howie, a communications technician, put his head around the door and told him. "Switch on your television, BBC World News."

He did so, and saw the headlines about a huge drug operation having been mounted by police forces in the UK. As he watched, a photograph of a ship came on the screen with the news it had been impounded in a British port for illegally carrying arms.

"Shit, that's bloody stupid of someone." He listened for a few more minutes before continuing with his call to London.

CHAPTER FORTY FOUR

The black, blank 44 inch plasma screen stared sightlessly down the length of the mahogany conference table at the only two occupants of a room designed to seat fourteen. Andy McNeish glanced across to look at Stewart, and saw that he was looking relaxed and rested. For himself, he felt as if every time he blinked his eyes would glue themselves shut and the sleep he longer for so desperately would overtake him. He was uncomfortable in this room, normally frequented by only the most senior officers and politicians. He mused that the walls could divulge some interesting facts and secrets if they could only speak.

Despite his best intentions to go home after the operation had wound up, and actually sitting in his car with that thought in his mind, he had not. Instead, he had visited each of the crime scenes and then sat and watched the interviews being conducted. Only when he was satisfied that everything was being done according to the book did he seriously contemplate home and sleep. He should have known from past experience that this would not be permitted. He was summoned back to his Edinburgh office for a meeting with the Chief Constable and a conference call from London.

He had wearily phoned his wife to inform her of the delay in getting home. She told him she had seen the news and understood, telling him it had cleared up all the mystery of the preceding few weeks. He had been surprised that it had made the news so swiftly, and quizzed her on the content. After promising to drive carefully, he hung up and concentrated on making it back to the office in one piece.

He had consumed three cups of strong, black coffee before being summoned to the Chief Constable's office.

"An excellent result, Andy. Well done to you and all your teams. I think I can safely say that we've never had anything like it before. The way you and the others put it all together is a credit to the Force."

Andy mumbled his thanks and felt oddly embarrassed by the praise being heaped upon his head.

"One other thing before you go off to take the call from London. It'll be in the conference room, by the way. The incident room is being dismantled as we speak. You may not know it, but a vacancy has become available in a new unit which will deal with Serious Crime in the area, everything from murder to serious fraud, a high priority case unit, if you prefer, and I want you to take charge of it. It will mean promotion to Detective Superintendent. You don't have to say anything yet, I know how tired you must be, God, I don't think I could have put in the sort of hours you have over the last couple of days. Think about it, put together your questions and a list of people you would want in this kind of operation, and come back to me on," he consulted his diary, "Tuesday, first thing."

He waited and Andy could feel his gaze on the top of his head. With an effort he looked up and across the desk. "Thank you, Sir. It's a bit of shock, and I appreciate the offer. Yes, I would like that job. I will take the time and get back to you. Thanks again."

The Chief Constable looked at his watch. "Right, you'd better get to the conference room, only ten minutes to go. Then home and get some sleep, spend some time with your wife, Jean, isn't it?" He made his way to the door and offered his hand and congratulated Andy again as he left.

Now sitting in the comfortable leather, high-backed chair, he could try to absorb what had been offered. Even his addled brain could appreciate what an opportunity this was. However, he pushed the thoughts to one side, resolving to think about it all after he had slept.

He and Stewart had only spoken briefly after shaking hands and taking their seats. Stewart could see how tired he looked and left him in peace to rest.

Andy focused on the red standby button glowing on the bottom of the screen, willing his eyes to stay open. After an eternity of waiting, it glowed green and the screen stuttered into life. Andy straightened in his chair and watched as the images on the screen came into focus. It was split into five, and he could see his colleagues from the Task Force in four of them and then Jane Bond appeared in the fifth.

She started speaking after a brief smile of greeting. "God, you guys look terrible. I won't take long over this, then you can go home. Firstly, thanks to all of you for a job well done. I have been asked to pass on thanks from everyone from the Prime Minister down. I won't bore you with the details, you're all aware of the size of the haul and the number of arrests. However, there is one new development, which I felt I had to pass onto you all. One of the suspects broke during his interview, and made a deal. He has given us the details of the extent of a fraud ring. The Serious Fraud unit had suspected that this had been operating in the country and had started an investigation. This new information has placed our friend Gregori as the brains behind the whole thing. His reach was greater than we had originally believed. Anyway, the long and the short of it is that there is a sophisticated network of computer crime, credit cards, accessing bank accounts details, identity theft, all that sort of stuff. It has been alleged that it is operating in London and we are now in the process of putting together a team to put an end to it. All this, we believe, is going to practically cripple Gregori's operations in this part of Europe. No one can sustain these kind of losses and survive."

She paused and smiled again. "OK, off to bed for you. Again, well done."

A few muttered thanks and the screen went blank, resuming its dark stare down the room.

Andy and Stewart said their goodbyes, assuring each other of their intentions to stay in touch.

Andy stopped on his way out and looked into his office and his team. He gave them a brief outline of what had been achieved and assured them he would see them on the Tuesday morning.

Outside, he sat in his car nursing yet another cup of strong, black coffee before starting on his way home. He knew that the supply of drugs would be interrupted only temporarily. The current shortage would force up the prices and would most likely result in a few deaths as more additives were mixed in the cut. He chided himself for being too cynical, but realistically, the drugs problem would never be effectively stopped.

CHAPTER FORTY FIVE

Gregori was furious. He was burning from the inside with his rage. He had switched on the BBC News to listen to the sports, and had heard about a drug shipment being seized in Scotland. The police had crowed about the size of the haul, the biggest in UK history, and the number of arrests they had made. Almost as an afterthought, it was announced that a freighter had been impounded for shipping arms under illegal documentation. He had sat for several minutes as the news sunk in. Then the anger started to burn. Why had he not been told? Why did he have to find out through a news channel? Someone had obviously betrayed him, but who?

He tried all the contact numbers he had, but all the phones went straight onto voicemail. He called his operations centre in London, but they could give him no details. They only knew what was on the news, adding that they had been unable to contact anyone apart from lower-end dealers. It appeared that most of the people involved in the drugs operation had been arrested. They had not even been able to pick anything out of the phone taps or police officers on the payroll.

Frustrated now, Gregori called his most trusted lieutenant.

"Yuri, I need you, you need to get here as soon as you can. We have a big problem. No, I'll tell you when you get here."

As he waited for Yuri, he began to receive more calls back from London. Informants had been called, both in the police and on the street. One of the first calls was from Southampton. The whole crew had been arrested and the ship impounded by Customs. Some of the crew were being released as having no knowledge of the cargo.

Other calls confirmed his worst fears. At the distribution centres, everyone had been arrested, and the drugs seized. Also, his yacht had been impounded; it had been seen sailing into Rosyth in Scotland with a Navy warship. Police informants were telling them that it had been a well-planned operation which had been kept secret until the last minute.

Gregori was no longer furious by the time Yuri arrived and sat down in front of him. He was as cold as ice. He told him everything.

Yuri's face showed incredulity then shock. "Everything and everyone?"
"Da, everyone of any importance. I have lost a fortune in a few short

hours."

Yuri waited. "They must have known all the details to work out such a coordinated plan." He knew he was stating the obvious, but was also aware that this was what Gregori wanted to hear.

"What about the arms? Only the Captain and his First Mate knew about them, although I'll bet they're talking to save their own necks."

"I agree, but to seize a ship which is only in transit, they must have known not only about the shipment, but about their destinations and the paperwork. It was too good to be picked up on a routine inspection. I'm afraid you are correct, old friend. We have a traitor among us. I am asking myself, though, if there is a way to have the ship and its cargo released."

Yuri thought for a moment. "I think that they will have checked the legality of the seizure before they did it. Probably some UN resolution which they can use to justify it. Something about supplying arms to the two countries. It's worth a try, but I doubt you'll be successful."

He waited, but Gregori appeared to be deep in thought. "What do you want me do?"

Gregori looked up from his desk. "Start digging here first, but also everywhere we work, including England. We have to find the traitor. I badly want to speak with him. Go now and keep me informed."

Yuri was glad to leave the office, and only relaxed when he had driven three blocks. He pulled over and saw that his hands were shaking from the built up tension. When Gregori had looked at him as he gave his instructions, it had felt as his eyes were boring into the very soul of him. It had been difficult to feign the shock and to carry it off. He had known for a full twenty four hours of the success of the operation in the UK. He had spoken to his handler on the Friday and had been instructed to pull out and make his way home.

Home, he thought, I haven't been home for almost three years. How could he call it home? There was nothing there for him. There was no-one waiting for his arrival. His parents had been killed in a car accident when he was twenty and any old girlfriends would surely have moved on, and were probably married by now. He would be absorbed into the mainstream of the agency and perform routine tasks for the rest of his working life. Unless Gregori decided to come after him. That was a very real possibility. Once he left, it would not take a rocket scientist to work out who the traitor was. Gregori would never forgive that betrayal, and would seek revenge as long as he breathed. He had not been told how he would be reintegrated into life in the UK. Not been told what his cover would be, how he would be hidden from the organisation's spies and informants.

As he pulled out onto the dark, quiet streets, he thought that his cover for placing him in Gregori's organisation had been painstaking and meticulous. The amount of work and training had been arduous and long. He hoped his extraction was as meticulously planned, but somehow doubted it.

He felt at home in Kiev. The last four years of his life had been devoted to this one job. To this one big coup. Ever since he had been recruited and offered this undercover work, it had been one big lie. His adult life had become one big lie. He did not know if he could tell the truth any more. He did not know if he could fit in and adapt to a normal life. He smiled to himself as he imagined himself being called Peter again. The use of English as his first language. But, he reasoned, it would be good to be finished with the continuous fear, the never-ending awareness of what he said or did. To get away from the brutality that had become such a big part of his life since he had grown close to Gregori.

It had taken six months of intensive training to fit in with the legend which had been built for him. As a child, he had seen the fall of the USSR and had decided that he would study Russian at school, with a view to going into the Intelligence arm of the armed forces or some other agency. He had applied for, and been accepted, by MI5. He didn't quite know how they had come to the decision to approach him for undercover work. But he had jumped at the chance. If only, he sometimes thought, he had known then what he knew now, he would have run a mile at the suggestion.

His cover was that he was running from the law in Western Europe after a botched attempt at a robbery. His legend showed him as a petty criminal from an early age and that he decided that the way to escape was to use his Russian and move to the Eastern European countries. He had not been given any further linguistic training as too much proficiency in the language would seem suspicious. Once he had arrived, he had become involved in petty crime, gradually working his way into Gregori's organisation at the lowest level. He had struggled for months to become Yuri. To think only in Russian and to forget the name and personality that was Peter Grant. Now he was Yuri, he thought as Yuri and lived as Yuri. He did not know if he could ever regain the person that was Peter Grant.

He had performed various duties as an ordinary foot soldier in the organisation; as a mule used to smuggle drugs, as a driver and slowly as an enforcer. That was the worst part for the Peter part of his persona. He had to be brutal and unforgiving in his treatment of the offenders. Some of the time he managed, with the help of his handler, to use subterfuge to show that a task had been completed. But at other times he was in the company of others and had to blend in with their version of discipline and the administering of it. He knew that he had come to accept this aspect of the job and hated himself for it. During the course of the first year he had been on the verge of quitting. The work sickened him. But time passed and he worked his way up the ranks, gaining a reputation for ruthlessness. Which was how he came to the attention of Gregori himself.

He had chased down and dealt with a defector who had been supplying information to Interpol. The story went that he had been particularly brutal with this person, resulting in his death. That was actually not the case; a story had been built after he had managed the capture and removal of the man. He was now safely ensconced in Scotland with a new identity. But it had been enough to gain the attention of the higher echelons, and he had found himself in the group surrounding Gregori. It was then only a matter of time, in fact it had taken over a year to gain his full trust.

It had been slow at first. He was more akin to a bodyguard than anything. It was after a late night drinking session when he was alone with Gregori that he had been questioned in depth. He had not been fooled by the drunken demeanor; he had observed how much he had actually drunk, and knew it was part of a test. He had apparently passed as he was drawn closer into the circle, moving from the role of a bodyguard to someone who drank with Gregori. One of the more onerous tasks was to use the constantly changing string of young girls. Although they appeared willing participants in the sex games, he could never lose the feeling that he was dirty, that it was rape. He knew they went on to brothels throughout Europe and passed their details onto his handler at every opportunity. He never was told if anyone had ever acted on that information.

Now he was at the height of his power in the organisation. He was privy to all that was happening, was involved in the planning and had access to every facet of the organisation. He knew that London had been surprised when he told them of the extent of the operation in the UK. In particular, the operations centre and their capabilities, which were equal to any police force. He knew that the next move was to take down the operations centre. That alone would save ordinary citizens from the scams on their credit cards and bank accounts. It would be yet another blow to Gregori. The centre controlled computer fraud across Europe and far beyond.

As he pulled up in front of the very utilitarian apartment block where he lived, he resolved to have his handler get him out of the country as quickly as possible. The thought of being caught out by Gregori was a terrifying one, and he was unwilling to frame someone else for the treatment in his stead. That would be a pointless cruelty, as his job was well and truly done.

I, Plague

CHAPTER FORTY SIX

James felt as if he had only slept for a couple of minutes, but when he opened his eyes daylight was streaming through the windows. His left arm felt numb and he flexed his hand, feeling the weight and then remembering that Mona was there. He looked to the side of the bed and saw Monique asleep in the chair. He had to get to the bathroom and tried to slide his arm from under the girl. She stirred briefly and turned on her side, releasing him.

When he returned, he found a terry bathrobe and donned it, moving to the window to look out at another sunny day. Saturday, he remembered, God, it had been two weeks since he left home. Today was a good day to go back; he felt he would recover more quickly in his own home, anyway. He had the pool and the gym. He felt a bit dizzy and returned to the bed, sitting on the same side as Mona and gently stroking her hair. Poor kid, she had seen too much violence. He hoped with all his heart that she would come out of it in one piece. He had seen grown men crack under the same pressure she had been under.

He felt her gaze and looked down into her eyes, saying nothing but still stroking her hair.

"I love you, James."

"I love you too, sweetheart. Did you have a good sleep?"

"Yes, and I didn't have any nightmares. A bad dream started, but I knew you were here and that I'd be all right." She pulled herself into a sitting position and put her arms around his neck. "When are we going to watch that movie you told me about? I bet you've forgotten our bet."

He had to laugh. "No I haven't, we'll watch it when we get home. The first night, I promise. Speaking of which, I think we'd better get up. I want to leave today. If that's all right with my nurse, that is?"

That made her jump up, saying that she had to pack and get ready. After a prolonged debate with Monique about his ability to get dressed by himself, he managed to persuade her to leave the room while he, at least, put his trousers on. She had found his modesty extremely funny, reminding him, and surprising him, by informing him it was she who had put him to bed.

He was sitting checking his guns and placing them in their holsters when Mike came in, followed by Lizelle and Ethan. "Good of you tell us you're leaving this morning. No, don't say anything. We've decided that Mona and Monique will go with you. Carmen and Lou want to stay here to get things back to normal. These two," indicating Ethan and Lizelle, "will be going with you. No arguments, Lizelle is leaving now to pick up some of her things, Mario will take her. It'll only take an hour, tops. I'm keeping on two of the guys here, just in case. Any objections?"

"None whatsoever, it's about how I thought it would be. One thing, though, when we leave we'll put in the defensive driving techniques, just to check we're in the clear. Who's riding shotgun, Lizelle? Probably should be you, you have the experience." They agreed and helped him down the stairs.

They had managed to leave after an hour and a half and it had been a cautious exit, and a necessarily devious route through London, until they reached the M1 and declared themselves free of any followers. James had noticed that Mona, who was sitting in between him and Monique in the back of the Range Rover, clung to him all the time. He kept his arm around her shoulders for the whole of the three hour drive.

The sight of the house at the end of the driveway and the paddocks, as always, amazed him. He still could not accept that this was his home. It was always the same; when he returned after his first excursion to London, when he and Marie had returned from Kenya and then their honeymoon. It excited him to watch it grow in the windscreen. As they pulled up in front of the main entrance, Madge and all the household staff came down the steps, closely followed by Vicky and Helen from the stables.

Madge was the first to reach the door and open it for him. "Master James, are you all right? Mona told us you had been hurt. Goodness, what a shiner you have. Come, let me help you out." She stopped gushing long enough to offer her arm, which he accepted to gain his balance on solid ground.

"This is Ethan and Lizelle. They're friends of mine." He left Madge to introduce them to the staff, while he made his way inside on distinctly shaky legs and threw himself on the sofa with a sigh of relief. He heard the bustle as everyone was shown to their rooms and shut it out as he relaxed, savoring the feeling of being home. Jean was the first to join him. She stood in front of him, looking unsure about what to say. He patted the sofa next to him and, when she sat, took her hand.

"It looks worse than it is." He smiled, gaining a small smile in return. "Really, it's nothing to worry about. I need to ask you a favour, well, you and everyone else. Will you take extra good care of Mona? She needs a bit of normality. She's been though a lot. I think she's a bit fragile, she might cry a bit, that sort of thing. Anyway, I know you'll all know what to do. Will you do that for me?"

"Of course, I will, but what about you? You don't look so good yourself." Before he could reply Mona ran into the room.

"Right, bed for you. Come." She would brook no arguments, taking a hand and half pulling him to his feet. Jean stood and took the other hand, between them leaving him no choice but to stand. Secretly, amid his protestations, he knew he should be in bed. The morning had taken more out of him than he cared to admit.

In his bedroom they helped him with his shoes, after seeing his grimace of pain as he bent. When he was down to his trousers he insisted they left. He had not missed the look of dismay on Jean's face when she saw the dressing on his side and back. He would have to think of some explanation for that later. She hadn't, however, batted an eyelid when he removed his guns, taking them and putting them in the wardrobe. He had pulled on a pair of shorts and climbed into bed before he called that they could come in.

"Right, as much as I hate to admit this, I need to sleep. So off you go. Both of you, I'll be fine. Mona, will you see how Darling is doing? Maybe go down with Vicky and Helen. Please tell them I'm fine and I'll see them later." They both hovered until he told them "Go."

He saw that he had slept for two hours, and listened to the quiet of the house. Taking advantage of being alone, he showered and dressed, making his way downstairs. Finding no-one in the living room, he went into the kitchen. There he found almost everyone busy at work counters, preparing the evening meal. He surprised them. "Looks like you're cooking for a small army?"

"Master James, you're up." Stating the obvious he thought. "Here, sit down, and have a coffee."

"I thought I'd have a chance to get away from the fussing, when I didn't hear anyone up and about." But he allowed himself to be seated, a mug of coffee appearing almost magically in front of him. "How many are you cooking for anyway?"

Madge informed him. "There are eight for dinner, your friends, Monique and the girls. Of course, you didn't know that Pippa and the others arrived this afternoon while you were asleep. Quite a house full. I convinced their father that it would be good for the sisters to stay here for the weekend, it gives them all a chance to catch up. They are all down at the stables now. I'm not sure where your friends are, but they're around here somewhere."

"Good. But listen you lot, no more fussing, I think I've got my hands full with Mona taking care of me. OK?" He thought the agreement was reached too easily, and knew that no matter what he said, there would continue to be a fuss over every move he made. "I'm going next door, to relax before the marauding hordes return."

He had deliberately left the coffee unfinished, and poured himself a generous measure of whiskey before sitting down. But peace was not to be his. Ethan and Lizelle walked into the room. James indicated that they should help themselves to a drink. "What have you two been up to?"

"Just walking around, getting a feel of the place. I suppose you could say we were securing the perimeter." James smiled at the terminology.

"What do you think of the old place? Been down to the stables to pester the girls yet?"

Lizelle was the one who laughed and replied. "I think the girls, as you call them, have found a new object of desire. Mr Smoothie here has been charming them. Nice place you have though. That Madge has been taking good care of us." She paused and lowered her voice. "Do they know anything? I mean, we don't want to say anything wrong."

"No, they don't. Jean, the one with short hair, knows about the guns I keep, and she's seen the dressings, I don't know what she thinks. But best if you act just like the guests you are. Enjoy yourselves while you're here. I'll soon be up and about, feeling better already, and then I'll show you around properly, have a couple of drinks in the pub. But we'll keep a quiet, discreet eye on the girls."

"No problem, boss" grinned Ethan.

"Boss, what movie's that out of? What happened to the old man?"

"*Cool Hand Luke*" he replied. "They called the guards 'boss'."

"James will be fine, thank you. Have you spoken to Mike? Is everything OK down there?"

"Yep, I spoke to him just after we arrived. Nothing untoward happening. There was a bit on the news, though. Seems the police have seized a yacht, which was smuggling a large shipment of drugs into the country. Biggest haul yet, they're saying. I'd take a guess that it was our friend behind it. That'll really piss him off, if it is his. Worth millions, they say."

The talk turned to the house and the business. He answered their questions about the set up, the children they tried to help and told them how Marie, as well as the others, had been responsible for keeping things going. They were on their second drink when sounds of hilarity sounded from the kitchen. Three teenagers descended on the lounge and James in particular. He was subjected to hugs and kisses on the cheek. Although embarrassed, he found it pleasant. They told him about their day, with Mona being solicitous about his wellbeing. He noticed Monique holding back, going to the bar to fix herself a drink. "I need this, they've run me ragged. Anyone else?"

The adults had another, and the girls Coke. James listened to their stories until they were sent to their rooms to change for dinner.

As they ate, James revelled in the light, laughter filled atmosphere. He noticed, however, that Mona never strayed far from his side, jumping when the door opened and glancing worriedly around as the courses were served. He tried to keep her involved in the conversation and her mind distracted.

They had been sitting in the lounge after dinner when James asked that he and Mona be excused. "I made a promise to this young lady and now is the time to keep it. You stay as long as you like. Someone will be around if you want anything." He stood and selected a DVD and gestured to Mona to follow him.

They went to his bedroom and lay on the bed as the movie started. Jean appeared after half an hour with some cold drinks and crisps. Sure enough, the tears started when Demi Moore realised that Patrick

Swayze was actually there. James had given up questioning why he was also so emotional during this movie. But this time he had a reason. He hadn't watched it since Marie's death, and now it had more meaning. It was stupid, he knew, but he hoped that maybe she was there with them. At the end, Mona's tears turned into a torrent. Good, he thought, he knew that it was only partly due to the movie, rather more of a release of the built up tension from the past couple of weeks. He allowed her to cry her eyes out, cradling her as her sobs racked her body. It took a while but eventually she stopped crying and lay quietly in his arms.

It was only after a long silence, during which he had been thinking about his dead wife, that he saw that Mona had fallen asleep. A deep sleep in which she looked at peace. She did not stir as he adjusted his position and pulled the duvet over her. He was thinking about going for some help to move into her own bed when Monique and Jean came to the door. He whispered to them. "I think she's cried herself out. I didn't know what to do. She's sound asleep now."

Mona woke at the sound of Jean picking up the glasses, and Monique's movement to pick her up. "I want to stay with James. Please, can't I stay here, just for tonight?"

It didn't seem right to James, and he said as much to Monique. She took him into the hall and told him. "You're her safety blanket, for the time being anyway. She feels safe with you. I can't say I blame her. It'll be strange not sleeping in the same room, even if it was in a chair." She thought for a minute. "There is one way to let her stay and maintain the proper decorum." He waited for her to finish. "I could stay as well." The shock must have registered on his face. "It's all right, we'll put her in the middle." He was dubious, but when they asked Mona if that was all right, she agreed and he was left with no options.

By the time Monique returned in her sweats and James had donned a track suit, Mona was asleep again. As soon as he lay down on top of the duvet she cuddled up to him, an arm thrown across his chest.

He did not have the most comfortable of nights, always aware of the unfamiliar feeling of an arm touching him throughout the night. He was glad when the sun rose and he was able to get up. She had stirred only a little through the course of the night, but had settled as soon as he soothed her by stroking her head.
After dressing, he watched the two sisters before leaving the room and making his way into the kitchen for some coffee. It was his intention to take a mug with him and walk down to the stables, to savour the bright,

crisp morning. The aches and pains of the previous two days were rapidly dissipating; he felt stronger and more alert.

As usual, there was someone in the kitchen. He could not remember a day when he had come down and found it unoccupied, but he did not linger and was soon walking down to the stables. He stopped at the bend in the drive and stood looking. He loved the sight of the horses' heads looking over the stall doors, the gentle whinnying as they waited for the grooms to arrive. He looked over the fields and saw the tree where he sat, the rise jutting up over the light ground mist, a mist that was quickly disappearing under the warmth of the sun.

The sound of a car engine broke the silence and his reverie. He stepped to one side and looked back. It was Vicky, one of the stable managers. She slowed as she drew level and asked if he wanted a lift down. He refused and watched her finish the drive and head to her office. He remained where he was, drinking his coffee and watching the day unfold.

"Are you all right?" He was startled by the question. He had missed the sound of anyone approaching and inwardly reprimanded himself. He swung round and saw Jean. "I saw you leave and thought I'd come and bring you another coffee, that one must be finished by now. I know how you like your three cups in the morning." She handed him a mug and smiled.

"Thanks, Jean." He thought he should say something about the previous night. "Mona's had a tough time, as I told you. It seems she only feels safe when I'm around, that's why she wanted to stay with me."

"We all saw that, we understand. She's a good kid." He had to smile. This from someone who was only just past the kid stage herself. "But James, are you all right? I mean the bandages on your side."

"I'm fine, Jean, really. I'll be taking you off to the pub, just like I promised, in no time."

She stayed with him for about ten minutes before she said she had to get back to prepare breakfast, taking the other empty cup with her. He continued down to the stables, walking along the horse lines, talking to each animal.

When he returned to the house, he felt that his life had returned to almost normal. That illusion was abruptly shattered by the cacophony of sound that hit him as he crossed the threshold. He had frequently wondered why teenagers could never converse at a moderate level. They all seemed to be talking at once, and what was more, appeared to hear everything the other had to say.

CHAPTER FORTY SEVEN

The two photographs lay on the desk. The faces of the four bodies were clear. They had been lain on their backs with their hands folded across the weapons on their chests. Gregori and Yuri started at them in silence. Yuri was aware of the close ties between the two, from their days in the army together, and held the silence.

"Ah, Anatoly, my old friend," Gregori reached out and touched a finger to a face. "There will be no more football games, no retirement dacha on the Black Sea. You were so close."

He forced himself up, pushing the photographs to one side of his desk.

"First the arms, then the drugs, now this." He stared very hard at Yuri. "Whoever did that was not police. No, they must be very good to have caught Anatoly and his boys. And this note," he pushed it across the desk to Yuri. "It's obviously a threat, some kind of a quote. You're English, what do you think?"

Yuri looked at the note and read it out loud. "*And there went out another horse that was red: and power was given to him that sat thereon to take peace from the earth, and that they should kill one another: and there was given unto him a great sword.* Yes, I'd say that was a threat. I think it's from the Bible. We must have really pissed someone off. If they took out Anatoly and his crew, then they are every bit as good as anyone I can think of. Any word on professional contractors coming after you?"

"Nyet, I would have heard. Besides, I haven't pissed anyone off lately, none that mattered anyway. No, I think this has to do with the old man. The guy I told you about from Paris. I have a feeling he is somehow tied into this. You think he is going to come after me?"

"He would have to be very, very stupid to come here and try to kill you. Might be better to beef up security for a while, just in case. I gather we have no idea what this man from Paris looks like? How were these delivered, did they come here or to your home? It would be bad if they did."

"No, it might be he was only a boyfriend of the girl. But Anatoly said his escape and evasion was professional. And no, they were delivered to one of our men in London with instructions to pass it on. Who knows, but you're right, we'll step things up for a week or two, just in case. Right, any more news on how the British found out about the shipments?"

Yuri was worried about the answer to that question. He knew how volatile Gregori could be if things were not going well. And right now, things were definitely not going well.

"Not much. I've spoken to Matt in London and asked him for all the phone records of everyone who could have known about the times and dates; so far nothing. We're also putting out a reward among the informers to come up with some information, but again, nothing so far."

Gregori's face was darkening, his glare almost ferocious. "What about here, could anyone here have made contact with some English agent?"

Yuri struggled to stay calm. He used a glance at his notes to hide any feelings he might show. He pulled a list from the folder and passed it across. "Here is a list of everyone who knew, including us. I'm checking phones, bank accounts, everything, but it will take time and so far I've turned up nothing." He passed across another sheaf of papers. "These are the phone records and bank accounts which I got so far, all of us who are close to you here are on that list. Nothing suspicious. Of course, money could be in an account somewhere else, I'm checking that, but it will be a while before I hear anything."

Yuri was dismissed and made his way outside to have a cigarette. It was time to get out, but that was not going to be the easiest thing to accomplish. In this air of suspicion everyone watched everyone else. It was very rare to be left alone long enough to duck and run. That would only point a finger at himself, and he would be picked up in very short time. He had to get hold of his handler and make some arrangements; his luck would not last forever. He decided to walk and clear his head. He checked frequently to see if he was being followed. There was no-one behind him as he neared the edge of the massive stadium car park. That meant nothing; he could be observed from the stadium for a long way. It wasn't necessary to follow him on foot. What he needed was a break, enough time to use a public telephone and get hold of his handler. It was a risky move; he could not be seen making a call like that.

He could not even rely on the privacy of his own apartment. His girlfriend of a year now lived with him, and he had a feeling that he could not trust her fully. She worked in one of the companies which laundered money, and her loyalties lay firmly with the organisation. He knew that her loyalty was inspired partly by fear, but that the lifestyle she enjoyed was far superior to anyone else of her age. It would be hard for her to compromise that. He had never tested her stated devotion and love for him. It would have been awkward if he had not agreed to the living arrangement, and he had prepared very carefully for it. He had arranged for his phone to be tapped by his handler to provide an early warning if she picked something up about his double life. He constantly checked for bugs placed around his apartment, and was cautious when it came to talking with her about his daily routine, always careful to give the impression that he was totally behind everything that Gregori did.

Getting away from her would be difficult in itself. She was always there in the evening; it had become their habit to spend most evenings together, the only time he departed from this he was either working or indulging Gregori's whim to go and get drunk. He had moved himself into a position where he was trapped 24 hours a day.

To make matters worse, he knew he was not immune to the surveillance he had ordered on everyone else. Gregori's paranoia would not exclude him from suspicion, and he was surely being watched. But he had to get away; time was definitely running out.

CHAPTER FORTY EIGHT

James was feeling strong and fit after three days of sessions in the gym. The initial tiredness and aches were quick to disappear. It was as expected; the blood loss had been the worst factor of his weakness. That Thursday morning he had taken advantage of a bright day to ride for the first time. Lizelle had accompanied him, proving herself to be a very capable horsewoman. It had given them the first real chance to talk and he had learned about her upbringing in the city of Welkom in South Africa, and she had amused him with tales of her days in the police in Johannesburg. Ethan had sworn that the only thing he would mount would have to have an engine.

Things had quietened around the house with only Monique and Mona being the remaining guests. He was not sure if he preferred the bustle of so many teenage girls or the quiet of an almost empty house. Sitting in the kitchen now, he decided he preferred the quiet.

A package had arrived for Ethan that morning and he had spent the last couple of hours in James' office setting something up. It was as he was about to refill his mug that he came into the kitchen with Lizelle and announced that he had set up a call with Mike in London.

Mike's face appeared on the screen and they stared into the webcam.

"Morning all," was the cheery greeting. "Good to see you looking better, James. Ethan, did you manage to install the equipment all right?"

Ethan told him that it had been relatively simple and tthat hey were ready.

"Good, that means we're on a secure line. Right, while you lot have been having a holiday, I've been busy. You ready?"

On being told they were, he continued. "Tickets for Kiev booked. We fly a week on Sunday and return on the Wednesday evening. We have to go from Heathrow on Austrian Airlines. The agent says the passports will be back with the necessary visas on Friday, Monday at the latest. I've also spoken with our friend in Amsterdam. Weapons are already there, we will be meeting with his contact in the hotel on Thursday night. I won't go into all the details now, I'd like to come up on Saturday and we can go through what we have in detail then. I have to say though, we don't have much. Anyway, I've bought us all tickets for a football game on the Wednesday evening. Seems our friend owns the club that's playing and will definitely be there. We have to be at the airport two hours after the game. OK so far?"

"How about travel arrangements?" James asked.

"Patience dear boy, patience." He smiled. "I thought that us two old men would travel together, just tourists, on the hunt for young girls. Dirty old men should suit us just fine. Lizelle and Ethan, you will travel as a couple. We're all staying at the same hotel, but will travel there separately. We can make it appear that we struck up a friendship in the bar. You know, Brits abroad."

He paused, "The down side of all I can gather is that we're going to have to recce the place, and decide a plan of action once we're there. It doesn't give us much time and we're going to have to improvise as we go. You know how much I hate having to do that. But as I see it it's the only way. As I said, what I'd like to do is come up on Saturday and we can all sit down and put our heads together. That OK by you?"

"Of course it is. We can have a chat in the meantime. But, I think you're right, we should make it up as we go along. Do you think the man in Kiev can give us more of an idea as to the opposition we'll face?"

"I'll ask. One thing I know from conversations setting this up is that our friend is very suspicious of everyone and everything since the drugs bust last week. It could make things a bit awkward.. Oh, one more thing. We'll be staying at the Hyatt Regency, supposedly the best in Kiev. I figured we deserve a bit of comfort."

"OK, Mike, we'll wait until Saturday for all the details." They signed off and the three of them sat quietly, each with their own thoughts.

"There's no point in discussing it now, let's wait until everyone has gone to bed tonight, then we can put our thoughts together and see what we've come up with. Agreed?"

The others agreed and James headed back to the gym. Now he had a time frame to work to he had to get in the best shape possible. He had finished his workout when Ethan and Lizelle came in and began a training session. He thought, as he watched them, how honed their bodies were, how easily they moved through their individual exercises. How he envied them that level of fitness. He had to work hard each day, and it was getting harder with each passing year, to keep the flab from around his midsection. He hated the ageing process with a vengeance.

Then he knew his mind was accepting the forthcoming operation. He was always the same, the guilt about taking others into danger never lessened. It sometimes felt that the responsibility weighed heavier every time. Now, as he watched the two youngsters, he had a vision of their bodies ravaged by bullet holes, blood seeping from their inert forms. He had never become accustomed to these thoughts and always found them disturbing. They were not visions, just thoughts about what might happen. He had grown attached to these two, he had to admit, and didn't want them to end up dead and forgotten in some far off country. Especially not on a job such as this. It would be such a waste.

This was the trigger he needed for his brain to kick into the mode he used when planning an operation. He banished the images and let his brain go wherever it wanted to. It would work out the details without any conscious effort from him. Somehow, it always clicked and everything fell into place.

After dinner, Monique and Mona went to their rooms quite early. They had, as they had since arriving, been busy all day and it left Mona, in particular, quite exhausted by the evening. It had been a deliberate act on James' part to ensure that all the stable hands worked her hard. Chores and riding were hard exercise; it would take her mind off things and, hopefully, ensure a good night's sleep. So far it seemed to be working.

With drinks in hand they sat in the lounge. The others waited for James to speak first.

"I suppose I'm right in thinking that this has been weighing on all our minds this afternoon." He continued without waiting for a response. "I'm going to say this, if only because I always say it. It's not going to be a walk in park, this is different from anything any of us has done before. We'll be operating in a country where we don't know the language, we don't know the enemy, and we don't know our way around. This ranks up there with the toughest job we've ever done and the chances of getting hurt or killed are in the high percentages. You don't have to do this. If you have any doubts – pull out now. It won't be held against you. Lizelle, you in particular, you owe us nothing, whatever we pay you might not be enough. I want you to think on that for a minute. Ethan – you don't owe Mike or me anything. The same goes for you, think about it for a minute."

Ethan was the first to speak, but James stopped him. "If you're going to say you've got nothing better to do, I'll smack you so hard you'll wake up next week."

Ethan gave him his injured little boy look. "It never crossed my mind. I'm in. I started this so I'll finish it. I wouldn't dream of letting you and Mike go off somewhere without me to look after you. Besides, Mike's said I've got a job at the end of this. It will get me out of soldiering for good."

James looked at Lizelle. "That's a good point; have you given any thought about what you're going to do when this is over?"

She shook her head and replied. "I'm in as well. I couldn't really tell you why. I guess I've grown to like you. Anyway, it's better to have two teams of two, than an odd number."

"To change the subject for a minute. And I want to assure you that this was not dependent on you're coming. I was going to ask you anyway. I wanted to know if you'd like to stay on here and work the stables? The girls could do with some help managing things and you know your way around horses. Also, there's a small apartment in the loft above the stables, which is vacant, fully furnished, and ready for someone to move in. It's yours if you want it."

Her face lit up. "That would be fantastic. I was getting tired of moving from job to job, anyway. Wow, that's great. Thanks James. If I knew you better I'd give you a big fat kiss."

"Don't even think about it," James laughed. "I have enough of that nonsense from the girls. Right, down to business. The way I see it is that we need someone to show us around, to take us to places where this Gregori works. Where he drinks, if he has offices, that sort of thing."

"We were talking about that – the problem getting around and locating him in the short time we have." Ethan looked at Lizelle who indicated he should carry on. "What about the man who'll be meeting us? We presumed he would be a local. If we made a good enough offer, he might be persuaded to help out. It would fit in with the tourist bit as well, picking up a guide, paying for him and a car to show us around. We could even arrange the first meeting to be accidental, just like we plan to do, in the bar, restaurant, somewhere."

"That's good, how about you put that to Mike? See if he can arrange things through the Amsterdam contact of his."

CHAPTER FORTY NINE

Gregori was drinking more than usual. His behaviour bordered on manic and this worried Yuri. He had seen this kind of pattern before, and it always preceded something violent. It was an intangible feeling, he could not have described it if he had to, but it was real. Gregori's laughter was forced, and he avoided looking at Yuri; it was as if he was restraining himself from saying whatever was on his mind. Despite the amount he had to drink, his eyes, whenever he looked at Yuri, were sober, questioning. Yuri had a good idea; Peter's cover had been breached. Gregori obviously did not have the confirmation he needed, was maybe hoping that whatever information he had was wrong. Whatever the reason, Yuri was being tolerated.

He had not realised that he had withdrawn from the conversation until Gregori spoke. "What's wrong Yuri, our company not good enough for you tonight? Maybe you have your mind on the lovely Natasha waiting for you with open arms, and legs."

"Nyet, I have eaten something, it's making me feel ill. I think I should go home. You have a good time. I'll go to bed and let Natasha nurse me." He forced a smile, and knew it was very half-hearted. He hoped the story of feeling unwell would explain it. He stood up and put on his jacket.

Gregori waved his driver over. Yuri protested that he was fine to get home by himself, but he was insistent. "Make sure he gets home safely." Then he was dismissed. He was now certain that he had been blown. If he made it home he would be lucky. If he had any time left, it was only a matter of hours.

He was relieved when it was only the driver who accompanied him to the car. He sat in the back seat and watched the streets pass, envying the carefree attitude of the customers of the sidewalk cafes. He wished he could share their laughter. He forced his mind to concentrate. He would have to neutralise Natasha; he did not want to kill her, he would have to find a way to keep her quiet, at least until morning, giving him a few hours head start.

He was still thinking about that when the car pulled up in front of his apartment block and the driver waited for him to get out. There were no pleasantries as he stood and watched the car pull away. Obviously word had spread about him. He glanced up and down the street as he walked to the front door, but could not see anyone in the rows of parked cars. They would be there; he guessed that there were probably two teams watching, waiting for the word to pick him up.

He strolled slowly through the lobby and waited for the lift. As he waited, he walked to and fro, each time trying to look through the windows opening onto the street. Nothing.

In the apartment, Natasha was sitting in their lounge, reading a magazine. The TV was on but the sound turned down low. Was it his imagination but did she seem a bit reticent in greeting him? He knew he could be getting paranoid, but she usually did not wait up for him. She was always in bed, sometimes asleep, sometimes reading. It was possible he thought, as he held her, that she had been told and, being loyal, had been trusted to keep an eye on him. The tightness of her grip around his waist tended to confirm that. It was almost as if she was hugging him for confirmation that the information was wrong. He held her until she relaxed her grip and told him she was going to bed.

"That sounds like a good idea. How about a drink?" He didn't wait for her reply, and went through to the kitchen. When he was lifting the glasses from the cupboard he searched for the medicines she kept, then realised they would be in the bathroom. He closed the bathroom door and turned on the tap. Searching through the small cabinet he pulled out every medicine bottle he could find. He searched the labels. He knew that she had been prescribed something to help her sleep, and now desperately sought it. Valium. He knew it was something she used to calm her, improve the dark moods that settled on her, but had no idea of the effect it would have. The label stated clearly that it was not to be taken with alcohol. He shook three into his hand and flushed the toilet before going back to the kitchen. He shouted through that he was making a sandwich and asked if she wanted one. She didn't, but it gave him an excuse to delay and make some noise as he crushed the tablets into a powder. He poured two generous measures of Vodka and added the Valium. The sediment was visible in the glass. He topped up the glass with Coke and stirred it with his finger. It appeared to dissolve; it would have to do.

He handed her a glass and toasted her. "You know I was thinking earlier how much I love you. I don't really tell you that very often." She watched him over the rim of the glass, taking large sips of the drink.

"I love you too, Yuri. Promise me that you'll never do anything to hurt me."

"Never, I promise." He decided to push a little to see if he could elicit any more from her. "Is everything all right, you seem a bit quiet, not pleased to see me?"

"No, everything is fine." She had finished her drink and lay back on the pillows watching him undress. By the time he climbed into bed her eyelids were beginning to droop. He picked up a novel and held it in front of him until she had fallen into a deep sleep. He switched the light off and went to the window.

Going from one side to the other he peered through the small gap in the curtain but could not see anyone in the parked cars. Going back to the bed he listened to Natasha's breathing and was satisfied that she was out for the count. He dressed quickly in the darkest clothes he had and lifted up a floor board in the kitchen. From the hole he took his passport, a Glock 9mm, spare clips, a box of ammunition and some local currency and dollars he had kept for an emergency. With a last look at the sleeping form, he let himself out of the door and made his way to the fire escape.

In the basement, he went to the door leading to the service alley. Slipping outside and concealing himself between two garbage skips, he scanned the shadows to his left and right. He remained motionless for ten minutes, during which time he heard and saw nothing. He was sure that his eyes were sufficiently accustomed to the dark and slowly slid along the wall, trying to keep behind the skips until he reached the entrance to the street. He was half a block away from the front of the building but he stopped in the shadows and scanned the street before moving. He pulled up the hood of his sweatshirt and, picking up an empty bottle from the garbage, staggered out of the alley and across the street to stop again in the shadows of the alley on the other side. Again he looked up and down the street but nothing moved.

He quickened his pace to a jog and skirted another two blocks, using the service alleys until he was sure he well clear of any surveillance.

One o' clock in the morning and he was conspicuous, walking alone down the deserted streets. There was no traffic, and he knew that there was a real danger that any car passing might contain Gregori's men. He had to get off the street and out of Kiev as quickly as possible. He reasoned that if his cover was blown there was no point in not using his mobile phone for one last call before ditching it. He dialled the emergency number he had been given and it was answered after one ring. Nothing was said on the other end and he spoke. "October, Red Dwarf." And immediately hung up. October identified him and Red Dwarf, taken from his favourite TV show, was the emergency code to say that his cover had been blown and he was now running. He slipped the card from the phone and dumped them in a nearby skip.

Now that he was truly on his own, improvisation was the only advantage he had. He would have to make another call once he was clear, to arrange a pick up, but first he had to get clear. He kept to the shadows, trying to avoid the glare of the street lights, hugging doorways if he heard a vehicle approaching. He worked his way into a residential area with tower blocks of apartments. In the car park he scouted for an older car, one that would not have a screeching alarm which would alert the whole neighbourhood. For once he was glad of the skills learned; stealing a car was an everyday occurrence, and he was in and driving in under a minute. With luck, it would not be reported as missing for another six or seven hours. Longer, if his luck really held. But he knew he could not afford to take that risk. Being picked up by the police was as bad as being picked up by Gregori's men. The end result would be the same.

Once driving, he decided to head towards Odessa. It was the lesser evil. If he could make it there he could go into hiding and try and contact his handler for an extraction. He found he could not think beyond that. At least Odessa had more options for escape. There was an international airport, a port and rail links.

CHAPTER FIFTY

He had to drag his eyes from the 9mm gun barrel, which was an inch from the bridge of his nose, and look Gregori in the eye. He did not like what he saw. Gregori's face was suffused with anger.

"Eight hours, eight hours," he screamed. "Your stupidity has given him eight hours head start on us."

"I'm sorry, I didn't think he would run." It was all he could say.

Gregori calmed his voice, but did not move the gun. "Why didn't you watch the back? An easy question, *why?*" Shouting the last word. Spittle spraying onto the face. He could not reply. The gun swivelled to his right and a shot deafened his left ear, leaving it ringing. Out of the corner of his eye, he saw his partner fall to the floor. He started to tremble at the knees. The gun barrel swung back to his forehead.

"Stupid, stupid." It was the last words he heard. A hole appeared, the edges blackened by the gunshot residue. He stood for a moment as the back of his head exploded, then crumpled to the floor.

"Get these idiots out of here." Gregori gestured to the two fallen. "As for you two, find him. Find him if you value your lives. Now get out."

Gregori went to the desk and sat down. How they could have let Yuri escape was beyond him. He had obviously gone home, drugged the girl straight away and left. He could be anywhere in the country. He had placed a bounty on his head, enough to encourage anyone to report a sighting. But Yuri had proved himself to be resourceful; it could be a hard task.

"Have we got men at all the airports?" he asked of the two men left in the room.

"Airports, cars on the roads at the borders, starting to set a watch on the rivers and Black Sea ports."

"If he has a handler, then he will come from the Embassy or a Consular office. Set up a watch on them and follow anyone leaving." He could not blame them for not having seen that Yuri was undercover. That was down to him and him alone. He hadn't wanted to believe the first reports, which indicated that he might have been. He had waited too long to confront Yuri and this was the result. He was angry, he could not remember the last time he had been this angry. He had looked on the man as a friend, had trusted him.

His organisation had never been in this much trouble before. He had lost tens of millions of dollars. There were the beginnings of other groups moving into his territory in some countries. He would have to move fast and hard to restore his power. He had already brought forward the dates for the next shipment from Afghanistan. But he had to find Yuri, or whatever his name was, and make an example of him.

He thought about the threat, if it was that. His people in London had not been able to find out anything regarding the men who had taken out Anatoly and his team. The only thing they could tell him was that there had been a group of mercenaries recruited to look after the old man and his family. Unfortunately most had now gone off on some job. Gregori was not concerned, though. He had decided that Yuri had been correct in this. They would be very stupid to come onto his home soil and try anything. He had a small army who would take care of him. No, he decided, as he picked up the phone, he could forget about them, at least until the Yuri business had been taken care of.

He dialled a number and spoke. "How are things in Odessa my friend? Have the arms arrived yet?" He listened for a moment. "Good, get them loaded and on their way. There should be no problems getting them out through the Black Sea." He listened for a few moments more and hung up.

Next he checked on the deployment of the men he had dispatched to search for Yuri. This time he would leave nothing to chance, he would not entrust others to do the job properly. He had men checking the hotels from Odessa to Zaporozhye, north to the border with Russia and in Russia. He would not evade him for very much longer. But he could not settle in his office and decided to go out and drive around his establishments. Maybe he could take his mind of the betrayal by keeping busy; he would find someone who had made a mistake and vent his anger on them.

CHAPTER FIFTY ONE

By the time he was approaching the outskirts of Odessa the persona of Yuri was being consigned to the rubbish bin of his mind. He was now Peter Grant again. He was thinking, with a bit of effort, in English. Now he had put some distance between himself and Kiev, he was beginning to think clearer, able to plan ahead. It was almost sunrise and he had to find a phone. It was also time to ditch the car.

He stopped on a street corner somewhere near the centre of the town. He would have to buy a map. Although he had been here before, it had been to specific locations and there had been not time for sightseeing. He would find the seediest area. It was bound to have cheap, no questions asked, accommodation, where he could hole up for a day or two. He had discarded the idea of going straight to the airport and trying to get on one of the first flights. He could not believe that his absence had not been noticed by now. He turned the corner, drove a short distance and parked the car at the kerb between two others. Now on foot, he walked in the direction of the sea. It was three blocks before he found a telephone and dialled the emergency number.

Again it was picked up after one ring. He gave his code and waited. A series of clicks as relays put him through to his handler. It was a cursory greeting. "Where are you? Give me a run down on what happened."

Peter did, taking only a minute to condense the events. It was arranged that a car and driver would be sent to pick him up. He would find someplace to hide for a day and then contact his handler again when he had found a safe place where the pickup would go undiscovered. In the meantime, flights would be arranged.

He walked through the streets of Odessa, turning randomly at corners, waiting for the morning crowds to fill up the still quiet sidewalks. He found a cafe open and, as he passed, hunger pangs and the desire for coffee welled up from his stomach. He turned back and went in. It was a small relief to sit at a back table and enjoy a breakfast. He lingered, taking his time over a second cup of coffee until the place started filling with the regular morning crowd on their way to offices.

Sitting watching the crowds he decided that anonymity was his best defense. He would lay low and wait. He reasoned that it would take some time for the plans to extricate him to be put into motion. The biggest problem was that he knew Gregori would mobilise his thousands of pimps, prostitutes and drug dealers to find him. He would check into a hotel which had a high turnover of guests, one used by prostitutes for their business, and remain in his room until he could move. Yes, he thought, get off the streets.

Finishing his breakfast, he walked towards the sea front and after an hour found what he was looking for, a rundown hotel with a worn, unpainted exterior and a flickering neon sign which incongruously named it as the Grand Hotel. Inside, the carpet was well worn, threadbare in places, from the constant stream of unkempt guests. It was the epitome of a seedy hotel in a B movie. Even the receptionist, sitting behind a wire cage, looked like he had been cast especially for the part. He was unshaven, with long greasy hair swept back from his forehead, and he was wearing a dirty white singlet. He barely looked up as Peter approached. He mumbled the price and asked for ID. Peter paid for two nights and took the key. As he climbed the stairs to the second floor, he asked himself if he had made a mistake; it was likely he would be remembered because of the two night stay. He mentally shrugged his shoulders, deciding that he needed some sleep before planning his next move.

The room was just as shabby as the rest of the building and, after looking at the bed linen, he knew he would not undress and use it. Too many people had left their mark on the sheets and blankets. He found a dirty glass in the bathroom and, wrapping it in a towel, put it on the floor and stood on it. He opened the door and sprinkled the broken glass in the corridor outside his room. He doubted that anyone would clean it up in the near future, not if the levels of dust and garbage outside the rest of the rooms was anything to go by. He closed the door and noted that it would not take much to break in; the wood surround was rotting and the lock was loose. He propped a chair under the handle; it might give him enough time to react if he heard someone outside. Satisfied that he had done as much he could, he lay on the bed, keeping the 9mm close to his hand, and closed his eyes.

Sleep did not come easily, his mind was working too hard, trying to work out what he would have to do to stay alive for the next day or two, but eventually he drifted into a light sleep. He remained on the bed, drifting in and out of sleep, as the shadows moved slowly around the room. The sun had set and darkness was enveloping the corners of the room when he heard the crunch of glass outside his door. Then nothing. He moved off the bed to the wall opposite the door, thumbing back the hammer on the pistol. The light from the window was enough for him to see the door handle. He was alert now, his every sense straining to hear, feel, what was happening in the corridor. If it hadn't just been someone passing the door there would have been more noise from the broken glass. He had to assume that the noise had made whoever was there freeze in place. He could imagine them listening at the door, trying to ascertain if he had moved, if they had indeed alerted him. After an interminable silence, he thought he saw the door handle being turned, a slight creak as the lock and rotting wood protested at the pressure. Again silence. Peter raised his gun and aimed where he thought chest height would be, his finger tightening on the trigger, taking up the slack. Even though he was expecting it, he was still surprised when the door burst open, coming completely off its hinges to fall to the floor. The whole door falling also surprised the intruder, catching him temporarily off balance as he rushed the room. Peter waited in the shadows and the man stumbled and tried to regain his balance, turning to face the bed. A second figure appeared in the doorway and it was then that Peter opened fire, putting two rounds into the chest of the man framed in the door before switching his aim and putting another two rounds into the chest of the first man.

The shots sounded like canon fire in the confines of the small room, and Peter's ears were still ringing as he checked each body. He hurriedly grabbed his bag and ran into the corridor. Looking each way, he did not see any prying faces; curiosity in a place like this could be fatal. Thankful for small mercies, he raced in the direction of the fire escape and leapt down the steps, praying that the door would not be locked and secured against people trying to leave without paying for services rendered. There was no chain and padlock, and he threw himself against the panic bar and the door swung open, leaving him standing in a back alley. No sooner had he stopped to take stock of the situation than an alarm sounded, the shrill bell echoing off the walls. Damn, he cursed himself, that was why there had been no locks; the door had been alarmed. Now anyone waiting would know his location. He swept his eyes around the alley, desperately trying to gain his bearings; which way was the hotel front? He quickly retraced his steps in his mind and turned to his left, breaking into a run in the direction he hoped was away from any pursuers.

He reached the street in seconds and stopped. His guess had been right and he walked quickly in the direction of the town centre, hoping to lose himself in the crowds. He used every technique he had been taught in training to try and spot any followers and was reasonably satisfied that he had escaped them for the time being as he again approached

Prospekt Square. He found a bench in the open and sat to gain his breath and think.

It was obvious he would have to move out of Odessa, and move very quickly. Now the police would be looking for him as well. An unwelcome complication, but at least he could spot them and avoid them. Getting caught by the Police offered no safety; Gregori would still be able to get to him, possibly even have him handed over to him. He stopped a couple passing by and asked for directions to the railway station. Fortunately, as they explained to him, it was close by. He thanked them and followed their directions, hoping that some trains would still be running. He looked at his watch for the first time and was surprised to see that it was only eight o clock.

He found the station and walked onto the concourse. Finding a timetable outside the ticket office, he looked to see what trains were next to leave. Glancing around, he saw the usual amount of police officers hanging around various points of the concourse, but reasoned that they had probably not been notified about him yet. It would take time, he hoped, for the facts to be established at the hotel and then for a description to be issued. He chose a train leaving in ten minutes for Zaporozhye. It was a four-and-a-half hour journey east along the coast. He bought a first class ticket and rushed to the platform to catch the train.

On the train, he anxiously watched the platform until the train pulled out on time, but no-one made any last minute dash to catch it. As the train gathered speed, he sat and relaxed for several minutes. He knew he had to do something about his appearance; the previous twenty four hours in the same clothes, without a shower, had left him in a less than desirable state. That was why he bought a first class ticket. It offered more facilities to clean himself up. He had to admit that he felt far better after he had done this and changed his grimy clothes for fresh clean ones.

He would spend the next four hours trying to work out the best way to hide from his pursuers. Obviously, using a cheap hotel had been a bad idea. That would be one of the first places to look; it was too easy to gain information about him, and there were too many people who might be on Gregori's payroll to spot him. No, when he arrived in Zaporozhye he would find a better class of hotel and try and blend in with the businessmen and tourists. It would also be unlikely that Gregori's employees would frequent a better establishment.

I, Plague

The night obscured any views of the passing countryside, only the occasional lights of an isolated farmhouse indicating their movement. Only his reflection stared back at him, and the hypnotic movements of the train took their toll. Sightlessly looking at the window Peter found himself thinking about the things he could do when he eventually reached England. He thought about his childhood and the ambitions he had harboured. He had achieved the first one when he joined the intelligence services. He knew he would like to meet that special person and settle down to a normal life. How would it be, he asked himself? Would they go for picnics in the country, lie in a meadow basking in the warm summer sun? Would they have fun during the winter months in front of a fire, reading, holding each other, spending Christmas together or with her family? Nights out in the pub with friends. It would be so good to lead a life without lies and constant deception. He could see, in his mind's eye, the village he had grown up in, the green where cricket was played, the local pub with the benches outside. With this picture, he felt his eyes grow heavy and closed them.

He woke with a start as he sensed someone putting a bag into the overhead rack. He saw a woman slightly older than himself struggling with her bag and she smiled apologetically at him. "Sorry, I didn't mean to wake you." She shoved the bag in the rack before he could stand and help her. Sitting opposite him, she smiled again, almost shyly. Checking his watch, he saw that he must have dozed for almost an hour; it was only another hour and a quarter until they arrived. He smiled back at her and asked where they were. She told him the name of a small town which he didn't recognize.

He watched her as she settled, taking a book out of a handbag and starting to read. Although her clothing was casual, he could see it was expensive. Her short light brown hair was pulled back from her ears and, in repose, he realised she was younger than he had initially taken her for.

Gradually they struck up a conversation, the way strangers do on trains and planes. She told him she was returning home after spending the weekend with her parents at their summer home on the Crimea coast. As she talked, she confirmed his thoughts that she was well-educated and fairly well-off, coming from a prosperous family.

It turned out she was a civil engineer, having attended university in Moscow. He encouraged her to talk, enjoying the normality of the conversation with someone who wasn't involved in any criminal activities. As he listened, he began to form the idea that possibly he could seduce her and use her and her apartment to hide in until he could leave. He quickly dismissed the thought, and, surprised at himself for even thinking in that way, he chastised himself. He would be placing her in danger; Gregori, he knew, would have no compunction about treating her very harshly if he found them together. No, it was better not to involve any civilians in his escape.

He found that he was enjoying her company and actually found her attractive. He asked her about hotels in Zaporozhye and she told him of the Sheraton which was the best in town. He decided to take a chance and asked if she would join him for coffee or a drink the next day, after she had finished work. She agreed readily, and they decided on the sidewalk cafe outside the hotel as the meeting place. She looked at him expectantly, and he knew that she was waiting to tell her something about himself. He told her he was an Englishman visiting the Ukraine on holiday. Touring around as the desire took him, thus the late night train journey. He had decided to use his real name and formally introduced himself. She introduced herself as Olga Semnova and shyly offered him her hand.

As they were going through the outskirts of the town, she asked if he had a reservation at the hotel and, when he told he did not, she took out her cell phone and offered to call and make one for him. His suspicious mind immediately jumped to the conclusion that she was checking on him, but he dispelled this thought as uncharitable; she was only trying to be helpful. The booking was made and they prepared to get off the train as the station platform came into sight. She offered to share her taxi, dropping him at the hotel before making her way home. He was grateful to this sweet woman who had made this interlude so pleasant. He almost felt normal again.

The formalities at reception were soon taken care of and it was with relief that he found himself in a clean and well-appointed room. It was identical to thousands of other hotel rooms, but it was clean and had every convenience. Because he knew his handler's phone was on a secure diplomatic line, he decided to phone from the room rather than take the chance of leaving the hotel and finding a pay phone.

He gave his code name and was put through.

He cut the formalities. "I had to leave Odessa in a hurry. There are two down at the hotel, but I expect they will have sent a cleanup crew. Anyway, I'm in Zaporozhye, the Sheraton. Any news on the extraction?"

The anonymous voice replied. "I have arranged a seat for you on a corporate jet leaving from here the day after tomorrow. You'll be travelling as part of a group of visiting businessmen. It's all arranged, we just have to get you there, and on board, then you'll be home before you know it." Peter thought he sounded very optimistic, but knew there were a lot of risks in between his hotel room and the seat on the plane. His handler continued. "I have a car standing by to pick you up. He'll leave in the morning, should be with you by the evening, then we time the drive to get you to the airport a few minutes before takeoff. How does that sound?"

"Fine by me," replied Peter. "The sooner I'm out the happier I'll be. Anything else?"

"What name are you using?" Peter told him that it was his own. Easier with hotels, he explained.

"OK. The driver will meet you in the lobby at seven thirty tomorrow night." There was a pause. "I debated whether or not to tell you this, and decided it's only fair you know." Peter waited. "We've noticed that our cars are being followed as they leave the compound. It has to be Gregori. We're letting them do it in the hope we can slip your car away unnoticed. So be alert, just in case. I'll do my best this end, and the driver I'm sending you is one of our best. Well, Peter, I'm sorry I never had a chance to meet you, but good luck."

Peter thanked him and hung up. Sitting on the edge of the bed, he stared at the phone. For the first time since he had started this job he felt alone. He felt a desperate need to phone back and have a conversation with his handler. He knew absolutely nothing about him, would not recognise him in the street. But he had always been there, particularly at the start, offering advice and encouragement, listening to his concerns and fears. Now there was nothing. Yes, he felt alone.

He lay on the bed and tried not to think of the last moves he would make in this country. He tried not to think about what it would feel like to be home. The thoughts he had had on the train came back to him unbidden. The things he could do, the places he could go, old friends he might be able to meet up with. With these thoughts on his mind, eventually fatigue took its hold and he drifted into an uneasy sleep.

CHAPTER FIFTY TWO

When things went well they went really well, but when things turned bad they went very bad, very quickly. Gregori sat in his office and stared out of the window, not seeing the view, his mind trying to work his way around his predicament which was getting worse by the hour. First the drugs and arms seized in England, then Yuri, or whatever his name was, now a shipment from Afghanistan had been taken by NATO forces near the border. Even his political contacts seemed to be shying away from him. Only that morning, one had been unavailable to take his calls. The moves against him were rapidly gaining momentum, and he had to do something quickly to regain control. If he showed weakness now there could even be moves by some of his own subordinates. The only loyalty they had was to money and the power it gave them. He now looked with suspicion upon everyone.

Maybe, just maybe, he mused, it was time to do what poor Anatoly had been going to do. Retire to a quiet dacha on the Crimean coast and enjoy the rest of his life without the hassles of trying to run his businesses.

A knock at the door broke his reverie and he pulled himself together. As soon as they entered he knew that his two lieutenants had bad news. Trepidation at having to tell him was etched deeply on their faces and the manner in which they sidled to the desk, half prepared to run from the room.

They stood in silence before him, each waiting for the other to start.

"Well, spit it out. I'm not a mind reader" he demanded.

"We found Yuri in Odessa. He had checked into a hotel we run as a brothel. We sent two men, the best we had, to take him."

"Let me guess. No, tell me."

The other took up the story. "They're dead. Shot as they broke into the room."

"And Yuri?"

"Nothing, no one saw him leave, he hasn't been seen on the streets, airport or anywhere else. He's disappeared."

At this Gregori exploded. "Disappeared, what is he? The bloody invisible man? He has to be somewhere. Tell those idiots in the south to get off their fat arses and start looking. Better yet, you two go down there and find him."

"What about business here? We'll lose our pickups."

"I don't care." Gregori was yelling now. "Find him and bring him back, or you won't have any business to lose. Understand?"

They nodded mutely and hurried from the room. Before they reached the door, Gregori stopped them. "Learn from this. Yuri is not an amateur like the people you send against him. He made a mistake allowing us to find him. He will not make the same mistake twice."

As the door closed, he regained control of his temper. What a pity that Yuri was working for someone else. Whereas before Yuri had always shown a reluctance to kill, which he could now understand, that was no longer an issue. He was smart and resourceful; it would take his most trusted men to catch him. The street people were no good in this type of situation. He had a small team he used for the more unpleasant tasks, and he would have to bring them in, ready to move whenever Yuri was located.

Next his main problem areas, France and Germany. There the migrant blacks were muscling in on him. He would have to send some people to crack down on them. The more brutal the better. It was the only thing they understood. A few bodies strategically placed would send the message that he was not down and out just yet. If that did not work, then if they wanted a war, he would give them one.

It gave him some satisfaction to start planning his campaign. He might even go himself to show his face and make everyone understand he was the one to be feared, not these bloody amateurs who were emerging.

But first he had to take care of this Yuri business; if word got out that the traitor had escaped it might encourage others. If he escaped his net, it would also be read that his grip was not as widespread as it had been. Not good messages to send out.

CHAPTER FIFTY THREE

Seven in the morning, and a long day stretched ahead of him. He ordered breakfast from room service and took a shower while he waited for it to arrive. After putting the tray outside the door he hung the "Do Not Disturb" sign on the door handle and lay on the bed. This was the worst part. The waiting. A sudden thought had him on his feet, reaching for his bag and throwing his few belongings into it.

If he didn't check out then it would be possible to find him just by making a phone call. Whereas if he checked out the hotel staff would tell any caller just that. It might buy him some time and he could seek the anonymity of the hotel lounges and bars until the car arrived. He stopped as he caught sight of himself in the mirror.

"Hold on," he said to himself. "No one can know your real name. The staff who checked you in last night will be in bed asleep by now. No one can give your description, so why make life complicated for yourself?" He smiled at himself. "And stop talking to yourself, it's the first sign of madness." With this he turned from the mirror and sat back on the bed.

He tried to think it through. There were ways he could alter his appearance without too much trouble. A hat of sorts, sunglasses... At this he glanced out of the window and saw that it was a sunny day, so no problem there. He checked his funds and knew he had plenty. He would buy a suit and shirt to look more the part of a businessman. That decided, he was about to leave the room. The ringing of the phone startled him. He hesitated momentarily before picking it up.

"Peter? Glad I caught you." The voice of his handler came through. "Sorry to break with protocol, but I had to take a chance and speak with you. A small problem, I'm afraid." He didn't wait for Peter to reply. "The driver has been unable to shake off the tail. He took a run at it and came back here. Couldn't take too much of a chance, sorry."

Peter thought for a moment. "OK. What now?"

"I'm trying to work a way to get a car out on legitimate business. From what they've been doing they lose interest if the vehicle doesn't seem to be going to pick you up. It might take a bit of time though, are you all right to stay where you are for another day, maybe two?"

"Yes, I think so. I'm trying to act the part of an English visitor. If I lay low I should be all right. When do you want me to phone?"

"How about tonight? I should have it set up by then."

Peter agreed and hung up. It was a bloody nuisance, but nothing could be done. He had to rely on his handler to know what was best. But right now he had to do some shopping. He found the room safe in the wardrobe and placed his gun, spare clips and passport in it. Leaving the room, he removed the sign from the door. It might raise questions in the housemaid's mind if she could not service the room.

In the lobby, he found the corridor with the shops and chose a pair of sunglasses from one before going to the clothing shop where he bought a suit and two shirts. He debated about a hat and found a dark fedora which would not look too out of place in a country where hats were a common sight. It had the advantage of good rim which he could pull low over his forehead. It also served the purpose of hiding most of his hair.

He hurried back to the room and changed quickly. Now was the hard part. How to lose himself for the remainder of the day? His first stop was the reception desk, where he checked if he could have the room for at least one more night. He kept his head down, pretending to examine one of the brochures while the computer was checked. It was one of those odd situations where it was difficult to know how much or how little to say. What would a visiting businessman say? As he waited, he explained that his meetings were running late and as a result he would not finish in time for his flight. A solicitous enquiry as to the hotel assisting in booking another flight was fended off by his reply that the company was taking care of it. Hoping he had managed to act the part, he left the desk and made his way out into the bright sunshine.

He didn't hang about at the entrance, making a left and walking down the street. Only after he crossed a road did he check his surroundings and the people in his vicinity. He walked another block, checking windows for anyone who might stop when he did, but there were only commuters walking quickly to get to their place of employment. He chose a cafe and sat inside with a good view of the door and the sidewalk. He ordered coffee and sat sipping slowly for twenty minutes before moving back outside. Checking around, he could not recognise any of the faces around him and, seeing a gap in the traffic, made a dash across the road. On the other side, he walked quickly to the right, checking the other side of the street and behind him as he did so. There were no hurried movements, no one was taking the slightest bit of interest in him. Satisfied, he stopped and bought a street map.

He continued walking aimlessly and found himself on Lenin Avenue. He passed through scenic squares, some with fountains at their centre, and all with up-market bars, cafes and restaurants. He noted one which seemed popular, but with a vacant table at the back near the large window. He bought a paper and took his seat, ordering coffee and croissants. Looking over the top of the newspaper, he watched the street and square in the direction he had come, but again noticed nothing out of the ordinary. Sipping his coffee, he saw that the headline concerned two British youngsters who had been arrested in possession of a kilo of drugs. Stupid kids, he thought.

They never seemed to be aware of the penalties for drug smuggling. They always thought it only ever happened to someone else. From what the paper said it looked as if there was no doubt about their guilt and they would be sentenced to lengthy prison terms. Although he believed it to be their own fault, he could not help but feel sorry for them. Prisons, he had heard, were not a comfortable environment for a young person.

As he finished his coffee he saw that it was not unusual for customers to linger, no one had left since he had sat down, so he felt able to sit, read his paper and watch the passing foot traffic.

His mind went back to the rendezvous he planned with Olga for that evening. Was it a wise move? Probably not. But there was the fact that it would, he hoped, be a pleasant distraction from his situation. He had always found that having time to dwell on a problem did not improve his frame of mind. Yes, he decided, he would go ahead with the meeting. There was, after all, risk in everything he did, some acceptable and some not.

With surprise he saw that it was nearing lunchtime and decided to move, find another square, another cafe and have something decent to eat. After that he resolved to find a cinema and spend the afternoon in the dark anonymity of the theatre.

He watched a dubbed performance of "Australia" with Nicole Kidman. It amused him to watch the actor's lips and the dialogue as it came over the speakers. But it was good to enough to distract him for a couple of hours. Coming out of the theatre, he made his way back to the hotel and took a seat to wait for Olga.

I, Plague

The sun was still warm on his face, and bright, reflecting off the fronts of buildings. He nursed a beer until he saw her walking towards the hotel. He stood and waved, catching her attention. He liked the way she smiled when she saw him. It lit up her face, small crinkles forming at the corners of her eyes. As she threaded her way through the tables, he thought that it was a shame that a naturally good-looking people should maintain a rather stern, unsmiling visage most of the time.

He held out a chair for her and summoned a waiter. He asked about her day and, after an initial hesitation began talking. He kept her talking about herself with the odd question. He was beginning to feel himself relax and enjoy her company. The conversation became more light-hearted, with both of them laughing at some absurdity.

The sun had sunk lower than the surrounding buildings and he was forced to remove his sunglasses. He had removed his hat out of politeness when she had arrived, and now he felt naked, his face exposed to anyone who wanted to look. After a moment's uneasiness, he turned his attention back to Olga and continued to spar verbally with her, much as two strangers have done for generations.

He did not know what made him glance out of the corner of his eye towards the hotel entrance. Maybe it was that he felt the intense stare directed at him by a man standing just outside the revolving door. He had been placing something in his jacket pocket, but had now taken it back out and was looking at it. Peter could not see what it was but knew that it was probably a photograph. He looked directly at the man. He was not one of the usual street people; he was well dressed in a conservative suit. He turned back to Olga.

"Please excuse me for a minute, I think I've just seen a colleague passing and I want to catch him." She smiled and he stood up, moving through the tables away from the entrance. He turned to wave to her and saw the man move to the sidewalk and start in his direction. Peter thought furiously, his mind racing over all the possibilities. He would have to make sure he had been identified; he could make a couple of turns to be sure before he did anything. Because of his walk that morning, he knew if he made a right turn he would come across a service alley. He would make his move there. He had not see anyone else in the vicinity and hoped fervently that the man was alone.
He made the turn and then, at the mouth of the alley, glanced back and saw his follower closing in on him. He entered the alley and rushed a

few yards to where there were a row a garbage dumpsters against the wall. He found a gap and squeezed into it. The hurried footsteps told him the bait had been taken and as they neared he moved out to stand squarely in front of his pursuers. He saw the pistol held in the right hand and acted. His own right hand shot up, fingers together and straight, the tips burying themselves in the throat. He could feel the cartilage being crushed as he pushed as hard as he could. The man let out a small breath and what sounded like a groan. Peter knew that he crushed the windpipe and larynx, it would only be a matter of time before he died. But he did not have time. At any moment a passerby might see what was happening and call the police. He grabbed the now stooped man by the hair and pushed him between the dumpsters. Moving his hands to the back of the head and the chin, he wrenched and heard the neck snap. He caught the falling body under the arms and propped him against himself while he lifted the lid of the nearest dumpster. With an effort, he managed to swing the top half of the body over the lip followed by his legs. He glanced in as he closed the lid and saw that it was only half full. With luck, whoever dumped their garbage would throw it in without looking. If he was really lucky the man might never be discovered. He checked his clothes, dusting off marks left by the wall and dumpster, then made his way back to the street. He paused at the entrance and checked around; nothing, he must have been working alone. He was probably just sent to check the hotel and make any report back for a team to be sent in to take him.

He made his way back to Olga.

"That was quick, was it your friend?" He realised that, although it had felt like an eternity, the whole episode of taking a man's life had in fact only taken minutes.

"Yes, I just wanted to check if he was on the same flight home. You know, arrange to sit together and compare notes on our trip."

He smiled, "Look, I know we only arranged to meet for a drink, but, would you like to have dinner with me? I'm sure they'll have a table in the restaurant."

He had to get both of them off the street. Something to eat, and then he would put her in a taxi and send her home.

In the restaurant, he saw that there were some tables at the back. There was comfortable leather covered bench type seating under a mirror which ran the length of the wall. He indicated one of the seats to the maitre'd and they followed him, sitting Olga under the mirror while he had his back to the room but could see everything in the mirror. Olga had explained that she and her friends only ate out very rarely, it was too costly for them, preferring to meet at each other's homes. It pleased him that she showed delight at the menu, which, in keeping with the Sheraton standards, was very cosmopolitan. They both ordered prawns and steak dianne. He chose a bottle of local red wine and they continued their conversation, mainly with him getting her to talk about her life, her childhood and her family. It proved to be interesting, especially when she talked about her grandparents. From his knowledge of the Soviet ear he knew she had had a privileged upbringing. Despite everything he found himself warming to her, and wished they had met under different circumstances. Over coffee he asked if she would like to stay in touch after he had flown home. She readily agreed and gave him her e-mail address.

All too soon it was over and he reluctantly led her into the lobby, asking the concierge to order her a taxi. He gave the driver enough money to cover the fare and turned to thank her for the evening. To his surprise she reached up to him and gently kissed him on the lips. Embarrassed, she immediately turned and got into the taxi. He waved at her as it left and, feeling slightly foolish at his reaction to the kiss, turned back into the hotel.

Walking through the doors he was aware that the concierge was watching him. He stopped and went across to the desk. He fished in his pocket, looking for the US currency he had.

"I would like to ask a favour." He smiled at the concierge. "As you probably guessed, that was not my wife." He saw the flicker of a smile and understanding on his face. "Anyway, my wife does not understand that a man sometimes needs a diversion." More understanding. "Anyway, I think she is checking on me. Perhaps you understand, and forget about me if anyone were to ask." He slipped a hundred dollar bill across the desk top. It was covered and disappeared in an instant.

"I understand perfectly, Sir. Discretion is my middle name. You were never here and certainly did not entertain a young lady."

"I was sure you would understand, thank you. For your trouble." He slipped another hundred dollars across the desk.

They parted, Peter with a smile hinting at the shared conspiracy and the concierge with a happy smile because he had just made the easiest two hundred dollars of his life.

CHAPTER FIFTY FOUR

Once in the room, he emptied the safe, placing the gun near the pillows and packing his few belongings in case he had to make a quick exit. Next, he dialled the Kiev number and was put through.

"Christ, Peter, you had me worried. You all right?"

"Everything's fine. I was spotted, but dealt with it. It should buy me more time." He briefly filled him in on the events of the evening.

"You're leaving quite a body trail. I hope you're right about the city cleaning this one up. Anyway, here's the plan. Bear with me, it's the best I could do. Well, we have two nationals in prison down there, on drug charges." Peter told him he had seen it in the papers and let him continue. "The thing is, they have to have some consular representation and two of the consular guys are going to be there tomorrow. One of them is a friend and has agreed to do me a favour. In a nutshell, you'll swap places with the driver and drive them back." He waited for Peter's response.

"Jesus, that's breaking all protocol, they'll have your ass in a sling if anyone finds out about it."

"They'll only find out if it goes wrong. Anyway, it's the only option so far. Let me worry about the Foreign Office. The thing in our favour is that it's a diplomatic car instead of one I would normally use. Also, with the uniform cap and sunglasses, it will be hard to spot the difference when you're driving. Another plus is that you'll drive straight to the diplomatic compound and be out of harm's way in no time. All things being equal, it should work. What do you think?"

"Sounds good, but I wouldn't want to be in your shoes if they find out. What's the timing? Where do we make the switch?"

"The prison is in an area called Pavlo-Khichkas. There are a lot of old, Soviet era warehouses and factories, mostly disused and empty now. You have to be at ZaporizhStal near the cargo port at 11h00. They'll pull over, ostensibly for a toilet break, and the driver will go to a doorway when he sees you. That's the swap. You need a dark suit, white shirt and dark tie. You make your way into the car, not forgetting to do up your flies on the way, and head back here. The driver is not local, so we have to be exact on the point, have you got a map?" Peter spread it out on the bed and they made sure they had the directions to the street clear.

"One last thing, Peter. If the interview overruns you have to be patient. Do not move, they will arrive, I just cannot guarantee the exact time. I have to admit, I'm looking forward to meeting you tomorrow. You take care. Oh, and please don't get my friend killed." Peter assured him he would not let that happen and hung up.

It was a restless night for Peter. He alternated between dreams of being chased down endless dark corridors and then waking with a start, unsure of his surroundings. Unable to sleep, he left the television on and dozed. It was with relief that he saw daylight breaking through the curtains. Opening them, he saw that it was going to be another fine, clear, sunny day. He prepared himself while waiting for eight o' clock when he felt he could go down for breakfast, figuring that it would be the busiest time and he would be lost in the crowds. His last task before checking out was to buy a dark tie and white shirt, which he donned before leaving the room. He knew that he could walk the distance to the rendezvous point and reckoned it would take him an hour to get there. He bought a paper and read it in the lobby, waiting until just before ten before leaving. He took the usual precautions after leaving the hotel, until he was sure he had not picked up a tail. Frequently consulting the street map, he started in the direction of the cargo port.

He walked through areas of increasing deprivation and rundown buildings. He could feel suspicious eyes following him from the darkened, filthy doorways and glassless windows. He adjusted the gun in the waistband of his trousers, and left his jacket unbuttoned for easy access. He smiled grimly to himself as he thought of the irony of being taken down in a street mugging. Worse yet was the thought of the delay it might cause him.

He was sweating by the time he reached the agreed street and started to walk down the left side, searching for a suitable doorway which would provide cover for himself but which would also allow room for the swap to take place unnoticed. He found such a doorway about one third of the way down the road, and stood in the shadows to begin the wait. Looking at his watch, he saw that he was fifteen minutes early. He regularly checked the street, but there was no movement that he could see. The empty factories towered all around him. Empty windows stared vacantly out on to the broad road. An occasional sea gull squawked as it circled in its search for a scrap of food. From what he had seen, he thought that the bird would be very lucky indeed to find anything apart from used hypodermics, empty drug bags, and used condoms. After twenty minutes, he began to imagine shadows inside the windows moving, fleeting glimpses of things unseen out of the corner of his eyes.

"Steady," He spoke quietly to himself. "You're beginning to jump at shadows."

He took a couple of deep breaths and stood stock still, with only his eyes constantly scanning the surroundings. Another look at his watch, and another fifteen minutes had passed. He was getting very jumpy, when at last he heard the low rumble of a car engine.

He sneaked a glance around the corner of the doorway and saw a black Mercedes with diplomatic plates crawling along. The driver saw him and indicated he had with a slight movement of his hand on the steering wheel. Peter slid back into the shadows and watched as the car drew level with him, and the driver exited the left door. He jumped the steps into the doorway, fumbling with his flies; for anyone watching it would appear that he was desperate for the toilet. Inside, he slipped his cap to Peter, taking his hat. He handed him his wallet. "Just in case, we look enough alike to pass a quick inspection. I'll pick it up when I get back. Don't worry, I have ID and money. I was followed out of Kiev, I don't know if they made it all the way here, I don't think so, but it'll do you well to keep an eye open. Here, take it and go. Good luck to you."

Peter hesitated; it was the first English voice he had heard, apart from his handler, in a very long time. He moved into the sunlight, pulling up his zipper, made his way straight to the car and got in the driver's seat. The engine was idling, and he put it in drive and made a wide U turn, turning left at the end of the road. The driver had left a map and instructions on the way back to Kiev on the passenger's seat and he followed them until hitting the freeway and the way north. Only on the freeway did the man sitting behind him speak.

"Glad to meet you, Peter. Heard a lot about you."

"Thanks for your help." Peter glanced in the mirror and saw the man smile back at him. "I know how much trouble you could be in, bringing me in using a diplomatic car."

"Don't worry about it. I'm Bradley, and this quiet fellow is my assistant,

Lee." Peter acknowledged him with a nod.

He settled into the drive routine as the undulating countryside sped past the windows. The road was not busy, but his attention was kept on the road as he negotiated the passing of slow moving heavily laden trucks moving their goods from the port to the inland cities and towns. The countryside alternated between vast fields of grain swaying in the warm, gentle breeze, huge combine harvesters contrasting with the horse drawn equipment used by the old farmers. The 21st century competing against medieval methods.

He thought that, in some ways, it was a pity that Western corporations were moving in, bringing their modern methods. But after the collapse of the Soviet Union, vast tracts of arable land had fallen into neglect and this investment was increasing basic food production to new levels. He wondered how much of the revenue was falling into the hands of corrupt officials. He knew from his time with Gregori how much corruption still prevailed in all levels of government. Gregori had most of the corrupt politicians and police in his back pocket. He could influence the outcome of local elections and, in some cases, national policy. The country would no doubt grow and develop, gradually changing the culture to one of honesty, but it would probably take a generation to accomplish this.

As he thought and mused the Mercedes ate the miles and he soon had to drag his attention back to the task of driving as the build up of traffic indicated they were nearing Kiev. Now on what had been his home turf, he mentally planned his route to the diplomatic compound. He had been regularly checking the mirror to see if he could spot a tail, and now increased his vigilance as any following car would have to close the gap to keep up with him in the heavier traffic. He could see nothing; perhaps the driver had been correct in the notion that they had lost interest. Three out and three in, nothing untoward there to someone observing from a distance.

He drove as fast as he could through the suburbs and into the city. With a relief he could feel sweeping through his body, he saw the consular buildings, and as he glanced in the mirror, could see the same relief on the faces of Bradley and Lee. He could manage a small smile at this; two diplomats playing at spook games. As they swept through the gates, he smiled at them, "Thanks again for the ride. It's really appreciated."

Bradley was the one to reply. "You're more than welcome, Peter. Look, there's Steve."

I, Plague

As Peter had never met his handler, he had to assume that Steve was the tall, lean man coming down the steps to meet them. As he pulled up, he moved to open the doors for the diplomats, thinking that was what a regular driver would do. Once they had made their way up the stairs he turned and waited, unsure what to do next.

"Peter, come inside and relax." He followed him up the stairs and into the lobby. There, Steve turned and offered his hand. "Good to meet you at last. Too bad it's under these circumstances. Glad you're here though."

Peter shook the proffered hand. "Good to meet you too. Thanks for getting me out of there. Another day might have been too much."

"Well, you're safe as long as you're here. Of course, the next problem is how to get you out of the country. The corporate jet would have been just the ticket, but, never mind, we'll think of something." He took Peter by the elbow and led him up the stairs to the second floor.

"This will be home until we can make the necessary arrangements." He indicated the room. It appeared to be a coffee room, easy chairs and sofas scattered around coffee tables. There was a coffee maker with mugs and all the usual paraphernalia in the corner. Steve indicated a small fridge, and told him that he would find some ready meals inside. The microwave was on a table in another corner of the room.

"Anything you need, just shout, and we'll get it for you. There are some blankets in the cupboard over there. Not quite the Sheraton, but I'm sure you don't mind."

"Definitely not," replied Peter. "But what about the others who use this room? Won't they be curious about me?"

"Not at all, they call this the haunted room." He laughed at Peter's quizzical look. "Inhabited by spooks. Only the security services use this place. Come and sit, I'll fix you a coffee, or would you prefer something stronger?"

"Well, I don't have to worry about watching my p's and q's for a while, so a whiskey and a beer would be great, thanks."
As they sat, Steve became more serious. "I'm not going to debrief you here, everything you told me has been passed on. They'll take care of

that in London. I suppose you're wondering who I am. I'm with MI6, attached here with the culture people. We have a small team here, two of us and one from SIS as well as technicians who deal with the all the communication stuff. The driver you swapped places with was my colleague; I couldn't take a chance on a civilian or one of the embassy drivers. By the way, he's phoned in and should by now be on a train back."

"Any thoughts on how I'm going to get out of the country? You know enough about the organisation that they reach everywhere."

"No idea. That's the simple answer." A rueful smile came with the answer. "In the good old days, we would have an organisation set up to deal with border crossings, defectors and all that. Unfortunately, with the demise of the cold war most of those methods died as well. We can't even afford to charter a plane; that would have been the easy answer. But, on the bright side, your boys in London are working their butts off to find an answer. I'm sure that between us we'll come up with something."

Peter answered all the questions about what happened while he had been on the run. He was not overly surprised to hear that nothing about the shooting in the hotel or the body in the dumpster had come into the open. As far as Steve knew, the police had not been involved, at least in an official capacity.

"Look, I can see you're tired so I'll leave you. I have some paperwork to take care of. You try and rest, we'll not disturb you unless we have to." He left and Peter lay back on the sofa. The whiskey was working its magic, and his mind was accepting the fact that, for the time being, at least, there was no danger, no threats lurking in the corridors. He permitted sleep to take over.

CHAPTER FIFTY FIVE

It had been two long days with no word from the south on Yuri. Gregori was beginning to think that he somehow had managed to escape the dragnet he had thrown around the country. It was costing him a small fortune to keep the police on the lookout for him; even in this society, bribing a senior police officer did not come cheap, but even they were beginning to complain that they could not keep the current level of surveillance up for much longer without throwing suspicion on themselves. And then there were the lower-level dealers and pimps who were spending much of their time on the search. They were getting slack as the need to make money took over as their priority. He had sent more of his best men to the south to help in the search, but nothing. Only one indicator that he might be in Zaporozhye was that a detective had gone missing. But he couldn't count on that being Yuri's work. It could be that he was holed up somewhere with his mistress.

But, he consoled himself, at least the time had not been wasted. He had set in motion the crackdown that he wanted. Starting in the suburbs of Paris, his teams would go in and quash independent dealers and suppliers. It would mean a crackdown by the Paris police and their drug enforcement agency as well as the Suretee, but that would be short-lived and only result in the loss of street dealers and lower-end suppliers. No one who could not be replaced. If they managed to get hold of the ringleaders, there were orders in place that they were to be held for his personal attention. That should get everyone's attention on who the real boss was in Europe.

He had even managed to re-establish links with the Afghan warlord who supplied the raw material from his vast poppy fields, and new methods of transportation were being put in place for the next shipment. Without Yuri feeding them information normal business should be resumed very quickly. He was, all in all, very satisfied with the efforts of the last two days.

He had arranged a meeting with all his major suppliers and distributors for the Wednesday. He had even persuaded the Afghan warlord to come, despite the fact that he detested the man's lack of personal hygiene and manners. He was too important to offend controlling as he covered a large percentage of the country's poppy regions. The meeting would take place in the opulent surroundings of the football stadium and they would all watch the game afterwards. The stadium served the dual purpose of providing security and also of convincing the others that there was nothing amiss with his financial status. If there was even the slightest doubt that he could fulfill his obligations with regard to payments, he would be finished.

Although he had hated to lose the money on the operation in the UK and the loss of the weapons, his personal wealth was still staggering by anyone's standards. He simply had too many offshoots in the business world to be hampered greatly. However, it still hurt to lose that amount of money. Although, he had to admit to himself that it was his pride which had suffered greatly, as well as his standing in the criminal fraternity.

As he always did, he was drawing up a game plan of how the meeting should run. He would have to assert himself in the strongest possible manner. Catching Yuri and taking care of him would go a long way to achieving this goal. He intended that Yuri's demise should be as brutal as possible, a lesson that no one could succeed in betraying him and that his network was capable of finding anyone, anywhere, no matter who they had behind them.

No, he told himself, he would have absolute control again by Wednesday evening. He would not tolerate any doubts that he was still in charge.

A discreet knock at the door and two well-dressed men in business suits entered, approached the desk and shook hands with Greogori. He indicated that they should sit and indicated that his bodyguard should give them coffee.

"You have both been advising me on business matters and handling my money for a few years now. You know that I have been moving into more legitimate businesses and you are the front men for these organisations." He paused deliberately, seeing their apprehension over what could be coming next. He smiled as he imagined their minds going over past transactions, trying to assure themselves that no mistakes had been made and readying arguments in their defense against any statement to the contrary. Gregori let the silence hang for a few minutes as he sipped his coffee.

"I am pleased with the results so far." He could see the tension ease, their shoulders dropped into a more relaxed posture. "But now I want to move more into the legitimate side of business. You are to use the money held in Lichenstein and make some acquisitions for me. Firstly,

I want to expand the shipping side; I think we could take on some cruise ships and operate out of the Baltic. Put together something for me to look at, whether we should build or buy into the market. Next, oil; I want to make a move into that and I think we can start buying up shares in one of the fairly new exploration companies." He paused to watch their reactions and waited for them to stop scribbling notes before he continued.

"The revenues from my other interests will continue to fund these moves. You, as usual, do not need to know anything about that side of things. I have always kept you away from that, because I need these businesses to stand on their own no matter what else happens. Do I make myself clear?" He waited for the assurances.

"The sooner this happens the better, as far as I'm concerned. Apart from the cruise ships and oil, I want you look at other fields we could move into, for example, the communications companies. I want an organisation of good businesses in the next year. At that time, I will assume control of them, keeping the two of you on as Managing Directors. I will, at that time, relinquish all control and involvement in my other interests to someone else."

"Right, your thoughts on what I've just said."

There was a long silence. Gregori knew that it was fear of contradicting him or saying something which might upset him that caused this, and added "Speak freely, we are starting a new era and it is necessary that you are able to advise me honestly. You are the experts I employ to do this."

Given this freedom ideas and suggestions started to flow. They were well paid for what they did, and were well versed in the business world. Gregori had paid handsomely for their services, poaching them away from the well established and successful companies they had been employed by.

After a two hour session all the details of the transactions had been agreed, the funds made available and a deadline set for the various stages of progress. Gregori was satisfied that he could do no more.

After they had left, Gregori settled back with the contented air of someone who had achieved something of importance. In a funny way, ironic really, he had Yuri to thank for this move to legitimise his ventures. He might have continued on with what he had been doing for years to come, had not Yuri betrayed him and thus made him aware of his vulnerability. He doubted that he would ever have gone to prison, but the world was changing so much and so quickly that he realised he had to change just as swiftly.

Yes, he decided, looking at himself in the bar mirror, lifting a glass of vodka in a silent toast to his reflection, it would feel good to be a respected and wealthy businessman instead of a criminal mastermind.

CHAPTER FIFTY SIX

Mike had arrived from London at ten on the Saturday morning and the four of them were sitting in the lounge drinking coffee, watching the breaking news story on the BBC about the drugs seizures and arrests which had been made nationwide. The atmosphere was subdued after the initial greetings, each lost in their thoughts about whatever the next few days might bring. As James watched the TV, with only a small part of his mind, he again asked himself if this was the right course of action. He had been arguing with himself over the points in favour of the operation and points against it. He could not resolve the issue in his own mind and was currently feeling less than confident about the whole idea.

On the negative side was the biggest issue of them all – none of them had ever embarked on something like this before. It was a completely new ball game from going to fight in someone else's war. They did not know who their enemy was, not even what he looked like, they did not know the environment they were travelling to and could not understand the language. Those problems made the exercise seem futile. On the other hand, he reasoned, they had probably made this Gregori really mad, and he could not reconcile himself to the belief that he might harbour his grudge and, at some point, come after them all again. It was this which had hardened his resolve to see the matter through to its conclusion; simply the fact that innocents could be harmed if Gregori decided to seek his vengeance at some point in the future.

James forced his doubts to the back of his mind, stood and offered more coffee to the others, before asking Mike to give them details on what he had been able to accomplish.

"My man in Amsterdam," he started, to be interrupted by Ethan.

"Who is this "Man in Amsterdam", that's all you call him?"

"He likes his secrecy; let's call him Anton if you prefer a name. We've always worked with him in the past, and he's totally reliable. One thing, though, when I told him what we were planning he was scared, really scared." He saw another interruption coming. "Stop. We always tell him what's on the cards. We found that, in the past, it was always the best option, he can give all sorts of help if he knows what's going on. Right, I'll continue, if I may?" He grinned at Ethan. "As I said, he is really worried about this gig of ours. This Gregori has a long reach and Anton says everyone is terrified of crossing him. Fortunately for us, Anton himself believes he is so well protected that even Gregori will not be able to get at him, even if we fail. It says a lot for his confidence in us, or lack of it, that he is comfortable with the failure option."

"OK, now for the details. We fly out on Monday, as I told you. I thought we would go in pairs as discussed and meet up at the hotel. Anton has arranged for a guide to meet with us, he will find us in the hotel after we arrive. Weapons have already arrived in Kiev, hand guns for the most part, but we will have access to long range weaponry if we require it. Alexander, that's our guide's name, will hold them for us and he will show us around the usual haunts of our target. He is originally from Kiev and knows the area well. He also knows our target and where he will most likely hang out. He has been there for a few days now, doing a recce, that should save us some time. Anton says we can trust him completely, he's apparently been with him for a long time and has been used on delicate matters before."

He paused and looked around the room. "That's about it. It's not a lot, I know, but then we haven't had much time. I think we're going to have to improvise as we go. Questions?"

James thought about voicing his fears and doubts but decided against it. They had all been asked if they wanted to pull out, and he was sure that if they had any doubts of their own they would say something. The silence held for five minutes as each digested the scant information they had been provided with.

It was Lizelle who broke the silence. "Well, I guess that's it, we leave on Monday. Anyone for a drink?"

The rest of the Saturday and Sunday passed with a palpable tension in the air. Each had their own way of relaxing. Mike and Ethan spent hours in the gym and swimming pool, James and Lizelle spent most of their time at the stables, mostly in the company of Mona who was riding as much as she possibly could. Watching the children come and go, their excited laughter and chatter driving away the dark clouds of foreboding, brought a ray, however small, of sunshine into their days and made it easier.

Monique had been conspicuous by her absence from the group. James guessed that the tension was rubbing off on her, and it was her way of concealing her concerns. He had tried to talk to her, reassure her in some small way, but knew that it had not worked. If anything he felt he had made the situation worse with his forced good humour.

It was, therefore, with an almost palpable sense of relief that it was time for them to take their leave and drive to the airport. There were hugs all round with a few soft spoken words of good luck and, for James, an explicable feeling of loss as they drove away from the house.

CHAPTER FIFTY SEVEN

"Right, here's the plan the bright boys in London have presented us with. I can't say I'm overly happy about it, but listen and then tell me what you think."

Peter had been ensconced in the consulate for two days and was feeling stir crazy. He had been well looked after, everything he had wanted he had been given. Everyone had tried to spend time with him, talking about home, girls and any sport they could think of, but it still felt like a gilded cage. He was now impatient to hear of anything that might get him out of there. The building had been particularly quiet on the Saturday, and now on the Sunday.

Steve told him that three "heavies" were flying in. They were all close protection specialists, one of them being a specialist driver. A new identity and legend were to be delivered in the diplomatic bag. They would alter Peter's appearance to conform to the photograph in his new passport. That would be nothing elaborate, dying his hair to black, puffing up his cheeks and jowls with padding and leaving the stubble on his face. They would increase his height by an inch with heightened shoes, and increase his girth with a padded corset. He would be taken to the airport by his minders and they would travel on an Austrian Airlines flight direct to London Heathrow on the Monday morning.

"My worry is," Steve continued, "that Gregori either knows, or is fairly sure that you are here. His intelligence is too good not to know. Add to that that he could have bought or coerced one of the local staff to pass on information. You've been here too long for some accurate guesswork not to be put together. London seems to have missed this, or have chosen to ignore it. If he does know, then no matter how hard we try to get you out of here it is going to be risky, if not downright dangerous. Also, no matter how good those three are, if Gregori wants to go up against them, you won't stand a chance against his firepower. On the plus side, if we do get you to the airport, your legend will stand up to any scrutiny. It's that bit between here and the airport that worries me."

They were both silent as Peter tried to work out the percentages. "How about a run for the Turkish border?"

"Only see the same problems, with one added concern. It gives them more time to mobilise and intercept you between here and the border. It's a good four hour drive. More than enough time to organise troops

I, Plague

down the road."

"No smaller airports to leave from, provided we can get a flight?"

"None which would give you a flight to a safe destination. Sorry, but I can't think of any viable alternative."

"Not your fault. It looks like we'll have to get set to do some creative make up work."

After a long silence; "When do we expect the bag and the minders to arrive?"

"Both are coming in on this afternoon's flight. We'll have tonight to work on you. All being well, you'll be on the 10h45 flight tomorrow morning."

"Well, at least it doesn't mean too much hanging about. It jangles the nerves, all that waiting. We might as well get on with it. What is it?" Peter had seen Steve almost debating with himself.

"One thing I can do. Before I go on, I have to tell you that I thought about moving you to a safe house tonight. Then I thought, if the three coming in are picked up at the airport and followed, then you wouldn't even get out there. So an alternative – I'm going to send out every car we have, each with two, three or four occupants. They'll leave in quick succession. You'll be in a group of four that leave at the same time. They'll all follow the same route, away from the airport and then split. My hope is that they won't have enough people on standby to follow all the cars. It'll be quite a break from the normal routine. Of course, once it's reported in they'll realise what we're doing and that you're on the move, probably to the airport. My hope is that it'll buy you enough time to get through immigration and on to airside where you should be safe."

"Sounds good. I bet you had a hell of a time convincing the boss man to agree to all that."

"Not too bad actually. I think he's desperate to get rid of you. It could be an embarrassment, your being here." They had a laugh at that, relieving the tense atmosphere.

"Well nothing to do now but wait. How about cracking open that new bottle and getting mildly drunk?"

"Now, as they say, that's the best idea I've heard all day." Steve stood and retrieved the bottle and two glasses from the sideboard.

Having a few shots of whiskey under their belts certainly made the process of dyeing Peter's hair a hilarious affair. Applying the dye using a mascara brush borrowed from one of the typists appeared to them even funnier, as his hands shook with the effects of both the laughter and the whiskey.

The dyeing process was nearing completion when the "heavies" from London were shown into the room. They looked exactly the opposite of what they were. They looked for all intents and purposes to be three businessmen, slightly crumpled and weary after their flight. But they went straight down to business, asking if the weapons were available for their inspection, and then the car. Only after they had satisfied themselves that their equipment was in order did they relax and join in the conversation.

The evening was a subdued affair after the temporary high brought on by the whiskey subsided. Gehan, Graham and Martin wanted to know all about Gregori's operations and what sort of opposition they were up against, if it came down to that. They talked late into the night and it ended on a fairly optimistic note for Peter, as he gained confidence in their abilities and thus the chances of actually making it to the airport.

CHAPTER FIFTY EIGHT

It was an early start with the efforts to change his facial profile with the judicious use of padding around his gums and some foundation makeup. When it was finished, he looked in the mirror and was surprised at the transformation a few bits of padding could make. His face was fuller, rounder and his jawline was now indistinct. The modified bulletproof vest added to his girth and chest, making him appear a lot heavier. He practiced talking and walking around in his platform shoes which had added another inch to his height. After the initial discomfort, caused mainly by the unfamiliarity, he found he was becoming accustomed to the weight and the restricted movements. He doubted if even his mother would recognise him at a cursory glance.

As the departure time grew close, goodbyes were said and the four made their way down to the back of the building and into the waiting car. Radio checks were made and they watched the procession of cars leave until it was their turn to drive onto the street. Martin, the driver, discarded the map he was revising; he had confidently informed them that he had the route firmly implanted in his mind anyway. They swept onto the street, turning left and picking up speed, the third vehicle in a convoy of four. As they wound through Kiev's city centre and into the business district, one by one the others radioed that they were making their turns until they were alone. Martin and Graham in the front were constantly scanning their rear. Peter could see their eyes continually moving over the mirrors and to the front and sides. He, as instructed by Gehan, kept his attention focused on his side and front of the vehicle.

"Hard to say," Martin answered the unspoken question. "Still too much traffic to be sure. If they are there then they're good, possibly changing the lead car frequently. We'll soon see."

He made a series of quick, unexpected turns, throwing the unprepared Peter against the door. "Nope, can't see the same car. You Graham?"

"Nothing"

Martin checked his watch. "We'd better get a move on; time's tight, and there's not much more I can do, anyway."

He drove and soon aircraft were passing overhead as they climbed off the runway. A series of right turns, and they were approaching the perimeter fence. A left turn, and they were on the perimeter road. In the distance, across the fields, runway and taxiways, the terminal buildings were clearly visible.

"Reckon another ten or fifteen minutes." Martin had sped up on the straight road. "Still nothing behind us."

As they approached a small wooded copse he had to slow to follow the road as it worked its way around the area, taking them away from the perimeter fence for a short distance.

"Shit," from Martin brought all their attention to the road in front. It was blocked by a car and a tractor. "Could be innocent. I can drive around them to the left there. But get ready just in case."

Clicks as hammers were drawn back on weapons and windows wound down were the only sounds above the whine of the slowing engine as Martin went down the gears. He drove onto the left verge and mounted the grass. As they drew level they could see two men arguing. One appeared to a farmer and thus the driver of the tractor and the other in casual clothes. They paid no attention to the passing car and there were audible sighs of relief as Martin guided the car back onto the road.

"Jeez, that had the old heart pumping there for a while" Graham joked, turning in his seat to grin at the two in the back. He soon swung his attention back to the front as Martin braked suddenly, slowly the car down to a crawl.

"We've got problems." He indicated to the front where, about a hundred yards away at a bend in the road, two cars blocked their way. This time they could see the armed men waiting for them. Martin put the car into reverse and started back.

"Stop!" Gehan yelled as he and Peter both saw that the tractor and car had changed positions and were now fully blocking the road. The farmer and driver had miraculously produced automatic weapons, which they were aiming in their direction.

"Bugger, like rats in a trap. Through the trees?"

Martin shook his head at Graham's question. "Too tight, ground probably too soft. Only thing to do is run straight at them. Start shooting and that might keep their heads down while I ram them." He put the car in gear and it jumped forward, rapidly gaining speed as he flipped through the gears.

The noise in the car was deafening as they opened up with handguns and Uzi's. It had the desired effect, as the men manning the roadblock sought cover behind their vehicles. The car was covering the ground at ever increasing speed, the engine screaming as Martin tried to gain maximum speed from each gear. Peter did not hear or see the Rocket Propelled Grenade which hit them. One second he was hanging out of the window, firing at the roadblock, the next second he was aware that the car was airborne. He was tumbled and thrown around the interior as it hit and started to roll.

He had no idea how many times it rolled before it came to a creaking halt. Stunned, he crawled through the window and onto the grass. He tried to gather his thoughts, shake his mind clear, clear the double vision and the ringing in his ears. He was aware of someone moving his legs and looked down to see Gehan's bloody face at the window. Automatically he reached down to pull him free.

"No, cover the road, they'll be closing in. I'll be fine."

Peter stood and leaned on the car, turning to where he thought the road was, only to see a wall of trees and thick undergrowth. He swiveled and, with his back to the wrecked car, faced the road. There were six men moving in a semicircle, very cautiously, towards the car. There was no cover for them and Peter opened fire, seeing one fall and the rest dive for the sparse cover available.

"Quick, round the other side, use the vehicle as cover." Gehan had found his feet and loosed two shots to keep their heads down.

Peter kept up steady fire over the roof of the vehicle. He was vaguely aware of how lucky he and Gehan had been to escape the wreck almost unscathed; the roof had been flattened by a good foot, and the doors were mangled bits of metal. Gehan had leaned through the window to check on Martin and Graham.

"Both dead," he pronounced, as he stood and shot again. "Lean in and see if you can reach their weapons and any spare clips."

Peter did as he was told, trying to get as far into the car as possible. This movement elicited a volley of fire, most of the rounds sinking into the already dead flesh of Graham. He managed to retrieve the Uzi, and two magazines, which he placed on the ground at Gehan's feet as he slid himself free of the window.

As he peered over the car, he saw that the two men from the backstop of the ambush were working their way up the road to join the fight.

Gehan pulled him down. "OK, we've no chance if we stay here. You have to move now. Get down on your belly and crawl into the trees. I'll hold them here for as long as I can. You've got to see if you can clear the wood and get to a road. Get as far from here as you can in the next five minutes."

"What about you?"

"Don't worry about me, I'll be right behind you as soon as I see you disappear in the trees. Keep low, but move as fast as you can. Go." The last word was an imperative. He turned his full attention back to the attackers.

Peter touched his shoulder but could find nothing to say.

"GO."

He went, but it was with the certain knowledge that he would never see this man again.

Flat on his belly, Peter crawled as fast as he could, unaware of the stones and thorns grazing his hands and elbows. He pushed through the undergrowth, tearing his clothes free from the cloying branches which entangled him and threatened to halt his forward progress. The additional padding he wore was making all his movements slower and a lot more awkward than he liked, but he did not have time to try and discard it. After a few yards he stopped, winded by his efforts, and looked around. There was enough cover for him to raise his head and take stock of the situation. Only then did he become aware of the gunfire behind him. He could hear the short, sharp crack of the Uzi and 9mm, the returning continuous fire from AK47's. He risked a look and could see that an encircling movement around the car was almost complete. Gehan, he knew, had only moments before he was cut down. At this he saw him take a couple of rounds which knocked him off balance and spun him out of the cover of the car. That was when he took on the appearance of a puppet, as round after round thudded into his body, jerking him this way and that until he eventually fell, his now lifeless finger still pulling on the trigger of the Uzi until the magazine was empty and the rounds had sped uselessly into the air. The attackers wasted no time on him, forming a group shouting in their excitement and gesticulating towards the woods. They seemed to reach a decision and spread out to form a skirmish line walking slowly and warily towards his position.

Peter knew he had to move. He did not stand a chance in a stand-up fight against such superior numbers. He dropped to a crouch and started to move cautiously forward, careful not disturb branches or bushes which might alert them to his position. He knew he had a slight advantage in that they did not know where he was. They would be careful in their approach in case he was waiting in ambush for them.

The only thing he could do was to keep moving; his brain, still fuzzy from the effects of the explosion, was putting out only one thought. Run. But where could he run to? First find some cover and try to think. He willed his mind to start working as he continued his movement deeper into the trees.

He stumbled across a fallen branch and fell heavily onto his right shoulder. A sharp spasm of pain shot down his arm and into his hand. In an involuntary gesture he dropped his gun. Ignoring the pain, he scraped about in the undergrowth until he found the barrel and pulled it out with his left hand. He looked at the branch which had brought him down. It might provide some cover. He seemed to be in the middle of the small wood; he knew he could not go much further without ending up with his back to the airport fence. Maybe he could stay here and remain hidden until they had passed, and then make his way back to the road and take one of the cars.

"Right," he thought. "That's what we'll do."

He flexed his hand and arm, trying to ease the pain and regain some movement at least in his fingers. At the sound of the undergrowth crashing behind him, he eased further down against the branch, trying to burrow his way through the rotting leaves and damp soil. He listened to the voices and tried to guess how far apart they were. They seemed to be constantly shouting at each other, maybe in an effort to quell their fear and apprehension. From the sounds, he worked out that one would pass within a few feet of him. He hoped he did not trip over the same branch.

Maurice Johns

He kept the gun in his left hand, and drew his knees up under his chest. He steadied his ragged breathing and concentrated on the noise of the man approaching. Lifting his face upwards, he caught a glimpse of the blue sky through the upper branches and thick foliage of the trees. Incongruously, he thought it was a good day to sit at some cafe and sip a cold beer. Startled by his own thoughts, he again had to force his mind back to the business at hand. The stalker came closer, ever closer. Peter felt that he was going to be close enough to see him if he looked down. Out of the corner of his eye he saw a movement to his left. He tensed. First a booted foot came into view, then the leg and then another foot. The man was moving slowly but his head was swivelling from side to side and to his front. He was not looking down. Another two slow and cautious steps and he had his back to Peter. Slowly, hardly daring to breath, Peter straightened his knees and came to a crouch. He remained motionless with his knees and thighs aching with the effort, while he looked to his left and right. He could hear the others crashing their way forward but could not see them. He straightened further into a half-crouch. His prey was now four steps to his front and slightly to his left. Gently placing one foot in front of the other he moved as the man's shadow, looking down to make sure he did not break any twigs. The soft ground absorbed any sound and he made a last minute lunge for the head and neck in front of him.

He threw his left hand round to the front of the throat, pressing backwards with the barrel of the gun. It was sufficient to halt the involuntary shout to a mere grumble coming from the back the throat. His right hand he brought down with as much force as he could muster against the right side of the neck. The blow, however, was weak and did not land with the power he needed for it to be effective in bringing his man to the ground. The blow further weakened his right arm, pain shooting from the wrist to the back of his head. He changed the position of his hand and moved it under the nose of the semi stunned man. He was beginning to struggle against the pressure of the gun barrel against his throat. He had dropped his own gun and, in an instinctive reaction had both hands fighting against Peter's own grip. As Peter was exerting all his strength to keep the barrel pressed against his throat and establish a grip on the man's face, an elbow dug sharply backwards into his solar plexus, forcing the air from his lungs. Something screamed at him that he had to finish this quickly. He could not get into a prolonged wrestling match with only one good arm. He found the base of the nose and pulled hard against it. It was not a killing blow, but the pain was bad enough for the grip on the barrel to loosen as hands were changed to relieve the pressure on his nose.

I, Plague

Peter used this to ram the barrel of the gun hard against the throat, twice, before he felt a lessening of the grip on his right hand. With a supreme effort, he jerked backwards with both hands, the neck bent backwards and, despite trying to throw his weight forward, the man started to fall. As he did so, Peter released his grip and turned to follow him down, his right hand moving to strike at the nose, again and again, each blow bringing waves of nauseating pain from the protesting arm and shoulder. He stopped raining blows when movement had stopped. He stayed motionless over the body and listened. The others appeared to have continued on their way, and were now to his front. He had to move again. He did not know how far it was to the fence, and when they would start working their way back to the road. That would probably mean the discovery of the body, and the knowledge that he had turned back.

He started moving fast in a low crouch, using the noise of the pursuers to cover his own retreat. The distance to the road was less than he expected. He almost burst through the edge of the trees and into plain view. He had come out away from the wrecked car and Gehan's still, blood soaked body, nearer to the roadblock than he could have planned for. He worked his way through the trees until he was opposite the parked cars. At first glance, he thought himself lucky that all the men had gone off in the hunt for him, but a cloud of smoke from a hidden cigarette dispelled that very quickly. He could not hear any voices, and lay flat to gain a view under the cars. No sign of feet and legs; that would mean that whoever remained behind had to be sitting in one of the cars.

Using the parked cars as cover he ran, covering the short distance quickly. He crouched behind the first car he came to and looked through the back window. There was no one inside. The second car was facing away and he could see the smoker in the driver's seat. He hefted the gun and moved it to his right hand, but it was numb from the fall and he could not rely on the grip he had. He moved it back, straightened and walked boldly across to the driver's door. The surprise on the face of the driver was almost comical and lasted only a second as the gun barrel landed on the bridge of his nose and blood started flowing. The dazed expression did not last long either as the barrel crushed bone under the repeated blows. Peter opened the door and pulled the body out to fall on the tarmac. He climbed behind the wheel and started the engine. Keeping the revs down he eased slowly forward and then sped up. Watching the rear view mirror constantly until he rounded the bend, he was relieved that no one came rushing out of the wood. Again paralleling the perimeter fence, he sped up, still watching the mirror. He found the ring road and drove as fast as he dared onto the airport grounds, finding the car park and driving to the top floor.

Parked, he felt the fatigue that follows such action, but had to brush it aside. He did not have much time to make his flight and, looking down at himself, he knew he was so bedraggled he would arouse suspicion as soon as he walked into a public place. He took off the jacket, checking the pockets to make sure his documents were still in the inside pockets. At least his shirt had been protected from the worst of the damage his crawling had done and was still in one piece.

He rolled up the sleeves to hide the dirty cuffs from view and stood beside the car to try and brush down his trousers with his handkerchief. The same cloth was used on his shoes. Still scruffy, but less so. He looked in the side mirror, adjusting the padding in his mouth and straightening his hair. He hid his gun under the driver's seat and locked the doors.

He had to hurry if he was to make his flight. The wonders of the Internet had meant that check-in had taken place online, and he had the boarding pass safely in the jacket with his passport. All he had to do was get to International Departures and he would be home free. Emerging from the car park and crossing the walkway to the terminal building, he anxiously scanned the incoming traffic for signs of pursuit. Mingling with the crowds, he still felt out of place, too scruffy to be taken for a businessman, but was only aware of a couple of curious glances in his direction.

He stopped in front of the departures board and found his flight. It did not indicate that it was boarding, so he took the opportunity to go into the men's room next to the entrance to immigration and customs. The cleaner he could be for immigration the easier it would be. Filling the sink with warm water, he washed as best he could, slicking back his hair and sponging down his trousers using the paper towels.

Exiting the men's room he fished out his passport and boarding pass and started towards the turnstiles blocking the entrance. He was waiting for a family in front to make their way through when he saw several men running through terminal looking all around. With impatience he watched a small girl in front playing and hesitating before being ushered on by her parents. It was one time that he wanted to scream at the child to stop messing about. He pushed his way through and mingled with the family in front of him. He did not dare glance back into the concourse but joined the queue for passport control. He produced his EU passport to the bored, indifferent officer and was quickly waved through, after only a cursory glance at the photograph.

He could not believe it. He had made it and was now only minutes away from being safely ensconced aboard the plane. A few hundred yards to the departure gate and that would be it. He knew that it was unlikely that Gregori's men would be able to follow him here.

He heard the instruction for his flight to proceed to Gate 32 where the aircraft was ready for boarding. He looked at the signs and started through the concourse to the walkway leading to the gate. With each step he felt more confident. He was walking briskly, trying to ignore everyone around him, his mind only having one goal, to reach the plane.

His right arm screamed at him as his elbow was grabbed and held. He stopped and turned; there were two policemen behind him. They were asking him in Ukrainian for his documents. He remembered his cover just in time from answering them, instead holding up his hands and shaking his head. One reached to his hand and took his passport.

"Mr Peterson?"

Peter tried what he hoped was a friendly smile and said, "Yes. I'm flying to London."

In broken and hard to understand English he was asked what was his business in the Ukraine.

"A holiday."

He was asked to wait and had no option in the matter as they flanked him. He expected them to radio someone, but instead one reached for his mobile phone. Now Peter's instinct was to run, somehow disable two armed policemen in a crowded environment, and run to the plane and board it. Even as he thought this he knew it was useless. They would hold the plane and then forcibly remove him. Or would they? If these two were in Gregori's pay, they had no official reason to hold him. As he stood he heard the second call for the passengers to London. Time was running out. He could not believe he had got this far only to be stopped in sight of escape.

He listened to the conversation. The policeman on the phone was obviously speaking about him and his appearance not matching the one they had. Good; he had doubts as to whether or not they had the right man. But that hope was swiftly dispelled as he heard the name Peterson. There had been a leak, it had to have been one of the local employees. Then it struck him how the ambush had been set up. They had to have known in advance which car he was in. Now he prepared himself for flight. He moved slightly, but immediately two pairs of hands grabbed his arms and held him.

His hands were handcuffed behind his back and they started leading him towards a door beside the ramp leading to the plane. He passed within two paces of the exit to freedom, down a series of steps and onto the tarmac, where they passed under the nose of the plane to enter another door, this time leading to a long dingy corridor. It was a stark contrast to the pristine condition of the terminal building above them. The fluorescent lights flickered, throwing awkward shadows against the dirty white walls, the corridors were largely un-swept, but he did not identify any potential weapons amongst the garbage. He was tightly escorted down corridor after endless corridor, he lost all sense of direction and only knew that he must be somewhere under the terminal. He had no chance of breaking free; the two policement kept him close between them holding tight to his arms. So tight that the pain from his right shoulder had returned with a vengeance, throbbing painfully and sending spasms through the muscles of his arm. The handcuffs were too tight to try and ease his wrists through them, and they began to chaff and rub the skin raw as his arms were pulled roughly, guiding him onwards.

When they emerged into the sunlight Peter was temporarily blinded and had to squint against the glare from the buildings. He was led to a police van and unceremoniously bundled into the back. The door closed and he could hear the keys being removed from the lock.

There was a small grille separating the back from the front compartment, not big enough for him to do anything with. He looked around the van. Wooden benches ran the length of each side and they were securely bolted to the floor. There were no sharp edges and no protrusions that could be improvised into weapons. He sat and thought. His only chance of escape would come when they stopped and opened the doors. It was possible he could surprise them by kicking the doors open, with a bit of luck stunning them and allowing him to incapacitate them.

He had barely finished accepting this as the only option when the van braked and stopped. He heard the police leave the cab and then the key in the back door. He positioned himself on his back with his legs drawn back to deliver the kick. The doors cracked open and he mustered every bit of strength he had to kick out and slam the doors back against their hinges. He tried to regain his feet to jump down but was faced with two men armed with pistols.

He thought he recognised them from the ambush. They spoke to him in Russian, "Step down easy, Yuri." As they spoke, another van with the side door slid back stopped at the side, and they gestured that he should climb in. He could see no other option but to comply. He had an idea what was going to happen, and thought he might provoke them into killing him. As he stepped into the van he threw himself back and slammed the back of his head into the face of one of the gunmen. Turning rapidly, but forced into a crouch by the low roof of the van he tried to kick the remaining gunman. A sharp blow to the back of his head and he dropped to the floor, semi-conscious. The van lurched as they climbed in and the driver put it in gear and started driving.

"That was very stupid, Yuri. Our orders are to deliver you alive, but no one said how alive you have to be."

Lying face down he saw four feet in front of him, two of the feet swung back and then forward straight into his ribs. He felt a rib crack before it was lost in the pain as blow after blow, kick after kick rained down on him. He was not aware of the pain stopping but of a welcome blackness.

He emerged from the darkness into a world of pain several times and each time he was beaten unconscious again. He was not aware of how much time passed between each brief spell of consciousness, only of the pain which wracked his whole body.

CHAPTER FIFTY NINE

Monday evening found James and Mike waiting in the lounge for Lizelle and Ethan. They were watching the other customers, trying to spot their contact. All they knew was he was called Alexander, and he would be wearing a black leather jacket with an Eagle logo on the right sleeve. The Amsterdam contact had assured Mike that Alexander would be able to recognise them. They listened to the different languages that were spoken by the mixed crowd of mainly men. They saw men sitting on their own, looking nervous, and businessmen talking in groups, mainly with American accents.

Ethan and Lizelle walked into the lounge and stood looking for a table. They made their way through the crowded bar area and weaved their way to a table behind James. They ordered drinks and James took the opportunity to order another for himself and Mike. This gave Ethan the opening he needed.

"Excuse me. I heard you order and that you were English. Here on business?"

"Partly, some leisure as well. Short trip, though, this time. Where are you from?"

They continued to chat between the two tables until Mike invited them to join their table. The casual acquaintance had been struck. They maintained the illusion until the nearest table was vacated and they could continue without being overheard.

It had passed seven o' clock, the rendezvous time agreed, and James looked worriedly at Mike. The whole thing would have to be called off if they did not have someone to guide them around. They did not have the time to look themselves and did not trust hiring a local. He saw Mike relax after twenty minutes and looked up to see the bomber jacket walking into the bar. He stood and looked around, seeing them and coming directly to their table.

"Mr Hawk?" At James' nod; "I am Alexander, your guide. I am sorry I am late, there was accident, and the traffic was slow-moving."

James invited him to sit and he ordered a coffee. After the waiter had left he continued. "My employer has explained in great detail what you want. But not why you want it." He held up his hand to stop an interruption. "And, I hasten to add, I do not want to know. I will take you to all the places I know, I will tell you all I know about Gregori, but once you have everything you need I will leave you. Understood?"

They agreed and Mike asked about the weapons.

"I have them safe. We can collect them tomorrow, you can either take them away then or leave them until you have a need for them. Everything is as you ordered."

"Where do we start?" asked Ethan, eager as always to get things moving.

"We can start tonight. I know of a club where Gregori likes to drink. It is his club and the girls are recruited by him, some say personally. We can go there later if you so wish."

"Great, what time should we leave?" Ethan asked.

"Not you and the young lady. It is not the establishment to which one takes a young lady. You two gentlemen are the type of clientele who might go there. It is quite popular with visiting gentlemen."

"He's right Ethan, remember you two are a couple. You'll have to sit this one out." James smiled. "Fits right in with our image, right Mike?" To Alexander; "How will we know if Gregori is in the club?"

"I will come in with you. That is normal for most guides. You will need someone who speaks Ukrainian. Anyway, there is a booth in the rear right hand corner which is reserved only for him. No one else sits there unless invited by the man himself."

Mike was curious about Alexander and asked him to tell them a bit about himself. "You know my employer? I am from here many years ago. I did some work for him and then moved to Amsterdam to work directly for him. I have been with him for fifteen years." He halted as if deciding what to say next. "I should tell you that even my employer has a healthy respect for this Gregori; he is a very dangerous man. If he had even the slightest idea that you are showing an interest in him, well, I would not like to be in your shoes."

They agreed that they should meet again with Alexander at ten o' clock. He told them he would be outside the hotel in a white old model

Mercedes. He had refused their invitation to eat with them, stating it would be unusual at this stage for a guide to be so friendly with his clients.

They left the lounge together, the four heading to the dining room where they ate a slow meal. The conversation was sparse, but light-hearted, keeping off the subject of the operation not only by the close proximity of other diners, but also because of the unspoken rule that once the planning had been done, any further talk on the matter only clouded the waters. James saw that Mike, like himself, was watching the others diners. Eventually he spoke.

"I wonder what all those men who were alone in the bar are now doing with attractive local women. Do you think they're on the game?"

It was Ethan who laughed and replied; "No, they're respectable locals looking for a husband in the West."

He laughed again as he saw the disbelief. "You two really are dinosaurs. There are websites where Western men can look for brides here and in the Russian Union. They write to each other, and then meet up to see what each other are really like. I don't know for sure, but there seem to be quite a lot of successful matches."

"Possibly something the two of you should look at when we get home." Lizelle said, joining in with the teasing. "I can't imagine either of you married and settled down, though." She jerked at the elbow in the ribs from Ethan. "God, I'm sorry James."

"Don't worry about it. I'll have a look, but only to see if I can find someone for Mike. He's not making much progress on that front; he needs a bit of a push."

"Let's change the subject, shall we?" an embarrassed Mike said. James knew that the dig about Monique had hit home.

At ten, James and Mike left the others in the bar, telling them to go to bed, and that they would brief them about the evening in the morning. They joined Alexander outside, finding him easily in the throng of the evening crowd. As he pulled away he told them;

"It's not far, but it is sometimes better to drive, especially on the way back to the hotel. The streets are far safer than they used to be, but what is the point in taking a chance? Unfortunately, the local thugs know that

Westerners carry lots of cash and there are always the credit cards. You wouldn't believe how stupid some are when they go out, flashing their money and wallets for everyone to see. They ignore the warnings not to carry all their money and credit cards."

Five minutes after leaving the hotel, and they were pulling up in front of a gaudy entrance. The naked women portrayed by the neon signs left no one in any doubt as to what sort of establishment it was. As they walked along the pavement, Alexander led them past the queue of men waiting for entry. There were two burly, dark suited doormen and Alexander went straight up to them, speaking and indicating his charges. James saw the note change hands and the rope barrier was lowered, allowing them entry. First impressions showed a lushly carpeted entrance hall with a reception or cashier's desk and cloakroom. The desk was expensive and the woman behind it well dressed in an evening dress. They paid their entry fee, and another well dressed woman appeared at their elbows and asked Alexander something. He turned to the two. "She wants to know if we want a table or to sit at the bar?"

Mike turned to James. "A table please."

Once inside the swing doors the music, which had been muted in the lobby, became loud and intrusive. As they were led to a table, they could see that the bar ran in a U shape around a raised stage on which four women clad only in G strings were gyrating around poles, performing various gymnastic feats and not leaving a lot to the imagination of the men seated at the bar. They were all glued to the performance of the girls, and there were plenty of raunchy comments being shouted to encourage them to perform. James supposed it was perhaps fortunate for the girls on the stage that the bar was separated by an aisle, which permitted the bar staff to serve drinks and, he saw, pass money on to a dancer.

Seated, Alexander ordered beer and vodka for them, and leaned across to indicate a booth to their left. "That is where Gregori sits. Don't worry, it's still early for him to make an appearance."

Waiting for their drinks, they had time to look around. The whole place was well laid out, every seat having a view of the stage. It was immaculately clean, and everything screamed that a lot of money had been invested in the furniture and fittings. James wondered if the girls who worked here received wages commensurate with the rest of the place; he doubted it.

Placing the drinks on the table, the waitress said something to them. Alexander translated.

"She asks if we want young ladies to sit with us. I suggest that you do this, it is, after all, why gentlemen come here. One thing; they will only drink champagne, and it is not cheap."

"Tell her yes; it could be good cover." Mike looked around and saw that most tables had girls at them. "We could draw attention to ourselves if we don't; Mike?"

"I agree, go for it Alexander. Just see if any of them speaks some English, will you."

He grinned at James. "If we've got to this for the sake of the operation, we might as well be able to talk to them."

"By the way, Alexander, was that money changing hands with doorman?"

"Quite correct, a guide receives, how do you call it, commission for bringing foreigners to the club. Unfortunately, I am not permitted to sample the wares on offer, which is why only two young ladies will be joining us. Look, here they come."

As they looked where he pointed, two girls arrived at the table. Alexander stood to allow one to slide in next to Mike and the other slid along the seat to sit next to James. "Ah," he thought. "That's why all the tables are in u shapes with continuous benches. Stupid old man not have realised it.

Alexander introduced Svetlana, next to Mike, and the other, Irina.

"I don't know about you, James, but I'm beginning to feel like an old pervert. Alexander, how old are these girls? They don't look much older than sixteen."

Alexander spoke rapidly to the girls, who laughed and replied in English. "No, we are both twenty."

They were beautiful. Their clean hair shone and glistened in the flickering strobe lighting. They had good, even, white teeth which they displayed a lot as they seemed to have permanent smiles on theirovely faces. As far as James could see, the smiles were genuine, little lines appearing at the corners of their eyes.

"I think I might have a look at that website after all" grinned Mike.

The bottle of champagne arrived and two glasses were poured. James paid the waitress, working out that it cost the equivalent of just over a hundred US dollars. Certainly not cheap, and it was probably watered down, if it was indeed champagne. Irina had a good grasp of English, and they were able to talk without too much trouble. Mike felt embarrassed as Irina slipped closer and closer to him. He didn't want things to progress any further than talk, and did not know if they provided "extras". He hoped not; he hoped that it was only their job to keep them in the place and spending their money. Mike, on the other hand, was enjoying himself enormously. James had to think that, at times, his conservative nature was a hindrance. He would concede, however, that the girls were good company.

He was beginning to think that it was about time to leave, before things with the girls progressed any further, when there was a small commotion as three men in suits pushed through the crowd at the bar, which had grown thick as the evening had progressed. Behind them was a tall, well-built man in a suit with a shirt unbuttoned half way down his chest, showing a think mat of hair and what looked like a gold St Christopher and chain. Behind him came two more well-dressed men. They made their way to the corner booth. Gregori had arrived. James felt that Mike's attention had been drawn to the group as well, and he tried to keep up the conversation with Irina while observing the group settle themselves. Only Gregori and one of the suited men sat at the booth. The others took up places on either side, and remained standing. Immediately, waitresses appeared with champagne, probably the real stuff, thought James. He glanced at Alexander, who confirmed with a nod that the man himself had arrived.

James studied the man who was now his enemy, the target.

He had seen from his walk and bearing that he was a tall man, but he also appeared to be in good shape; there did not seem to any spare weight on his lean frame. He had moved like a dancer; a dangerous man who knew how to handle himself, James concluded. Now with a glass in his hand and joined by three girls, he appeared to be in good spirits, laughing and joking with all who came into his orbit. He sat there radiating his ego outwards. They watched as he greeted those around him. They in turn were respectful, half bowing as they shook his hand.

But their posture indicated something else. Fear. It took a while to realise it, but the deference shown was a cover for fear.

He caught Irina watching him, looking where he was looking, and had to stop and devote more of his attention back to her. He tried to catch Mike's eye and indicate that he thought it was time to leave. They had seen their quarry and had achieved what they had wanted; to be able to identify him again.

Mike handed James his mobile phone and asked that he take a photograph of him and Svetlana. Mike took it and pointed it, turning it slightly to put Gregori in the frame. To keep up appearances Mike took one of him and Irnina. Then James suggested they take one of Alexander and took the camera back. He asked him to stand and managed to get a photograph of the men with Gregori.

When they were ready to leave, they promised the girls that they would come back and ask for them. They deliberately went close to the back booth and, as expected, the bodyguards moved to intercept them, guiding them away from the table. "Tight," whispered Mike as they approached the exit.

It was two thirty when they arrived back at the hotel, and James was surprised to see that the bar was still busy, although now the crowd had become a lot louder. They told Alexander to return at nine, and made their way to their own rooms. They would not get a lot of sleep, but then again they did not have a lot of time.

CHAPTER SIXTY

The police inspector looked around at the girls dancing on the stage as he made his way through the occupied tables to the booth in the corner where he could see Gregori watching his progress. He smiled in relief as he saw that Gregori was in good spirits. He was a terrifying man when angered, as the inspector knew only too well, having witnessed the brutal and swift punishments meted out in the name of discipline.

He slid into the booth and sat waiting for Gregori to speak. He was ignored for several minutes, during which time a drink was placed before him. When at last Gregori turned to him he still said nothing, but slid an envelope across the table. The inspector lifted it and placed it in his inside pocket. He did not look at the contents; he had learned at the very beginning of his association that to do so was perceived as an insult. It was inferred that he did not trust Gregori to do the right thing. It was a lesson he had never forgotten. The ache in his hand during the cold weather reminded him frequently of the pain caused by the broken hand.

"The shooting at the airport – who is in charge?" The question was put so quietly that he had to strain and lean forward to hear over the music and chatter.

"Stanislav."

"It is a dead end. There is not enough evidence for it to lead anywhere." This was given as a statement of fact. The inspector wanted to protest, to tell him that there was not much he could do. To tell him that Stanislav was one of the new breed of policemen who had risen rapidly under the new regime. He, however, knew better and nodded mutely in acquiescence.

"Is there anything else that has been reported which may interest me?" That meant did he know of any raids, any information which had been given to the police about his activities.

"Nothing." He was always surprised at his one word answers. He was normally verbose in the extreme and he knew that it was fear that kept him stilling his tongue to prevent any pain being inflicted on him.

"Good. Go." he was dismissed with a wave of the hand. Gregori had already turned back to his companions before he even got to his feet, ignoring him completely as he left the table.

CHAPTER SIXTY ONE

He was fifteen and cycling with three friends from school along a country lane in the south of England. It was the summer holidays and the four of them had decided to have a picnic somewhere in the countryside. The sun was beating down on their bare arms and faces, the banter was light and regularly interspersed with laughter and giggles from the two girls. They moved through shadows on the lane cast by great, old oaks and elms. Cattle and sheep grazed lazily in the adjoining fields. Only the sound of their voices and bicycle tyres on the tarmac broke the quiet. They saw an old oak standing alone in a field, its long leaf-laden branches providing welcome relief from the sun, and made their way there, dropping their bicycles on the ground and taking off their rucksacks to lay out their sandwiches and cans of soft drink. Peter lay back on the soft grass, letting a soft breeze fan his face. Next to him lay Angie. He had had a crush on Angie since they had started High School together. Nothing was said by them. They listened to the other two horsing around and the squeals and giggles. He propped himself on his elbow and looked down at Angie. Her eyes were closed and he wondered if she had fallen asleep.

"What are you staring at?" she murmured. He could say nothing. He wanted to kiss her, but was unsure of how to go about it. She looked up at him and he saw her lips part. He slowly dropped his head and brushed her lips with his. But it hurt. The slight pressure with which she had responded had hurt him badly. He recoiled in shock as she slowly disappeared in front of him.

It was the pain that brought on consciousness. His body was racked by it, it was the only thing that filled his mind. He kept his eyes closed and his chin resting on his chest as he tried to marshal his thoughts. He knew he was now sitting upright and felt his hands and feet securely bound to the chair. He opened his eyes and knew that they were swollen to such an extent that his vision was very limited and blurred. He could barely make out his legs. His face ached and he guessed that his cheekbone, nose and jaw were probably broken. It was excruciating to breathe and he surmised that he had sustained broken ribs during the prolonged beating he had taken. As hard as it was, he willed himself not to move, or give his watchers any indication that he had regained consciousness.

Indistinct voices filtered through the pain. Again, he focused and could make out the conversation about the football game the previous Saturday. Some instinct made him test the bindings. They were tight and he knew that the circulation to his hands and feet was severely restricted. But then, he reasoned, his comfort and well-being was not the highest priority on his captors' minds. The realisation that all he could hope for was a quick end to this slowly dawned on him. Maybe it would be possible to provoke them into being over zealous with their next beating.

A mobile phone broke into the conversation and he heard a voice raised as it was answered. The conversation was brief. Whoever had called had been told that he was still alive and they were waiting. Cold, naked fear wrenched his gut. He now knew that Gregori himself would be coming to finish the job, and he knew that it was going to get far worse. He had seen Gregori at work in the past and the object was to inflict as much pain as possible. There would be some questions, but the pain would continue no matter what the answers.

He wished he had heeded the warning from London to leave prior to the shipments being seized. If only, he thought, if only, funny how life was a series of 'if only's'. It had been wrong, maybe even arrogant, to assume that his cover would remain intact after the arrests. The intervening two and a half weeks had only served to reinforce his belief that he was not suspected. Stupid. But it had been close; he had believed he had been in the clear and on his way to Kiev Airport.

It was no consolation, as he sat bound to the chair, that his years undercover working his way up the ranks to be a friend and trusted confidant of Gregori had paid off. No-one would ever know what had happened to him. Yes, they could surmise that he had been taken, but his body would never be discovered. They would never know what he would have endured during his last hours. He did not know if he had the strength of mind or body to stand up to whatever the next few hours were going to bring.

The only thing he could be certain of was that he was scared, very scared. Barring a miracle there was no way to escape, even if he could free himself he knew he was too weak to make even a token resistance against two men. God, what a way to end it all. He tried not to think of the things he had seen Gregori do to others who had betrayed him, stole from him or lied to him.

He allowed himself to slip back into the darkness. Better that than think on what lay ahead.

I, Plague

His head was jerked brutally back and he felt the welcome taste of water on his cracked lips. He tried to lick as much as possible into his parched mouth but was stopped with a hard slap, slamming his head to his right and reawakening the pain in his cheek and jaw. He felt a rough cloth being dragged over his eyes and could feel the dried blood being washed away. He managed to open his eyes, and standing right in front of him was the hard, stone cold face of Gregori.

"So my friend, do I call you Yuri, or will you tell me your real name?" He spoke quietly and he struggled to hear the words.

He croaked, "Peter." At least he could die under his true identity.

"Peter, good. I am disappointed in you, Peter. Did you not think I would find you? Did you not think that I have one of my people working the British? The only thing your friends did with all those cars was waste petrol. You and your friends killed some of my best men in your futile efforts to escape from me. But do you know the thing that has hurt me the most? All this time I thought you were my friend. I trusted you. We drank and whored together. Now, well now, you have cost me millions of dollars, tens of millions of dollars. But you know what, Peter?" He raised his chin to look into his eyes. "It is not that which angers me as much as the betrayal. It is for that you have to pay. I don't even want to know what department of which agency you work for. I am not even interested in which government. Did you not think I would find out that there was an informer in our midst? No. Very arrogant of you. I have to set an example to others who are thinking of betraying me. You understand that, don't you?" He moved Peter's head up and down in a nod. "Good."

He allowed Peter's head to drop forward onto his chest again as he moved away. Peter heard him moving about and opening some kind of case. He did not want to look to see what was coming but had little choice when his head was pulled back again. What he saw brought sheer terror. In vain he threw himself against his restraints and the arms holding him. Gregori smiled at him as he walked slowly towards him. He was still three feet away when he switched on the Black and Decker hand held drill. The screech filled the air. Standing directly in front of the helpless Peter, he switched the drill off, the whine dying slowly as the drill bit halted.

"What is the saying in England? This is going to hurt you more than it hurts me. Think of it as payback for the pain you caused me. Think on that, Peter."

He switched the drill on and Peter was forced to watch it drop level to his right knee. Gregori moved it slowly forward and he could feel the draught brushing his trousers as it drew closer. Suddenly the pain was searing through every nerve end in his body. He screamed as the bit drilled into his kneecap. Strangely he was aware of the smell through the pain, the burning of skin and bone as Gregori continued to push the bit deeper and deeper. The pain was unbearable; he continued screaming, jerking his head from side to side against the restraining hands, his back arched and strained against the chair. The whine of the drill ceased, but not the pain. It was a constant, consuming him in a tsunami of agony. He felt the hands release his head and it dropped back onto his chest. He prayed for the blessing of unconsciousness, but it would not come. He barely heard Gregori give an instruction and saw the booted foot swinging towards his knee. When it connected the shock of searing pain coursed through his body. But still it did not bring the release of darkness. He heard Gregori's voice in his ear, almost whispering.

"No, my friend, you will not die so quickly, you will not suffer so much that you pass out. You, Peter, will feel everything."

The drill started its whine again and he felt the same excruciating pain flood from his left kneecap through his body. He screamed and bucked. When it was extracted he slumped. The level of agony was unbearable, it felt as if his blood was boiling in his veins. He didn't know if he pleaded out loud but plead he did, anything to stop. Again he felt his head pulled back and this time his jaw was forced open.

"Now a souvenir for your friends in England. Let them see how we deal with traitors here."

He only knew what was going to happen when he felt rough fingers reach into his mouth and pull the tip of tongue forward, so far forward that it felt as if it was going to be ripped from his mouth. Then the coldness of a blade at the back of his tongue. A sharp downward thrust and his tongue was severed. He felt the blood fill his mouth and his throat and gagged. Opening his eyes he could see it pour down his chest in a bright red river. He tried to breathe but again his throat filled and he gagged. He heard Gregori's harsh voice.

"Fool, keep his head forward, he is choking on his own blood. There is one more souvenir to collect."

Peter barely felt his trousers being cut away at the crotch. He barely felt the hand grasping his penis and scrotum. He felt a sharp searing pain as a blade cut away his manhood. But it was now only one additional pain among the multitude of pains. He felt hot breath against his ear.

"One more thing for your bosses to think about before they send someone else." He pulled back and stood looking at the broken man before him. Blood loss would bring death in a matter of minutes. He motioned his men away and moved back to watch the life drain slowly out of the mangled body.

Peter felt the pain recede slowly, and knew that death was imminent. He hoped they didn't intend to prolong the torture. The natural reflex of the throat to choke and gag on the blood was fading, he was drowning in his own blood, he could vaguely feel the flow of blood pooling in between his legs. In the quiet, he thought he could hear it dripping onto the floor. The darkness came slowly, he welcomed it, allowed himself to be enveloped in it.

Gregori signalled to his driver that he was ready to leave, and waited for the car to be brought into the warehouse. "Leave him here for a couple of days. Let the others see what happens if they betray me, then dump the body. Send those things," he indicated the severed appendages, "to the English."

CHAPTER SIXTY TWO

The sun was still low on the horizon as Gregori climbed into the back seat of his car and instructed the driver to take him to his apartment. He felt exhausted, drained. He had spent all Monday night at the club, and had drunk too much champagne and vodka before he came to the warehouse. He had been savouring the moment when he would confront Yuri, Peter, whoever. But now it was done, there was a feeling of anticlimax. A dark mood was settling on him; he felt a sense of foreboding. Perhaps he should cancel the order to send the bits to the English. It would make them really mad, and that could lead to a lot of complications. He leaned forward, tapped the driver on the shoulder and told him what to do.

He sat back and closed his eyes. No, he was just tired. He would go home, avoid the club, and then do some business the next morning before the football game in the evening. That would see him right. There was nothing to worry about any more. The Yuri business was closed, and the Paris end of the business was coming back in line after a series of brutal and bloody murders, which had the French press baying for law and order. The smuggling route from Afghanistan had been changed, and the next shipment would arrive in the next two weeks. All right, he would have to hold off on the UK operation for the time being, but that would come.

He looked down at his trousers. The sharp crease was still in place, but there were flecks of Yuri's blood up and down the front. With annoyance, he rubbed at them. He decided that it must have happened when he used the drill on his knees. Such a shame; it had been an expensive suit, and now he would have to get rid of it. He knew from experience just how hard it was to get rid of the blood stains. When he examined himself more closely he saw, with distaste, that the specks of blood had also stained his jacket sleeves and the cuffs of the otherwise pristine white shirt he was wearing.

A small price to pay, he thought, for the lessons that would be learned from the body of Yuri. He knew he had been overly harsh, even by his standards. He had even somewhat regretted the actions he had taken. But he had been so angry at the betrayal, had been so obsessed with the need to make an example of him. He sighed audibly, drawing a glance from his driver in the rear view mirror. He closed his eyes and willed himself to relax.

CHAPTER SIXTY THREE

They had met Alexander early on the Tuesday morning, James and Mike tired from their late night at the club. As they had breakfast they told Ethan and Lizelle of their impressions of the man they hunted. They had agreed with Alexander that they should, under the guise of tourists, continue their recce with visits to places where Gregori was known to conduct his business. Alexander informed him that there were only three prospective locations; two warehouses and a shipping office for his fleet of ships.

They drove to the shipping office first and watched for half an hour. It was a hive of activity, container lorries arriving and leaving with annoying frequency, office workers and visitors always going in and out of the building. Apart from the storage area and a car park, the building was surrounded by others all conducting thriving businesses.

The sun was making the interior of the car hot as they drove to one warehouse and then another. The results were the same; they were securely locked and obviously only used when a shipment arrived or left. There was no sign of activity at either, although the other businesses in the area maintained a steady flow of traffic.

James was beginning to worry that it would be difficult to find a place to mount an assault on Gregori as they continued their rounds. He asked Alexander if he knew where Gregori lived.

"He has a penthouse apartment in a very expensive and up-market block" he replied, glancing briefly at James as he spoke. "I had a look and there are two entrances, a tradesmen's and the main foyer. There are three elevators up, only one of which goes to the penthouse. Access to the penthouse is by a key card. Also, Gregori has someone in the foyer all the time, in the guise of a doorman. Asking around, I found out from maids that there are also men stationed outside the door of the apartment and that all visitors are checked before they are allowed entry. Very difficult, if that's what you were thinking."

James thought about it and looked at the others in the back seat. All he received in return was a shrug of the shoulders. He settled back and watched the industrial area pass by the windows. They were approaching an area where the buildings were poorly maintained and mostly empty.

"This is a throwback to the old days of the USSR, when industry was at its peak. These buildings are mainly used by the street people as shelter, drug dealers for buys, that sort of thing. It would be a good idea to take the weapons out of the trunk when you leave me."

Another few minutes and Alexander pulled up at the end of the road. Looking down, they could see an endless run of loading ramps. Paper and cardboard swirled and was tossed in the eddies caused by the wind whistling between the buildings. As they opened the doors there was only silence.

Typically, it was Ethan who spoke. "It looks like something out of those old spy movies. You know, Quiller Memorandum, that sort of thing."

Having retrieved weapons from the trunk, chambered a round and fitted silencers, they started off, climbing onto the ramp and moving in file towards the doors Alexander had indicated. Mike indicated to the others the tyre marks on the road. "Someone's been here, but not recently, maybe a few hours ago, maybe yesterday."

Vigilance was increased, each covering their own field of fire as they clung to the wall and reached the roller shutter door. James indicated to Lizelle that she should join him on the right side of the small door they had located. Mike and Ethan took the left side. James tried the handle and was surprised when it turned and opened. He looked across at the others and gently pushed it open. It creaked as the rusting hinges protested. They waited, but there was only the silence and moaning of the hinges as the door moved gently in the wind. A nod, and Mike went diagonally through to the right, James moved to the left, quickly followed by Ethan and Lizelle. Now inside they froze. The contrast from the bright sunlight to the gloom meant that all they could see was a wall of darkness. As their pupils adjusted to the gloom they could make out pallets stacked with cardboard boxes at odd intervals stretching the length of the cavernous warehouse. The daylight was filtered through murky windows placed high on the walls, breaking it into irregular patterns and casting long deep shadows over the floor. Through the patches where the sunlight did gain access, dust motes floated in the air, blown by the breeze which came through the open door.

James indicated that they should move forward, each pair taking one side. They moved cautiously but quickly around the pallets. James tried to see what the boxes contained, but could not make out the shipping labels in the gloom. They progressed further and further, leapfrogging each other. Lizelle had taken the lead, and James was about to move when he was aware she had stopped and was staring at something he could not yet see. He motioned to the other two to freeze and waited, maintaining their visual sweeps of the areas, waiting for her to take the lead.

"Oh, God," They turned towards Lizelle to see what had brought on the horror in her voice. They saw her turn and run to corner of the room and start vomiting violently.

"Sweet Jesus," Mike had been the first to reach the chair where the body of a man was strapped. They were speechless as they looked on the mutilated, beaten body.

"Mother of God, I hoped I had seen the last of this sort of thing. I wonder who the poor bastard is." Even Mike had paled at the sight of the injuries inflicted. "Whoever did this is one sick son of a bitch."

Ethan had moved to a nearby table and was looking at some clothing lying on it. He picked up the jacket and went through the pockets, carefully avoiding the blood stains. James had moved to the body and pulled a piece of ragged cardboard into the light.

"English traitor, looks like he pissed someone off, maybe informed on them, see, the tongue's missing." He was thinking out loud. "English. Maybe that implies he was working deep cover for someone." He was interrupted by Ethan, holding up a small book.

"I found this in the jacket. British passport says his name is Peter Grant. You're probably right. If he had this then he was more than likely running. Jesus, what a mess. No one deserves this. Anyone thinking this might be Gregori's handiwork?"

Mike answered, "Seems likely. This is his building. Leaving him like this, with the sign, is a message for others not to betray him."

Lizelle had rejoined them, "Sorry about that. God, it's awful what they did to him. What are we going to do about him?" - Pointing but not looking at the body. "We should tell someone, we can't leave him here. Jesus, I think I'm going to be sick again." She turned away, dry retching racking her body.

James thought and answered her question. "She's right, we can't leave him here. How about we phone the Embassy or Consulate? There's bound to be someone there who could take care of this."

"Yes, MI6 or SIS, some organisation like that. Maybe the military or cultural attache. At least that's what they are in the movies. I'll try the Embassy." He asked for the military attache, arguing that he was not going to give his name, but trying to stress the urgency. After a brief wait, he was speaking again. He gave the address of the warehouse and a description of what they had found, including the name in the passport. He was silent for a couple of minutes, which ended up in him taking paper and pen from his pocket and writing down a number.

Turning to the others he explained. "Bloody fool. Said he doesn't know of any of those agencies working in the Embassy. Said I should send proof of what I said. Gave me a mobile number to send photographs to. Ethan, bring that passport across, will you? Be careful." He stopped as Ethan picked it up. "Don't leave your fingerprints, everyone be careful. We don't want to end up being investigated for this."

He took a photograph of the passport and then of the body and sent them.

"We've done all we can. Let's get out of here. Mike, chuck that phone when we get away from the building." He watched Ethan take Lizelle's arm and steady her as they carefully exited the building and made their way back to where Alexander was waiting.

The silence lasted during the drive back to the hotel and while they sat in the lounge waiting for double shots of whiskey. Alexander was wise in keeping quiet, knowing that something was not right, patiently waiting for an explanation.

"Damn, I can't get that picture out of my head. I don't think it will ever leave me. What kind of animal would do that to another human being?" Lizelle was still very pale, a slight flush on her cheeks appearing as she put the question.

"I can't say I blame you; we've seen stuff like that before but, like Mike says, I didn't think I would see it again." Ethan took her hand. "Look, it won't go away, but it'll fade and get easier. Try not think about it. I know, easier said than done."

"You know if you want to talk, any time, we're here for you" James added. "If you want we'll put you on a plane this afternoon, no problem."

"No. I'll stay. I'll be all right, I just need some time." She tried and failed to smile reassuringly.

"I'll get more drinks." James stood. "Ethan, you want to give me a hand?"

As they waited at the bar James turned to Ethan and lowered his voice, smiling to hide what he was about to say from the others.

"If the worst happens, and Mike or I can't do it, I want you to promise me that you won't let Lizelle be taken by that pig. Can you do that?"

Ethan stared hard at James before replying. "All I have to do is think of that poor bastard. Yes, I think I can. I don't even want to think about what would happen to her if she fell into his hands. Yes, I'll do it."

The drinks arrived and they picked them up. James was about to turn to go back to the table when Ethan stopped him. "It makes killing this bastard all the easier, doesn't it? Any doubts I've had have disappeared."

James couldn't think of anything to say in reply and just nodded grimly. "Too right, kid," he said. "This is one time when I think it will be a pleasure." He was startled at the thought. Any killing he had done had always been against an enemy, something which was only business, something he had been contracted to do, and, always as a soldier. This had become very personal.

Back at the table, James knew he had to get their minds off what they had seen.

"Let's review where we are so far. The nightclub looks to be out; too many people, too many of his men and the likelihood of civilian casualties too high to be acceptable. Also it would be unlikely that we would get out of there alive. Two, the shipping company and the warehouses. The first two are out for the same reasons as the nightclub, the third looks as if it is only used infrequently. That leaves us with only the one option. The football stadium. Alexander, how sure can we be that Gregori will be there to see the game?"

"One hundred per cent, barring something major coming up" was the swift response. "As far as I can find out, he attends all the games, home and away."

"Good, well, if we all agree, it will have to be there. I suggest we take a quick look this afternoon, make some plans and then visit it again tomorrow to iron out anything we might miss. Agreed?"

They all nodded their agreement. James knew that lethargy was setting in and told them "There's no time like the present. Alexander, let's go now and this time you have the cover to accompany us, guide us around this marvellous stadium."

They knocked back their drinks and stood, waiting for James and Mike to take the lead out to the car.

CHAPTER SIXTY FOUR

Steve hung up the phone after the call. His mind was spinning; he had only just received news about the bodies on the airport perimeter road. He had gone to the morgue and identified them. Something had gone horribly wrong. There was all hell to pay. The phone from London had been burning with the number of calls; everyone was demanding an explanation as to how three close protection officers and Peter had been taken out so easily. Steve had nothing to tell them. Now it appeared he did. His mobile phone chirped to show he had a message. He opened it and went to the first attachment. It was the photograph of Peter's passport. He slid to the second photograph and his stomach lurched and bile rose in the back of his throat. He could not recognise the face but it was obvious that his mystery caller had been correct. They had even left the sign across his chest.

He put the caller to the back of his mind and started to call trusted colleagues to get a car and a van to drive to the address he had been given.

The black Mercedes SUV and van pulled up in front of the deserted warehouse. Two men left the SUV with drawn handguns and moved to the entrance. They heard the same silence, saw the same litter blown in the wind and moved to the same door which had been closed. They moved cautiously through the warehouse until they were confronted by the figure in the chair. Steve was aware of a never ending string of expletives from his right, but could not find anything to say as he looked on the body of the man he so recently put in a car to the airport. If he had not known he would have had a hard time recognising the face before him. He looked down the body and gradually he became aware of the other atrocities committed. It took time before the horror sunk in and the need for action forced him to move.

"Get the trolley from the van" he instructed, his voice hoarse, and pulled a switchblade from his pocket. As he heard the running footsteps disappear in the direction of the door he leaned forward and started hacking at the ropes which bound Peter to the chair. Once free of the restraints, the body fell to the side and Steve had to lean forward and catch him, gently lowering him to the floor. As he waited for the trolley, he looked around and found the clothing and passport about which he had been told. He took it back to the body and knelt by it until the others arrived.

They gently lifted the body onto the trolley and wheeled it out into the bright sunshine, moving to position it to slide into the rear of the van.

The question which had bothering Steve was eventually asked in the car.

"How are we going to get him home? Are we going to involve the locals?"

"Definitely not. Too much red tape, too many questions. I think we have to resort to a bit of old-fashioned subterfuge. We'll wait for the others to be released, then our friend here will ride piggyback with one of them. It'll cost us, but I'm sure we can get the undertaker to do it. Not too dignified, but I don't suppose he cares."

His anger was boiling, bubbling like lava just below the surface. "God, how I wish it were the old days. Then we could take on this bastard at his own game. Christ, I hate having my hands tied by these namby-pamby politicians. Let's see if we can move things along as soon as we get back. God, what an almighty cock up, they're not going to like this in London."

CHAPTER SIXTY FIVE

The five sat in the car park looking at a modern eye-catching stadium. There were only a few cars parked near the gated entrance to the playing field. A coach was disgorging some tourists at the glassed entrance, the voice of the guide reaching them clearly as he tried to group them together, issuing instructions about not walking on the playing field when they eventually reached it. They could hear him still as he shepherded them, now telling them about the history of the structure, his voice eventually fading as they made their way into the building.

Alexander told them that the same entrance was also the VIP entrance and led to offices and some of the private boxes. Gregori's box was also his office, and at the top of the structure. It could be accessed either by an elevator or by the stairs, which they could see winding their way up through the glass front, which stretched from the ground level all the way to the roof.

"All right, Alexander, good. Now let's take the tour, shall we?" Alexander drove to park near to the coach and they formed a group. The security on duty paid them no attention as they entered the building and stood listening to Alexander. James had to concede that he had done his homework and was playing the part of the guide very well. They moved on following the route taken by the preceding group.

It took almost half an hour for them to complete a half circle of the grounds. Alexander stopped them on the terraces and pointed out the boxes, in particular Gregori's office high on the opposite side of the field. "It is the only box that is totally enclosed with glass."

Ethan looked back and up. "Any chance of a shot from up there? It's not too far, it's protected from the wind, it shouldn't be a difficult shot."

"Windows, Alexander?" He had to confess he did not know. Mike turned and looked. "The kid's right, it's an easy shot, but if the windows are reinforced and the first shot doesn't take him, then we're screwed. Trouble is, I don't suppose there's any way of finding out. I shouldn't imagine that they'll let us walk into his office, and, looking at the other boxes isn't going to tell us much about his. Think we should make our way back to the start and have a look at the stairs and elevator, and take it from there."

Alexander led them around the stadium, giving his guided talk if they approached anyone. James could see that the others were examining all aspects of the ground, their minds working as they figured out trajectories and escape routes. But by the time they had reached the main lobby no definite ideas had taken shape.

Alexander stood before them. "We are permitted to look at one of the private boxes so we will go up in the elevator." He led them up to the top floor. "This is as far as we are permitted. Greogori's office is on the next level."

They saw a security guard patrolling the area, and went into the vacant box. It was comfortable, with seating for twenty people outside the windows which gave a panoramic view of the whole field. Inside, there was a well stocked bar and tables and chairs where, as Alexander explained, meals would be taken prior to the game. They moved outside, but could see the office from that level.

Outside, they took the stairs down to the ground level and left the building. Once inside the car, James told the others to think about what they had seen, and use the drive back to the hotel to come up with suggestions that they would discuss in the lounge.

James started the discussion after arranging to meet with Alexander the next lunchtime.

"I think that must be the place. The box affords us privacy and the chances of collateral damage are minimal. We have to consider that anyone in the box with Gregori is an associate and in some way connected. They will not be considered innocents. I would also guess that any staff are in his pay anyway. Thoughts?"

Mike was the first to speak. "I agree. Security first. I think that on game day it will be beefed up. Anyone going to boxes will have to show some kind of pass. We're not likely to get on the invitation list of anyone, so we have to consider taking out any security at the elevators or stairs before going up. Once we've reached that level there will be more security and we will have to take them down before moving into the office. If what we've seen at the club is anything to go by, I would say that there might be as many as four, possibly only two in the corridor. Then once inside, we cannot afford the time to pick and choose targets. We have to assume that everyone there is hostile and take them all down."

"Agreed. First the elevator and stairs. Ethan, did you get that knife you wanted?" At the affirmative he continued. "We don't know how many security guards there will be on game day. My guess would be two, to check passes, maybe one at the elevators and one on the door, but we'll have to wait and see. Right, Ethan, you deal with any security on the elevators. Use Lizelle as a distraction. Ideally wait for the doors to open and take him inside with you. Mike, depending on the position of other security, we may have to deal with them. We will wait until the game is under way, that should mean there will be less people milling around in the entrance. One thing in our favour is that it is the VIP entrance and therefore likely to be quiet."

Lizelle added, "Let's not forget surprise. Hopefully he will feel safe in that environment. The last thing he'll expect is the four of us bursting through the door."

James watched them each running the scenario in their heads. "One thing, Mike and I go through the door first, Mike to the left, me in the centre. We know what he looks like and we'll both take our first shots at him. Ethan, you come into the room on the left, take out anyone who poses an immediate threat. Lizelle, you'll have our backups in the corridor, in case anyone walks into us." He saw the protest forming on her lips as he finished and stopped her. "No, don't. Someone has to be in the corridor and you have the training to tell the difference between a threat and a bystander. You will react better out there. We will be relying on you to get out of the place as undetected as possible. Anything else?"

"If we want to remain undetected then it's important we don't spray the room. If we hit the window the game will be up and the place will be swarming with police and security guards in no time flat."

James looked at them before turning to Lizelle. "One thing you should know about us, we have learnt that no plan is ever written in stone. Nothing is ever as it should be, there is always something that happens which no amount of planning can account for. If you think the plan is loose it's because it is. Flexibility is the name of the game. Once things kick off we will deal with each obstacle as it occurs."

He turned to Mike. "Cameras?"

"One in the entrance foyer pointing towards the door, none in the elevator or in the corridor."

"Bit light in that department, aren't they?" Ethan asked.

"Not necessarily. Remember it's a sporting stadium; most of their attention would be on break-ins when the place is closed." Mike put their minds at ease with a smile. "Think about it, if you were in charge of security would you plan for an attack on some of the spectators?"

"Thanks Mike. One more thing." James had been thinking about the cameras as well. "Clothing. I think we should blend in with the crowd. From what I've seen I think that jeans, sneakers the home team's shirt and their baseball caps would be the order of the day. The caps will cover our faces and the rest means we will be able to melt into the crowd. How do they identify us among twenty odd thousand other supporters?"

They sat for a while in silence thinking through the operation, looking for weak spots which they could cover before going in. James could see none, none that they couldn't deal with on the day, anyway. Ethan stood and brought another round of drinks to the table.

In the light of what they had found in the warehouse he was still concerned about Lizelle. After dwelling on it in the time since they had finished the discussion he spoke directly to her.

"Listen, Lizelle, and don't take this the wrong way. I'm not sure if it's the best thing for you to come with us. Wait, let me finish. It's not that you don't have the skills or that I think that you can't do the job." He started to fumble his words, not sure of how to carry on. "It's just that I think it would be better for you to take a back seat. At least you could get out if things go really badly for us."

Ethan decided to add to his argument. "Don't worry about James, he's not used to having women around on an operation. A bit of a male chauvinist is our James, but I think he may have a point. Mike?"

"Yes, he does have a point. It would be good to have someone get away if things did go wrong. At least the people back home would know what had happened."

Lizelle was silent for a couple of minutes. "No, I know what you're trying to do. I think that you're all trying to protect me, that you remember what we saw in the warehouse and that's the reason for this.

Well, stop." She saw the rebuttals coming. "Think logically; if we get into the box then the threat is going to disappear with our entry, correct? If you fail inside the box it will be because of heavier firepower than we can plan for; I'm correct again. In that case we will all be dead." She paused and looked around, her gaze staying on Ethan the longest. "Besides, I may not have worked with you long, but I trust you guys. I can guess that one of you will be watching me with instructions to put a round in my head before I would be taken." She smiled at the look on Ethan's face. "You, is it?" Ethan looked as if he was about to protest, stopped and nodded. "I'm coming, and that's final."

There was a long, uncomfortable silence before Mike spoke. "Well, I guess that's that then. Stand or fall together, as Ethan would probably quote from one of his movies."

"One last thought," said Lizelle. "How about tickets for the game? We will need them to get into the stadium area."

"Way ahead of you there," replied Mike. "Alexander should have them already. My friend in Amsterdam bought them for us when we first talked. He bought four for every game in the time we might have been here. I thought when we first looked at the feasibility that it was best to cover all our bases."

CHAPTER SIXTY SIX

A heat haze rose from the warm tarmac, the cars and coaches blurring and blending colours. Over the stadium, four tall floodlight towers stood already lit, guarding against the approaching dark. The car park was full of thousands of fan streaming towards the entrances, their brightly coloured shirts mixing and swirling as each jostled for a place in the lines. The noise was incredible, as each group of fans vied with the next to vocalize their support in songs and yells. The invading armies of Genghis Khan centuries before could not have made more racket or been more colourful.

James and the others left the Mercedes and mingled with the throng, close enough to stay within sight of each other, but with enough distance between to ensure no-one would take them to be together. They were jostled and shoved as they neared the front of the line. James slid the barrel of the Beretta further inside the waistband of his trousers, the bulbous shape and additional length of the silencer making it just a bit uncomfortable. They passed through the turnstiles and the crush eased as each group made their way to the stairs leading to their seats. James and Mike walked along the concourse underneath the stands, past concession stands selling everything that an avid football fan would need to support his team, with hamburger and hot dog stalls by the dozen. As the kick off time neared the crowds became thinner and the four were able to join up and buy hot dogs, standing eating them as the concourse emptied until it was deserted apart from a few latecomers running to gain their seats.

They knew they were now becoming conspicuous and moved slowly along until they were near the VIP entrance. They did not have long to wait before there was a deafening roar from the crowd as their teams came on to the field. There was a period of quiet as the National Anthem was played, followed immediately by another roar.

It was time, and they sauntered to the glass doors. Lizelle and Ethan led the way, looking at their tickets and making every effort to look lost and confused. They pushed their way to the doors and stood looking at the signs. James was relieved to see that there were only two security guards on duty, standing together just inside the door. He and Mike entered and made straight for the elevators, passing Ethan who was talking to the bemused guards in English while Lizelle smiled at them. One broke away and rushed across to Mike and James, obviously asking for passes and trying to stop them entering the lift. Mike started arguing with him in English, buying time until the lift arrived and the doors slid open.

While this was going on James glanced behind him and saw Lizelle skirt the other guard and make for the elevator. The guard responded by trying to move in front of her and block her way. Ethan followed and the guard held his arms out to try and stop them moving backwards under the pressure of their forward movement.

As the lift doors opened, Mike gave the guard in front of him an almighty push into the, thankfully empty, elevator. The guard stumbled back, trying to regain his balance and Mike sprung forward, hitting him with a flat hand on the throat. As the guard dropped to lie on his back, wheezing and desperately trying to draw a breath, Mike brought the heel of his shoe down on the centre of his chest. They could hear the candid crunching of broken bone and smell the fetid, cigarette laden breath being forced from his lungs, whistling as it tried to clear the crushed windpipe.

At the same time, Ethan had pushed against his guard and slid the blade of his knife between the ribs, keeping the momentum going until they too were in the elevator. Lizelle joined them and James stabbed at the button for the fifth floor.

They laid the two guards against the side of the elevator and pulled their weapons from their waistbands, thumbing back the hammers just in time for the lift to stop and the doors to slide open. James and Ethan were first out, swinging to left and right.

The corridor they stepped into was more lush than the other floors. The carpet was thick, their feet sinking into it, and the dim lighting was provided by lamps hidden under the ceiling skirting board. The noise from the stadium was more muted, only a low rumble penetrating the sound proofing.

There were two men standing outside the double doors, slightly to the left of the elevator. They had not moved as the doors had opened, and their surprise at being confronted by two armed men was etched across their faces. Even as Mike and James levelled their weapons, their hands were diving under jackets to try and reach their guns. Neither of them succeeded in doing more than touching the butt of guns hung in belt holsters. Four gentle plops and two holes magically blossomed on the shirts of the two. A very slight dribble of blood, and they fell back against the wall and slid down to continue staring at the elevator doors, only this time it was through sightless eyes, already glazing over.

The four moved soundlessly on the carpet to the double doors. They could hear nothing through the thick wood. Time was now of the essence, as someone might chance along the corridor at any moment.

James whispered to Ethan and Mike to drag the two guards into the elevator and disable it, jamming the doors shut. They did so, and Ethan drew his knife, digging it into the key hole which controlled the doors. He twisted and was rewarded with the doors sliding shut. He eased out between the two sliding doors and, once they were firmly closed, he tried the call button. Nothing happened, and he grunted in satisfaction, making his way back to the double door. Like the others he now held a spare clip in his left hand, hefting his weapon in his right hand. Mike was on the side next to the door handle and reached out to gently turn it. They all watched in silent fascination as it moved and then stopped. James had the sudden thought that the door might be locked.

But then Mike eased it open a crack. With a sigh of relief he watched as Mike moved his face to the crack to peer through.

"Everyone has their backs to us, watching the game. I couldn't see much of the room though. Me to the right, Ethan to the left and you in the middle. Ready to go?"

James had a last glance at Lizelle, but she had her back to them, constantly turning to left and right as she scanned the corridor. Satisfied, he nodded to Mike.

Mike swung the door wide open. It moved on well-maintained hinges and stopped at its widest. Soundlessly the three stepped into the room, taking in the layout and the position of the spectators. They all had their backs to them; even the two dressed as waiting staff were absorbed in the game below them. At the first glance, James was sure that the gathering was an all male affair. There was a large easy chair with a high back in the middle of the serried ranks of watchers. It was too high to make out the occupant, but James was willing to bet that it was Gregori who had the most comfortable seat in the house. He levelled his gun and sighted it on the middle of the chair.

The chair jerked as the two rounds hit. Heads on either side swivelled to look at the occupant, taking a second to register shock at what they saw. No sooner had the sight registered, than people were were falling as round after round was fired into the seated mass. It would have been hard to miss, even for a very poor shooter. Most did not have time to raise themselves from their seats before they were hit. Even in the heat of the moment, James could see that most hits, like his own, were in the centre of the back or chest. The low load, hollow point rounds were not exiting, the fragmented metal doing terrible and irreversible damage as they careered round the rib cage. James heard the click of an empty chamber and thumbed the magazine release. It dropped to the floor and he had a replacement in and the slide forward in one smooth well-practiced movement.

With a full magazine, he stepped forward and started forward to the rear of the easy chair. On the periphery of his vision he saw the others doing the same and moving in from either side, checking the bodies as they moved. They stopped beside James and they surveyed the carnage they had inflicted. Bodies lay sprawled in the grotesque ballet of death. The first to die still wore the expressions they had worn when watching the game. Other faces were in limbo with a mixture of surprise and incredulity. It had been a massacre such as James had never inflicted on anyone before. He felt sick at the thought of what he had done. He had to physically shake himself to pull himself out of the trance-like state he was in.

James was standing at the back of the chair. He could now see up close who this man was who had caused him to travel so far back down a road he wanted to abandon. Ethan and Mike were standing watching him. He looked back at the door and saw Lizelle also watching, waiting.

"Ethan, Lizelle, pull those into the room and see if you can find a key to lock the door behind us." Still, he hesitated before putting his hand on the headrest and swivelling the chair to face him. To his surprise, he saw that Gregori was still alive, his eyes open, staring. However, the life was draining from him rapidly, he was past the point of pain and only surprise registered on his face. He must have been leaning forward or to one side when the bullets struck. James raised his gun to administer the coup de grace but was stopped from pulling on the trigger by a weak sound from the man in front. He leaned forward, pressing the muzzle against his forehead.

He spoke in Ukrainian and James only said the one word. "English."

Surprise was replaced by understanding. "Ah, the message. But why?" James now had to strain to hear the words, spoken in a thick, heavy accented voice.

"You wanted to hurt my friends." This was the only thing that James could think of to say. He pulled back, straightened and pulled the trigger. The round entered the middle of the forehead and the body slumped into its final pose. He stood looking at the figure before him, his mind filled with thoughts which moved in and out of thinking so fast he couldn't keep up with them, until he was interrupted by an urgent, "James."

He turned and saw the others waiting. Ethan was at the door placing a key in the lock.

"Let's go." He moved into the corridor, and, seeing it empty, replaced his gun in the waistband of his trousers. The others, following, did the same. He started for the stairs and heard the sound of the key being turned behind him as he opened the door and started down. The urge to race down the stairs was overpowering, but he maintained a steady, unhurried pace. Through the windows, he could see a car's headlights starting towards the entrance. They left the building as the Mercedes pulled up in front of them. Once inside, they busied themselves changing into fresh clothes, dumping the football shirts and jeans in a bag, swiftly followed by the weapons.

The change of clothes was completed in silence, and they settled back to watch the dark city pass before them as Alexander drove as quickly as he could to the airport.

"Fifteen minutes to check in," Alexander told them needlessly as he pulled up in front of the departures terminal. Each shook his hand, climbed out and took their bags from the trunk. They split into the pairs they had arrived in and went to the check-in desks. After checking in, they passed through immigration and into the airside lounge to see that the departure gate had already been posted. They wasted no time in joining the stream of passengers down the moving walkway to the gate. Inside, James saw that Ethan and Mike had separated themselves and were in a serious discussion. Lizelle was fidgeting impatiently with her hand luggage. She looked pale and nervous. James put a hand on her elbow to try and reassure her. The returning wan smile showed her gratitude for the small touch.

"I'll be fine."

Mike rejoined him and Lizelle went to Ethan.

I, Plague

"What was that about? I think I can guess."

Mike moved closer and told James. "He was feeling a bit sick about what happened. I told him we were feeling the same. That none of us had ever done anything like that before. But to remember the warehouse, Lou and his family." Mike paused before carrying on. "That's it, James. I'm finished. There's going to be a lot of shit in my mind for a long time to come."

James had to agree. He could almost predict the nightmares, and the cold sweats that were going to plague his sleep for the next weeks and months.

To take their minds off the events, he told them to keep an eye open as they were not safely out of the woods yet.

He could see the others constantly looking at their watches, as he was. The hands dragged round very slowly, minute by agonising minute until the flight was called and they made their way on to the plane.

Seated, Mike voiced the thought which had been running through James' mind. "Half time is gone, do you think they've found the bodies yet?"

"The only way we'll know is if they stop the plane from leaving. But think about it, how will they identify us as non-Ukrainians? Also, there's the time it will take for the police and others to swing into action. It might also be the case that they won't be found until full time. It is possible that anyone wanting to go in would see the locked door as a sign that he didn't want to be disturbed. It might be another thirty minutes before someone goes into the room."

CHAPTER SIXTY SEVEN

Steve had followed the undertaker's cars to the airport and had signed the documentation with customs to permit the caskets to be cleared for their flight. He had moved heaven and earth to have three bodies released. It had helped that the matter was being, as he was informed by a senior police officer, handled discreetly. An investigation was underway, but he regretted that the men must have somehow got themselves involved in a gang land shooting. Steve thought he could smell Gregori's hand in this, but was thankful to him insofar as it cleared the way for the release of the bodies. The undertaker had not been a problem either. A substantial payment in US dollars had ensured his cooperation and his silence. Peter's body had been moved to the undertaker's offices in an anonymous black body bag and was safely ensconced under the body of Gehan.

But, he had been correct in his guess that there was going to be hell to pay. The wires from London had been burning with the messages sent, inquiries demanded, reports to file with every agency which existed. It did not help that the close protection officers had been with the Metropolitan Police and had only been on detached duty, on loan. Then there was the Serious Crime Unit, Organised Crime, Drug Enforcement Agencies as well as the security services. Everyone wanted to know what had gone so badly wrong. And he did not have the answers they wanted to hear. It was obvious that someone inside the Consulate had tipped Gregori off about the movement, but he did not have the faintest idea who that might be out of the thirty or so locals employed. A new series of vetting was underway, but he doubted if they would turn up anything worthwhile.

He followed the caskets onto the tarmac and stood beside the plane as they were sent up the ramp and into the hold. He was leaving when some impulse made him turn and raise a hand in farewell to the man he worked with so long, but had known only through his reports. He had liked the person he had met so briefly during the stay at the consulate and felt real regret that he was going home in the hold instead of in the cabin.

CHAPTER SIXTY EIGHT

James sat looking out of the small window on the starboard side of the Airbus A300. He watched the ramp moving slowly back into its resting position and the flurry of activity under the belly of the aircraft. He thought it strange that the hold door had not yet been closed, and was watching as the activity waned as the baggage handlers waited.

The preflight safety information was going out over the PA and he absently watched the cabin attendant demonstrating the oxygen mask and the life belt. She saw him watching and smiled at him. He wondered if he looked particularly nervous. He had never enjoyed flying, but had not thought that this was so obvious. Maybe it was the waiting for the aircraft to get airborne that was making him more jumpy than usual. He smiled absently back at her as she completed the demonstration.

It soon became apparent as to the reason for the delay. A small tractor pulled a trolley and parked next to the loading belt. Three caskets were removed and slid slowly up the belt into the hold. He elbowed Mike, sitting next to him, dragging his attention away from the female cabin attendant who was securing the overhead lockers.

"Three coffins have just been loaded into the hold. I wonder if our friend from the warehouse is among them?"

"I hope so, it would be nice to think they could get him home so quickly." He leaned across James and looked at the small knot of men who were watching the loading. They were turning away as they felt the soft thud of the hold door being secured. One of the onlookers turned briefly and raised a hand in a half-salute before turning and walking rapidly to catch up with his companions.

"If I were to take a wild guess, I'd say that he was. Those guys didn't look like the usual officials you see around there. I guess we'll never know."

Once airborne they each ordered Glenfiddich and raised their glasses to each other.

"Now, at last, a long and happy retirement. No more of this work for me."

"Agreed. To a long and happy retirement, old friend."

CHAPTER SIXTY NINE

It was a sombre group sitting around two tables in the village pub. The Rose and Crown lived up to its name. It was almost medieval in decor, with a low ceiling, oak beams and a bar which ran the length of the lounge. The landlord, dressed in a white shirt and black tie, had not opened the pub until he had returned from the funeral. He had told them as they had ordered their first drinks that he had known the lad and his parents, had served him his first pint of beer and been at the parents funeral before he went off to London.

A funeral with full honours was always a poignant affair, but this one was even more so because no one could speak of his achievements, of his contributions.

The group surrounding Jane Bond was the complete task force which had been assembled all those weeks before. They had been invited to close the case finally, she had told them, adding that she would explain all after the funeral.

She now cleared her throat, gaining their attention. "Where to start?" She looked at each of them. "Well, we know that the operation was a resounding success, no small thanks to our friend Peter. I know we have been deliberately vague about him throughout the whole affair but I can now tell you everything. As you've probably guessed, he was in deep cover for years to be able to provide the information he did. He was supposed to get out after our side was complete, but he wanted to stay and provide anything that came up with regard to future plans. It was a decision that cost him his life. Before he died he was able to tell us that the hit team which was here were all dead. Shot, obviously not by us, but by some other party. We now know their identities but have not found, nor do we expect to find their bodies." Here she managed a wan smile.

"I shouldn't say this, but the good news is that Gregori is dead. He was assassinated a day after Peter's body was discovered. His organisation, by all accounts, is in chaos. Peter's body was discovered in a warehouse. He had not died easily. I'll not go into any details, but believe me when I say that I am not the only who is glad that Gregori died. Unfortunately, he did not die in the same manner as Peter." She stopped again and took a long swig of her drink. "Another aspect of this affair was that three others were killed in an attempt to extract Peter.

They were all Close Protection Officers, and all good men."

"I know that I can rely on your discretion on this. We think that the hit was done by a group of UK and South African citizens. There is absolutely no evidence that they were involved. It could very well have been a coincidence. Three were from the UK, and one woman was from South Africa. Three men, ex-Army and mercenaries, now all settled and perfectly legitimate. The woman is an expert in Close Protection. We also believe that they are the ones who took care of the hit team here in London. Also, we believe it was one of them who phoned the Military Attache at our Embassy in Kiev and told them about Peter. How did they know he was English? Well, some bloody idiot had hung a sign around his neck saying "Treacherous Englishman". No doubt he was left as a warning to others. Probably just as well he did, otherwise we would never have known what happened to him. No action will be taken against these people. Why? Because they have not committed any crime on UK soil, as far as we know, we only have Peter's unsubstantiated report on the fact that someone took them out. Gregori had no idea who it was and apparently could only guess that they had been hired for the job. And if they did kill Gregori, it was Ukrainian soil and therefore none of our concern, unless the police there ask for our help. So far, they have nothing to go on; it was our security services who picked up on their travel to the Ukraine, and some bright spark put it together. The group have behaved as tourists and have done nothing at all to raise any red flags. If it was them, they are very good. Lastly, we do not expect to hear from them again; this seems to have been a personal thing with them, for reasons we do not know. We are happy to let sleeping dogs lie."

It took a few minutes for this information to sink in. It was Andy who took the lead with the question he imagined was on everyone's minds.

"How can you be so sure these people won't come back on our radar again? After all, they have proved to be very effective in that line of work, maybe they've done something like this before?"

Jane didn't hesitate before answering. "I thought that might come up. The three men, all resident here, have worked abroad. They have never taken a job which has been against our national interests. In fact, they have indirectly worked for both us and the CIA. MI5 has kept tabs on them; two have retired from soldiering and one is now looking to retire, according to word in that circle. The woman has always been totally legitimate. Never a foot wrong. No, we don't think we have anything to worry about from them in the future." She laughed suddenly, surprising them. "In fact they could be handy assets to have up our sleeve. Sorry that was a thought only, a joke. Please forget I ever said that."

She stood. "Gentlemen, I propose a toast to Peter Grant, a brave young man who no one knew, but who will be remembered."

They all stood and raised their glasses. Andy noticed that groups at other tables around the pub did the same. He found it quite a moving moment.

The conversation turned to more mundane matters after that, each passing the time until they could leave and catch flights or trains or their drivers picked them up. During the small talk Andy found that he was not the only one who had received promotion. He was now a Superintendent, a rapid jump but a welcome one. He could now lead a more ordinary life, vowing to spend more quality time with his wife. That's the thing about funerals, he mused; it tended to put matters in better perspective.

CHAPTER SEVENTY

The night sky was clear, the full moon's light strong enough to cast shadows from the buildings. All the horses had their heads over the stall doors and were watching as James worked his way down the line, stopping and whispering to each, a tidbit in his hand. He enjoyed the feeling of the soft muzzle nuzzling his hand, the feel of the strong necks as he stroked them. The unquestioning loyalty and dependence showing in their eyes.

As he moved, he saw the loft window again lit. It had been a long time since its warm glow suffused the stable yard. Not since Marie. He knew there was no-one home; Lizelle was at the house attending the impromptu party which had been thrown. Still, there had been a time... Stop, he thought. He would not allow the pain to return, by remembering when he and Marie had spent so much time together, how it had all started with her staying in the loft.

He was halfway down the line, still talking softly to each animal, when he was aware of a presence behind him. He turned, still with an arm around the animal's neck, and saw Monique standing quietly watching him. The moon rays reflected off her dark hair, placing her face in shadow. He looked in her eyes, and he could see the concern there as she returned his gaze.

"Get bored with the chatter, then?" It was the only thing that came to mind.

Still holding his eyes she moved towards him. "Yes, I missed you and came to see if you were all right."

She was now standing directly in front of him. "You always talk to them." - Indicating the horses.

This caused a small laugh. "Always. They listen, but never talk back, never judge."

She leaned forward to stroke the muzzle. "And what were you discussing tonight?"

"Oh, just telling them about the last week. We were remembering other times, when all this first started." He swept his arm around the yard. "This was the original stable building, and most of these were the horses we started up with."

They moved on to the next stall. "Can I feed her?" He gave her a carrot. "Is that all? Seemed to me you've been very quiet since you got back."

She was very perceptive, he thought. "I've been telling them about the youngsters. They seem to have grown used to having Lizelle around and like her."

"That's not what I meant, and you know it."

"I know." He thought for a moment. Well, if he couldn't trust her, then who could he trust? "I feel like I've become the kind of person we were hunting." He put a finger to her lips to stop her replying. "No wait, I've thought about all the arguments. They were a very real threat to you and me. They were cruel and vicious people who had no regard for human life. They probably deserved to die. And, yes, the world might be a little better off for not having them around. But the thought keeps nagging at me. I hunted them, as I would an animal. I felt nothing when I shot them. I never ever thought I would do that kind of thing. At least as a soldier you know what the parameters are. Here we made the rules up as we went along. And that is the thing; there were no rules. Just the end product."

They had moved to another stall down the line as he spoke, and he silently held his hand out and felt the warm breath of the horse on it. He rubbed the ears and ran his hand down the long neck, enjoying the feeling as the horse nuzzled against his chest, searching for the carrot hidden in the pocket of his jacket.

Monique said nothing, waiting for him to finish putting his thoughts together.

"I suppose its post-op blues. The let down of returning to normal life after the rush of the operation. One thing I do know for sure," he turned his head and looked at her, "I am never doing anything like that again. I'm finished with guns, criminals. I only want a quiet life here."

She took his face in her hands, forcing him to look her in the eye. "I know there's something you, and the others, aren't telling us about what went on over there." She must have seen something in his eyes as the memory of the broken and tortured body flashed across his mind. "I know it. Whatever it was must have been pretty terrible. But it's over now. I know this sounds asinine, stupid and totally inadequate but we're all grateful for what you've all done. You didn't have to do it, none of you, but you did. You're right, people like that sometimes have to be killed. The law can't touch them." He saw a tear form in the corner of her eye and escape to run down her cheek. "I'm so sorry. So very sorry." Now another tear was forming and he didn't know what to do or say. The last resort was to put his arms around her and pull her to him. He held her and stroked her hair as she sobbed.

When she had quietened enough he pushed her gently away and held her at arm's length. "Enough of this, here, dry your eyes." He handed her a folded handkerchief and watched as she dried the tears from her face, smudging makeup on the pristine white of the cloth.

"Come on, let's get back. People will be beginning to talk." He permitted her to slip an arm through his as they walked slowly back up the drive.

"I suppose that a couple of good things have come out of this." He said, trying to lighten the mood. "Ethan will get his wish to retire from soldiering and learn an honest trade, thanks to your dad and Mike. And, of course, Lizelle is here. She seems to be settling in, says she doesn't miss the old life too much. She's turned the loft into quite a comfortable pad, made it a home for herself. Me? I'm just glad to be back. Glad to have friends around, like you."

As they rounded the bend in the drive and could see the back of the house, almost every window lit and shining down on the back garden, they could hear the muted sound of music, laughter and chatter through the open door and windows. He stopped them, and turned to look over the fields, still bathed in the ethereal glow of the moon.

Monique stood next to him and whispered. "It's so beautiful, so quiet, so still."

He looked down at her. She had nestled under his arm and her head was almost resting on his shoulder. She felt his look and turned to look at him. Slowly, without any conscious effort, his neck bent and his head moved slowly downwards. At the same time she raised her head. He could feel the length of her reaching up to meet him.

Their lips touched. The exquisite gossamer touch of the first kiss. Silken skin brushed against the rougher skin of his chin and cheeks. When he moved a fraction back, it was as if a butterfly was flitting away in a flurry of delicate wings. He moved in response to her and their lips touched again.

The moon behind them cast one shadow over the white fence and onto the grass beyond them.